Peter Watt has spent [...] prawn trawler deckh[...] real estate salesman. [...] geant and adviser t[...] Constabulary. He [...] Aborigines, Islanders, Vietnamese [...] Guineans and he speaks, reads and writes Vietnamese and Pidgin. He now lives at Finch Hatton in Queensland where he also works as one of the part time emergency ambulance drivers. Fine fishing and the vast open spaces of outback Queensland are his main interests in life.

Peter Watt can be contacted at www.peterwatt.com

Also by Peter Watt

Cry of the Curlew
Shadow of the Osprey
Flight of the Eagle
To Chase the Storm
Papua
Eden

Excerpts from e-mails sent to Peter Watt since his first novel was published:

'Keep up the wonderful writing – your books are so full of interest and hold the reader from the first page till the end. They are hard to put down. Just what a reader wants.'

' . . . thank you for the hours of entertainment you have given me . . . '

'They are the most enjoyable books that I have read in a long time . . . I look forward to reading more of your books in the future.'

'Novels on PNG are so rare . . . coming across *Papua* was a good thrill.'

'Thanks for getting me interested in reading again.'

'All your books are so powerful with detail of their period. Brilliant reading. Riveting.'

'Keep up the great work . . . you are a credit to the writing world.'

'I wanted more! . . . no superlative would be sufficient to describe your work.'

'Your books are marketed here [UK] as being as good as Wilbur Smith . . . or your money back. They certainly live up to that billing. Keep writing!!'

'I can honestly say in all my years of reading, your books have to be on my list of the best ever.'

'Fabulous, wonderful, brilliant.'

'Thanks for being one of those rare writers that has the gift to lose you in a different place and time, plus the added bonus of leaving the reader feeling as they have learnt something of the past and its people...Thanks for the escapism.'

'Australia's Wilbur Smith. Keep them coming.'

'I must say in all honesty I have never read a novel that has so captivated my imagination and heart and sent my mind and emotions on such a rollercoaster ride!'

'Gripping to the very end.'

'Your storytelling seems to get better with every book.'

THE SILENT FRONTIER

PETER WATT

PAN
Pan Macmillan Australia

First published 2006 in Macmillan by Pan Macmillan Australia Pty Ltd
This edition published in 2007 in Pan by Pan Macmillan Australia Pty Ltd
1 Market Street, Sydney

National Library of Australia
cataloguing-in-publication data:

Watt, Peter, 1949–.
The silent frontier.

978 0 330 42292 5

I. Title.

A823.3

Set in 11.5/13 pt Bembo by Post Pre-press Group
Printed in Australia by McPherson's Printing Group

Papers used by Pan Macmillan Australia Pty Ltd are natural,
recyclable products made from wood grown in sustainable forests.
The manufacturing processes conform to the environmental
regulations of the country of origin.

For my sister, Kerry, and her husband, Tyrone McKee.
With my love and gratitude to you both for being there.

PROLOGUE

Sunday, 3 December 1854

'To arms! California Rangers to the front!'

Awakening from a deep sleep, ten-year-old Lachlan MacDonald heard the shouted order and opened his eyes slowly. He could barely focus on the canvas roof above his camp stretcher and heard his father curse in the semi-dark of the early morning.

Following the shouted order Lachlan heard a shot and recognised it as coming from a rifled musket. Fear and confusion overcame him as he lay on his back in the sweltering heat of the summer's day on the goldfields of the Victorian colony of Ballarat.

'Get up, Lachie,' he heard his nineteen-year-old brother Tom shout at him from inside the tent the boy shared with his family. 'The bloody red-coats are attacking on the Sabbath.'

Lachlan sat up and then tumbled from his bed to stand uncertainly. His other brother, John, two years older than him, was holding their little sister, Phoebe, who was only five, in his arms. She was whimpering, torn from her sleep to the sudden crashing sound of a volley of musketry from a short distance away.

'God almighty,' Lachlan heard his father say. 'It's started. God have mercy on our souls. Thomas, get your brothers and sister out of here now. Run for the hills and hide in the bush until I come for you. Take this,' Hugh added, tossing a heavy leather money belt to his oldest son. Make sure you take it with the kids.'

Tom quickly strapped the leather belt around his waist under his shirt. He knew it contained a small fortune in five-pound sterling coins resulting from his father's sale of the profitable gold claim they had owned. The rest of the money they had made from the claim had been converted to paper currency and stored in a small tin, which his father was even now recovering from its hiding place under the earthen floor. The Scot was not a great believer in banks, which he saw as an extension of the detested English establishment.

While his father was recovering their savings, Lachlan could hear men cursing, shouting, crying out for help and even screaming out as the lead balls tore into yielding flesh on both sides of the palisade fence of crossed timbers. The Eureka stockade was under attack and Lachlan was confused why this should be so when the evening before his father had said they were safe on the Sabbath. If nothing else, his father had said, the British were a God-fearing nation and would respect Sunday as a day set aside for God.

2

'Da,' Thomas said, 'John can take Phoebe and Lachie to the bush. I will stay with you.'

Hugh MacDonald, a powerfully built man with a distinctive Scottish brogue, grabbed his oldest boy by the shoulders. 'Don't argue, lad,' he said, shaking his son. 'Get them out of here. I said I will join you.'

Tom turned to look at his younger brothers and little sister staring back at him, their eyes wide with fear. 'C'mon,' he growled reluctantly. 'Follow me and don't get lost.'

Tom snatched up his little sister and placed her astride his shoulders once they were clear of the tent entrance. It was then that Lachlan saw what was taking place all around him. Men dressed in the dark blue of the goldfields police and soldiers in their red coats with the distinctive white strap between shoulder and waist were pouring into the fortified enclosure to clash hand to hand with the rebellious miners. Long bayonet against axe-like pike, revolver against musket. Lachlan looked over to where the great flagpole stood with its blue flag and silver southern cross emblem flapping gently in the first rays of the summer's morn. He could see Lieutenant Ross, a Canadian miner who was said to have designed the flag of rebellion, fighting under it. Horses galloped all around them raising clouds of dust as Tom hauled his young charges after him towards the dimly lit outline of the tree-covered hills that lay to the west.

Tom placed his sister on the ground and swung around to glimpse back to where they had come from. 'God, no,' he whispered under his breath and turned quickly to John. 'Keep going with your brother and sister. Don't stop running until you get to the hill and hide in the trees until I come for you.'

John understood and took his sister's hand to half-drag, half-trot with her towards the increasingly distinct ridge of trees. He did not look back, as he was afraid of what his older brother may have seen. Lachlan followed reluctantly.

Tom sprinted back to the tent, where he saw his father clutching a small tin box. He had been confronted by a goldfields policeman who had a bayonet-tipped musket levelled at his chest.

'You are my prisoner,' the policeman snarled. 'Yield in the Queen's name, rebel.'

'I'm not a bloody rebel, man,' Hugh MacDonald shouted. 'I just want to get out of here and join my family – so step aside.'

Tom had almost reached his father when a red-coated officer galloped up to the tent. The officer was wielding a sabre that caught the first rays of the sun along its silver blade as he waved it over his head. 'Don't argue, trooper,' the officer shouted. 'Kill the rebel.'

Hugh MacDonald was momentarily distracted by the arrival of the mounted officer and the police officer lunged forward to bury the pointed tip of the long bayonet into the Scotsman's chest, running the blade through until it came out Hugh's back. The big Scot buckled at the knees, dropped the tin box and collapsed onto the dusty earth.

'No, you bastards,' Tom screamed at the top of his lungs, launching himself at the mounted English

4

officer. 'He wasn't a rebel, he was just trying to get out of here.'

The sabre fell and Tom felt it bite through the bone and flesh of his shoulder. He cried out with the searing pain before crumpling to the earth into an oblivion of merciful darkness.

The officer astride his horse glanced down at the ground where the two men lay. The policeman grunted, struggling to withdraw the bayonet from the body of the big man at his feet. He placed his foot on Hugh's chest and gave a powerful tug; the bayonet came free, followed by a steady flow of blood.

'That tin, man,' the mounted officer said. 'What does it contain?'

As the policeman scooped up the tin and opened it, the expression of surprise on his face was not missed by the English officer.

'Money, sir,' the policeman blurted. 'A bloody lot of money.'

'No need to curse on the Lord's day,' the officer said irritably. 'Here, be a good chap and hand it up to me.'

The policeman eyed the English officer suspiciously, gripping the tin to his chest, reluctant to part with his sudden and wonderful find. 'A trophy of war,' he said. 'With all due respect, sir, this money is mine to keep.'

'It is considered looting, sir,' the officer said threateningly. 'And I am authorised by Her Majesty the Queen to shoot you down without trial for the crime.'

The policeman hesitated. His eyes darted around the enclosure to see if there were any immediate witnesses if he were to carry out the thoughts that had gone so quickly through his mind. When he glanced up at the officer he was startled to see that the Englishman had him covered with a small revolver. 'Hand it up, man, and I will overlook this infraction of the rules,' the officer said grimly.

The policeman could see that he had no choice. He had already discharged his musket in the early stages of the attack on the rebels' stockade and had not had the chance to reload the single-shot weapon. Now he was out-gunned by the officer who had a sabre and revolver to enforce his command. The policeman handed up the tin box which the officer slipped inside his coat, before wheeling around his mount and galloping away, leaving the policeman alone with the bodies of the two men they had struck down.

The policeman felt something snatch at his coat and realised with horror that a stray musket ball had punched a hole through his jacket sleeve. It was enough to make him think of the battle still raging around him. Already the miners' tents were blazing, set alight by the rampaging troops of the two British regiments engaged in the attack aided by the goldfields police. What had commenced as some cross-fire had very quickly turned into a massacre of anyone found within the confines of the stockade. The overwhelming arms and numbers of the attackers were sure to bring the fighting to a short end. Forgetting the two bodies at his feet, the goldfields policeman secured cover from any more musket balls. He did not know that Tom MacDonald, as badly wounded as he had been, was still alive, although ignored by the soldiers pushing forward, seeking out anyone still standing.

Breathless and exhausted, John was able to cross the hard-packed earth road and get his equally tired and weary brother and sister to the edge of the bush, where they all fell to the ground to get their strength back. It had not helped either brother that they had taken turns carrying little Phoebe on their shoulders, turning the flight from the camp into a stumbling, ankle-twisting trot.

'Where is Da and Tom?' Lachlan gasped. 'They should be with us.'

John raised himself to his elbows and stared in the direction of the miners' camp. The gunfire was tapering off and he could have sworn that he could hear women keening their grief. 'They will be here soon,' he panted. 'But we must go further into the bush and hide like Da said.'

With his last statement, John forced himself to his feet, picked up his sister and staggered into the dry scrubland that ran up the side of the hills. Lachlan followed. They were not alone. Many others who had fled from the encampment were also seeking the safety of the distant hills.

Duncan Campbell had been awoken by the distant rattle of musketry. It was an all too familiar sound from his past life serving the British Crown on many foreign battlefields – from Waterloo, as a young drummer boy, to the Indian campaigns of the North West Frontier. The little mongrel dog lying asleep beside him awoke to lift his head off his paws and sniff the air with a low growl.

'Easy,' Duncan said, patting the dog's head. 'It's not in range.'

The Scot stood up stiffly to peer into the semi-gloom of the early morning. His head hurt from the excess of rum he had consumed the night before whilst sitting by his camp fire and wagon.

Duncan Campbell was a formidable figure and the red beard and thick, fiery hair hanging down to his shoulders were splashed with streaks of grey, denoting the fifty years he had lived on earth. He had the broad shoulders and barrel chest of his highlander ancestors and although he stood just over average height his powerful build made him seem taller. For three years he had plied his itinerant trade in the colonies of Victoria and New South Wales, a pedlar of trinkets, cloth, medicines, pots and pans.

'Ah, but there is mischief on the fields,' he murmured to his little dog. 'I dinna think it will last long from the sound of it. No time to reload. It will come down to cold steel.'

He had seen all the signs of an impending battle on the goldfields and had expected a bloody clash. It was not in the nature of the British authority to allow armed men to contemptuously drill in sight of the Royal regiments and, knowing it would only be a matter of time before the Crown moved to teach the rebels that they could not pull the lion's tail without it biting them, he had trundled his horse-drawn wagon out of Ballarat, past the fortified encampment to seek a quiet place to camp.

Duncan reached for his battered old pipe and filled it with a plug of tobacco. Sitting with his back to the wagon wheel, he lit up and watched the grey smoke curl away on the light, early morning breeze. He remained smoking until the sound of gunfire drifted into sporadic shots and eventually into none at all.

With a sigh, he rose to his feet and went to his horse hobbled a short distance from the wagon. It was time to return to Ballarat.

Crying softly, Phoebe huddled against her brother John while Lachlan stood among the trees gazing in the direction of the stockade. He was too far away to see anything of the battle but the disturbing sounds drifted to him on the early morning breezes.

'Why haven't Da and Tom come?' he asked without turning. 'I think something bad has happened to them.'

'They will come to us,' John said firmly. 'They said they would.'

Lachlan was not convinced. He did not know why, but he felt a dread he had never experienced before. The waiting was terrible and a man with a dreadful wound to his head had stumbled past their hiding place only moments earlier, only heightening his feeling of fear.

'I will go back to the tent,' Lachlan suddenly said.

'No,' John protested. 'We are to stay here.' But, before he could rise to his feet and stop his younger brother, Lachlan had broken into a run in the direction of the stockade. John was about to go after his brother when he realised that would mean leaving his little sister alone to the mercy of the bush. Torn by his duties, John chose to remain with Phoebe, to protect her. 'It will be all right,' John said soothingly to his sister. 'Da, Tom and Lachie will be back soon for us.'

In the stockade women were moving amongst the dead and wounded. Their anguished cries rose into the sky with the flames and smoke from the burning tents. Walking slowly amongst the carnage, oblivious to the troopers and soldiers around him, Lachlan could hear the agonised cries of the wounded. It was hard to tell where his father's tent was, as the orderly rows had disappeared into burning heaps. But he did recognise the body of the man being thrown onto a wagon by red-coated soldiers sweating in the searing summer heat of the day.

'Da!' he cried out, stumbling forward to reach the blood-stained wagon.

A hand grabbed him by the shirt collar. 'Where you goin' boy?' an Irish-accented voice asked gruffly. 'There be only dead'uns on the wagon.'

'My da,' Lachlan gasped, struggling against the strong hand that held him. 'You are taking away my da.'

'Sorry, lad,' the gruff voice softened. 'Not something a young lad should see, so come away with ye.'

Lachlan glanced up at his captor and saw the ruddy face of a soldier wearing the red coat of the British army.

'Let the boy go, sergeant,' a voice from behind said. 'Only right that he sees – and remembers – the fate of those who would oppose the Queen's peace.'

The grip was released and Lachlan turned to see a mounted British officer. The man had very fine features, hair the colour of corn and was about his brother Tom's age. Lachlan did not thank him but immediately went to the wagon to take his father's limp hand in his. Tears spilled from the young boy's eyes, splashing the ashen face. His father's eyes stared with an opaqueness Lachlan had seen in his mother's eyes only two months earlier when she had lain in a coffin awaiting burial. The consumption had killed her, people said in whispers behind his back. Now it was his father's turn to have that same look of death.

'What was your father's name?' the young English officer asked.

'Hugh MacDonald,' Lachlan, sobbed, without turning to address his questioner. 'He was my da.'

'Well, he has paid for his treason,' the officer said callously. 'I dare say he will answer in the next world for betraying the Queen.'

'Sir,' the Irish sergeant growled, 'I think that the little fellow does not need to hear that. He has lost his father.'

'Scottish scum do not deserve sympathy, Sergeant,' the officer said, bringing a furious look to the Irish sergeant's ruddy face. The sergeant knew that this pompous officer also considered the Irish soldiers who served loyally in the British regiment as little more than scum themselves. At least the Scots and Irish had the same Celtic blood, which the English had lost to the Angles and Saxons centuries before.

'Get the bodies to the morgue,' the officer commanded. 'And be quick about it. The rising sun will soon make them stink.'

'Yes sir,' the Irish sergeant replied dutifully but with a note of barely concealed contempt. 'Come away, lad,' he said to Lachlan. 'Your da will be looked after.'

Reluctantly, Lachlan stood back as the wagon was moved on to seek out more bodies for transport.

'What's your name lad?' the sergeant asked gently.

'Lachlan MacDonald,' the boy answered, wiping away the tears from his face with the sleeve of his dirty shirt now covered in his father's blood. 'Have you seen my brother Tom?'

A faint smile appeared on the Irishman's face. 'I'm sorry, young Lachlan,' he said. 'But I do not know your brother.'

'Tom stayed with Da,' Lachlan explained, looking up into the face of the red-coated soldier where he thought he could see a hint of kindness. 'Tom is old, like Da,' the boy patiently explained.

'Maybe you should stay beside me for the moment,' the Irishman said. 'I don't think it is wise to wander around here alone right now. Besides, you might bump into Lieutenant Lightfoot again and I don't think that would be a good idea, considering his comments about your father.'

Lachlan knew that this friendly Irish soldier was

somehow the enemy but he appeared to care for his welfare and so Lachlan warmed to the man. They walked towards the road that defined the rear of the roughly built palisade of timber and carts when the Irish sergeant suddenly stopped.

'Duncan Campbell, would that be you?' he called.

Lachlan's attention was drawn to a covered wagon drawn by a single horse and driven by a solid-looking, red-haired man sitting on the wagon seat.

'Would that be Paddy Rourke addressing the likes of me?' the man asked, a slow smile creasing the corners of his eyes.

The Irish sergeant quickened his pace to the wagon, where he was met with a great bear hug.

'I thought you would be dead by now,' Paddy said. 'I thought one of those heathens in India would have taken your God-cursed Gaelic soul to hell with him.'

Duncan stood back. 'And I heard the sounds of a great battle here just a few hours ago,' Duncan said. 'I never guessed my old comrade in arms would be in the colonies fighting the good cause for the Queen, God bless her.'

The Irish sergeant frowned. 'I don't think what has happened here today will appear on the regiment's battle honours, Colour Sergeant Campbell,' he said in a quiet voice. 'Many of the boys of St Pat faced kith and kin here today and did not feel good about killing fellow Irishmen – regardless of which side they were on. It was not a battle so much as a massacre.'

'Who is the wee laddie with the long face?' Duncan asked, turning his attention to Lachlan.

'One of your own,' Paddy replied. 'A MacDonald, who goes by the moniker of Lachlan.'

Duncan broke into a broad smile and extended his big, calloused hand. 'A fine name for a Scot. An honour to meet you, Master Lachlan.'

'Sergeant Rourke,' a voice called from the stockade. 'Get your men together and form up for a sweep of the hills.'

'Sah,' Paddy replied.

'Now.'

'Sah.'

'I would be asking you for a small favour, Duncan,' the Irish sergeant said. 'I would be asking you to look after the wee lad until I get back to you. His father was one of those rebels who was killed in the fighting.'

'I will do that for you, Sergeant Rourke,' Duncan answered. 'For old times' sake and our serving together under the colours.'

'Mr Campbell will look after you, lad,' Paddy said, patting Lachlan awkwardly on the back.

Paddy turned his back and marched smartly over to a detail of red-coated soldiers awaiting further orders. Behind them Lieutenant Lightfoot sat astride his fine mount surveying the burning tents of the stockade and the grief-stricken women moving amongst the soldiers and wounded miners now being taken prisoner.

'Well, laddie,' Duncan said when Paddy was out of sight. 'You look as if you could do with a tot of water.'

Realising how thirsty he was, Lachlan gratefully

accepted the canteen passed to him from the side of the wagon.

'I have to go back to John and my sister,' he said when he had taken a long draught. 'They will be worried about me and Tom will be angry if I don't get back now.'

'I can take you to your brothers and sister,' Duncan said. 'Where are they?'

'In the hills hiding,' Lachlan replied. 'I know where.'

Duncan frowned. Already, the soldiers and police were spreading out to track down any wounded rebels who had fled into the thick bush on the hills behind the stockade. It was going to be a long day.

Some time after the soldier and officer were gone, Tom regained consciousness. He glanced over to where his father lay and knew immediately that he was dead. Then Tom felt for the money belt under his shirt; it was still intact. For some unknown reason they had not searched his body, leaving him for dead. All around him Tom could hear the sounds of the massacre and smell the pungent aroma of burning canvas. He lay for a moment in the dust and felt the terrible pain bite at his shoulder. When he tried to move his left arm he screamed in pain; the sabre had inflicted a deep and deadly wound. The fighting shifted away, leaving him alone in its wake.

With great effort, Tom forced himself to his feet, trying not to cry out. Stumbling like a drunken man, he weaved his way through the stockade, which was filled with galloping, mounted police and the red-coated infantry who seemed to ignore him as they sought out those who were still able to resist.

Eventually he reached the foothills where he had sent his brothers and sister. Then the pain became too much and Tom sank to the earth with a loud groan. He knelt on the road, forcing himself to remain conscious.

'I'll give you a hand,' a voice said, as if from afar, and Tom felt an arm under his good shoulder, hoisting him to his feet.

'It don't pay to be caught here with your wound,' the voice said and Tom vaguely recognised the accent of a young American miner around his own age, with whom he and his father had been friends.

'Luke Tracy, leave me,' Tom said. 'Get away while you can.'

The young American ignored Tom's plea. When Tom was able to focus on his helper's face through the haze of his own pain, he could see that Luke had sustained a terrible wound. The side of his face had been slashed from his jaw to his ear. Blood streamed down the clean-shaven, handsome face. 'I will get you into the bush and try to hide you,' Luke said. 'Then I will go.'

'You get chopped with a sword?' Tom asked as the American helped him to his feet.

'God-damned Limey red-coat stuck me with a bayonet,' Luke replied with a wince. 'Got a feeling that I am not going to look too pretty if I ever get to dodge a hangman's rope. The British aren't going to look kindly on anyone who belonged to the California Colt Revolver Brigade after this.'

'We weren't even party to the rebellion,' Tom said as they struggled across the road into the bushland at the base of the hills. 'And the British murdered my da and tried to kill me. They slew him for nothing.'

'Not nothing,' the American rebel said. 'We stood for our God-given rights – as it says in our American constitution – where all men are equal and deserve a voice in how things are run.'

'That was a bit overlooked in Her Majesty's colony of Victoria,' Tom said, as Luke helped him into the cover of the dry bush and its trees. 'Hotham doesn't understand that we never wanted to rebel – just air a grievance.'

When they were deep in the bush, Luke helped Tom down to the ground and examined his wound. As a younger man on the California goldfields of '49 he had seen similar serious wounds and knew instinctively that his Scottish friend would most likely die.

'How's it look?' Tom asked with his eyes closed and vainly attempting to stem the pain.

At first, Luke did not know how to answer. 'Is there someone I can fetch for you?' he replied and Tom understood.

'I have to find my brothers and sister,' he said. 'I have something very important for them. They should be somewhere around here if they did what they was told.'

'What are their names?' Luke asked.

'My brothers are John and Lachlan. They are

twelve and ten. My sister Phoebe's just a little mite. I know that I am done for, but what is most important is that I have something for them before I die. Please, Luke, find them for me before I go.'

Hearing the plea in the dying man's voice, the American disregarded his own wound. 'I will leave you for a short time, Tom, and see if I can find them before the red-coats start sweeping the hills. Just take it easy and I will be back.'

John was huddled with his little sister when he saw the blood-stained face of the young American rebel.

'You young John?' Luke asked, standing over the two.

'I am,' John replied, staring in horror at the terrible wound to Luke's face.

'Where is your brother Lachlan?' Luke asked, glancing warily around the bush for any sign of the British troops.

'He went back to the camp to find Da and Tom,' John replied. 'He hasn't come back yet.'

'I've found Tom for you,' Luke said. 'He is only a short distance away and has been hurt. I think you should come with me to see him.'

Obediently, John rose to his feet and took his sister's hand. They followed the American through the bush until they came upon their brother, lying on his back in a slowly gathering pool of blood. Tears rolled down John's face. Little Phoebe, who did not quite understand what was happening, stood quietly by her brother with her thumb in her mouth.

'John,' Tom gasped weakly, 'Da is dead. I saw him slain at the camp. You have to look after Lachie and little Phoebe from now on. I want you to swear to me on the blood of our ancestors who fought at Culloden that you, as now the eldest in the family, will keep your brother and sister with you. Do you understand what I am saying to you?'

John nodded, forcing back the tears lest his brother think that he was a coward. 'I promise, Tom.'

'Good,' his dying brother sighed. 'I have something for you to make sure that you are looked after in the years ahead.' With a great effort, Tom slipped the lacing loose and Luke helped pull the money belt out from under the dying man. 'Luke, on your word as a Christian, I want you to bury this at the base of the tree over there,' Tom said. 'And when that is done, mark the tree with a slash. There is a fortune in that belt and I want you to swear that you will tell no one of its existence. Swear your oath to a dying man on the fate of your eternal soul.'

'I swear,' Luke said. 'Your wish will be respected.'

'Take this for your help,' Tom said and opened his hand to reveal thirty pounds sterling in five-pound coins.

'I don't want your money, Tom,' Luke said. 'You give it to the little ones.'

'You will need it to get out of the colony,' Tom gasped, as the pain came over him in a searing wave. 'I know that you are a good man with an honest soul, Da told me.'

Reluctantly, Luke took the gold coins; the dying man had better things to say before leaving this world. He took the heavy leather belt and commenced digging a hole a few yards away at the roots of a tall eucalypt. When the belt was buried, he used his bowie knife to carve out a deep notch in the trunk. When he turned to speak to Tom he realised that the young Scot was already dead. John knelt by his brother whilst Phoebe stood staring at her eldest brother's lifeless body with a confused expression on her pretty little face.

'Soldiers coming,' John said quietly, spotting the flash of sunlight on a bayonet and then glimpsing a distinctive red coat. 'You should go.'

Luke could see what the young man had spotted and was torn deciding between whether he should stay with the young boy and girl or flee. It was an agonising decision, but he had to believe that the soldiers would not harm defenceless children. As for himself, well, they would probably shoot him down on the spot as the bayonet wound on his face marked him as a rebel. He would be no good to the children then anyway.

'Take care of your sister,' Luke said, grasping John by the shoulder. 'And always remember where this place is.'

John nodded as Luke rose to his feet and quickly disappeared further into the bush, away from the cordon of soldiers sweeping the hills. When they arrived they only found two children grieving over the body of a young rebel. They were kind to the children and did not harm them, but the children were taken to the soldiers' camp and in the night strangers came and the children were separated. John realised that he had lost more than his father and brother to the massacre. He had lost his whole family.

It was near evening on that terrible day on the Ballarat goldfields when Duncan finally returned to find Lachlan with his little dog in his lap by the wagon.

'No one has seen or heard about your brothers or sister, Master Lachlan,' he said gruffly, sitting down with his back to the wagon wheel. 'There is a lot of confusion around us. The army is half expecting a counterattack tonight. I heard that there might be rebels up in the hills even now, forming up for an attack.'

'I have to find my brothers and sister,' Lachlan replied. 'They will be worried about me.'

'Not tonight, lad,' Duncan said. 'You could get yourself shot by a nervous picquet. You stay here and have something to eat. Then you get yourself some sleep. My old comrade Paddy Rourke can help us tomorrow.'

Reluctantly, Lachlan accepted Duncan's offer and ate a hearty meal of boiled meat and cabbage. It was not long before he drifted into sleep with the Scot's dog curled up beside him.

Duncan placed a blanket over the boy who slept soundly under the wagon. 'Ah, you poor wee laddie,' he murmured. 'I hope that we find your family.'

Duncan sat down beside his camp fire amidst the carnage of the stockade. He lit his pipe and stared at the starry night. He was a long way from his beloved green fields of Scotland but his life had always been like that, serving the British Crown on foreign battlefields and travelling across three continents. It had been a lonely life, despite the wonderful comrades he had served alongside. For most of his years he had only known the life of the Scottish Regiment. First as a drummer boy and then to the rank of Colour Sergeant near the end of his service. Finally, he had taken his retirement and meagre pension to seek a life in the Australian colonies as an itinerant salesman of home wares.

The brief blaze of a shooting star lit the southern sky and tapered off to a trail of heavenly sparks. Duncan watched the astral display and sighed. Today something had happened here that instinctively he knew would change the face of the Australian colonies. But for now, his only concern was his temporary custody of this little Scot and the responsibility of reuniting him with his family.

The sun rose hot and dry over the goldfields, now almost deserted of miners. The numerous pits dotting the landscape were empty of their diggers and the pall of grief after the massacre still lay heavy on the encampment. Duncan rose early as was his habit from his many years in the army and woke the lad. Together, they went in search of his brothers and sister. They found the Irish sergeant, Paddy Rourke, busy at work on Soldier's Hill among his men. When he saw Duncan his face broke into a broad smile but the smile faded when he noticed Lachlan beside him.

'The miners identified your brother Tom amongst the dead,' Rourke said sadly to Lachlan. 'We buried them yesterday. I'm sorry, lad.'

At first, Lachlan could not believe that he had lost his eldest brother as well as his father. It had been bad enough that his mother had died only weeks earlier, but now he barely knew how to react to the sudden loneliness the news had imparted to him.

Duncan could see the stony expression on the young man's face and had a partial understanding of what it meant. 'Well, laddie, time that we went and found your brother John and your wee little sister,' he said kindly, placing his hand on the boy's shoulder. 'I'm sure the government can do something for you.'

Duncan spent three days searching for Lachlan's brother and sister but it seemed that the children had simply disappeared. When Duncan asked questions at the military headquarters, still tense with an expectation of a counterattack by the armed survivors of the massacre, one harassed officer irritably snapped that orphans had been kindly taken in by miners' families departing the goldfields. When he went on to say that he could not find any records of who had adopted the rebel's children, even at ten years of age, Lachlan realised that he was alone in the world with just the company of a tough Scot and his little dog. The future looked bleak; all the little boy had to cling to was the former soldier of the Queen.

Part One

THE DREAMER

1862

The Colony of New South Wales

ONE

The great wedge-tailed eagle circled over the vast, sun-baked plains, high above the stunted trees and desiccated grasses which shimmered from horizon to horizon. Far below the bird's flight, a tiny wagon and horse sheltered from the heat under the tall river gums. The river of cool, clear water which snaked sluggishly through the plains provided the only relief from the searing summer sun.

In a reflective silence Lachlan MacDonald sat by the lifeless body of Duncan Campbell. The old Scotsman had been everything to Lachlan as he had grown into manhood. He was now eighteen years of age, of medium height but broad-shouldered and equally broad-chested. His grey eyes held an inherent intelligence and his thick hair curled at its ends. He was clean-shaven and had strong, handsome features. His face and arms were darkly tanned by exposure to the sun during the years he had been with Duncan Campbell, wandering the colonies of Victoria, South Australia and New South Wales as he plied the trade of a salesman of home goods.

They had been relatively happy years for Lachlan as the assistant to the Scot who, rather than describe Lachlan as a waif he had collected in his travels, passed the boy off as his nephew. Duncan had taken Lachlan under his wing and ensured, even while on the road, that the boy learned to read and write. Soon Lachlan was devouring every book he could lay his hands on. Duncan had been self-taught and had an insatiable appetite to educate himself, so was pleased to be able to pass on his skills to his young protégé. Lachlan's Christmas and birthday presents always consisted of expensive texts on mathematics or books of poetry. The great Scottish poet Robbie Burns' books were prominent amongst Lachlan's collection.

But Duncan taught him more than reading, writing and arithmetic. Around the camp fires he regaled him with stories of faraway exotic lands the former soldier had campaigned in – from the cold, snow-covered hills of northern Victoria to the arid, sun-baked plains of South Australia and New South Wales. These tales fired Lachlan's imagination and he dreamed of one day becoming a famous explorer in the mysterious new colony of Queensland, a place Duncan had told him was inhabited by fierce war-like cannibals and giant, man-eating alligators.

'You have to be good at mathematics,' Duncan would warn him, as stern as any school master when

Lachlan flagged in his studies while they were on the road. 'Explorers have to know how to make measurements, navigate and make precise sketches for maps. You have to have the skills of a master mariner – but on land – to be an explorer.'

Duncan had never been demonstrative in his love for the boy he had unofficially adopted but Lachlan sensed his fatherly love in everything he did for him. Once, after a beating Lachlan had taken from the local toughs years earlier in a town they had visited, Duncan had taken the bruised boy aside and taught him how to fight. Not just in the manner of the bare-knuckle boxer but also in the rough rules of the mean streets of Glasgow. Duncan himself had learned the hard way and after years of constant practice was second to none, be it in a street fight or in the ring. Lachlan learnt quickly and had eventually been able to earn a little money aside from what Duncan paid him, by fighting in the improvised boxing rings of many of the towns they passed through. Very rarely did he lose and his reputation had grown to the point that he was remembered with respect when they passed through those towns again.

It did not matter that the old man did not express his words in intimate gestures or words. What counted was that the Scot had always been there for him and that he had been kind and gentle in his gruff way.

Now he was dead.

The annoying clouds of bush flies buzzed around the body lying beside the wagon. It seemed to Lachlan that Duncan had known his death was coming the night before. The chest pains had become more and more frequent and even more painful. In the dark night lit only by the gentle flames of a dying camp fire he had called softly to Lachlan.

'Lad, get over here now,' he had gasped.

Awoken by the call, Lachlan had scrambled to the side of the Scot. 'You all right, Mr Campbell?'

'No, laddie, I'm dyin'.'

The statement, so frankly uttered, shocked Lachlan. 'I'll saddle up the horse and get you to a doctor,' Lachlan said.

'No need,' Duncan groaned. 'Waste of time. I just want you to know that you can bury me out here. I thought it might have happened many times when I was younger, that I would be buried in some foreign land. At least here I will be buried in the earth of a Christian country.'

Unconsciously, Lachlan took the old man's hand in his. Never before had he allowed himself such an intimate gesture, as it would have embarrassed them both.

'There is something I think that you should know, laddie,' Duncan said with some effort. 'You have to sell up all that I have when I'm gone and follow that dream of yours to become an explorer.' Lachlan made to protest, to say that he would continue the trade of his mentor, but Duncan cut him short. 'You are different, laddie, you have a fire in your soul that sees beyond the far horizons. One day, you may stand before the honourable gentlemen of the Royal Geographical Society in London and speak of the places that you have blazed for God and the Queen in this big country. I have always thought that you would be the man to explore that new colony of Queensland. You can do better than that mad Irishman, Robert O'Hara Burke, who got himself killed last year. I know you can. This is a time for young men to make their name in the annals of the Empire. Don't waste your life being an ordinary man, like I did, be an explorer and make a dying Scot proud. Go find those silent frontiers and shout out your name for all to hear. Make the land echo with the voice of a Scot.'

Lachlan had been stunned. How was it that the old Scot could understand his own restlessness to seek those unseen places beyond the horizon?

Suddenly, Duncan had arched his back, gripped his chest and slumped back against the earth. A strange gurgling sound came from his throat.

'Mr Campbell?' Lachlan said, desperately shaking the old man's shoulder. Then he kneeled, his ear to Duncan's chest. Lachlan sat up and squeezed the hand he still held. It was now soft and yielding to the touch and the young man knew that the kindly, gruff man he had loved as his adopted father was now dead.

It had been many years since Lachlan had truly cried. The last time had been the night after the rebellion when the full impact of the death of his father and brother had finally hit him. The young boy had sobbed himself to sleep under Duncan's wagon; the little dog, now long dead himself, had attempted to console him with licks to the face.

Duncan had sat by him throughout the night and had let him cry until he could cry no more.

Now, alone on the flat, desolate plains of western New South Wales, Lachlan rocked back and forth on his haunches, sobbing and holding the dead Scot's hand. For the first time in his life he felt truly alone. A fleeting memory of his brother John and little sister Phoebe came to him in his grief. He had never given up looking for them and Duncan had always asked questions, whenever he was in a Victorian town. Neither had received any news about the missing pair. It was as if they had vanished into thin air. Finally, Lachlan came to accept that the Scotsman was the closest thing to family he had.

Finally, Lachlan lay down beside the dead man and fell into a troubled sleep. When the early morning sun rose over the Hay Plains he sat up to stare at Duncan's body. Lachlan went to the wagon and secured a shovel. He looked around the camp site by the water hole and noticed a site overlooking a sweeping bend in the river. There he commenced digging a grave and by mid-morning had finished a reasonably good-sized hole. Satisfied that it would be deep enough, he took the body under the arms and dragged it over.

When he had shovelled earth over Duncan's body, Lachlan went back to the wagon to recover the battered Bible from which the Presbyterian Scot had read for at least an hour every Sunday. Lachlan did not know what he should read, so placed the Bible on the mound of fresh, grey earth under the wooden cross that he had hastily made to mark the grave.

He was through crying, he told himself, it was time to remember the Scot's dying words.

After washing himself in the river, Lachlan hitched up the cart-horse to the wagon. He knew from past experience that it would take him two days to reach the next reasonably sized town to report the death to the police. Then he would make his way east to Sydney. The future was still blurred but at least he had a goal: to reach Sydney, where he would sell the horse, wagon and all its goods. With the money he would seek out his new occupation. Although, as he admitted reluctantly to himself, he was not quite sure how to go about becoming an explorer of great note.

Even as Lachlan trekked east towards the Great Dividing Range heading for Sydney, which lay beyond the blue-hazed hills and ancient sandstone escarpments, another young man had finally reached his destination outside the town of Ballarat in the colony of Victoria.

John MacDonald was now twenty years old and had saved enough money to travel from Hobart in Van Diemen's Land. His apprenticeship as a printer in a Hobart printery had been completed and he was now free to go in search of a dream. Determined to honour the dying wishes of his brother, John had, as a child, scribbled on a piece of paper a rough map of what he could remember about the place where his brother died.

But what if his memories from that terrible day

so many years past had just been a figment of his imagination? John trudged the last mile to the foothills of the mountains that had provided temporary sanctuary the day of the rebellion. And what if the treasure had long been found by someone else? The question was like a dagger in his belly. He had spent just about every penny he had saved to purchase his ticket for the voyage to Melbourne and had just enough left over to pay for travelling costs to the old goldfields at Ballarat. If the gamble did not pay off, he would be stranded in a colony he scarcely remembered without any means of support.

The sun was still high in the heavens and the weather hot, bringing a sharp and disturbing memory of the day of the massacre when he had lost his family. At last, John began to recognise landmarks from his youth. But the stretch of bushland was daunting. There was a maze of possible routes into the hills. Where had he entered the bush from the road? John stood on the road, looking up at the hills in the distance. One tree looked much like another.

He made a decision, left the road and entered the bushland. For hours he meandered amongst the trees searching for the one that had a slash on its trunk. But time, as the young man realised, had healed many wounds, including ones inflicted on trees.

Despair began to set in as thirst and the hot day took their toll on him. He drank the last drops from his canteen and gazed up at the hill which was slowly falling under the shadow of late afternoon. He decided to give the search one more hour before returning to Ballarat and his lodgings at the boarding house.

John stood and slowly scanned the small clearing. His gaze fell on one particular tree. He walked towards it and ran his hand down the bark. There it was! The scar of a knife blade etched on the trunk by Luke Tracy so long ago!

John dropped to his knees, reached for a piece of branch on the ground and, with his heart pounding, began digging into the soil at the base of the tree. Within moments the tip of the branch struck something solid and John discarded the makeshift tool to claw at the yielding earth with his fingers. A rolled-up lump of leather was revealed and with both hands John pulled the heavy object from the ground. A partially rotted compartment tore open to spill the golden five-pound coins at his knees.

'Oh, God, thank you,' John gasped.

He had found the small fortune secreted by his eldest brother before he died of his wounds. John's gamble had paid off and he knew that he was now a very rich young man. He had in his possession half the small fortune his father had made from a gold strike and then a good sale for his claim. Now it was time to consider how he could invest his new-found fortune in an enterprise and make it grow even further.

His thirst and the heat of the dying day were easily forgotten as he made his way back to his lodgings, the gold coins concealed in the carpet bag containing all that he owned. But the small fortune was not his alone. John had sworn an oath to his dying brother to look out for Lachlan and Phoebe. All he had to do was find them – but that was likely to be a much harder task than uncovering the cache of coins.

TWO

In the village of Parramatta, Lachlan drove a hard bargain. He sold the horse wagon and its wares to a merchant with a rapidly growing clientele and the money in his pocket gave the young man the euphoric feeling of being rich. Tempted as he was to celebrate his windfall in the main bar of a local hotel, Lachlan chose wisely to continue his journey to the city of Sydney by boat.

The river brought him at length to the heart of the Pacific city where the harbour retained its charms, despite the intrusion by Europeans into its once pristine environment. The masts of sea-going ships at anchor rose majestically to blue skies. Little boats puffed out smoke from their funnels as they crisscrossed the harbour, taking commuters from one shore to another and leaving a white wake trailing behind their sterns.

But from the shore drifted the pungent smells of civilisation: the reeking tanneries spilling their odious effluent into the harbour waters, chimneys clouding the skyline with smoke from wood and coal fires, the reek of raw sewage wafting from open or cracked drains. Besides the odious smells were sounds alien to a country boy: the clatter of shod hooves on the streets, the rickety wheels of wagons and cabs, the babble of voices from pedestrians on the busy streets and the banging of builders' hammers as another warehouse took shape to cater to the needs of merchants shipping their produce to the far-flung ports of Europe and the Pacific.

With his swag of personal belongings over his shoulder, Lachlan stepped ashore in the shadow of the Rocks to gaze about his immediate surroundings. News boys stood by paper stalls, calling out the headlines of the day to finely dressed men in tall hats, tight-fitting trousers and frock coats. Women strolled past in their fashionable crinolines, shading themselves with parasols, stopping occasionally to look into shop windows. Rowdy, drunken sailors on leave and surly, gaudily dressed young men loitered along the thoroughfares.

Lachlan had to admit to himself that he was just a little frightened and confused, as he had never been in such a big town as Sydney before. He hoped that his condition would not be noticed by those who passed him by and, with a determined stiffening of the back, the young man strode out in the late after-noon sunshine to walk up a narrow street of two-storeyed buildings. He had no real idea where he was going but as a tramline featured as part of the road he felt that it would take him in the direction of somewhere important. What he did know was that before he could realise his dream of becoming an explorer he needed to make more money. Sydney held the promise of work and hopefully the knowl-edge to launch him on his path to fame. He hoped that he would not have to ask directions to a board-ing house, as this would definitely set him apart as a stranger from the country.

After a long walk following the tram tracks, Lachlan found that the heart of the city seemed to be behind him. Signs indicating that boarders were wel-come were becoming more apparent. He stopped at one building displaying a sign welcoming good and sober Christian men to stay for a reasonable rate.

Lachlan took a deep breath and walked up the wooden steps to the verandah of the two-storeyed, wooden house with its peeling paint and was met at the door by a ruddy-faced, middle-aged stout woman who eyed him with something between hostility and suspicion.

'What do you want?' she immediately asked, blocking the entrance to the house.

'I, ah, saw your sign,' Lachlan replied. 'I was hop-ing that you might have a room to let for at least a week, as I fit such a description.'

'Where you from?' the woman asked.

Lachlan could smell the pungent aroma of boiled

cabbage wafting from somewhere inside the boarding house. 'Melbourne,' he lied.

In their travels Duncan had taken Lachlan as far as the towns surrounding Melbourne but never into the city itself, as he had a strong dislike for cities. At least if he said he was from Melbourne the woman would not think that he was some kind of country bumpkin.

'Melbourne,' the woman echoed with a slight shake of her head. 'No wonder yer came to Sydney. You pay a week up front, no women allowed on the premises, no strong liquor, no animals, no blaspheming, no gambling, no fighting, no stealing from the other residents and yer get an evening meal thrown in – at an extra cost fer meat.'

Lachlan shrugged. 'How much?' he asked, and the woman gave him a price. Lachlan fished in his pocket for the right amount and counted out the coins into her podgy, outstretched hand.

'Me name's Melba Woodford,' she said, eyeing the small pile of coins in her hand. 'You can call me Mrs Woodford. What's yours?'

'Lachlan MacDonald.'

'Well, Mr MacDonald, I will show you to yer room,' the landlady said, turning her back and walking inside.

Lachlan followed her up a set of dimly lit stairs to a row of rooms with closed doors. She stopped, turned a key in a lock and stepped aside to allow Lachlan to enter. It was a small but functional room with a single bed, chair and table. He could see a tall wardrobe with a cracked mirror and there was the scent of stale sweat and dust in the room. Rising damp was apparent in the stains on the faded wallpaper.

'Yer put the candle out before you retire fer the night,' Mrs Woodford said. 'Don't want no fires here. And yer buy any candles yer need, other than the one in yer room which yer can have fer free. Yer got any questions?'

'Er, ah, where is the dining room?' Lachlan asked, feeling the effects of hunger after his long and arduous day.

'Downstairs. The evening meal is served promptly at six and if yer not there yer miss out. The outhouse is down the back stairs at the end of the garden – just in case yer got to go. Any more questions?'

Lachlan shook his head and dropped his swag onto the saggy bed. This was only a temporary abode until he found something better, until he came to grips with how he would eventually become an explorer.

'I'll see yer at evening meal,' the woman said gruffly, closing the door behind her.

Standing in his room, Lachlan suddenly felt sad and lost. He sat down on the bed and stared out the tiny window at the smoke-stained brick wall facing his room. Sweat trickled down his chest under his shirt. He had faced opponents on the dusty paddocks outside the country towns he and Duncan had travelled through and fought more tough country boys than he could remember for prize money. He had taken the painful blows and never once shown fear, but now tears trickled down his face. What the hell had he expected? he cursed to himself. No family, no friends and there was no certainty of immediate work prospects. As for fulfilling his dreams, they seemed far removed from the reality of his circumstances. At least he had a reasonably good supply of money until something came up.

Lachlan wiped away the tears. Only women cried, he told himself. It was time to take stock of what he did have and work towards achieving his ambitions. He would somehow make his dream come true. Sitting by the camp fire, old Duncan often used to say, 'Laddie, when one door closes in life, another will open. Just be certain to go through it.'

Fortified by his memories of the old Scot's words, Lachlan rose from the edge of his bed and went in search of the dining room. Downstairs he found a large room where seven men were sitting around a wooden table eating a meal in front of them consisting of boiled cabbage, potatoes and mutton. They were eating in a hearty manner, using slabs of bread to mop up the juices on the plate, and hardly gave Lachlan a second glance. From their suntanned faces and working man's garb Lachlan guessed the men were labourers of some kind.

One young man around Lachlan's age beckoned for him to take an empty seat beside him. Lachlan smiled his thanks and sat down as Mrs Woodford placed a generously piled plate of meat and vegetables in front of him.

'What's yer name?' the young man asked between mouthfuls of food.

'Lachlan MacDonald,' Lachlan replied, picking up a knife and fork.

'The name's Jimmy Graves,' the other man said, introducing himself without shaking hands. 'Yer working around here?'

'Just got in,' Lachlan replied. 'Haven't had a chance to look for work.'

'What were you doing before you got in?' Jimmy asked.

'I was working as a traveller,' Lachlan replied.

'You look like you could do a hard day's work,' Jimmy said, pausing in his eating to study the newcomer. 'Our crew has a vacancy since the Dutchman fell off a ladder and broke his back. You up to working on buildings?'

Lachlan was pleased to find both a good meal in front of him and an immediate offer of work. Maybe a door was opening.

'I can give you an honest day's work for a fair wage,' he replied.

'Hey, Harry,' Jimmy said across the table to an older, wizened-looking man ploughing through his meal. 'We got a replacement for the Dutchman. Lachlan here says he can start with us.'

The man barely glanced at Jimmy but nodded his head. 'He starts tomorrow – and he better not be bloody late,' he growled.

Jimmy turned to Lachlan, thrusting out a calloused hand. 'I'll make sure you get to work on time,' he said.

The following day Lachlan joined Jimmy to set out for work. Mrs Woodford had prepared each of the working men in her boarding house a sandwich for their lunch and Jimmy packed Lachlan's sandwich with his.

The building site was only one block from the boarding house and Lachlan was surprised to learn that they would only be working an eight-hour day. It was hot and the work a lot harder then Lachlan had expected. Sweat poured down his body as he hefted loads of bricks to the bricklayers, mixed cement with a shovel and unloaded more bricks from the horse-drawn carts arriving with their loads. The men were contracted to build a store house of great size and hauling the bricks on a hod up the many levels of planks was back-breaking work. The men worked mostly in silence and the midday lunch break was especially welcomed by Lachlan, who collapsed next to Jimmy.

'Here's yer sandwich,' Jimmy said, handing Lachlan a couple of dusty pieces of thick bread encasing slabs of cold mutton and pickles. 'Yer get a mug of tea with yer sandwich.' A battered enamel mug containing sweet black tea was handed to Lachlan.

'Yer get used to it,' Jimmy said, noticing how stiff and sore his new friend appeared. 'The money ain't much – but it's sumthin' at least.'

'Just glad we only do this eight hours a day,' Lachlan sighed after a sip of his tea. 'It was a lot easier selling wares to country ladies.'

'Yeah, well, unless there were lots of young ladies out in the country then you wouldn't find me swapping jobs,' Jimmy said. 'At least in Sydney yer get to meet plenty.'

Lachlan was interested in Jimmy's comment. He was a young man and had never had the opportunity to really get acquainted with the opposite sex. His itinerant life on the road with Duncan excluded a steady romance, although he had often caught the eye of a pretty young lady from time to time and town to town. Like all young men of his age, his thoughts were often plagued with curiosity as to the physical charms of the heavily dressed but shapely bodies of the pretty young ladies he had looked at shyly.

'Where do you meet young ladies in Sydney?' Lachlan casually asked.

'Lot of places here you can meet the fairer sex,' Jimmy said, finishing the last of his tea. 'Yer got the Domain, Hyde Park, Randwick race track that was opened this year, but that's not as good as the Domain, or if yer have some money, you can go up to Lane Cove on a picnic and meet a lot of single girls.'

'So, what's at the Domain?' Lachlan asked.

'The flash lads and lasses up there are more my crowd. Yer don't get them with the stuck-up airs of the toffs yer find around the Lane Cove lasses,' Jimmy said. 'I get to meet some of the lads from the Rocks at the Domain. They are a tough crowd but if yer get in with them they ain't so bad. The coppers leave them alone. What did yer do for fun when yer were working out in the country?'

'Did a bit of boxing for money,' Lachlan said. 'Or read books when I could.'

'How good a fighter are you?' Jimmy asked.

'I seemed to win more than I lost,' Lachlan shrugged.

'Yer look like yer got a fighter's build and if yer were any good then you can make some good money around the inns here, fighting bare-knuckle for a good-sized purse.'

'I don't know if I'm that good,' Lachlan answered honestly.

'So, when did yer win most of yer fights?' Jimmy asked.

'All my last fights,' Lachlan answered, remembering the pain-racked, bruising bouts of the last year behind the hotels in the little towns he and Duncan had visited.

'That means yer got a handle on what to do with yer fists,' Jimmy said. 'I reckon it is worth having a crack around here before Christmas. Hey, Harry,' Jimmy called. 'Who's that big bastard fighting fer the Shamrock Inn?'

'The Irishman, Kevin O'Keefe. Why?' Harry answered.

'I reckon we should put Lachlan here up against him. Win a few shillings on the outcome.'

Jimmy's statement attracted attention from the rest of the crew but the mumbled conversation that ensued was cut short by the call back to work. Lachlan heaved himself stiffly to his feet to face another few gruelling hours under the hot summer sun. If nothing else, he had a job and if today was anything to go by it would toughen his body unlike anything else he had known.

That night, Lachlan ate a stew prepared by Mrs

Woodford, washed himself down in the backyard from a tub of water and climbed the stairs to his room to collapse on his saggy bed. Before he knew it, he fell into a dreamless sleep to be awoken in the early hours of the following day to do what he had done the day before. This ritual went on for a week before his body slowly became inured to the physically hard work. Then the weekend finally came around – and Sunday meant a day away from the dusty, hot construction site to go with Jimmy to the Domain and meet some of Sydney's lasses.

The smartly dressed young man sitting in the sombre offices of a Victorian bank waited patiently as the bank manager, sporting a bald head and great bushy sideburns, pored over the table of accounts on the polished timber desk between them.

'Mr MacDonald, you have quite a considerable sum of money deposited with us for someone so young,' he said, glancing up at John MacDonald. 'I would strongly advise that you put your money to work.'

John took a deep breath and fiddled with the hat that lay in his lap. 'I intend to do that, Mr Craven, and that is why I asked to see you personally.'

The manager, a man in his late forties, sat back in his comfortable swivel chair. 'You are somewhat of a mystery man around Melbourne,' Craven said, eyeing John with just a hint of suspicion. 'May I ask how you suddenly came by such a large amount of money?'

'I came by it honestly,' John replied. 'It was bestowed to me in a family legacy. My father was a miner who did well out of the Ballarat fields some years ago but he has since passed on, as has my mother, and now you are the custodian of my moderate wealth.'

'Please forgive me, Mr MacDonald, I was not casting aspersions on how you came about your windfall,' Craven hurried to say, lest he insult one of his recent best depositors. 'I can assure you that our services will always be available to you when it comes time to invest your money.'

'I feel confident that you will, Mr Craven,' John replied. 'I do have some ideas, but first I wish to purchase some real estate for a residence. I do not envisage spending a lot on a place to live at this stage.'

'A wise idea,' Craven replied with the faintest of smiles, relieved to know that this young man before him was not going to whittle away what he had in the bank in a foolish search for pleasure as was the habit of most young men his age.

The bank manager rose from his chair to indicate that the interview was over and thrust out his hand to John. John accepted the gesture and was struck by how limp and clammy the older man's grip was. They parted, John walking past the tellers to the busy street outside the bank and slipping on his hat. To passers-by his appearance was that of a successful young man of probable good breeding – and that was what John wanted people to think.

Losing his family that terrible day of the massacre

had all happened in confusing circumstances; the killing of his father and brother by the red-coat guns and bayonets, Lachlan's disappearance, and the forced separation of himself and Phoebe the day after the fall of the stockade. Confirmed orphans, Phoebe had been adopted by a good Christian family. But where they had taken her John had never known.

As for himself, he had been put in an orphanage in Van Diemen's Land and eventually apprenticed to a printer in Hobart. It was there that he had slaved to improve his grasp of reading and writing as he worked diligently to master the trade of printing.

The young man who walked the broad streets of Melbourne had come a long way from the miner's son working with his family in the dust of the goldfields at Ballarat. But he returned to his hotel with a dream. One day, the wealth that he intended to increase many times over would assist him in finding his lost brother and sister. As young as he had been at the time, he had sworn an oath to his dying brother that he would keep them all together. Now the ancient, clannish blood ran hot in his Scottish veins and John knew he would not rest until his promise had been fulfilled.

THREE

Sunday came bright and sunny and after a wash, Lachlan donned his best clean clothes. He stood outside the boarding house with Jimmy who was dressed in his best shirt and trousers, finished off with a red scarf wrapped around his neck. Jimmy had slicked his hair with copious quantities of grease – although a stubble of whiskers remained on his chin.

'We are going to Hyde Park,' Jimmy declared.

'I thought you said that the Domain was the place to be,' Lachlan countered.

'Ah, but the regimental band will be playing at the Park and it will be your chance to see your opponent for the big fight,' Jimmy declared. 'I knows he goes there with one of his lasses of a Sunday to strut about like a flash man in front of his push.'

Lachlan shrugged. At least he would be away from the dust and heat of the building site and could relax and take in what the sprawling town had to offer. Listening to a band from a British regiment stationed in Sydney would be a pleasant diversion.

However, Lachlan was pleasantly surprised to see that there was an abundance of young ladies parading with friends and family through the park. Ladies wearing dresses which cascaded to the ground and wide-brimmed hats and carrying parasols could be seen on the arms of stiff-backed young officers in the bright uniforms of Her Majesty's regiments. Other young men wandered amongst the strolling crowds, their seemingly inherent disdain for the socially more advantaged ensuring they kept their distance from the higher classes. Lachlan felt just a little self-conscious of his working-class clothes, especially after receiving a nudge from Jimmy. 'Yer seem to be getting a couple of looks,' he said from the corner of his mouth. 'Must notice that yer a country yokel. Ah! Over there,' Jimmy suddenly exclaimed. 'It's O'Keefe himself.'

Lachlan glanced in the direction Jimmy had indicated and noticed a tall, well-built young man, not much older than himself, strolling with an adoring young lady on each arm through a small grove of shrubs. He was well dressed and had the air of a man confident in his abilities to command those around him.

Lachlan groaned inwardly. If this was the man that Jimmy had announced to all that he was to fight, then he was not feeling so confident. O'Keefe stood a head taller and was many pounds heavier than himself.

As if reading Lachlan's mind, Jimmy commented, 'He might look like a big bugger but he hasn't had a good fight in months. He has been seeing Kate Duffy from the Erin Hotel lately and I hear he is a bit sweet on her. It has taken the edge off his fighting skills.'

Lachlan was surprised to hear that the man he appraised over the twenty paces between them was courting a young woman, when the two lasses hanging off his every word and gesture looked much more than passing friends. Duncan's strict Presbyterian morality had rubbed very much off on Lachlan, and he immediately disapproved. 'He's got a longer reach than me,' Lachlan said quietly.

'Yer an unknown around here,' Jimmy said as they stood gazing in O'Keefe's direction. 'Me and the boys at work are game to back you for a win against O'Keefe.'

Lachlan turned to his friend. 'You have never seen me fight,' he said in surprise. 'How can you be so sure that I can take this O'Keefe?'

'Just sumthin' about you,' Jimmy said, scratching the tip of his chin reflectively. 'It could be all that country air you soaked up in yer travels, but I reckon you could easily take O'Keefe in a bare-knuckle bout. It would mean good money. The publican at the Victory Hotel would put up a good purse and then there are all the side bets on the outcome. He's not keen on O'Keefe. Doesn't like Irishmen and would pay to see O'Keefe go down to a Scot.'

Lachlan turned to once again appraise his potential opponent. Lachlan loved the art of bare-knuckle fighting. It was hard to explain to himself why facing another man with fists raised and a howling crowd around you made the sport so good. Maybe it was just that; the pain inflicted was bearable when there was always the chance that you might win against the odds, and hearing the crowd howling for your blood certainly urged you towards a victorious outcome. Whatever it was, the more he stared at O'Keefe, the more he felt the need to face him growing in the pit of his stomach.

'I'll do it,' he said quietly and felt Jimmy slap him on the back.

'That's my fighting Scot,' Jimmy said with a grin. 'Show that son of an Irish convict just what a Scot can do. Now it's time to introduce ourselves.'

Jimmy led Lachlan over to O'Keefe, who glanced curiously at the two approaching men.

'Mr O'Keefe,' Jimmy said when they were within paces of the three. 'How the devil are you this fine day?'

'Well, Mr Graves,' Kevin O'Keefe replied cautiously. 'And who's your friend?'

'I'd like yer to meet the man who is going to put you on yer arse,' Jimmy said with a cheeky grin. 'Mr O'Keefe, meet Mr Lachlan MacDonald, undisputed champion of the Mudgee district and soon to be undisputed champion of the Redfern village – that is, as soon as he puts yer down.'

Kevin O'Keefe thrust out his hand to Lachlan and with an ironic smile replied, 'Pleased to meet you, Mr MacDonald. Sadly, I must admit that I have never heard of you before.'

Lachlan was surprised at the lack of animosity in his future opponent's voice but did not miss the facetiousness of his comment. The grip was hard – a test of strength met by Lachlan, whose own hands had hardened already with the tough work of handling bricks. They released their grip and eyed each other with slight smiles of mutual confidence.

'I have to admit that I have never heard of you either,' Lachlan said gallantly. 'Jimmy tells me that you are the best around here.'

'Not quite the best,' Jimmy interjected. 'Mr O'Keefe has yet to fight Michael Duffy from the Erin. Then, after you have put Mr O'Keefe down you get to do the same to Michael Duffy and all will know that you are the best around Sydney Town.'

Lachlan was embarrassed by Jimmy's puffed-up boasting, which he had not yet earned. He would ask Jimmy later why he had applied the non-existent title of Mudgee district champion to him, when he had never fought in that pretty little town on the other side of the Blue Mountains, west of Sydney. Lachlan suspected that Jimmy did a fair share of hustling and wondered at his friend's motives for being so keen for him to take on an obviously good fighter. However, his thoughts about fighting O'Keefe were distracted by the sight of a beautiful young lady sitting alone in an expensive carriage just beyond where they stood. Her face was framed by lustrous brown hair and her large, dark brown eyes appraised him with more than casual interest. He guessed the young lady to be in her late teens and was struck by her full-shaped lips and pale, unblemished skin.

'Damn!' O'Keefe suddenly swore and Lachlan could have sworn that the big man facing him had paled. 'You have to do me a favour, Jimmy,' he said, slightly nudging the girls on his arms away from him. 'You and Lachlan have to pretend to be with Molly and Gertrude.' Both Lachlan and Jimmy blinked in confusion. 'Michael Duffy is here,' O'Keefe continued, without going into detail.

Jimmy was first to move and stepped beside the older girl, Gertrude. Lachlan was left with the younger one he now knew as Molly. No sooner had they taken their places beside the two young ladies than O'Keefe stepped away to walk in the direction of a tall, broad-shouldered man in the company of a young woman with striking features.

'That's Michael Duffy's sister with him,' Jimmy grinned, 'Kate. She's the one O'Keefe is courting.'

Lachlan glanced over and could see O'Keefe greeting the young man and woman warmly.

'Well, ladies,' Jimmy said, bowing gallantly at the waist and sweeping his hat off in an old-fashioned gesture, 'as you can gather, me and me friend Lachlan are your beaus for the day. May we presume to call you by your first names?'

'As you wish,' Gertrude answered in an annoyed tone that well and truly bespoke her annoyance of being parted from the arm of the charming Irishman.

Lachlan turned to Molly and saw the same displeasure in her expression.

'May I also call you Molly?' Lachlan asked politely, without presuming Jimmy spoke so forwardly for both of them.

'You may not,' Molly snapped petulantly. 'I think my sister and I would rather be in the company of Chinamen than be seen with Jimmy Graves and his friends.'

'How did you know my surname?' Jimmy asked.

'Mr O'Keefe saw you enter the park and warned my sister and myself of your reputation,' she said with a snort of indignation. 'I would presume that your friend may have much in common with you.'

Lachlan was stung by her comment. It was obvious that Jimmy was well known in certain social circles and Lachlan was beginning to think that those circles were less than reputable. Instead of defending his reputation, Lachlan remained silent.

'I see Mr Bell and his family over there, Molly,' Gertrude said. 'Are you coming?' Molly turned on her heel and joined her sister, leaving the two young men standing alone. But Lachlan was secretly pleased that the two young women had chosen to take leave of their company. While talking to Gertrude and Molly, Lachlan had noticed that the very beautiful young woman in the expensive carriage had continued watching him.

'Excuse my dust,' Jimmy said, 'but a Graves does not give up that easily.' Lachlan watched him hurry off after the sisters who had snubbed them.

Lachlan did not know where the courage came from but impulsively he turned and walked towards the carriage, stopping at its side to glance up at its occupant, although now he could see that the lady was desperately pretending not to notice him.

'Do you know,' Lachlan blurted, 'that you are the prettiest lady in the park.'

The young woman's smile was slow and warm. 'You are being very forward,' she replied. 'But thank you for your compliment – although I doubt it to be true.'

Lachlan felt awkward at his confession. Being tactful was not something he'd had the opportunity to learn from Duncan's brusque interactions with others on the road.

'I did not mean to be forward,' Lachlan quickly countered. 'It was just something I felt.'

'Well, if that be so,' the young woman said sweetly, 'then I accept your compliment as more than an attempt at flattery.'

Lachlan shook his head in his exasperation. He was suddenly out of his depth. This young lady spoke with an intelligent voice far beyond his limited experience with members of the opposite sex.

'I am not very good at this,' Lachlan finally sighed, giving in to defeat at his awkwardness. 'My name is Lachlan MacDonald and I am new to Sydney Town.'

'Then I should introduce myself, Mr MacDonald. I am Miss Amanda Lightfoot. I noticed you in the company of Mr O'Keefe.'

Lachlan recognised her cultured tones and English accent; they marked her as a lady well born.

'Do you know Mr O'Keefe?' Lachlan asked, curious at her knowledge of the man reputed to be one of the best fighters in Sydney.

'My brother, Captain Charles Lightfoot, is an

avid follower of the pugilistic scene in the colony,' Amanda replied. 'He once took me to witness a bout between Mr O'Keefe and a brute of a man from a visiting merchant ship. Mr O'Keefe soundly thrashed the man.'

Lachlan did not want to hear that and mumbled, 'I am contracted to fight Kevin O'Keefe.'

'You are going to fight Kevin O'Keefe!' Amanda exclaimed 'Do you think that wise when you do not know of his reputation?'

'I was talked into the match,' Lachlan said. 'Jimmy thinks it is a quick way to earn some money.'

A worried expression creased Amanda's pretty face. 'You seem to me on first impressions to be a nice young man,' she said. 'You could be seriously hurt in a fight with Mr O'Keefe.'

'It is a risk every fighter is aware of when they step into the ring with another fighter,' Lachlan replied. 'We will not know the outcome until the match is ended.'

'What profession do you practise, Mr MacDonald?' Amanda asked.

'Profession? I do not have a profession,' Lachlan said. 'I am a working man who labours on building sites.'

'I am surprised at that,' Amanda said with a note of genuine surprise. 'From the manner of your speech I would have thought you a man of letters, albeit a very young one.'

'Now it is you who are being complimentary,' Lachlan replied with a slow smile. 'It is just that I love reading and was fortunate enough in my growing years to have a teacher who fiercely believed the way from one station in life to another was in learning from books – and speaking like a toff.'

'You had a good teacher,' Amanda said. 'You could pass as a gentleman in Sydney were it not for the manner of your dress.'

'Well, another compliment to you, Miss Lightfoot,' Lachlan said warmly. 'From your manner of speech and bearing I would have taken you for a lady of good breeding.'

Amanda burst into a short, soft laugh. 'My father was a merchant from the north of England. But he was much wealthier than our neighbours with their ancestral titles. My pedigree has been bought – not inherited. Until my parents passed away I was considered a rebel by my family because I had a desire for learning not necessary for a woman from a privileged home. I have read many books on a great diversity of subjects and I also have a love for colonial literature and poetry. Have you read Mr Kendall and Mr Harpur's poetry?'

'I am afraid that I have not heard of them,' Lachlan replied honestly.

'If you have a love for poetry,' Amanda said, 'then I do recommend both men's works. They have a beautiful way of putting into poetry the very nature of the Australian colonies. I think Mr Kendall's book *Poems and Songs* is extraordinary and believe that one day he may be nominated as our first poet laureate to the Queen.'

'Then, I shall endeavour to read Mr Kendall,' Lachlan said. Without knowing it, he had been drawn into a world far away from the gruelling labour of the construction site and his loneliness in this new, crowded place.

'Would it be forward of me to invite you to take a walk through the park?' Lachlan asked, at the same time holding his breath and expecting rejection.

'I would be delighted, Mr MacDonald,' Amanda said, offering her gloved hand for him to assist her down from the carriage.

They strolled together through the crowds in the park, engrossed in each other's company, talking on so many subjects. Time flew so fast and it was obvious that Amanda found him interesting company.

'You do not talk on sport as so many other young men do,' she commented. 'It is so refreshing to engage in conversation on the arts. You are very much a contradiction, Lachlan,' Amanda said, frowning. 'You appear so very physically strong, yet you have a gentle mind. I wish you were not going to fight Mr O'Keefe as I fear he may hurt you.'

Lachlan felt his face flush. Her concern seemed genuine and for that he felt a surge of warmth for Amanda. 'It may be that I hurt O'Keefe more than he hurts me,' he said in defence of his pride. Amanda did not reply.

Jimmy strolled over to them with a triumphant expression on his face.

'Well, young Lachlan,' he said. 'It has all been arranged. You fight O'Keefe for a purse being put up by the publican of the Victory over in Paddington. Next Saturday afternoon, so it's about time we got you into shape.'

Lachlan noticed Amanda's look of concern. 'I think that I should join my brother,' she said quietly. 'He may be missing my company.'

As Amanda walked away without bidding him a good day, Lachlan was mystified by the sudden change in the young woman. He looked at Jimmy, who had also noticed her abrupt coolness. He shrugged and slapped Lachlan on the back. 'There are plenty more like her,' he said.

But his answer did not please Lachlan. No, Miss Amanda Lightfoot was unique, he thought. He knew that he desperately wanted to see her again and in the back of his mind hoped that she might come to see the fight on Saturday.

In the distance, the regimental band struck up a marching tune and the Sunday crowds moved as one towards the sounds of music filling the hot summer's afternoon. But Lachlan was not one of them. He felt an emptiness in the pit of his stomach as he realised just how much he truly wanted to share Amanda's company again.

The next week on the building site went quickly. Each day as Lachlan hauled the bricks and mixed the cement he was occupied by thoughts of Amanda Lightfoot. Even when he went home after a heavy day of labour he still found himself lying on his bed in the dark, stifling room staring at the ceiling and thinking about her. He would wonder what her body was like under all those clothes, and the ache of the thought caused him a restless sleep. He would attempt to admonish himself for his less than honourable conjecture about the young woman – but his desire would not go away.

At work Lachlan noticed that he was being treated with a great deal of respect from the others on his team – but he was less than pleased to hear that already bets were being laid on the outcome of his upcoming fight with O'Keefe. Although the purse was twenty guineas to the winner, a sizeable amount of money, the real money would be made in the wagers. Jimmy had done a good job in spreading a false rumour that Lachlan was the undisputed champion west of the Great Dividing Range and many of the bets favoured him for a win. These came mostly from the Protestant factions who followed the fight scene in Sydney Town. They saw the young Scot as the great hope to prove to the Papist Irish that the Protestant way was the one granted as true and correct by God.

On the Saturday morning Lachlan was not required to work. Jimmy was also granted the day off to help prepare his champion for the fight, which would take place not far from the Victoria Barracks.

That morning Mrs Woodford served up a great pile of bacon and eggs. 'Yer goin' to need all yer strength,' she sniffed uncharacteristically to Lachlan before turning away lest her tenant think that she was a bit sentimental about him. Lachlan already had gleaned that beneath his landlady's hard exterior was a soft heart and she treated her tenants very much as she would her own family.

Jimmy paid the expense of a horse-drawn cab to

the Victory Hotel. When they entered the main bar a cheer rose up and calls of 'Put that Mick on his Papist arse' rang out from many of the patrons. Ales were pressed on Lachlan but Jimmy elbowed them away from his fighter, knowing that Lachlan would need all his wits to face O'Keefe's formidable skills.

A sweating, stout man wearing a sleeveless vest and fob watch on a chain pushed his way through the crowded bar to Jimmy. 'This is Mr Fielding,' Jimmy said to Lachlan. 'He is the publican here and is putting up the purse.'

Lachlan shook hands with the stout man.

'Jimmy tells me that you are the undisputed champion from the Mudgee district,' Fielding said. 'You had better be,' he added with just a hint of menace. 'A lot of my clientele have backed you to win.'

'I do not intend to lose, Mr Fielding,' Lachlan replied and the publican grunted his satisfaction at the answer before moving away.

'Well,' Jimmy said. 'It's time to go down to the paddock.'

As always, Lachlan felt the awful fluttering in his stomach. As much as he liked to fight, it was always the same before a bout and he would be glad to get it over with.

It was around four thirty in the afternoon when Lachlan finally stood waiting for O'Keefe to arrive, stripped to the waist surrounded by a very large crowd of men – both drunken and sober – who had come to watch the much-advertised contest. Lachlan had never seen as many people at any one of his country fights before and was awed by how much interest his unproven skills had attracted. Either Irish or Scots honour would prevail at the end of the day.

On a slope adjoining the paddock, Lachlan noticed an expensive carriage drawn by two greys. In the carriage sat a young army officer in his dress uniform and alongside him was Amanda, holding a parasol to shield her milky skin from the dying rays of the summer sun. Even at the distance they were from each other, Lachlan was aware that she was staring at him.

'Do you know who the officer is with the lady I met at Hyde Park?' Lachlan asked Jimmy, who was soaking a rag in a wooden pail of water.

'Who?' Jimmy asked, glancing in the direction Lachlan was staring. 'Oh, that is Captain Lightfoot. The captain always attends the fights around Sydney and I hear that his sister likes them too. You know how to pick 'em, Lachlan MacDonald. But I think that she is a bit out of our class.'

Lachlan's attention was distracted when a low buzz from the gathered spectators became a roaring cheer. O'Keefe had arrived in style, a cigar jutting from his mouth. It was obvious that the crowd in attendance were divided into two camps, as booing was also mixed with the cheers.

Kevin O'Keefe was not alone. Beside him were two men. One, Lachlan had seen the previous week at Hyde Park and knew as Michael Duffy whilst the older, very solidly built man, he did not know.

'Ah, O'Keefe has brought the referee with him,' Jimmy said. 'His name is Max Braun and he taught Duffy to fight. Max works at the Erin Hotel with the Duffy family. He will guarantee a clean fight.'

Lachlan was reassured by this news, as Braun had a fearsome appearance. From his scarred and broken face it was obvious that he had seen many a brawl in his time. When O'Keefe saw Lachlan he waved in a friendly manner. Lachlan returned his opponent's gesture.

Max Braun went to the centre of the area left open for the fighters. It was dusty and a silence fell over the spectators as this well-known personage in the world of bare-knuckle fighting took up his position.

'Ladies an' gentlemen,' Max said in a guttural way that left no doubt as to his Germanic origins. 'Today vee haf Mr Lachlan MacDonald challenging Mr Kevin O'Keefe for the purse of tventy guineas. Vinner take all.' Max raised his hands to indicate that the two fighters should step forward to him.

O'Keefe stripped off his coat and shirt so that he also stood half-naked in the paddock. Both men were bare-footed and their skin-tight trousers accentuated the muscles in their legs.

'Go and show him how a Scot can fight,' Jimmy whispered in Lachlan's ear. 'Fer the honour of bonny old Scotland.'

Lachlan moved forward to meet O'Keefe.

'You two must fight clean,' Max said when the men were face to face. 'No biting, scratching, kicking or vrestling. I will stop the fight if I think enough is enough.'

Both men nodded their understanding, intently eyeing each other.

'You start fighting ven I drop the handkerchief,' Max said, stepping back and holding a red cloth in his hands.

The cloth fluttered to the ground and a cheer rose up from the spectators. Lachlan stepped back with his hands raised in the classic stance – as did O'Keefe. Lachlan knew only too well that his opponent had a longer reach and a few more pounds of body mass over his own.

It was O'Keefe who made the first move with a quick left-hand jab for the face. Lachlan parried the punch, knowing it was simply a feint to see how he would react and before O'Keefe could recover from the punch he let fly with a left and right for O'Keefe's own face. But he did not stop there. Lachlan knew that he must stay in close to his opponent to negate being held at arm's length. The suddenness of the attack took O'Keefe off balance and he stumbled back with a sudden respect for the unknown young fighter.

A roar rose from the crowd and Lachlan was vaguely aware of shouts of encouragement. He continued to hammer his opponent with hard, stinging punches to the stomach region. O'Keefe had his guard up and many of the punches slammed into O'Keefe's forearms.

Then Lachlan felt the first heavy punches as his opponent found the target of his own head and torso. O'Keefe was dancing away to use the advantage of his longer reach. But the distance also helped

Lachlan as the punches had lost some of their sting when they connected. 'Get in close,' Lachlan could hear someone in the crowd yell. It was good advice but also a strategy O'Keefe was aware of as he kept Lachlan at bay.

The fight settled down with Lachlan advancing, throwing a couple of good punches and hurting his bigger opponent, and then O'Keefe countering at a distance to continually sting Lachlan. The stinging effect was beginning to work, as Lachlan felt the attack sap his strength. Torrents of sweat stung the eyes of both men, interfering with their respective techniques.

After what seemed an eternity, Lachlan suddenly found himself sitting down on a short wooden stool with water being splashed over his body. He was gasping for air and vaguely aware that his nose was broken. Blood washed over his lap with the flow of water.

'Keep in tight,' Jimmy hissed in his ear. 'The big bastard doesn't like yer punches. Yer really hurtin' him. No one can remember anyone goin' this long with O'Keefe. Yer just might beat him yet.'

Lachlan did not know whether he should laugh or cry. Sure, he knew that he was hurting O'Keefe, but not often enough. His only chance was to wear his opponent down, maybe causing him to tire and drop his guard. But it was Jimmy's last statement that stuck in Lachlan's mind. '*Yer just might beat him yet.*' What did that mean? Was he not here this day to beat O'Keefe?

Before Lachlan could dwell on an answer, the

fight was back on, and the slugging began again. But this time it had settled down to punch for punch. Dust rose to cling to the two men and the crowd roared. Blood – from Lachlan's broken nose and O'Keefe's split lip – splashed each opponent until they were both sprayed with red. Lachlan could feel the pain in his swollen knuckles and each blow was beginning to be agony. Never before had he faced such a challenge.

Then it happened.

Lachlan hardly knew what hit him. An explosion of red stars blurred his vision before the black night came and ended the fight. Lachlan did not hear the roar of approval from the Irish supporters as O'Keefe won by a knockout and remained the undisputed champion of Sydney Town.

FOUR

'You did very well against O'Keefe,' an unfamiliar voice said as Lachlan slowly recovered his wits. He could taste blood in his mouth and his head throbbed. He knew he did not want to open his eyes and lay for a moment in his world of hurt. But the worst hurt was the knowledge that he had been soundly beaten in front of Amanda.

A wet cloth splashed his face, easing just a little of the pain. Lachlan opened his eyes and attempted to sit up, but a hand gently held him down. 'Take it from me,' the unfamiliar voice continued, and Lachlan detected the influence of an Irish accent, 'it is best to get your wits about you before you attempt to take on the world again.'

'Do as Mr Duffy says,' Jimmy said. 'He knows what he's talkin' about.'

Lachlan lay for a brief moment before opening

his eyes to focus on the ring of faces looking down at him.

'Ah, that looks better. I'm Michael Duffy and I saw you fight O'Keefe. He had the reach and weight on you – but you held him well. You are a real fighter.'

Lachlan sat up with a groan and with help from Jimmy got to his feet to face the handsome, well-built, tall young man with striking grey eyes. Duffy was around Lachlan's own age, with a charisma that was palpable. Michael held out his hand.

'Lachlan MacDonald,' Lachlan said accepting the firm grip. 'I am pleased to make your acquaintance, Mr Duffy.'

'Michael will do. I ought to get old Max to give you some pointers. You tend to fight like someone more used to country pub bouts.'

'You are right on that point,' Lachlan replied, with a weak smile. 'I think that was my first and last fight in Sydney.'

'I wouldn't say that,' Michael said. 'I think that you have a big heart.'

'Thank you,' Lachlan answered, warming rapidly to this virtual stranger. 'But I think I will not be very popular in Sydney after losing the wagers my friends placed on me for a win.'

Michael chuckled at Lachlan's rueful reply. 'Put it this way, don't go drinking at the Victory, but you are always welcome at the Erin.'

Jimmy coughed at Michael's comment and Lachlan looked at him. There was something strange going on he was not a party to. 'What does that mean?' Lachlan asked, glaring at Jimmy, who was unable to look his friend in the eye.

'I got yer a bit of money,' Jimmy mumbled. 'Me and the boys kind of bet against yer winning and I put some money on fer you without revealing where it came from. Yer just personally made five pounds by going down to O'Keefe. But it was touch and go fer a moment. It looked like yer just might put him down an we all would have lost our bets. Yer really are good – like Mr Duffy says.'

Lachlan did not know whether he should punch Jimmy or admire him for his canny financial foresight. He opted for the latter and shook his head with a wry grin.

'Well done, my good fellow,' a voice said from the side and they turned to see the immaculately uniformed officer of a British regiment. Beside him stood Amanda. 'I was hoping to see that upstart Irishman get his just deserts when you faced him off. Here, take this as a token of my respect for a man of courage.'

The gold coin spun in the dying light of the day to be caught by Jimmy, who immediately handed it over to Lachlan. Caught unawares by both the compliment and the coin, Lachlan did not reply. There was also the distraction of the beautiful face of Amanda appraising him. Lachlan was suddenly conscious that he was covered in blood, dust and sweat, but this did not seem to deter Amanda's frank gaze.

'Thank you,' Lachlan finally blurted. 'I accept your kind words.'

'Well, if you were a part of my regiment,' the

captain continued, 'I am sure that you would be our champion. You have a good, strong Scots name with the shoulders to go with it. Now I shall bid you all a good evening. My sister was cheering for you, Mr MacDonald. She seemed to be very upset at your defeat.'

With his farewell, the officer turned to walk back to his carriage with his sister, who had remained silent.

'Bloody British,' Michael spat in the dust. 'Curse them all to hell.'

Lachlan could see that Michael Duffy was not a patriot of the English crown but he did not hold this against him. 'Why?' Lachlan asked, sensing something personal in the curse.

'It was English officers like Lightfoot at the Eureka stockade,' Michael replied, turning to face Lachlan with fire in his grey eyes. 'His kind slaughtered a lot of innocent men that day. I know, my family were there.'

'You were at Ballarat that day!' Lachlan exclaimed. 'So was I!'

Suddenly, the flame in Michael's eyes was extinguished, to be replaced with brazen curiosity and a kind of empathy. ''Tis truly a holy sign of St Patrick and St Andrew,' Michael said. 'We were meant to meet.'

'My mother died on the fields from consumption,' Lachlan continued. 'My father and oldest brother were killed that day. I was made an orphan and separated from my other brother and sister. I have not seen them since.'

Michael and Jimmy stared at Lachlan. ''Tis a day of strange coincidences,' Michael said, 'that we should be here today with the stockade as a common bond. But it is back to the Erin with you, where you will be truly welcomed. Even if you are not of the true faith, there is at least Celtic blood in your veins.'

He grasped Lachlan's arm and Lachlan sensed that he had made a good friend in this enigmatic but charismatic Irishman. They both shared the wound of the massacre and, although divided by religion, still shared the spirit of the brotherhood of rebels.

The return to the Erin Hotel with Michael and Jimmy opened up a whole new set of friendships for Lachlan MacDonald. In the kitchen of the hotel – owned by the gruff Frank Duffy and his kindly wife, Bridget – Lachlan met the rest of the Irish clan including Daniel, who was a leaner, more serious version of Michael, and Michael's sister Kate. He also got to know Max Braun, who took him through the fight with O'Keefe blow by blow, patiently explaining where it had gone wrong for Lachlan.

The talk around the kitchen table was accompanied by a bottle of good Irish whiskey and the night soon mellowed into a medley of Irish songs. Lachlan joined in heartily, despite his strict upbringing by Duncan Campbell.

From Monday to Saturday the following week, Lachlan rued his brief attempt at glory and prize money. His body ached and his broken nose was setting at a slightly awry angle, adding a tougher look to his normally pleasant face. The bruising to his knuckles and face was beginning to fade away and the foreman did not press him hard on the work site – after all, he had made good money on Jimmy's tip to back O'Keefe.

By Saturday evening, Lachlan sat in the backyard of the hotel with Jimmy planning their Sunday outing. Jimmy was not surprised to hear his friend suggest that they go to Hyde Park again. It had not gone unnoticed that Lachlan seemed to be a different man ever since meeting Amanda.

In Melbourne town, John MacDonald well and truly knew the subtle signs, and suspected strongly that he was not alone in his dark and terrible secret. He sat alone at his linen-covered table in the expensive hotel dining room, supping on an excellent pea and ham soup. There was only one other diner.

John knew the other man's name, as from time to time they had passed each other in the hotel foyer and exchanged polite greetings. Now John watched the other diner with more than passing interest. He was about ten years older than John, with the fine-boned features of an aristocrat. His face was clean-shaven and his hands manicured. Even in their brief encounters John had noticed the dreamy quality of the other man's eyes when they exchanged brief glances. They reminded John of the eyes of a poet.

'Why don't you join me, Mr MacDonald,' the man suddenly said, as if reading John's thoughts. 'We seem to be alone this night.'

Startled, John almost dropped his spoon but recovered his senses to smile, stand up with his bowl and walk over to the other man's table.

'Thank you for the invitation, Mr Busby,' John said, sitting down carefully, lest he disgrace himself by spilling his soup over the table.

'I would rather you call me Nicholas,' Busby said with a faint smile, 'if I may call you John.' He held out his hand and John accepted the gesture, noting how smooth and soft the other man's hand felt in his own. 'Despite your dress, speech and manner I suspect that you are *nouveau riche*,' Nicholas said, sipping at his soup. Before John could speak to defend himself Nicholas raised his free hand. 'That is a compliment, my dear chap. Something refreshing, when one considers my origins in merry old England and her class system.'

'You are very perceptive,' John replied. 'I am the son of a gold miner from Scotland and my wealth is an inheritance as a result of my father striking it rich and selling out his claim at a good price.'

'Ah, as for my good fortune,' Nicholas said, leaning slightly back in his chair, 'I am fortunate enough to be the third son of Lord Busby. Born on the right side of the bed, you might say. But now I am what you colonials call a remittance man, one who has been exiled forever from the fair shores of England to live on a stipend allocated from the family estates.'

'I was under the impression that a remittance man was someone sent out here for some kind of indiscretion.'

'True,' Nicholas answered with an enigmatic

smile. 'Mine was to resist the temptation to marry well, sire a brood of little brutes and continue the family line in the time-honoured tradition. What is the dark secret of one who originally hailed from Van Diemen's Land?'

John was surprised at how much Nicholas knew of his life. It was both flattering and disconcerting at the same time.

'Why would you think that I would have a dark secret?' John countered uncomfortably.

'Because we all have secrets,' Nicholas said with that same smug look of knowing. 'What are your dreams in life?'

'To find my brother and sister,' John let slip. 'And make a fortune along the way.'

'Maybe I could be of assistance – at least in the latter part of your dream,' Nicholas offered. 'It all depends on how we may find our future relationship in life.'

John felt his heart skip a beat. His suspicion that the other man was inclined in the same manner as himself was being played out in their little game of verbal cut and parry. From the very first time he had first seen Nicholas in the hotel foyer he had to admit that he had been attracted to him. Now, this beautiful man was practically telling him that the feeling was mutual.

'How could you do that?' John asked, feeling as if he needed air to breathe.

'If nothing else, my dear father is hoping that I will manage his estates in these colonies with some financial success,' Nicholas replied, delicately wiping the side of his mouth with a perfectly starched linen napkin. 'I sense that you are a young man with much talent, despite your origins.'

John did not resent the comment, rather he desired Nicholas more than before.

They finished their soup and the kitchen staff came in to reset the tables for breakfast. Both men retired to their respective accommodation. In the early hours of the morning John plucked up the courage and made his way very carefully and quietly to Nicholas Busby's room. A gentle tap on the door was all it took to change both their lives forever.

Lachlan had been invited to share Christmas day of 1862 with the Duffy family at the Erin Hotel and was welcomed as if he were a member of the family. He found himself very much in the company of Daniel Duffy, who was enjoying a break from his training to be a solicitor.

In the European tradition, Bridget had prepared a feast of roasted vegetables and a haunch of beef. There was even the luxury of a couple of roasted chickens and a huge ham. Lachlan could not remember a Christmas before that he had enjoyed so much. Most of his Christmases had been spent on the dusty tracks outside one little town or other west of the Great Dividing Range.

Ale and rum flowed throughout the day, while Bridget and Kate worked in a sheen of sweat to keep up to the demand by the hungry and thirsty men. A rich plum pudding covered in yellow custard took them into the evening when Frank Duffy, the publican, broke into nostalgic songs of old Ireland, bringing forth tears to the eyes of both the tough Michael Duffy and his gentler cousin, Daniel. Only old Max Braun seemed to be immune to the sentimentality and sat quietly sipping his tots of rum.

When Lachlan finally staggered home from the evening he found Mrs Woodford uproariously drunk, sitting with the rest of the boarders around the dining room table. It was the one day of the year she allowed alcohol in the boarding house and the empty sherry bottle on the table testified to her indulgence. Lachlan was greeted warmly by his friends and reeled up to his room to collapse on his bed.

There was no work during the Yuletide break and the men in Lachlan's team luxuriated in the days away from the gruelling work site. Early in the new year, Lachlan found himself drawn to Hyde Park, where he wandered amongst the holiday-makers enjoying the open air. He was always on the lookout for Amanda and was rewarded one day when he saw her strolling with a tall young man at her side. Lachlan felt his heartbeat increase, watching the two walking together. Then for a moment the young man at Amanda's side disappeared, seemingly to fetch something for her, and Lachlan hurried across.

'Hello, Miss Lightfoot,' he said and she turned to face him under her parasol.

'Oh, hello, Mr MacDonald,' she responded in a startled way, glancing around her quickly. 'Happy new year.'

It was clear Amanda appeared uncomfortable in his presence and Lachlan suspected strongly that it had something to do with the young man.

'You must know that I am in the company of a dear friend,' she said, averting her gaze. 'I don't think that it is appropriate that you and I be seen together.'

'I am just a friend greeting you a good day,' Lachlan answered, concealing his hurt. 'I hardly think that is inappropriate.'

'Well, Sir Percival Sparkes will be back soon and it might be better if you take your leave,' Amanda replied, this time looking him directly in the eyes.

'I was hoping to see you. I had a small gift for you – a token of meeting you. I realise Christmas has passed but I would like you to have it anyway.' He reached into his pocket and produced a pearl at the end of a gold chain. He held it out and placed it in Amanda's hand. She stared at the pretty piece of jewellery, her mouth partially agape in her surprise.

'I cannot accept this,' she said quietly. 'It must have cost a small fortune.'

'It is nothing,' Lachlan retorted, attempting to shrug off the expensive item, which had cost him his entire winnings from the wager he had inadvertently won against himself. 'One day I will be a famous explorer like John McDouall Stuart who I have read has just returned after his journeys into the centre of South Australia. Then I will be rich and buy you more pearls.'

'Mr MacDonald,' she said, 'I do not want you to have the wrong idea, but both society and my situation dictate that we can only ever be acquaintances.

Sir Percival is my beau and it is possible that we may wed in the future. He has prospects in his family business and we have known each other for many years.'

'And I am nothing more than a labourer you know very little of,' Lachlan said, the bitterness edging his reply. 'I do not intend to remain a labourer for the rest of my life.'

'I believe that you are a highly intelligent young man who will one day make something of your life,' Amanda replied sadly. 'But, for now, you must find your way as I am finding mine. I am sorry, Mr MacDonald, if you were under some misapprehension about our brief meeting before Christmas. Please, you must take your gift back.'

Amanda attempted to hand back the necklace but Lachlan shook his head.

'It is yours to keep,' he said. 'You don't have to tell anyone where it came from. Keep it to remind you of the man you met in Hyde Park who thinks that you are the most beautiful woman he has ever come across in his life.'

Lachlan turned, and walked away quickly to prevent Amanda seeing the terrible pain of rejection in his face. He did not turn back to see her standing alone with tears in her eyes clasping the pearl necklace in her hands.

The Christmas and new year period of 1862 had been one of the most wonderful times in John MacDonald's life. He and Nicholas found love in each other's company, although their relationship had to be kept a closely guarded secret. Neither society nor the law were sympathetic to what was termed the abominable crime of sodomy and their unacceptable affection for each other could get them arrested as felons.

When Nicholas purchased a cottage on Port Phillip Bay, they had a retreat to which they could escape from the world that would punish them for their feelings. It was a place of peace where they were able to stroll along the foreshore, read books and poetry together as well as share intimate meals.

As summer came to an end, John had not as yet invested his money and while sitting outside one starry night with Nicholas and sipping a fine port he raised the matter of returning to the real world of commerce.

'I cannot continue to avail myself of your kind hospitality, Nicholas. It is time that I put my money to work.'

Nicholas leaned back to stare at the constellations wheeling slowly overhead. 'I think that you may be able to take advantage of a very opportune time coming up,' he said. 'If there has been one thing that has made fortunes for the speculator, then it has been when England has gone to war. Men of foresight have always seized the opportunity of feeding the war machine of Her Majesty, God bless her.'

John glanced at his lover with surprise. 'But Britain is at peace. We have not had a major conflict since the war in the Crimea against the Russian Tsar.'

'Ah, but you do not follow the journal reports of

that island to our east, New Zealand,' Nicholas replied smugly. 'If you had, then you would realise that the Maori have not been defeated and from what I can glean from the reports, Governor Grey has engineered a road from a place called Drury to Pokeno. That gives him access to the Waikato district from Auckland and the Maori have ordered all white settlers to leave the Waikato district, because they see the road as being a colonial effort to seize their fertile traditional lands. If I know British pride, the Empire will not tolerate being dictated to by its brown-skinned colonised peoples. There will be a war waged and you and I are in a position to supply government tenders with two vital commodities: rum and beef.'

John knew little of the colony of New Zealand – except that it consisted of two islands to the east of Australia across the Tasman Sea and that it had once been under the jurisdiction of New South Wales. He also knew that the country was inhabited by a fierce, war-like native people who practised cannibalism from time to time.

'Do you really think so?' John asked in his ignorance.

'Well, I am going to play my hunch and speculate that there soon will be a call for tenders to supply the military commissariat. All one has to be is in the right place at the right time to satisfy the demand and I have a rather good idea how we can do that using a new invention designed by a fellow Scot of yours by the name of James Harrison. His invention has not been exploited to its full potential but I can see it could help us make a fortune.'

John was intrigued. The seemingly indolent Nicholas Busby was forever reading articles from the library and perusing the newspaper journals from cover to cover.

'What invention?' John asked.

'It is something called refrigeration,' Nicholas replied. 'In a nutshell, he has invented a device that can turn out around three tons of ice a day. It is currently being used in the Geelong brewery to cool the building. It seems Harrison got the idea when he was cleaning typeprint with some ether and noticed how it left the metal surfaces cold to the touch. So he extrapolated from that and by putting gas under pressure was able to come up with a device that cools the air to the point of freezing. But you colonials, being as stupid as you are, have resisted his invention and Harrison has gone bankrupt, losing his newspaper the *Geelong Advertiser* to creditors because he put his money into his invention.'

'Refrigeration,' John mumbled. 'But how does that help us?'

'You can be rather obtuse, Mr MacDonald,' Nicholas sighed. 'Imagine if we could buy up a lot of beef at a cheap price, have it slaughtered and then keep it cold to avoid decomposition. We could then have the meat canned and sold off to the army. The refrigeration would help us stockpile meat. Who knows what else will come from Harrison's invention. No doubt, the colonies will one day be shipping lamb and beef to old England herself by using refrigeration.'

John could see Nicholas's vision – if not

Harrison's dream – but still felt a pang of fear. What if Nicholas was wrong? He questioned himself. Was it possible that he would lose all he now had?

'I have always sworn to find my brother and sister so that they may share in the legacy left to us,' he replied quietly. 'This venture could cost me all that we have in this world.'

'I know of your crusade,' Nicholas said gently. 'But I am offering you the opportunity of a lifetime to turn what you have into a fortune beyond even your dreams. Then you would be able to allow your brother and sister to share that fortune with you. All you have to do is trust me.'

John pondered on the proposed venture, staring into the dark night. 'I trust your instincts,' he finally said. 'I must have to have met you in the first place.'

Nicholas smiled and leaned over to take John's hand. 'Now, all we have to do is get hold of a refrigeration machine, buy a meatworks and build a cannery,' he said. 'I will warn you that we are in for a lot of hard work and will have to trust each other's decisions in matters pertaining to the enterprise. I can assure you that I have most of the working capital that we may need and you can consider that my dowry bestowed to you in our union.'

The die was cast and John felt both elation and fear at what was ahead of them. All they really needed for their product was the promised war in New Zealand that Nicholas had forecast. If he was wrong then they could find themselves living on beef for a long time to come – along with the debts incurred in setting up such a large enterprise.

FIVE

Winter had come to the Southern Hemisphere. In the dark, early hours of the morning, Lachlan lay on his bed under a thin blanket, feeling the Sydney cold and knowing that in a few minutes he would have to rise to prepare for another day on the work site. So much had happened in the past few months in the small world around him. He had lost two good friends; one to death and the other to God knew where.

His friend Michael Duffy had been accused of the murder of a well-known Rocks criminal and had fled Sydney. A rumour had circulated that the killing was the result of an impossible love match between Michael and a high-born young lady; another rumour said that he had been seen in the colony of South Australia. Even Kate Duffy was gone from Sydney. Married to Kevin O'Keefe, she had journeyed to the colony of Queensland.

And Jimmy had died. The doctor said it was pneumonia and Lachlan had watched day in and day out as the insidious sickness ravaged his young friend's body. Jimmy had refused to miss work and eventually this had been a contributing factor in his demise. That had been in April, three months earlier, and Lachlan, along with old Harry the works supervisor, had stood in the rain at the cemetery, watching the muddy earth shovelled into the grave. Jimmy's last resting place, unacknowledged by any impressive monument, had simply a wooden cross with his name and length of life inscribed on it. Other than the grave-diggers, Harry and Lachlan had been the only two to say farewell to Jimmy that day. Afterwards they allowed themselves the luxury of retiring to a hotel to get drunk to the memory of the man who had been a firm friend to one of them and good employee to the other.

A cold wind whipped at the loose tin sheets on the boarding house roof and in the dark Lachlan eased himself from under his blanket to dress for another day on the construction site. For a moment he sat at the edge of his bed and reflected on his dream of being an explorer. He had allowed the mere fact of surviving financially from day to day to keep him from his dream, he knew. But apart from the twenty pounds in the bank from the sale of old Duncan's property, he had little else in the world other than the clothes on his back and a couple of battered books of poetry. The loss of Jimmy had hit him hard and this, coupled with Amanda's rejection, made him feel lost and alone. He cursed himself for the self-pity. At least it was Saturday morning and, all going well, old Harry just might give them an early break if the rain persisted. Lachlan knew that he would go to the Erin Hotel and get very drunk. The alcohol made him forget his situation for a while and it was something that he was doing much too often lately so it was also having an adverse effect on his income. Life had seemed to come down to hard work and equally hard drinking. Old Duncan Campbell would have rolled over in his grave if he knew about the drinking binges, Lachlan thought, slipping on his trousers over his long john underwear. Breakfast would be on the table downstairs and the young man suddenly felt a flash of warmth for the kindly landlady who never missed ensuring her boarders were well fed before they departed for work.

Driven off the construction sites and streets by the rain, the Erin Hotel was packed with working men, smoking pipes and sitting around tables drinking hard spirits. Lachlan felt the warm glow of the rum seeping through his body as he leaned against the bar. He was drinking alone, sometimes chatting to Max Braun who was working behind the bar, and had been pleased when he saw Daniel enter the public house.

'I see that you are back again,' Daniel said by way of greeting, pushing a space between Lachlan and a drunken tannery worker who smelled of foul chemicals.

'Not much else to do with myself,' Lachlan slurred.

'I don't know about that,' Daniel replied with a frown. 'You have always struck me as a man with prospects, despite your current circumstances.'

'Nice to know that someone has a bit of faith in me,' Lachlan replied. 'Because I don't know where to go from here.'

Max placed a tumbler of lemonade on the bar in front of Daniel. 'I don't think drinking is going to help,' Daniel said, raising his glass.

'It doesn't hurt,' Lachlan replied and raised his glass in a mock salute. 'It has a nice way of making the world go away. Why is it that you aren't having one on this fine Saturday night?'

'I have to study this weekend,' Daniel grimaced. 'I have mid-year exams for law this week.'

'Ah well, I shall raise my glass to the up-and-coming lawyer and to my old but brief friend Michael Duffy, wherever he may be in this big world,' Lachlan said, somewhat unsteady on his feet when he straightened up.

Daniel was concerned for the young Scot, having noticed his deterioration over the last month, and he glanced at Max for support. Max understood what young Daniel meant and leaned forward to speak quietly into his ear. 'I vill make sure he gets a bed here tonight,' he said quietly.

Daniel nodded his appreciation. The streets of Sydney were dangerous for anyone after the hotels closed. Even Michael Duffy had learned that when he had once been ambushed by a couple of thugs from the infamous Rocks district.

Lachlan continued to drink until he remembered nothing more of the evening.

He awoke on Sunday morning between clean sheets and for a moment was completely mystified as to where he was. It was a small room cloaked in semi–darkness. His head hurt more than usual after a night of heavy drinking and he felt very ill. At least the ceiling was not spinning but deep down he thought death might be preferable to the way he felt.

Muffled voices came from beneath his feet and when he strained his ears he could recognise Bridget Duffy's voice chiding Daniel to get out of bed and go to Mass. So he was in the Erin. But how had he ended up in a bed? The question nagged him but his answer came when the door opened to frame the stocky build of Max Braun.

'Goot morning, my friend,' Max greeted, holding a pail of water in one big hand. 'I thought you might need this to clean up.'

Lachlan half raised himself into a sitting position and yelped his pain. His ribs hurt and he did not know why.

'You haf a bit of pain,' Max said, setting the pail down by the side of the bed. 'It must have been from the fight last night.'

'What fight?' Lachlan asked softly lest his head fall off at loud noises.

'The fight you had vif me,' Max grinned. 'You lost.'

'Damn!' Lachlan swore. 'Did I really have a fight with you?'

'Ja, but you did not mean it,' Max answered

graciously. 'It vos too much drink and not enough sense, my young friend.'

'I'm sorry, Max,' Lachlan groaned. 'You know that you are one of the few friends I have and I would never mean to fight with you.'

'That is all right,' Max grunted, waving off what he considered an unnecessary apology. Clearing the bar of drunken trouble-makers was second nature to the old seaman, who had brawled his way through some of the most infamous sea ports of the world, from San Francisco to Hamburg and many others in between.

'You must clean yourself up,' Max said. 'You have a fine gentleman visitor who wishes to meet with you.'

'Who is it, Max?' Lachlan asked, sitting up in the bed and clutching his head in his hands. 'God, I swear I will never drink again.'

'I do not know,' Max shrugged. 'He has a pretty red-coat uniform and a fine pair of horses for his carriage.'

'I think I know who he might be,' Lachlan said. 'But what in Hades does he want to see me for? That is the question.'

'Then you must clean yourself up and find out,' Max said, exiting the room to join the Duffys downstairs.

Lachlan eased himself out of the bed and pulled on his clothes that lay on the floor in an untidy heap. It was obvious that Max had undressed him for bed the previous evening and not Bridget. For that, Lachlan was grateful.

He stuck his head in the pail of water and wiped down his face with a towel he found on a sideboard with a mirror. When Lachlan stared at his reflection he noticed two very red eyes looking back at him. Stubble dotted his chin and his hair lay flat against his head where it had been wetted down.

By the time he stumbled downstairs the Duffy family had departed for church, leaving only Max and a parlour maid to look after the hotel. Lachlan saw the officer standing in the bar in his bright dress uniform.

'Good morning, captain,' Lachlan said with as much dignity as he could muster for a hangover. 'How may I help you?'

The officer turned to Lachlan and sneered, looking him up and down as if inspecting one of his troops on parade. 'You do not look very formidable, Mr MacDonald,' he said with a snort. 'Not in your present condition.'

'I can assure you, captain, that the present condition is only a temporary affair,' Lachlan replied stiffly. 'But your presence here, seeking me, is of interest. How did you know that I would be here?'

'I have visited your lodgings and spoken to your landlady,' Lightfoot sniffed arrogantly. 'She said that I might find you here – or in the gutter somewhere on the road back to her establishment.'

'Well, you found me here,' Lachlan said politely. 'What can I do for you?'

'I have a proposal for you,' Charles Lightfoot said. 'I am about to steam for New Zealand to take command of a militia unit being raised to confront the Maori threat. Before I depart these shores I have promised my fellow officers a boxing match to remember. For some reason my sister has suggested that I choose you to fight our regimental champion, Bill Williams.'

'Why me?' Lachlan countered.

'My sister was very impressed with the way you fought that Irish chap,' Lightfoot replied. 'I would have preferred to have O'Keefe but it seems he has wed and gone north with his bride to Queensland.'

'How much?' Lachlan asked, trying to stem his excitement that the beautiful young woman had remembered him.

'Say, a purse of a fifty guineas.'

Lachlan kept his composure. Fifty guineas was a lot of money. 'Win or lose?' he asked.

'Winner takes all,' the English captain answered brusquely. 'There is no second prize for losers.'

Lachlan wished that his throbbing head would settle. He did not have to really consider the proposed fight. He knew he needed the money if he were to find a way out of his current predicament stuck in Sydney. 'I will accept the challenge,' he replied. 'When and where do I fight?'

'Two weeks from now at the same ground you faced the Irishman,' Lightfoot said. 'I only pray that my sister chose wisely,' he added, looking at Lachlan contemptuously. 'I have promised a fight to remember.'

'You will get that,' Lachlan said proudly.

'Well, I shall bid you a good day and see you on the field of battle in two weeks' time, Mr MacDonald.'

Lachlan watched the haughty English captain

exit the hotel and turned to see Max hovering in the shadows.

'I know of this Bill Williams,' Max growled. 'He is a goot fighter but you are equally matched in weight and size.'

'How good?' Lachlan asked.

'You must give up the drink and train hard,' Max replied, stepping from the shadows. 'I vill train you – as I haf Michael and many others – and you vill vin.'

'If I do win,' Lachlan said. 'Then I would like you to take a quarter of the winnings for training me.'

'I do not want money,' Max answered in an annoyed tone. 'I want you to vin, nothing more, and a promise that you vill not drink anymore.'

Lachlan was taken aback by the condition. 'I promise,' he finally said, giving in to the old German's offer.

'Das is gut,' Max said, turning back to his chores for the day's trading.

Lachlan trained hard and kept to his word not to drink. He risked a week off work with permission from old Harry, the supervisor, who was happy to oblige when he learned of what Lachlan was setting out to do.

'Me an' the boys will be backing you this time,' he said with a tobacco-stained smile. 'I reckon you have it in yer to beat Williams.'

Lachlan was cheered by the boss's confidence in him.

'So, take the time off an' get ready fer the fight.

Me an' the boys will be there to cheer you on.'

Max was also given some time off to coach Lachlan and in the backyard of the Erin Hotel they trained hard. Despite his large frame and big belly, Max proved to the much younger man that he was still a formidable fighter. His reflexes were fast and his jabs thrown at lightning speed stung Lachlan with the impact. Lachlan was just glad that old Max pulled his punches before they truly made contact.

Max concentrated on Lachlan's footwork and stance. 'You must dance like one of those ladies who ballet,' Max said, shuffling his feet. 'You hit hard but not let the other fighter hit you.'

Every day, Max made Lachlan toughen his knuckles by punching continuously into a bucket of sand and then bathing his hands in water laced with salt. Max would shake his head and mumble in German that he needed more time to toughen the young man's fists but told himself that Lachlan would not have to hit his opponent too many times. Just that one good punch to end the fight . . .

Sit-ups, push-ups and a run through Fraser's paddock a short distance from the hotel helped Lachlan sweat away the past couple of months' heavy drinking.

In the evenings Daniel would share a lemonade with Lachlan and over the two weeks their friendship deepened. The hours on dusk as the three men sat in the backyard of the hotel surrounded by empty wooden crates were good times, although when Lachlan returned to the company of Mrs Woodford at nights she would look hurt by his absences. She knew of the coming bout and Lachlan had heard from one of his work mates that she had put ten shillings on him to win. This knowledge alone was enough to stiffen Lachlan's resolve to win. The woman with the sharp tongue and big heart did not believe in gambling, rating it as a mortal sin alongside murder and adultery – but she was prepared to show her faith in him.

On the eve of the bout, Max produced a bottle of English ale. 'Just this once only,' he grunted, handing the opened bottle to Lachlan with a shrug of his broad shoulders. 'Vee drink to your victory.'

Daniel had joined them with his usual glass of lemonade. 'You know,' Daniel said, 'it was in this very backyard that Michael thrashed Kevin O'Keefe one night.'

Lachlan looked at his friend in surprise. 'I heard that they never fought each other – although the match would have brought out all Sydney to watch.'

'Ja,' Max said with a wide grin. 'But it was a fight of honour.'

'Over what?' Lachlan asked.

'Mine little Katie's honour,' Max replied, taking a long gulp on his beer.

Lachlan was tactful enough to know that he should not ask any more questions. He was just pleased that he had never had to face the absent young Irishman who could thrash O'Keefe. All he had to worry about was this Bill Williams who Max was confident enough could be beaten by any man he trained. Lachlan prayed that he was right.

• • •

A cold wind whipped at the green grass in the paddock, now filled with a much larger crowd than had witnessed Lachlan's first fight in the same place. The dust was gone, to be replaced with mud. There were many colourful military uniforms and on the slight rise that acted as a natural amphitheatre above the paddock many fine closed and open carriages were parked. Lachlan also noticed many more ladies attending the bout. As he stood stripped to the waist, attempting not to shiver against the bite of the late afternoon winter's wind, an expectant hum filled the air and Lachlan was very aware of the many eyes appraising him.

'I didn't think it would be like this,' he said in an awed voice.

'Ja, many people saw you fight O'Keefe and admire the way you fought,' Max said, massaging Lachlan's shoulders with his broad hands. 'They have come to see you win.'

Lachlan smiled inwardly. As nervous as he was, he was actually looking forward to stepping up to his opponent but his cheer dimmed when he saw the army's fighter step out from the crowd. He was Lachlan's height but had a massive barrel chest and a head that seemed stuck onto his bovine-like shoulders. A long, handle-bar moustache topped off his fearsome expression. He was older and appeared confident. He glanced at Lachlan from across the paddock, snarled and turned to say something to his seconds, who laughed at his joke.

'Don't let him trouble you,' Daniel said quietly in Lachlan's ear. 'Poor fellow, he does not know what awaits him.'

'Thanks, Daniel,' Lachlan said with little conviction. 'The other chap looks like he should be working in a slaughter yard rather than the army.'

'You vill beat him,' Max grunted. 'Just remember to dance.'

'Mr MacDonald?'

Lachlan heard the voice from behind him and turned to look directly at Amanda. Her deep brown eyes were locked on his and Lachlan felt his stomach knot.

The young woman was given a path to move through the small circle of spectators directly around him. She was carrying a brilliantly coloured waist sash of deep blue in both hands and held it out to Lachlan. She was so close that he could smell the eau de cologne she wore.

'I would like you to wear this for your fight against my brother's champion,' she said.

Lachlan felt his heart thump. He took the sash from her hands and wound it around his waist. A small cheer rose from those spectators closest to him at the gesture. 'I am honoured, Miss Lightfoot,' he said with a smile. 'I will win this fight for you. I am your champion – as in a Byronic poem.'

An unexpected look of surprise swept across Amanda's face. 'Have you read any of Mr Byron's work?' she asked.

'His and many others,' Lachlan replied.

'You seem to have hidden depths, Mr MacDonald,' Amanda smiled sweetly. 'Somehow that does not surprise me.'

'It is time,' Max said. 'The referee has arrived and beckons.'

Lachlan wished that he could share some more moments with Amanda but he could see his opponent was already by the referee. When Lachlan turned back to bid Amanda his best wishes, she had already been swallowed by the crowd.

They were hammering blows, Lachlan thought in his exhaustion. For a good twenty minutes the fight had ebbed and flowed in either direction. Blood ran down both men's faces from cuts above the eyes and from split lips.

Gasping, punching, grunting in clinches, both men probed with their fists for a weak point on each other's bodies. Lachlan had heeded Max's good advice and kept his distance from what he had come to learn was a stronger opponent. Bill Williams's massive shoulders were reservoirs of power and Lachlan knew a well-delivered straight punch could end the fight with a loss to himself.

The earth under their feet was slippery and Lachlan was no longer aware of the crowd roaring with each punch delivered by either fighter. At one time, early in the fight, he had noticed Amanda sitting in her brother's open carriage on the earthen terrace above the field. But that seemed an eternity ago as he fought to keep on his feet.

'Go down, lad,' he heard Bill Williams rasp when they went into a clinch. 'Yer can't take much more of a beatin' from me.'

Lachlan ignored the advice and realised that Williams was in worse condition than he had thought. His plea for Lachlan's capitulation was not delivered out of kindness but a subterfuge for himself to win the fight before he lost all his reserves of strength. This gave Lachlan a boost in his own inner strength and he broke the clinch to land three good punches into Bill Williams's midriff, expelling air from his opponent's lungs. Lachlan followed with three more quick punches to the head and his opponent reeled. Without letting up, Lachlan waded in with a continuous barrage of punches to both the head and body. Williams continued to reel back, blood splashing them both from the serious cut above the older fighter's eye. Now Lachlan was aware of the crowd roaring. They too sensed a change in the pace of the fight as Lachlan continued to deliver his punches.

When Bill Williams dropped his guard, Lachlan knew he would win. The exhausted fighter fell to one knee and Lachlan stepped in to deliver the coup de grace of boxing. With all his remaining strength, he swung a punch that caught Williams in the side of the head. He toppled on his side to lie at Lachlan's feet.

All Lachlan could remember was standing momentarily over the army's unconscious champion and the crowd sweeping forward to hoist him onto their shoulders. His eyes had closed so badly he could not see Amanda in her carriage, but he hoped that she would be pleased. He had been true to his promise to her.

SIX

The evening was drawing nigh and the cold of winter was turning bitter. Amanda Lightfoot was snuggled against the leather seat of her brother's carriage with a warm fur coat and muff warming her hands.

'You chose wisely in your fighter,' her brother mused opposite her in the carriage, a cheroot between his lips. 'One would think that you have an eye for the sport, my dear sister. Our father would have been pleased at your intuition. May I ask why you insisted that this young man should be the one you suggested?'

Amanda gazed out at the tall gum trees bordering the road into the city. 'I thought that he fought with courage in his fight before Christmas against that Irishman,' she replied. 'Nothing more.'

Charles Lightfoot was not satisfied with his sister's

answer. As her older brother it was his duty to ensure that she make a good match in any liaison that might lead her to a good marriage, which was why he had introduced her to the eminently eligible Sir Percival Sparkes. Amanda knew where her duty lay but it seemed as though recently she had been neglecting her suitor and Sir Percival had spoken to him about the situation. She did not give any reason but simply declined accepting visits from her beau. Charles was puzzled and concerned at her sudden change of heart.

He and his sister had been orphaned not long after Charles had departed on a military posting to the Australian colonies. His first action had been at the Ballarat goldfields and a short time later he had received a letter from his uncle in England informing him of the death of his mother and father from a fever when they had been visiting London. The letter went on to say that his sister was being sent to the colonies to join him. With his limited financial means as a vicar in an English county, his uncle could not ensure she made a suitable debut into refined society.

Charles's father had been a relatively well-to-do merchant with a warehouse just outside London and Charles had been able to purchase his first commission into a middle-ranking regiment. The money he had taken from the dead Scotsman at the Eureka stockade had been used to purchase his captaincy, with enough left over to ensure a comfortable cottage not far from his regiment. There he had been able to curry favour with his fellow senior officers with games of cards and bottles of good port.

It was at cards that the captain had proved to be lucky. Charles Lightfoot was a born gambler, who had added boxing matches to his list of wage-earning gambles. He had respected his sister's choice of the young Scot against his own regimental champion as the odds were long against MacDonald to win. Charles, wisely, secretly backed Lachlan, however, and had won a large amount on the fight.

The arrival some time ago of his beautiful young sister in the colony of New South Wales had ensured his popularity with the young, unwed officers of the regiment, many of whom vied for her company. Charles had been careful to vet each officer's pedigree with the hope that one of them was only marking time in the army until an inheritance from a substantial family estate came through, either freeing him to return to wealth in England or allowing him to pursue further fortune in the Australian colonies, where already several expatriate officers had demonstrated their keen nose for a good business venture. Sir Percival Sparkes had been the perfect choice. Now, it seemed as if she had rejected him. In her brother's eyes she was far too independent and educated for a woman of some means. She even found the stark beauty of the colonies appealing and seemed to immerse herself in its coarse culture devoid of the genteel softness of home.

But now Charles had been asked to take command of a militia being formed in New Zealand to confront the Maori warriors, and this was his prime concern. All that worried him was a small but nagging doubt about his sister's interest in the young

Scot. It was just something about the way she had looked at the man, Charles brooded. The way she seemed to react when MacDonald took the punishing blows as if she were feeling them too. No, she may think that she was infatuated with the Scot but he had nothing to offer the sister of an officer rising in the regiment.

Although he had little to do with his sister when they were growing up – and his postings in the army had taken him away from home – Charles was coming to learn that Amanda was a far more complex creature than most women he knew. She loved to read and yet was quite outspoken at gatherings of his fellow officers when she should have remained quiet. She had a passion for life and the colonies seemed to agree with her. Charles was able to put on airs and pass as some kind of English aristocrat but Amanda spurned such behaviour. She was kind towards their housemaid, a young girl of fourteen, and did not speak down to anyone she met, whether rich or poor. This interest of hers in the young Scot troubled him more than he liked. But he had a plan.

'Amanda, I would like you to accompany me to New Zealand for the duration of the campaign,' he said, watching the grey smoke of his cheroot whirl away on the cold breeze.

'I would like that,' Amanda replied, her lack of hesitation surprising her brother. 'I have read much about the people there and the land. It seems to be a fascinating place.'

'Good,' Lightfoot replied. 'Then you can arrange our luggage for the voyage.'

Charles Lightfoot breathed a sigh of relief. The Tasman Sea would surely dampen his sister's strong feelings for a young man of no consequence other than his ability to use his fists. After his service in New Zealand he would ensure that his sister was reunited with Sir Percival and was made to realise her duty.

Lachlan was in no fit state to enjoy the victory celebrations held for him at the Erin Hotel. Washed and freshly dressed, his face told the story of a hard-fought win. Both his eyes were nearly closed and the congealing blood from the cuts to his face marked what would be scars for life. The prize money had been delivered and a small amount of it had been used to pay for drinks all round. Despite Lachlan being raised a Presbyterian, the predominantly Irish Catholic patrons of Frank Duffy's pub had supported him to a man, as had the popular publican himself.

As Lachlan had given his word to Max not to drink alcohol again, he slipped from the rowdy crowd in the hotel to find a quiet place in the dark of the backyard amongst the stacked empty wooden crates. He ached all over from the heavy blows he had received and sat on an empty crate, the silk sash spread across his lap. He cherished this gift from the beautiful Amanda Lightfoot. He felt that it had brought him luck and knew that he would never part with it. If only he could speak once again with the young woman and listen to that soft, gentle voice, he sighed.

John MacDonald stood in the cold room of the newly completed storage area for the sides of beef that would soon hang from the meat hooks. Nicholas had been a master in organising the joint enterprise into which they'd invested all their savings but they now had a working meat canning complex situated not far from the wharves of Melbourne.

Nicholas had been able to track down the trades-men and engineer who had worked on installing the cold works for the brewery and explained what he wanted. The engineer soon put together a system to cater to their requirements and the building had gone ahead without any real hitches.

John had been able to win a contract for meat to be supplied to the British army in New Zealand and now all they had to do was deliver. Along with the meatworks they had been able to corner the market on rum. All going well, they expected to see the money roll in within a short time.

'This is not a good place to be in the middle of winter,' Nicholas said, entering the large cold room. 'But not so unpleasant in summer.'

John turned to greet him and they decided to exit the room for the comparatively warmer air of the Victorian winter day.

'Well, my dear John,' Nicholas said, rubbing his hands against the chill of the late afternoon, 'it is going as I predicted it would. The British army is recruiting men in Sydney, Hobart and here in Melbourne to join an expedition to New Zealand fighting the Maori. We have put ourselves in the right place at the right time and will reap the profits.'

'That's good,' John replied, yet without the enthusiasm Nicholas expected.

'What is wrong, my dear chap? I thought our imminent fortune might make you as ecstatic as I am.'

'I was just thinking that finding my brother and sister would have truly made our probable success a happier occasion. It all seems so empty without being able to fulfil my promise to my dying brother.'

Nicholas placed his hand on John's shoulder. 'The money we earn from our enterprises will be the key to finding your brother and sister,' he reassured. 'Money can open a lot of doors.'

John accepted the reassurance. Yes, he would use the money they earned to track down Lachlan and Phoebe. Nicholas was right.

After two weeks back on the work site, Lachlan's body had healed and all he sported now were the tiny scars on his face which marked his fight with the army's champion. He was well treated by his work comrades, as they had all won good money on the outcome of the match.

He still missed the larrikin ways of Jimmy, who, when Lachlan thought about it, had been the catalyst for him to meet Amanda Lightfoot. Not that briefly meeting the beautiful and charming young woman would ever lead anywhere, Lachlan had to admit to himself. He was but a poor, hard-working young man of no foreseeable means of any worth, and only a dream to cling to.

He had read about the colourful explorer John Jardine establishing an outpost at Somerset on Cape York Peninsula in Queensland only months earlier and would have given his right arm to have been with him as he forged north through the wild, unexplored country. Lachlan had been impressed by the news earlier in the year of the massive funeral held in Melbourne for the ill-fated Burke and Wills, who had died at Coopers Creek a couple of years earlier. He read of how a huge crowd formed the funeral procession estimated at around four thousand strong. The bodies had been carried on a copy of the Duke of Wellington's funeral carriage and escorted by a contingent of dragoons. Shops had closed and it had been the Victorian colony's first state funeral.

Australia knew how to treat its glorious explorers, Lachlan had remembered thinking when he read the article. To be a famous explorer was to make a place in history and be remembered for all time. He was determined that he would one day establish his place in history, regardless of having already carved out a reputation in Sydney Town as a bare-knuckle boxer. But others would follow in the sport and he knew his feats as a pugilist would soon be forgotten. No, it was as an explorer he wanted to be remembered.

As he sat on the steps of the boarding house this winter's day watching the horse-drawn drays, fancy carriages of the well-to-do and the pedestrians pass by the door, Lachlan pondered on his future. It was in poetry that he often found solace and the young Scot made his decision. He would go to a bookshop and lose himself amongst the words and thoughts of those who spoke with wisdom and experience from the volumes on the musty book shelves.

Lachlan loved the smell of books. He stood perusing a pile of poetry volumes neatly stacked on a table. The older woman who ran the store knew Lachlan from previous visits and had bid him a pleasant day with her smile when he entered the shop. Lachlan was so engrossed in flipping through the pages of a collection of John Donne sonnets that he was startled by the voice behind him.

'So it is true that you really do have a romantic soul, Mr MacDonald.' Lachlan turned to gaze into the brown eyes barely inches from his own. 'Miss Lightfoot,' he spluttered. 'I would never have expected to meet you here.'

'And why not, Mr MacDonald?' Amanda teased with a gentle smile. 'I can read and as it happens I consider Mr Donne's poetry the best that was produced in Elizabethan times. I would think that you also have a love for his fine poetry.'

'Er, ah, I do,' he replied.

'You are blushing, Mr MacDonald,' Amanda said with a twinkle in her eyes.

Lachlan was lost for words.

She had caught him unawares and was consolidating her ground.

'I suppose I was going to say that you are the finest lady I have had the honour of meeting. A lady born to privilege.'

'You may see me as one born to the manor, but my parents were simple country people who struggled to build a business,' Amanda said quietly. 'In England we did not receive invitations from the gentry as you might think. I think that my brother wishes to forget our humble origins and pretend to be above what we really are.'

'Despite what you say, Miss Lightfoot,' Lachlan said, 'you are still the finest lady I have met.'

'Thank you,' Amanda replied as a slight blush stained her cheeks. 'I see that you have recovered well from your hard-fought victory.'

'I was lucky,' Lachlan replied modestly. 'And I attribute my luck to the beautiful sash that I wore in your honour.'

'You won because you have the heart of a lion,' Amanda said, meeting his gaze directly. 'And the mind of a poet.'

Lachlan felt that time was standing still and he wished it would remain that way for the rest of his life. He was in the company of an angel and could feel himself short of breath. He realised that his hands were growing clammy and hoped not to embarrass himself in her company.

Amanda broke her gaze and looked away quickly. 'I must offer my apologies, Mr MacDonald, but I am here to pick up a book and depart,' Amanda said. 'Meeting you so unexpectedly here has been very pleasant,' she added.

Amanda did not want to break her contact with Lachlan but she knew that her brother waited for her in their carriage outside and she did not want him to come looking if she remained too long in the book shop. She sensed that her brother suspected her feelings for the young Scot. Not that he had said anything to her but she knew him well enough to know some of his comments about Lachlan were less than subtle hints that he did not want her to see the boxer again.

Lachlan sought some way to delay her from leaving, but Amanda had already turned to walk over to the counter. 'Miss Lightfoot,' Lachlan said suddenly to her departing back, 'I would like to purchase this volume of Donne's sonnets, as a gesture of my thanks for having faith in me as a fighter.'

'That is not necessary,' Amanda said, turning to face him. 'The book is very expensive and you have already given me a beautiful present in the necklace, which I cherish.'

'Call it my payment to the lady who got me the fight,' Lachlan grinned, thinking that he could see an interest in his proposal in Amanda's eyes. 'I would like to inscribe it to you.'

'On that condition I would be flattered that you might present me with such a beautiful gift,' she said with a shy smile.

Lachlan paid for the slim, leather-bound book, borrowed a pen and dipped the nib in an inkstand. Very carefully he formed the words in his best copperplate handwriting just inside the cover: *A gift to the most beautiful woman in the world. That she may remember me in the years ahead as an explorer of this land.*
L. MacDonald

Lachlan blotted the wet ink and carefully closed the book, passing it to Amanda, who accepted the gift in her gloved hands.

'I would rather you not read what I have written until we part,' Lachlan said.

'I will do that,' Amanda replied, pressing the book to her breast. 'Thank you, Mr MacDonald. I hope that our paths may cross again some day.'

As she walked away Lachlan knew that no matter what else he achieved in his life, winning the heart of Amanda Lightfoot was the most important of his aspirations. He would march through hell if necessary to gain her love.

SEVEN

The day came when the last brick was laid in the construction of the great building, that would now become a warehouse. Old Harry announced to his team that they would have a couple of weeks break before the next contract was ready to begin. The enforced lay-off was hard on finances and one or two of the team had decided to seek work with other contractors to ensure that they continued to receive an income. Lachlan however decided to make the most of the break between jobs to see a little more of this rapidly growing city on the great and magnificent harbour. And there was always the Erin Hotel, which by now had become something of a second home to him.

Max was busy in the bar when Lachlan finally made his way to the Erin, but Daniel was at home and greeted Lachlan. 'You must stay and dine with us tonight,' he said.

'Thank you, Daniel,' Lachlan replied as they stood in the bar of the hotel, which was rapidly filling with patrons from the nearby factories, workshops and building sites. 'I would enjoy that. Your mother is a fine cook. Have you had any word from Kevin and Kate?'

A dark shadow fell across Daniel's face. 'My mother received a letter from Kate in Rockhampton. She has lost a baby and that bastard O'Keefe has deserted her,' he replied angrily. 'Michael never trusted O'Keefe, but Kate was besotted by him. He is lucky Michael is not around to give him a thrashing.'

'I am sorry to hear about that,' Lachlan said.

'A perception of love seems to have brought nothing but tragedy to my cousins' lives,' Daniel said. 'First, with Michael being besotted by that squatter's daughter, Fiona Macintosh, and then Kate wedding that no-good son of Irish convicts. Both loves have left nothing but sorrow in their wake.'

After hearing Daniel's bitterly delivered tirade against love, Lachlan decided to keep his feelings for Amanda Lightfoot to himself. Sharing a meal with the Duffy family in the Erin's kitchen, he felt just a little awkward when Bridget said grace in the Catholic fashion. Although not a devout Presbyterian, he still harboured the old religious animosities Duncan had instilled into him. And he was well aware that while his MacDonald ancestors had stood at Culloden as Catholics loyal to Prince Charlie, the family had since converted to the religion of Scotland.

When dinner was over, Max joined them and the three men retired to the backyard for Max to smoke his battered old pipe under the stars. Mugs of tea in their hands, they chatted on subjects of the day. Popular was the matter of the bushranger Henry Manns being hanged at the Darlinghurst prison back in March. He had been convicted of his role in a robbery whilst under arms of the Eugowra gold escort. The law firm where Daniel was articled as a clerk had some involvement in the unfortunate man's defence. Hangings in Sydney were not uncommon and Lachlan knew that Michael Duffy had made his escape, although Daniel swore that he had been innocent of murder. It was not worth the risk of losing a case and having him end up on the gallows despite any facts that might prove his innocence. None of the family had any idea where Michael had fled. All they had gleaned from friends was that Michael had jumped a Yankee schooner returning to America.

Eventually a silence followed and it was Max who spoke next.

'That pretty lady, the sister of that Captain Lightfoot, is travelling to New Zealand with her brother,' he said, puffing his pipe.

Lachlan looked at him sharply.

'How do you know?' Lachlan asked.

'I hear a soldier from his regiment talk about it at the bar,' Max answered.

'She is a nice lady,' Lachlan replied, appearing not to have any great interest in the matter but feeling crushed by the news of Amanda's impending absence. He had hoped that he might find a way to see her again.

'I thought you might like to know,' Max continued. 'I think she was sweet on you.'

At the old German's statement, Lachlan frowned. 'Why do you say that?' he asked, curious to know what was going through his friend's mind.

'No reason,' Max answered, staring ahead into the night and listening to the rowdy drinkers in the bar.

But Lachlan suspected that Max was not letting on to something and only the enigmatic expression on his face gave him away.

'It might be that she left a letter for you with me today,' Max finally allowed, a broad smile over his battered face as he handed Lachlan an envelope addressed to *Mr Lachlan MacDonald*. 'It is not usual for such a fine lady to leave letters with simple barmen unless they have good reason.'

As Lachlan took the letter he noticed his hand was trembling.

'You will need the light of the kitchen to read your letter,' Daniel suggested. But Lachlan was already making his way back into the kitchen.

Opening the letter carefully, he could smell Amanda's eau de cologne.

My dear Mr MacDonald,
I have sat down to pen these words to you as I will be departing tomorrow with my brother for the islands of New Zealand.

I have read the book of poetry that you so kindly gave me as a gift and also read the beautiful inscription that you penned within the cover. I would like to express my gratitude for both the book and the words.

It may be possible that some day we may meet again as friends and discuss the finer subjects of which you appear to have such a wonderful grasp.

Yours in all sincerity
Miss Amanda Lightfoot.

Lachlan read the letter once more, hanging on every word. When he had finished a third time, he carefully folded the missive and placed it back in the envelope.

New Zealand, Lachlan thought. He stood up from the table and rejoined Max and Daniel.

'How do I go about joining Colonel Pitt's volunteers for the New Zealand campaign?' Lachlan asked.

Even in the dimly lit backyard, Daniel's surprise was apparent, but Max did not appear so taken aback.

'You would go to be a soldier, then,' Max said, rather than asked. 'Ja, why is this no surprise?'

'I heard that Colonel Pitt has been recruiting men to join militias to fight the Maori,' Lachlan said. 'I believe that there was a promise of land to those who served.'

'So, it is for land that you vish to go,' Max said slowly, savouring his knowledge of his young boxing protégé's unspoken desire to follow the woman he was infatuated with. Max had seen much of life and

Lachlan's feelings for the aristocratic lady were no secret to him. He was surprised that the educated young Daniel Duffy was not aware of his friend's infatuation, as he had spoken of her enough times in their presence. Perhaps romance was far from his mind as he struggled with the technicalities of the law.

'I am without employment here,' Lachlan answered without much conviction. 'And I have always had a desire to see the world as surely you must have when you were a sailor.'

'A soldier is not a sailor,' Max replied. 'You must think carefully on what your travels to that land of savages may entail. You could get killed.'

'Jimmy never went near a war and he up and died only a few months ago from his fever,' Lachlan said. 'At least I will get to see some of the world before it is my time.'

'If you truly wish to serve in New Zealand,' Daniel said, 'I can arrange to have papers written up saying you are a man of good character. According to the terms of enlistment, you will need them.'

Lachlan looked to Daniel with gratitude. 'Thank you. I just have a feeling that it is time for me to set out on the first leg of the search for my real dream.'

'And what is that?' Daniel asked.

'One day, I will be an explorer,' Lachlan replied quietly. 'I think my service in New Zealand may assist me in doing that.'

'Not the hand of a beautiful young Englishwoman?' Max asked with a broad grin.

'Er, ah,' Lachlan spluttered. 'Not really.'

'Tomorrow, I will have the references drafted,' Daniel said, oblivious to Lachlan's untruth. 'I am sure that you will be granted a berth on one of the steam ships travelling to New Zealand before you know it.'

Lachlan only wished it had been the same ship transporting Amanda to New Zealand.

The Melbourne inn was far less salubrious than the type of establishment where John MacDonald would have chosen to meet someone. But the semi-literate note that he had received at his hotel stated the writer had information of great value to him. He was to bring twenty guineas with him as payment for that information.

'I will go with you,' Nicholas said when John informed him of the note. 'I know the place your mysterious writer intends to meet you and it does not have a good reputation.'

John was pleased to see Nicholas's concern and readily accepted the offer.

Now the two men sat in a corner of an inn frequented by Melbourne's underworld of pickpockets, thieves and other persons – both male and female – who made their living on the borderline of respectability. It was early evening and a cold draught of air blew through the door each time it was opened. Nicholas had ordered a couple of rums, which sat in front of the two untouched.

After some fifteen minutes, a thin, poorly dressed man sidled over to their table. He had been standing at the bar when John and Nicholas walked in.

'You Mr John MacDonald?' the man asked, leaning on the table.

'I am,' John responded, recoiling from the smell.

'You bring the money – like I asked?'

'I have,' John said, and a satisfied expression replaced the flat stare of the man facing him across the table.

'But don't even think about taking it,' Nicholas hissed quietly, 'without services rendered.'

Affronted, the man turned to glare at Nicholas. 'What makes yer think I couldn't just call me mates at the bar to take anything we wanted from you?' he asked in a belligerent tone.

'The pistol I have under the table pointed at your groin, my dear chap,' Nicholas said with an evil twinkle in his eye.

The menace in the man immediately evaporated and he sat down without invitation. 'I was only jestin',' he added quickly with a half-hearted attempt at a smile. 'I heard Mr MacDonald has been askin' around with a certain private detective about those who were on the Ballarat fields back in '54. I've just come down from Sydney and I think I might have some information about his family worth the money I ask.'

'You tell me what you have,' John said, 'and I will judge if it is worth it.'

'It's about yer brother, Lachlan,' the man explained.

'You will have to do better than that,' John responded. 'I have left that name – and that of my sister – with many that I have spoken to in the last few months.'

'Yeah, well I've seen him and he even looks a bit like you,' the man offered.

'Still not sufficient proof to earn the money.'

''E's got a reputation as a bare-knuckle fighter around Sydney,' the man continued, desperately groping for more information.

John sighed. 'I am sorry, but that could be someone completely different to my brother.'

Exasperated, the man leaned back in his chair. 'Oright, why don't you go to Sydney to find out if I'm right and when you do, give me the money when you get back.'

'That is a fair enough proposal,' John agreed.

'An' I wouldn't make any plans to renege on the deal either,' the man hissed, leaning forward with a fire in his eyes. 'Because next time I will have the drop on you an' you will pay with yer skin for trying to doublecross me.'

'If I travel to Sydney to confirm that your information may be correct, how would I find the man to identify him?' John asked.

'That's easy,' the man said. ''E hangs out at the Erin Hotel in Redfern. I even saw him fight the army champion. 'E's a bloody good fighter.'

When they had finished their business with their informant, John and Nicholas stepped outside to their waiting carriage and valet.

'Do you believe what he told you?' Nicholas asked, shoving his hands in his pockets to protect them from the bitter wind blowing.

'I don't know, he's not exactly trustworthy,' John replied, as they stepped up into the carriage. 'But I must at least attempt to find out if the man is my brother.'

'And if he is,' Nicholas said quietly, 'how will he react to the news that his older brother is a sodomite?'

Startled, John blinked at the question. He had never really considered the matter. Until now his love for Nicholas was a well-protected secret. What would his brother think of his relationship with another man? John did not have an answer.

All the Duffy clan came to say goodbye to Lachlan when he embarked on the ship to New Zealand. Daniel had, as he'd offered, been able to secure the necessary papers for Lachlan to enlist in the militia recruited from the Australian colonies by Colonel Pitt.

Lachlan was going to war. But not for the British Empire, as his friends imagined, but for the vague hope that he might once again find Amanda, and prove his worth to earn her love.

The steamer set its course and soon the twin heads of Sydney Harbour were mere specks on the horizon.

Part Two

THE SOLDIER

1863–1864

Waikato,
New Zealand

EIGHT

Sergeant Samuel Forster was drunk and swayed on his feet inside the crowded, wooden hut filled with around twenty men at the Otahuhu military barracks, south of Auckland. The biting rain had turned the encampment into a field of sludge and the volunteers were happy, despite the cramped conditions of their accommodation, to be inside.

'Youse are in for a big shock if yer come over here to fight the Maori an' think yer goin' to go home alive,' he slurred. 'I've bin here fer a lot longer than youse an' can tell yer that the Maori is a cunning bugger and as good as any Queen Victoria's best have ever had to fight.'

Lachlan sat on his field cot, his Enfield musket between his knees. He had crossed the Tasman to disembark in the town of Auckland on the North Island of New Zealand. Around him in the tent were his companions, who had enlisted in Sydney with the promise of a 50-acre farm and free rations for a year once their service against the rebel Maori warriors was complete. While serving they would be paid two shillings and sixpence per day as privates and prior to embarking had received free rations.

Married men with families had been given priority but a lack of suitable applicants had resulted in single men being signed up. Not all volunteered for the reward of land; many had simply sought glory and adventure in this campaign against an enemy the likes of which the professional had never faced before. The British army was used to fighting set-piece battles, capturing land or villages and considering this the sign of a decisive victory. But the fierce Maori warriors fought a running fight of hard-hitting skirmishes followed by the tactic of melting into the wild and rugged countryside before reappearing.

Lachlan had heard stories coming over on the ship of how the regular British troops had taken heavy casualties, often against lesser numbers of Maori, who had also perfected the entrenchment that made them virtually immune to the artillery of the attacking force. From his readings about the Land of the Long White Cloud he knew that the war against the rebellious warriors of Polynesian ancestry had its roots in a conflict as far back as 1845. This campaign was fought for possession of rich farming lands, with the inhabitants fighting to keep the colonisers from taking their lands and the colonisers being motivated by a fierce desire to control this new land. Lachlan did not think much about the moral issues of the war. For him, this was an opportunity to both escape the drudgery of working as a labourer and be closer to Amanda Lightfoot. He was a young man, and his sense of adventure had been a guiding factor in his decision to volunteer.

'Have you seen much action, Sergeant?' Lachlan asked quietly.

Sergeant Samuel Forster swung his attention to Lachlan, focusing on him in the dim light of the tent. He was a stocky man of about forty years of age with a full-blown beard like that of many of the other soldiers serving in the campaign. Behind the beard, his eyes were hard, devoid of any emotion other than hatred. 'You questioning me?' he asked belligerently and Lachlan regretted his innocent question.

'No, Sergeant,' he replied. 'I was just wondering what you had seen at first hand of the Maori.'

The sergeant glared at the newcomer. 'I've seen action from the Eureka rebellion to the Taranaki campaign. You questioning my right to wear my rank, boy?'

'No, Sergeant,' Lachlan quickly answered, sensing that he had inadvertently made an enemy. 'We are fortunate to have you as our sergeant.'

His tactful reply appeared to appease the drunken sergeant. 'Be sure of that,' the sergeant answered grimly. 'Make sure your muskets are cleaned and in proper order fer tomorrow's drill,' he said, leaving the tent to make his way to the mess for another bout of drinking.

'I heard that Forster is a real bastard,' a young man sitting opposite Lachlan said. 'My name is Andrew Hume.' He thrust out his hand.

'Lachlan MacDonald,' Lachlan replied, accepting the grip. 'I have a feeling that you could be right.'

'A friend of mine was under Forster last year and said that the man is a drunken bully. He only got his promotion because he has some kind of patronage from our new commander, Captain Lightfoot.'

At the name of Lightfoot, Lachlan felt his heartbeat quicken. He had been mustered into the volunteer militia unit under the command of Charles Lightfoot and wondered at the coincidence of being a part of the man's company. It was a good omen and augured well for giving him a better prospect of meeting with Amanda. Little did the young Scot know that Lightfoot had specifically requested that Lachlan be recruited into his regiment so he could keep an eye on him, a job which he'd requested Sergeant Forster to undertake.

The English officer didn't trust his sister's denial of feelings towards the young man and had no intention of letting some Scottish upstart spoil his plans for bettering himself through the marriage of his sister to a wealthy beau.

'Where are you from?' Lachlan asked his new acquaintance, whom he had taken an instant liking to.

'Moreton Bay,' Andrew replied. 'I was a surveyor up in the colony of Queensland. And you?'

'Sydney Town,' Lachlan replied. 'I was doing navvy work.'

'You don't give me the impression of being a navvy,' Andrew said, wiping down the mechanism of his musket with an oily rag. 'I would take you for an educated man.'

'I read a lot and my guardian was a man who always taught me to keep learning about the world.'

'So, that is why you are over here,' Andrew said.

'You could say that,' Lachlan answered.

Over the next two weeks of drilling, musketry and more drilling on the parade ground, Andrew and Lachlan cemented their friendship. They had much in common. Both were self-educated, of Scottish blood and Andrew had lived and worked in the colony Lachlan dreamed of one day exploring.

Captain Charles Lightfoot was not seen for those two weeks and he eventually joined his company after a period spent in Auckland. In the meantime Forster had done his best to single out Lachlan during their training and included Hume when he noticed that the two had become friends. The sergeant's reputation as a bully was fully evident. The sergeant did not have to have any reason to dislike any particular soldier but even so Lachlan and Andrew seemed to get more picquet duty, standing for longer hours on guard duty around the camp in the cold, wet nights than the others of the company. Their officer in charge, a young lieutenant, had been acting as the company commander until the latter returned to assume his duties and thus had paid little attention to his men, leaving the routine of training to Sergeant Samuel Forster. So Lachlan and Andrew had little recourse to complain to their superior about the unfair treatment that was being meted out to them.

'All men are to fall in with arms,' Forster roared through the barracks in the hour just before dawn. 'Your commanding officer, Captain Lightfoot, will inspect you at dawn.'

Lachlan slipped from his bunk, snatched his uniform and dressed quickly. The discipline of the army was making him more organised, at least. The recruits drew their muskets from the store and assembled on the parade ground. A weak sun broke through high, scudding clouds as the men shivered against the early morning cold while the roll was called.

When Charles Lightfoot appeared on a thoroughbred horse wearing a beautifully tailored uniform, Forster barked out his orders for the men to shoulder arms. When he had taken his parade through the drills, he brought them back to attention.

'All parade present, sah,' Forster bellowed, coming to attention and saluting his superior officer.

'Thank you, Sergeant,' Lightfoot replied, returning the salute. 'My parade, Sergeant,' he continued, taking formal control of his company. 'Parade, stand at ease, stand easy.'

The men went through their drill and were thankful to their company commander for allowing them to relax in military style, their musket butts beside their boots. Lachlan was in the front rank beside Andrew.

'Men, I am your commanding officer, Captain Lightfoot,' Charles said in a loud voice that could be heard by all. 'I have good news for you. I am satisfied that you are ready to join your British brothers in the war against these rebellious savages and so today we join the advance against their fortifications. You will be briefed by your senior non-commissioned officers on your duties after breakfast parade. That is all.'

Concluding his brief speech, Lightfoot handed the parade back to Sergeant Forster, before riding away.

The militia marched south along the track known as the Great South Road to set up camp in their bell tents just north of Drury close to Manukau Harbour. There, they fell into the routine of mounting pic-quets to guard against a surprise attack and it was then that Lachlan had his first direct contact since Sydney with his company commander.

In the early hours of the evening Sergeant Forster came to fetch Lachlan from his tent. 'Captain Lightfoot wants to see yer,' he said belligerently. 'Yer bin up to somethin'?'

'Not that I am aware of, Sergeant,' Lachlan replied and followed the sergeant to the tent designated as an orderly room and company headquarters.

'Private MacDonald reporting to you, sah,' Forster barked, threw a formal salute and stood back.

'You can leave us, Sergeant,' Charles Lightfoot said, dismissing the burly man.

Lachlan stood before a portable camp desk and saluted the Captain.

'Stand easy, Private MacDonald,' Lightfoot said curtly. 'I was perusing the files and noticed your name. It seems that my hunch was right and that you are one and the same Lachlan MacDonald whom I saw fight our regimental champion. I was also pleased to see that you had volunteered for service here and even more pleased to be able to ensure that you were enlisted in my company.'

'I also was pleased to see that good fortune had me posted to your company, sir,' Lachlan replied uncertainly.

'Well, so much for the greetings and salutations, Private MacDonald,' Lightfoot said. 'I feel that the same good fortune has put you in the right place at the right time. You see, I was hoping that I might have a man of considerable pugilistic talent in the company. While I was away in Auckland, I bumped into Gustavus von Tempsky, a remarkable chap with an over-inflated impression of himself and his men.'

'The Forest Rangers,' Lachlan offered. He had heard of their remarkable exploits fighting the Maoris. Von Tempsky and Captain Jackson had gained considerable publicity with their small units in scouting for the British army, as well as their forays into the bush to seek out and ambush Maori war parties. An old hand in their company had said that the Maori warriors had a great respect for the Rangers' prowess.

'Ah, I see that you are aware of the Rangers,' Lightfoot said with an arrogant smile. 'The Von and I had a chat and he boasted that he has a man in his company, an Irishman, who can beat anyone in the British army. I think that he is wrong. Do you think that you are still of the standard you were in Sydney?'

'I do, sir. I think that we can give the Von a bloody nose, if I may use such an expression.'

Lightfoot broke into a oily smile, rose from behind his desk and slapped Lachlan on the back.

'That's a good chap then,' he said with forced camaraderie. 'I will ensure that you have time off from your normal duties to train for the fight. I think we can organise the bout for the early weeks of September.'

'Could I ask a great favour, sir?' Lachlan asked, almost holding his breath for the liberty he had taken.

'What is that, Private MacDonald?' Lightfoot responded.

'I would need assistance in preparing for the fight. Would it be possible to release Private Hume to be my second?'

Lightfoot frowned but replied, 'If you think that he could assist then I will inform Sergeant Forster that he is also released and that you are both free of guard duty et cetera.'

'Thank you, sir,' Lachlan answered, relief flooding him.

'If that is all that you require you are dismissed,' Lightfoot said, returning to his chair and beginning to flip over a sheaf of papers on his desk.

'Thank you, sir,' Lachlan responded.

'Send in Sergeant Forster on your way out,' Lightfoot said dismissively from behind his desk.

Lachlan saluted and stepped outside the tent where he saw Sergeant Forster waiting. 'Captain Lightfoot wants to see you,' he said. 'I think that he has good news for you about me and Private Hume,' Lachlan added, unable to control his delight at being freed from the bullying NCO's persistent needling.

Without waiting for the sergeant's reply, Lachlan marched back to his tent to inform Andrew that he was now in the business of managing a fighter. But he had hardly settled in the tent and briefed Andrew on the developments when Sergeant Forster suddenly marched into their tent.

'Yer think that yer smart,' Forster snarled into Lachlan's face. 'Just cos yer got off some duties with yer friend here yer think that yer out of my hands. Well, I got news fer you. The Captain an' I go way back to the Ballarat goldfields rebellion an' there are things that the Captain wouldn't want people to know. So me an' the Captain are pretty tight too. Jus don't give me an excuse to call in a favour.'

With his parting statement delivered with spittle spraying the air and a wild expression in his eyes, the sergeant turned his back and stormed out of the tent, leaving Lachlan and Andrew staring at each other.

What had Forster meant about the Eureka stockade? Lachlan wondered. Had it not been for his own personal involvement, Lachlan might not have thought twice about the threat. But the statement stuck with him and was the catalyst for a dreadful nightmare. He was once again ten years old. On that hot, summer's day at Ballarat, the musketry exploded all around him as the bloodied face of his father stared at him with dead eyes. He was helpless to call out but could see what he thought was either accusation or a plea in his dead father's eyes. It did not make sense.

For the next couple of weeks life in camp was

good for Lachlan and Andrew; no guard duty and a minimum of other duties around the camp. Each day they would find somewhere a short distance from camp for Lachlan to train and rest up. They were focused on the impending fight, but always aware of the menacing presence of Sergeant Forster, who continued to seethe at having the two men he disliked most out of his clutches.

When the day arrived for the fight, the whole unit were given leave to attend. An area had been cleared for the match and Lachlan once more was able to wear the blue silk sash that Amanda had given him. Stripped to the waist, he stood at the edge of the grassy clearing with the members of his unit standing behind him. Many slapped him on the back to wish him well and already the bets were being placed, despite military regulations forbidding such a pastime.

'That must be the Von,' Andrew said, catching a glimpse of a tall, handsome man standing with their commanding officer. 'And that must be his fighter, O'Flynn,' he added when an equally well-built young man stripped off his shirt.

Lachlan stared hard at his opponent's hard, muscled back, finally catching his eye when he turned around slowly to face him.

'God almighty,' Lachlan gasped.

'What?' Andrew asked in his alarm.

'I know that man,' Lachlan said under his breath, so that only Andrew could hear him. 'His name is Michael Duffy.'

NINE

On the Friday evening the bar in the Erin Hotel was busy and Daniel had been assigned to help Max and the pretty barmaid serve the thirsty customers. The men jostled at the bar, vying for attention of the voluptuous blonde in preference to the dour German.

As Daniel placed five bottles of imported beer on the bar counter, his attention was drawn to the man who was pushing his way forward to be served. He had a vaguely familiar look about him but his expensive, well-tailored suit meant he stood out amidst the sweating working men around him.

'What will it be?' Daniel asked when the man had found a place at the bar.

'I would like a scotch straight – and possibly some information,' the man said.

Daniel poured a shot of whisky into a small

tumbler and slid it across the bar. When the man paid him Daniel could see from his roll of bank notes that he was well financed.

'I was hoping that you might have information concerning a Mr Lachlan MacDonald,' the stranger said, taking a swig of his drink.

'Why do you want to know about Lachlan?' Daniel asked suspiciously, naturally protective of the young man who was his friend.

'Lachlan MacDonald is my brother,' the stranger said. 'We were separated many years ago and I have recently received information that he had contact with this establishment. My name is John MacDonald.'

Daniel could see the strong family resemblance. It was as if he was looking at an older version of Lachlan.

'I think we should speak somewhere a little less crowded, Mr MacDonald,' Daniel said, wiping his hands on his apron.

John finished his drink in one gulp and followed Daniel through the bar into the kitchen. Daniel gestured for John to take a seat at the kitchen table. 'My name is Daniel Duffy,' Daniel said, offering his hand over the table. 'My father is the licensee of the Erin.'

'Mr Duffy, do you know my brother?' John asked.

'I do,' Daniel replied, taking a bottle of good quality Irish whiskey down from above the stove. 'And I believe you are who you say you are. Lachlan has spoken much of you and you look so very much like him. But, I am afraid to say, Lachlan volunteered for the campaign in New Zealand and has been away this past few months. We are yet to receive a letter from him as to his whereabouts. Your brother is very much favoured by myself and my family.' Daniel poured out two tumblers of the whiskey, handing one to John.

'You have just given me the best and worst news of my life,' John said, accepting the drink. 'I have finally been able to track down my brother only to hear he is serving in a war where he may lose his life.'

'Lachlan is a fighter,' Daniel smiled grimly. 'It would take a good man to put him down, Mr MacDonald. 'As soon as he makes some kind of contact with us, I can assure you that I will immediately inform you,' Daniel continued. 'Where are you staying while in Sydney?'

John wrote down the name of the prestigious hotel and handed it to Daniel, who raised his eyebrows at what had been written on the back of John's calling card. Lachlan's brother was indeed a prosperous man to be able to afford those daily rates, he thought.

'I would be grateful if you could tell me a little about my brother,' John said. 'I have spent many years wondering about his fate.'

Over a half bottle of the good Irish whiskey, Daniel told John as much as he knew from the stories he had been told by Lachlan. Daniel spoke of Duncan Campbell and Lachlan's days on the bush tracks beyond the Great Dividing Range and his prowess as a bare-knuckle boxer in Sydney. John was pleased to hear how his brother had become a self-educated man and realised that they both had independently sought learning to better their station in life.

When Daniel had exhausted all he knew about Lachlan's past – both distant and recent – John had a gloomy thought. How would his brother react to learning that his long-lost brother was in a relationship with another man? Would the issue divide them when they finally made contact?

Lachlan could see from the startled expression on Michael Duffy's face that the recognition was mutual.

'Who is Michael Duffy?' Andrew muttered in Lachlan's ear.

'Probably the best fighter who ever came out of Sydney,' Lachlan replied. 'And I am going to get the opportunity to fight him.'

'Well, why does he go by the name of O'Flynn?' Andrew persisted, rubbing down Lachlan's shoulders.

'A long story,' Lachlan replied in a low voice. 'And I would warn you not to utter the name of Duffy to anyone.'

Andrew shrugged. It was of no consequence to him who the opposing fighter was. All that mattered was that Lachlan should beat him and the money wagered by their unit be won in the fight.

The referee appeared at the centre of the grassy field, beckoning to the fighters to join him. Both Lachlan and Michael moved forward to face off, two paces apart. Lachlan's questioning expression said it all and was returned with what Lachlan interpreted as a plea not to reveal what he knew of Michael's identity. The referee, a colour sergeant from a British regiment stationed nearby, reminded the two fighters of the rules.

'Shake hands like the gentlemen that you are,' he concluded, stepping aside.

The crowd fell into a hush as the two men raised their fists. It was Michael who struck first and despite their friendship Lachlan realised that he was in for the fight of his life. He parried the probing punch and the crowd roared its approval. The fight was on.

Afterwards, Lachlan could only remember how fast and furious the blows came but he also knew that his punches were hurting Michael. At one stage they fell into a clinch, the sweat from their bodies drenching them despite the cold air of the New Zealand afternoon.

'What the hell's going on?' Lachlan gasped into Michael's ear in the clinch.

'I'll tell you after I beat you,' Michael replied in a hoarse voice.

'Like hell,' Lachlan said, forcing himself apart from the clinch. 'You can tell me when I beat you.'

His defiance brought a crooked grin to Michael's face and the fight resumed.

'To arms!' the cry came from somewhere in the crowd and was followed by a bugle call for assembly.

Lachlan and Michael broke contact and stood a few paces apart, looking to the spectators who were already moving away. The referee signalled for the end of the fight and strode away.

'What in hell is going on?' Lachlan asked Michael.

'It looks like the Maori have struck somewhere and we are needed.'

'Lachlan!' Andrew called from the edge of the field. 'We have to stand to. We are being called to action.'

'I have to join my unit,' Michael said, thrusting out his hand to his old friend. 'You fought bloody well, but I reckon I would have beaten you.'

Lachlan accepted the hand with a firm grip of his own. 'We just might get a chance later to find out who the better fighter is, Michael Duffy,' he grinned.

'Just promise me that you will tell no one of my real identity,' Michael said.

'I swear on the blood of my ancestors that your secret is safe with me, Michael,' Lachlan answered with conviction in his voice. 'Maybe we can catch up and you can tell me what happened after you left Sydney.'

'A promise,' Michael replied. 'As soon as we can – but for the moment take care. If you are going into action against the Maori you will need to be on your toes. They are a fierce and courageous foe.'

'Lachlan,' Andrew called again. 'We have to go.'

Lachlan turned and hurried across to Andrew, who held up a towel for him to wipe the drying sweat from his body.

'I just heard that the church at Ramarama is under attack from a big force of Maori,' Andrew said. 'We have to go and relieve them with an ammunition re-supply.'

Fronted by a ditch four feet deep by six feet wide, the church at Ramarama was a wooden structure with an incomplete log stockade with loop-holes for firing through. Defensive bastions had been set in the diagonal corners of the improvised fortress which was manned by a few militia men and local farmers whose families had been evacuated to Auckland. Amongst the defenders were members of the McDonald family – fourteen-year-old grandson, father and grandfather.

The first warning of the attack had come when a Maori scout was sighted by one of the defenders the day before. The Maori warrior drew an inordinate amount of fire from the twenty-three defenders and that afternoon senior officers visiting had promised a re-supply of ammunition for the next day.

Confidently awaiting the re-supply the next day, the men lounged about after breakfast smoking. A militia man gazed down the road to the church and commented to his comrades, 'Look at those cattle on the road, see how they are looking into the bush. I know there is something wrong.'

His comrades turned their attention to the road.

'It is nothing,' one of the soldiers said, getting to his feet and trailing his rifle with him. He winked at the men around him and mocked, 'Come on boys, there is some bloody work before you this day.' He raised his rifle and fired randomly into the scrub.

All hell broke loose as his cynical ploy at humour returned him a huge volley from the hidden warriors in the scrub. A mad scramble for the safety of the church ensued as the bullets flew around the men who only seconds before had scoffed at their comrade.

The defenders returned fire from the church as

the warriors closed the gap between them, attacking through the graveyard and from the south. The church was surrounded and the defenders seriously trapped.

Young McDonald gripped his rifled musket and his attention drifted curiously to a white pigeon perched unconcernedly not far from them. But for now he must concentrate like his father and grandfather on the howling Maori warriors as they came on courageously into the line of fire from the church defenders.

The cross-fire continued for a good couple of hours with neither side gaining advantage. At around 11 a.m. someone observed that the Maori seemed to be gathering for an all-out attack.

'Fix bayonets!' The order from the senior NCO was bawled so loud that the attackers also heard it. It was obvious to all that this would be a fight to the last defender.

A fine-looking warrior chief standing a good six feet tall attempted to rally his men for a charge. He stepped into the open and roared his challenge to the defenders in English, 'Come on, you cowards. Be men and do not stop behind the logs.'

He was flung on his back by a sniped shot from within the church. The sniper shook his head. It was a sad day to have killed such a courageous foe but in such a bitter fight there was no time for remorse.

By midday an audit of supplies revealed that each man was down to ten shots and water was scarce. There was no sign of the promised re-supply or of any reinforcements and young McDonald kept close to his father. He was afraid but knew he could not show his fear in the company of the men. The despondent defenders were cheered somewhat by the sergeant, who went about the confines of the church clapping his hands and saying, 'Go it, my lads. This is a glorious day.'

Young McDonald interpreted the tough sergeant's exaltations as meaning it was a good day to enter the gates of heaven. At least he would do so in the company of his father and grandfather beside him. He gripped the stock of his rifle and curled closer to the wall, peering out at the white pigeon which still perched serenely on the church steeple. Young McDonald wished that he could be that pigeon and fly from this terrible place and his certain death against such overwhelming numbers of Maori warriors.

As the smell of cooking fires drifted to the defenders, one of the soldiers noticed through a rifle slit that smoke was rising from just below the crest where the graveyard was. 'The bloody heathens are cooking their meal!' he exclaimed. 'Confident buggers that they are.'

Suddenly, the call of a British bugle sounded and young McDonald was startled to see the pigeon fly from its perch. A soldier staring through a gun port exclaimed, 'It's the 70th Foot from Springfield.'

His observation instantly brought a rousing three cheers from the defenders and at the same time curses from the Maori warriors who had been preparing for another assault on the church. Although now reinforced by twenty-five men from the nearby British regiment, the ammunition still had not arrived. It was bogged down in carts being brought forward by

Lachlan and his companions under the command of Captain Lightfoot, who cursed the delay getting to the battle raging ahead of them.

Young McDonald watched as the approaching reinforcements fought their way to them. A sergeant toppled forward, shot through the leg, but he turned to fire at his enemy and saw the Maori warrior drop from a fatal wound. With so few men to reinforce them, all knew that the fighting was far from over.

But Charles Lightfoot's dreams of glory were also suffering. His company was rapidly being overtaken by soldiers from the 18th and 65th Foot regiments. The militia men struggled, sweating to get their two wagons through the mud. The badly needed ammunition for the besieged defenders was heavy and Captain Lightfoot cursed the delay. They could hear the distant gunfire, drifting on a stiff breeze towards them.

In the late afternoon the faint sound of a bugle carried down the muddy track to Lightfoot. He recognised the call for a charge. 'Private MacDonald,' he called down from his mount, dismounting at the same time, 'to me.'

Lachlan left his post at the rear of one of the wagons where he had been pushing for all he was worth to assist the horses drag the wagon on the muddy track.

'Yes, sir,' he said, coming to attention and saluting the officer.

'You and I are going on ahead to reconnoitre the situation. Mr Grimes,' Lightfoot said, turning to a mud-spattered young officer, 'you are to assume command until I return.' The young lieutenant saluted his acknowledgment and turned to supervise the remaining soldiers.

Unslinging his rifled musket from his shoulder, Lachlan checked that the primer was in place and followed the captain, who had drawn his revolver and sword. At a hurried pace they ran towards the slope of the hill around a bend in the road.

The men of the 65th Foot had arrived under the command of Captain Saltmarch. He quickly ordered all the British regulars to form up and charge down the hill to clear the Maori warriors, who now found themselves on the defensive. The bugler raised his instrument to his lips to sound the charge and it was sent spinning from his hands as a full shot of lead took away his face. He fell to his knees clasping his hands to his shattered jaw.

The charge went ahead and the first of the 65th fell. The Maori who had shot him advanced to retrieve the dead soldier's rifle but in turn was wounded when Captain Saltmarch stepped over the body of the fallen soldier to fire two rounds from his pistol into the warrior's chest. The Maori swung his double-barrelled shotgun at the officer and the blast took Saltmarch squarely in the throat. The tough warrior was hit again by a rifle shot but refused to fall. When he turned to retreat he was speared by a long bayonet hurled by an enraged soldier. The fighting went on into the late afternoon.

Within ten minutes of setting off, Lachlan and Charles Lightfoot arrived to witness the skirmishing at the base of the hill. The soldiers from the British regiments that had arrived to relieve the defenders were locked in hand-to-hand combat against the Maori warriors who by now were making a retreat. It was long bayonet against heavy war axe and club. Rifled musket against double-barrelled shotguns.

For Lachlan, it was his first sight of a battle and he felt a tightness in his stomach and chest. He did not know whether it was fear or excitement at what was to come.

'Damn it to hell!' Lightfoot swore. 'It's almost over and we have missed it.'

He had hardly spat the words when Lachlan saw a blur from the corner of his eye. As if from nowhere a giant Maori warrior wielding an ornate axe of greenstone had risen from the ground to spring at the officer. Lightfoot was so focused on the fighting at the base of the hill below the church stockade that he did not see the threat at his back. Lachlan could not remember how it had happened but the rifle he carried was at his shoulder and fired in the same blur of movement. The musket shot alerted Lightfoot, who spun around to see the giant Maori warrior crumpling a mere pace behind him as the smoke curled from the end of Lachlan's musket barrel.

'A damned close-run thing,' Lightfoot muttered and glanced at Lachlan's face that was pallid with shock.

Lachlan did not reply but instinctively went about reloading. His training had kicked into action. Later, he told himself, he would reflect on what had just happened in his young life but for now it was a case of keeping alive against an opponent as fearless as any the British army had ever faced in its many colonial wars.

'Captain Lightfoot,' a voice called from a distance. 'The ammunition is up.'

Both Lachlan and Lightfoot turned. Not only had the wagons arrived under the command of Lieutenant Grimes, but the Maori had left the battlefield. The sounds of the fight faded as the warriors fell back to consolidate their forces. It was over for the moment and a peace descended on the breezes of the late afternoon.

Young McDonald came out from the church to gaze with awe at the setting sun. He was still alive. Even at fourteen years of age, he understood what it meant to be a survivor. He stared with guilt at the bodies of the dead Maori scattered about the churchyard.

TEN

Following the battle at the church, Lachlan and the rest of his militia unit returned to garrison duties at their camp. On the first evening back, he was summoned to company headquarters where Charles Lightfoot thanked him with bad grace in private for saving his life.

'I am granting you a three-day leave pass, Private MacDonald,' he said, signing a form and passing it across his desk. 'You will see that it is effective as from eight o'clock tomorrow morning.'

Lachlan thanked his commanding officer and took his leave to return to his tent. Lightfoot watched him depart. He had best keep the young Scot under his thumb while he was with his company, the officer brooded. Despite his dislike for the private he had to respect him for his courage and visually reward him to keep up the show. But that did not mean he would be sorry if something untoward were to happen to the young man.

'Where will you go?' Andrew asked.

'Auckland,' Lachlan replied.

'What's of any interest there?' Andrew queried. 'You don't even drink.'

Lachlan's promise to Max Braun still held and he had given his daily rum ration to Andrew. 'Let's just say that I have to find that out for myself,' Lachlan replied, and Andrew did not ask any more questions.

Lachlan was able to obtain a ride in a wagon returning to Auckland for supplies. Along the way the wagoneers decided to stop at Rogers Criterion Hotel at Otahuhu for a meal and a couple of ales. Soldiers in the regimental dress of British units, some farmers and a few locals hung around the entrance to the hotel. The campaign had brought prosperity to the publican and his business of helping soldiers fill in the dreary hours away from home.

Lachlan followed the two men inside and was not surprised to see Michael Duffy sitting with a group of men dressed in dark blue who were sitting around a table, playing cards and drinking rum. Lachlan recognised them as members of the elite Rangers unit. Michael was similarly dressed, sporting the broad chevrons on his arm to indicate his rank as a sergeant. He glanced up at Lachlan.

'Ah, Lachlan MacDonald,' he said with a broad smile, pushing back his chair and crossing the bar. 'Come and join us.'

It was obvious to Lachlan that Michael wished to speak to him, away from the company of his comrades.

'What brings you here?' Michael asked softly, his arm around Lachlan's shoulders so that they might appear to be two drunken friends carousing. 'Have you deserted?'

'No,' Lachlan answered, affronted by the suggestion of desertion. 'I have three days' leave.'

'That's okay then,' Michael replied in a relieved tone. 'The bloody British still flog a man for being absent without leave.'

'I'm actually on my way to Auckland,' Lachlan said. 'But this unforeseen opportunity to meet with you here gives me the chance to ask what the hell is going on. Have you contacted your family in Sydney to tell them where you are?'

Michael sighed. 'Let's go and sit at that empty table in the corner, and I will tell you what has occurred since I last saw you,' he said.

'The ship that got me out of Sydney made a stop at Auckland,' Michael commenced explaining. 'I was at a bit of a loose end wandering around the town and was actually making some sketches of the buildings when the Von spotted my work. He is a painter of some talent himself and we fell into a discussion. Next thing you know he has me signed up with his unit of Rangers and for the last few months I have been out bush getting into the occasional skirmish with the Maori. Seeing you that day came somewhat as a shock and I am glad that you did not betray my true identity.'

'You know that I would not do that,' Lachlan said. 'But have you written to your family?'

Michael stared at the rough-hewn table top, stained over the years by many spilled drinks. 'I do not think that would be wise under the present circumstances,' he replied. 'Not until a decent amount of time elapses. I need to wait for the matter of the killing to blow over and be forgotten by the police. If I make contact with my family, it may put them in a situation where the law can say that they were aiding and abetting me, and don't forget I'm a man wanted for questioning on a capital crime.'

'From what I heard,' Lachlan said quietly, 'you were only defending yourself.'

'The other bastard got his story in first,' Michael replied bitterly. 'I don't trust British justice. I remember too well the stories my da told me about Ireland.'

'Well, I could contact them to say that we have met and that you are well,' Lachlan offered.

'I would rather you did not,' Michael countered. 'At least, not until I think it is safe.'

'That is fair enough,' Lachlan accepted.

'Private MacDonald,' a drunken voice bellowed across the room. 'What are you doin' here, my lad?'

Both Lachlan and Michael turned to see Sergeant Forster swaying on his feet beside the bar. His eyes were bloodshot and although it was only just after midday it was obvious that he had been drinking for some time.

'I have a leave pass, sergeant,' Lachlan answered.

'Get to yer feet, soldier, when you address me,' Forster slurred.

The scene had attracted the attention of the Rangers as well as the rest of the patrons in the crowded bar. 'You're drunk, sergeant,' Michael said menacingly before Lachlan could respond to the order. 'I suggest you leave us alone.'

Michael's defiance enraged Forster and he stumbled forward. 'You think yer a man becuz you fought our precious Private MacDonald here, do yer?' he said into Michael's face.

'You need a hand, O'Flynn?' one of the Rangers asked.

'Stay out of it, you colonial upstart.' The voice came from a British corporal. 'You can see that the sergeant is in his rights. You bloody colonials are a disgrace to the Queen. Won't get yer hair cut or take orders from your betters.'

A chair rasped along the floor, and suddenly the Ranger flung himself at the corporal. Within seconds a full-scale brawl had erupted; colonials against British regulars. Somewhere in the melee, Sergeant Forster went down, and both Michael and Lachlan made a hasty retreat through a back door.

'I think that you should continue your journey to Auckland,' Michael said with a grin. 'I have a feeling the provosts won't be far away.'

'Good idea,' Lachlan replied, shaking Michael's hand. 'Are you going to be all right?'

'I am kind of used to this sort of thing,' Michael replied. 'By the way, have you thought about joining the Rangers? The Von has been called on to form a new company under his command. I know that he would appreciate having the second-best fighter in these parts with his unit as well as the best.'

Lachlan broke into a rolling laughter. 'That is yet

to be decided, Michael Duffy,' he said. 'But I like the idea of the better pay and less drill that I have heard you fellows enjoy.'

'Then you will be one of us,' Michael said. 'Just leave it to me.'

'One thing, Michael,' Lachlan said in parting, 'I have a friend who I know would also like to get away from the good sergeant inside. He's a fellow Scot by the name of Andrew Hume. You think you could put in a good word for him?'

'I don't know,' Michael said with a broad smile on his face. 'The Von is looking for real fighting men – like us Irish. I'm not sure if he will take second-best with you Scots.'

'Anytime, Duffy, anytime,' Lachlan growled without malice. 'Look after yourself and keep your head down.'

By the time Lachlan returned to the front of the hotel he was not surprised to see the two wagoneers preparing to leave.

'We're goin' to find a pub where yer get a peaceful ale,' one of them grumbled as he flicked out the end of the whip to put the wagon in motion. Lachlan was pleased to be on the move again.

Lachlan was let off by the friendly wagoneers at the end of the Great South Road into Auckland. He trudged into the town, overlooking the sweeping harbour crowded with British warships and cargo ships, steam-propelled as well as driven by the traditional sails that still guided ships across the seas.

Alongside were smaller river gunboats capable of navigating New Zealand's rivers and coastlines, and carrying aboard marines and heavy guns for use in bombardment of Maori earthworks.

The town itself had fine, well-established stone buildings alongside the newly sprung-up wood and tin buildings hurriedly built to take advantage of the financial boom the war in the Waikato had brought to many enterprising merchants. The streets were alive with soldiers and sailors in the uniforms of the British Empire and the islands' capital had the look of a military establishment. Lachlan spent an hour asking about the location of Captain Lightfoot's cottage and at length a soldier was able to point him in the right direction.

The little cottage was at the edge of town and when the door opened to his rap a young Maori girl wearing European dress stood before him.

'Yes?' she asked.

My name is Lachlan MacDonald and I wish to pay my respects to Miss Lightfoot,' Lachlan answered.

'I will see if Miss Lightfoot is accepting visitors,' the maid replied, but before she could close the door Amanda stood there with a startled but pleased expression on her face.

She was as beautiful as he remembered.

'I must apologise that I do not have a calling card to announce my visit, Miss Lightfoot,' Lachlan said with genuine apology for his breach of social etiquette. 'The army does not seem to have much time for such niceties.'

Amanda was at a loss for words. Before her stood the young Scot she thought of so often, in his crumpled militia uniform stained with the signs of his journey. Eventually, she was able to find her voice. 'You appear to have journeyed a long way Mr MacDonald, and it would be very impolite of me not to offer you tea. Annie, please go and prepare tea for my guest,' she asked, turning to the young woman who was suspiciously eyeing the bedraggled soldier on the doorstep. The maid left, leaving the two alone in the doorway.

Lachlan removed his cap and wiped his boots on the doorstep before stepping inside the small but comfortable cottage. It was not a grand place, but warm and clean.

Amanda gestured for Lachlan to take a chair and poured the tea, which the maid had brought in and placed before them, into two china cups.

Lachlan was not sure if Amanda was pleased or angry at his unannounced arrival and wondered if it had been such a good idea to visit her. But he countered his doubts with the fact that she was the primary reason he had travelled to New Zealand in the first place. He opened the conversation by telling her that he was serving in her brother's unit and that he had actually signed his leave pass.

'Does my brother know that you intended to visit me in Auckland?' Amanda asked.

'I just happened to learn that you were in Auckland,' Lachlan replied lamely.

'I'm not sure I believe you,' she said with a smile. 'Why is it, Mr MacDonald, that I feel you have gone to all the trouble to travel from my brother's camp simply to see me?'

Lachlan sipped at his tea. He did not know how to reply. He might as well have been back in the book store in Sydney when he had given her the book of poetry. He was helpless in her hands and they both knew it. He was never sure of her true feelings, as she liked to tease him. 'Well, yes, if you want to know,' he finally answered. 'I had a great desire to see you again.'

Suddenly, the smile on Amanda's face faded. 'Is that why you volunteered to come to New Zealand? For if it is I feel that you have placed your life in danger and I hold grave misgivings for your safety. It was bad enough watching that man you fought from my brother's regiment in Sydney inflict the savage blows on you. I . . .'

She dropped her gaze, suddenly bereft of words. 'Lachlan,' she said, lifting her eyes misty with tears, 'I do not think that this is the time or place for us to discover what we may feel for each other. I fear that if my brother learns of your feelings for me – and I must confess, mine for you – that he may do something terrible. I followed my brother to this country as a loyal sister should. I had hoped that we might see each other when I returned to Sydney and could never have known that you would enlist for the war here hoping to see me.'

'Oh, I trust that you did not interpret my being here as any foolish attempt to win your affections, Miss Lightfoot,' Lachlan said, hoping to retain his pride, but only too aware that she had called him by his first name. Such intimacy warmed his heart. 'I am aware that I am but a lowly private soldier in your brother's company and that I do not have any great fortune to my name,' he continued. 'I have yet to be recognised for what I feel I may achieve in the future.'

'I believe that you will achieve whatever you set your mind to, Lachlan,' Amanda said.

'Well,' Lachlan said, standing abruptly and taking his cap from the table, 'I must beg your leave, Miss Lightfoot, and commence my journey back to camp. I just wanted to pay my respects while I was in Auckland.'

'I hope that I may see you from time to time,' Amanda said with a warm smile, causing Lachlan to feel a surge of fresh hope.

'Thank you for the tea,' Lachlan said, showing himself to the door. 'Goodbye, Miss Lightfoot. I too pray that we shall have the opportunity to meet again soon.'

Outside the cottage, Lachlan could feel the cold wind against his cheek. 'You bloody fool,' he swore at the wind. 'Why didn't you just tell her what you truly felt for her?'

Standing in the doorway, Amanda watched Lachlan trudge away. She wanted to say something more, but she knew a penniless, handsome young man would never be accepted by her brother as a suitable beau for her. She turned away from the door, tears welling in her eyes. Oh, how she hated this class-ridden society that she had been born to.

• • •

Lachlan reported to the company orderly room that he was back from his leave, but as he stepped from the tent to return to his quarters he saw Sergeant Forster hurrying towards him with two armed soldiers in tow.

'Private MacDonald,' Forster roared across the hard-packed parade area, 'stop where you are.'

Lachlan ceased walking and waited for the sergeant and the two soldiers with him to approach.

'Private MacDonald,' Forster said when he was a couple of paces away, 'you are under arrest. Guard, escort Private MacDonald to the cells.'

Lachlan knew the two men who had been detailed to escort him to the small timber building used as a lock-up mostly for drunken soldiers. He looked at them and they both replied with shrugs and blank looks as if to say that they had just about as much clue as he did why he was being arrested.

'On what grounds are you having me arrested?' Lachlan asked Forster angrily.

'A small matter of a riot you caused at Rogers Criterion Hotel a couple of days ago,' Forster snarled. 'And the ensuing assault upon the person of meself.'

'I never hit you – or caused the fight,' Lachlan responded. 'And you know it.'

'Doesn't matter what I know, Private MacDonald,' Forster sneered, thrusting his face into Lachlan's. 'What matters is that you are under arrest an' when yer found guilty, yer get at least fifty lashes of the cat-o'-nine-tails at the triangle.'

Lachlan fought inwardly to control his temper.

He wanted to smash his fist into the sergeant's face, but knew plain well that would get him a court-martial and a hefty prison sentence, so resigned himself to being escorted to the lock-up. No doubt Captain Lightfoot would hear the charge and dismiss it, Lachlan thought as he was led away.

That evening Andrew was able to secure an unofficial visit to Lachlan in his cell. The two guards looked the other way as the two friends spoke through the barred window.

'We heard the news when Forster came back from Rogers Criterion,' Andrew said. 'He really has it in for you.'

'I know Captain Lightfoot will listen to my version of what happened,' Lachlan replied. 'Forster was drunk and spoiling for a fight. The man is mad.'

'Captain Lightfoot is away at the regiments' headquarters,' Andrew said gloomily. 'Lieutenant Grimes is in charge and Forster has been boasting that he will do anything that Forster tells him to do. The men are saying that Grimes is frightened of Forster. Is there anything we can do for you?'

'Not really,' Lachlan replied. 'But thanks for the offer. It looks as if I will have to take my chances with Grimes.'

The following morning Sergeant Forster came for Lachlan and ordered the guards to escort him to the orderly room. They passed a British regular soldier wearing his best dress uniform and the chevrons of a corporal. Lachlan was curious as to his presence outside the orderly room and when the soldier caught Lachlan's eye he looked away with an expression akin to guilt.

Lachlan was marched into the orderly room, where Lieutenant Grimes was waiting for him behind a desk cleared of all articles except a couple of sheets of paper. Lachlan came to a crashing halt, saluted the officer, removed his cap and waited at attention. Forster stood behind him and the two guards took a pace back. Grimes read out the two charges of assaulting a superior officer and disobeying a lawful order.

'Private MacDonald,' Lieutenant Grimes said, clearing his throat, 'how do you plead?'

'Not guilty, sir,' Lachlan replied, staring beyond the officer's head to where a picture of a young Queen Victoria hung on the wall.

'Sergeant Forster, present your evidence,' Grimes said.

Forster recited his story in martinet fashion, accusing Lachlan of striking him during a brawl that Forster claimed Lachlan had instigated when he had been ordered to produce his leave pass for inspection. Lachlan listened to the litany of lies spilling from the senior NCO's mouth.

'And I have witnesses from the British regulars who were present that day,' he concluded. 'Corporal Martingale is outside if he is required to give his statement of facts to corroborate my version of events, sir.'

Lachlan now knew that the soldier waiting outside must have been a drinking partner of the militia

161

sergeant and prepared to lie in support of Forster. 'Sir,' Lachlan spoke up, 'I did not instigate the brawl and I would like it noted that Sergeant Forster was drunk when he ordered me to produce my pass. I did not have the opportunity to do so as a fight broke out and I wisely departed the hotel bar to avoid becoming involved in what eventuated. At no time did I knowingly disobey Sergeant Forster nor strike him. If he was struck, it was not by me. I have a witness to verify what I am saying is true and a correct version of what happened that day in the hotel bar.'

As if deep in thought, the officer stared at Lachlan before speaking. 'Can you produce your witness, Private MacDonald?' he finally asked.

But thinking now about Michael Duffy, Lachlan realised that he would be drawing attention to his friend when the last thing he needed was scrutiny. 'I am afraid my witness is not currently available,' Lachlan replied.

'Then, if I should call on Corporal Martingale, a man with an impeccable record of service to the Queen, and he can corroborate Sergeant Forster's version of the events, it will leave me with no other recourse than to punish you to the full extent of the army code of conduct. What do you say to that?'

'I would prefer that Captain Lightfoot hear the charge, sir,' Lachlan replied quietly.

This seemed to anger the young officer. 'Captain Lightfoot has passed on the command to me, Private MacDonald, and in his absence I have his powers of command. That also means his powers to hear all charges of this nature.'

Lachlan was not sure if this was correct, but recognised that he was in a tight spot. If the British corporal gave evidence, he would no doubt damn Lachlan with his lies.

'I still plead not guilty to the charges, sir,' Lachlan said softly.

The British corporal was called in and presented his evidence. Clearly he and the Australian sergeant had conspired to get their stories straight enough to sound convincing.

After presenting his evidence the corporal was excused. 'I can only find you guilty of all charges, Private MacDonald,' Grimes said, shuffling the papers before him. 'But since your recent show of courage in saving Captain Lightfoot's life I am empowered to show leniency,' he said, fidgeting with the charge sheets. 'I am going to sentence you to fifty lashes at the triangle at 10 a.m. tomorrow morning. The unit is to be paraded to witness your punishment as a deterrent to others who may consider committing such serious offences. There will also be a three-month stoppage of pay. You will not, however, be cashiered from the army and hopefully after your punishment you will prove to be a good soldier. Do you have anything further to say, Private MacDonald?'

Lachlan continued to stare at the wall behind the officer. 'No, sir,' he replied and could almost feel Forster's pleasure. At least he would remain in the army and New Zealand.

● ● ●

Lachlan waived breakfast the following day and was marched out to the parade ground where the wooden triangle was set up. He was stripped of his jacket, tied by his hands to the wooden frame and the two soldiers assigned to deliver the punishment stepped forward with the thonged lashes in their hands. Across the frame Lachlan could see his comrades glaring malevolently at Lieutenant Grimes and Sergeant Forster, who were standing by to supervise the punishment.

'Stick this in yer mouth,' one of Lachlan's guards said under his voice as he tied Lachlan's hands. It was a piece of stick, which Lachlan accepted gratefully between his teeth. 'You don't deserve this, as all the lads know,' the guard muttered quietly, lest he be overheard.

A drum rolled and Lachlan felt the first lash from the cat-o'-nine-tails strike his back. The pain seared through his body and he bit down on the stick in his mouth. It was followed by another lash. One by one the lashes were counted off. At twenty-five the second soldier took over and Lachlan felt the sweat of pain roll down his face. He refused to cry out and give Forster the pleasure of knowing he was being hurt. Instead, he grunted with each lash until, mercifully, it was complete, and the drum beat fell silent. Lachlan was still on his feet but could feel the blood running down his back.

When the regimental surgeon stepped in to examine him and ask if he was well, Lachlan merely glared at him. The surgeon stepped back and nodded his head to Lieutenant Grimes. Then the bindings were untied from Lachlan's wrists and he felt himself being gently lowered to the ground. The parade was dismissed and Andrew ran over to Lachlan's side.

'The bastard will burn in hell,' Andrew spat bitterly. 'Can you stand, old chap?'

Lachlan struggled to his feet with a tight grin on his face. 'Is it over?' he asked with a crooked grin. 'I was just starting to enjoy it.'

ELEVEN

When Captain Charles Lightfoot returned from regiment headquarters, he was informed of the punishment and Lachlan was called up to his office. The wounds inflicted by the lash were still painful.

Lightfoot was standing by a window with his hands clasped behind his back. 'Private MacDonald,' he said with a pained expression on his face as he turned to face Lachlan, 'I am bitterly disappointed in your behaviour. I had thought very highly of you until now, but what you did is not tolerated in Her Majesty's colonial forces.'

'I was not guilty, sir,' Lachlan said quietly.

'Damn it!' Lightfoot exploded, turning his back on Lachlan. 'You were found guilty on the evidence of two fine NCOs. The army is incapable of making mistakes and it does not serve you well to continue defending your supposed innocence to the charges.'

Lachlan had not expected this reaction from the man whose life he had saved, but he weathered the explosive outburst, realising that it was futile to attempt to defend himself.

'What else do you have to say for yourself?' Lightfoot asked, turning to glare at Lachlan.

'Nothing, sir,' Lachlan answered.

'Then you are dismissed,' Lightfoot spat.

Lachlan saluted, turned about and marched out of the office. He stood in the early evening breeze, confused. Had he been foolish to even consider that Captain Lightfoot might have been sympathetic to him? Lachlan knew that Lightfoot had as much as called him a liar and that rankled more than anything. The young Scot's upbringing had impressed the importance of honesty, but he was growing to recognise that the captain was far more treacherous than any of Australia's deadly snakes. Was it possible that Lightfoot suspected his feelings for his sister? It could well be so.

Lachlan hardly marched back to his tent. It was more like a shamble. Michael Duffy's invitation to join the Rangers was appearing a more inviting proposition with each miserable day that passed.

John missed Nicholas more than he wished to admit. But the friendship he had forged with the Duffy clan and Max Braun helped pass the days of yearning.

As it was, both he and Nicholas had decided that he would explore any possibilities in Sydney for expanding their enterprises. The profits that flowed from the lucrative contracts with the army and navy in New Zealand required reinvestment. Both men were growing richer and had cemented their business partnership with a formal document. They were now MacDonald & Busby, Merchants, and it had been Nicholas who had first mooted the potential of the newly established sugarcane growing industry of southern Queensland. Sugarcane was the basis of rum and the far-off American war between the states had seriously curtailed the local industry.

John spent his days in interviews with bankers and men who had some understanding of the sugar industry in the Caribbean Islands. He had been fortunate when Daniel introduced him to a couple of the Erin's patrons who had worked in the cane industry as supervisors on slave plantations. The possibility now loomed that he and Nicholas might expand to landowners in the still somewhat mysterious colony that had claimed the lives of so many illustrious explorers.

John sent a telegram to Melbourne to report on his progress and said he was looking forward to sharing an evening with Daniel, whom he found to be an extremely intelligent young man. When he arrived at the hotel, he was warmly welcomed by Frank Duffy.

'Max has someone in the bar he thinks you might like to meet,' he said, opening the back door to the kitchen. For just a moment, John's hopes soared. Was it his brother returned? 'A fellow, who knew your father on the goldfields,' Frank continued, dissipating John's optimism.

John made his way into the bar. It was not a busy night and Max greeted him. 'The man over there,' he said, indicating a table where a man sat nursing a tumbler of rum. 'He knew your father and older brother.'

John ordered a whiskey and made his way to the table, accompanied by Max.

'My name is John MacDonald,' he said, standing in front of the table. 'Mr Braun has told me that you knew my brother and father at Ballarat.'

'My name's Joseph Leeson,' the man said, glancing up at the two men. He was in his late fifties, bald and had a long, black beard streaked with grey. His clothing gave him away as not being from the city. 'Have a seat.'

'I was talking to Max last evening when he just happened to mention how you had been at the Eureka stockade the day the red-coats came,' Leeson said. 'He said that you lost your brother and father in the bloody massacre.'

'That is right,' John replied, curious as to where the conversation was leading. 'My father was Hugh MacDonald and my brother was Thomas.'

'Thought so,' Leeson continued. 'I saw them struck down. I was only a few yards away but fighting for my own life at the time. I was not able to help them, I'm sorry.'

'You need not feel any guilt, Mr Leeson. You are probably lucky to be here today, considering what happened.'

'It was bloody murder, what they did to your father and brother,' Leeson said, taking a long swig of his rum. 'Your father wasn't even armed and that bastard trap Samuel Forster slew him with a bayonet. Then that bastard red-coat officer Charles Lightfoot hacked down your brother with his sabre.'

John almost forgot the drink on the table in front of him. 'I gather that you mean my father and brother were murdered,' John stated coldly, remembering the promise sworn to his dying brother.

'That is what I saw,' Leeson said. 'Cold, bloody murder. I heard later around the camp fires that Lightfoot took a fair bit of money from your father and used it to further himself in the army.'

'Do you know what became of the two?' John asked.

Leeson shrugged. 'Lightfoot probably returned with his regiment to England and as for Forster, well I would be surprised to hear that he is still alive. He had more than a few enemies amongst the miners. There'd be plenty prepared to meet him on a dark night and settle scores for his treatment of us on the fields. He was a real bastard. Some said mad. If he had a set on a miner for no particular reason, he would make his life hell. I kind of hope that is where he is right now.'

John thanked Leeson for his information and sat quietly for a moment, stunned by the news.

The old German patted John roughly on the shoulder. 'I know this is a hard thing for you to hear,' he added quietly. 'But there is something else you should know. When Lachlan last wrote to us, he told us about his new life in the army.'

John stared at Max intently and the bartender

shook his head with a frown. 'That man Mr Leeson was talking about? That bad red-coat, Charles Lightfoot? He's your brother's commanding officer.'

Lachlan and Andrew found themselves stationed with a detachment of their comrades at a wooden stockade located near a creek mouth south-west of Drury. Lachlan welcomed the garrison and guard duties away from the hated Sergeant Samuel Forster. He was washing his pannikin in a metal tub after breakfast when he heard the gunfire. From his reckoning it was coming from the direction of a feature only a mile away known as Bald Hills where he knew a company of the Mauku Forest Rifles were stationed in a fortified church.

'What do you think it is?' Andrew asked.

'I don't know,' Lachlan replied. 'But there is a fair bit of it going on. No doubt someone will tell us soon enough.'

Lieutenant Perceval, commander of Lachlan's militia detachment, called his men to arms and waited. Within the hour a rider galloped to their stockade. He did not bother dismounting and all watching could see his excitement.

'Sir, with Mr Lusk's compliments, the natives are massing in the valley between the hills. He requires your men to defend the church. He has dispatched a messenger to Drury for other reinforcements.'

Lieutenant Perceval was a young officer with no combat experience to date and Lachlan was not surprised to learn that he had been ordered to the creek mouth stockade to garrison the wooden fortress. The captain was putting all his less experienced men and officers away from his company in the event that he be called on to engage the Maori in a significant engagement.

Already Lachlan and the others had grabbed their kit, readying themselves for a fight. Rifles were given a closer inspection to ensure no parts were faulty. Corporal Power had the men fall in for a parade and awaited further orders from their commander. The orderly had already galloped away to rejoin his unit at the church and inform Lieutenant Lusk that the message had been delivered.

'Men fully kitted and ready to march, sir,' Corporal Power barked, when he was approached by the young lieutenant.

'We are not going to join Mr Lusk,' Perceval said aloud so that his men could hear him. 'We are going to move to the right for Titi Hill where, according to my calculations, we will be able to outflank any attack on the church and thus surprise the natives. I am sure that is a much better idea than joining our comrades in the defences.'

Lachlan felt uneasy. He caught a glimpse of the expression on the corporal's face and knew that it was one of disagreement. But like a good soldier, the corporal knew to obey orders from superiors, and so ordered the thirteen men of the detachment to set off with the young lieutenant in command.

The wounds to Lachlan's back had not healed completely and the strenuous effort of hiking through the timbered country took its toll on his strength. Beside him, Andrew kept a wary eye on his friend.

'Do you think Perceval knows what he is doing?' Andrew asked in a hushed voice as they made their way in a skirmish line through the timber, always alert to a sudden ambush.

'He's the officer,' Lachlan grunted as they struggled towards the crest of Titi Hill.

Then it happened. Over the crest swarmed a great mass of semi-naked Maori, screaming blood-chilling war cries, and coming down on the small detachment rapidly.

'Get to the felled timber!' Perceval bellowed. 'Make every round count.'

Lachlan and Andrew scrambled over a huge fallen log and threw themselves into a firing position. Even at a rough guess, Lachlan calculated that they were outnumbered ten to one. As the warriors quickly surrounded the fourteen men of the militia, Lachlan caught sight of a huge Maori wielding an old musket over his head and signalling his orders for the dispersal of his warriors. For a brief moment, Lachlan had a grudging respect for the decisive tactics of encirclement. He drew a sight on the giant warrior and fired. The rifle bit into his shoulder. A cloud of smoke temporarily obscured where he had aimed but as he began to reload he noticed that the warrior was not to be seen. Whether he had hit him or not was irrelevant. None in the small detachment at that moment entertained any hope of surviving. The young officer had clearly blundered and led them to certain death. Beside him, Lachlan could hear Andrew mumbling a prayer as he fired and reloaded.

'Over here,' Lachlan heard Corporal Power yell at the top of his voice and between the stands of timber he caught sight of European uniforms. A small relief party had stumbled on them, led by an officer Lachlan recognised as Lieutenant Norman, who had been sent to Drury to pick up their pay.

The defenders in the timber could see the small relief force fighting for every inch of ground as they battled their way towards them. Still vastly outnumbered, they fell in beside Lachlan and his comrades, just as the Maori warriors broke through the gunfire to engage in hand-to-hand combat.

Lachlan had already fitted his rifle with a bayonet. The irony was lost on the young Scot that he and his enemy were now on equal ground. It would be bayonet and rifle butt against war axe and club.

Out of the corner of his eye he saw Andrew suddenly stand and wield his rifle over his head like a club. A Maori warrior had leapt over a fallen log to bring his axe down in a wide swing at Andrew's head. It caught on the stock of the rifle, crashing it down to the earth, leaving Andrew helpless against another attempt with the axe.

Lachlan lunged forward and with the tip of his bayonet caught the warrior in the thigh. The warrior stumbled back, as Andrew scrambled on his hands and knees for his rifle. Although wounded, the warrior roared his defiance and this time came at Lachlan. The world had come down to a tiny place on the earth for Lachlan. This was not the arena of the bare-knuckle boxer who was most likely to walk away from a fight but a case of being up against a man who had every intention of killing him. All around in the forest, similar scenes were being played out. Men cursed and cried for their mothers as they fought to stay alive.

Lachlan was only concerned with his own plight, as already Andrew was engaged in battle with a Maori armed with a greenstone war club. The half-naked warrior Lachlan was facing was wearing only a small grass skirt but the mass of ornate tattoos over his body made him a fearsome spectacle. He was shouting words in his own language and his rage was obvious. Lachlan realised that even if he had fought this man in the boxing arena he might have come off second best.

The warrior did not launch into an attack imme-diately. He was sizing Lachlan up, the axe steady in a two-handed grip held to the right of his shoulder above his head. Lachlan stood with one foot slightly forward to balance himself in the classic stance of the bayonet thrust, his rifle fully extended from his body to keep the warrior at bay.

The Maori made a half lunge forward but Lachlan did not fall for the trick. Instead he allowed the huge man to come forward but the warrior was not fooled by Lachlan's attempt to lure him onto the point of the bayonet and flashed a savage, disconcert-ing grin at the young Scot.

'Die Pakeha!' the Maori roared as he swung the axe in a wide arc, inches from Lachlan's face. Only Lachlan's years of fist fighting had prepared him for this moment. The heavy brass butt plate slammed into the Maori warrior's head and he dropped senseless to the forest floor. Lachlan recovered his stance as the Maori attempted to rise from the ground. Without thinking, Lachlan lunged forward to drive the bayonet square between the warrior's shoulderblades.

The warrior staggered to his feet and turned to the man who had beaten him. For a moment the two men's eyes locked and then a stream of blood erupted from the warrior's silent scream.

Now, all Lachlan had to do was retrieve his rifle, but having ripped right through to his chest the bayonet was stuck firmly. Lachlan unlocked the bayonet boss. What had taken seconds felt like hours but all around him men were still fighting for their lives.

Andrew lay face down, blood welling from the terrible gash to his head. The warrior who had felled him now came at Lachlan, swinging the blood-stained war club and yelling his ancient war cries.

Lachlan gripped his rifle by the barrel and roared his own defiance. Club struck rifle butt with such force that the weapons were plucked from the men's grips and they stood face to face unarmed.

Lachlan grasped his new opponent in a head lock as the man clawed for his eyes. He sank his teeth into the Maori's neck and was rewarded with the taste of blood.

A blow to the side of Lachlan's head shook him loose and the warrior staggered away, screaming and holding the bleeding wound to his neck.

Lachlan searched around him and found the

warrior's club. He scooped it up and ran at the wounded man, who in the last split second attempted to shield himself from the blow. The club came down with a sickening crunch of bone.

'To me, boys,' Lachlan heard through the din of battle. He glanced down and knelt to examine his friend. Andrew's eyelids were flickering, so Lachlan hoisted him over his shoulder. He bent down and retrieved Andrew's rifled musket and staggered to a group of soldiers he could see regrouping a short distance away in the trees. They were delivering aimed fire into any Maori appearing in the openings between the trees.

Lieutenant Lusk stood at the centre of his men, calmly issuing orders. One group was to provide covering fire while another moved back in the direction of the fortified church at Mauku.

'Have you seen Mr Perceval?' Lusk asked as Lachlan placed Andrew gently on the ground.

'No sir,' Lachlan answered, quickly preparing his rifle for action.

'Damned man,' Lusk swore and turned his attention to the fight. 'Corporal, prepare your men to fall back.'

Lachlan bent down to scoop up Andrew once again. Bullets chopped away at the foliage as he ran in a shuffling jog until he reached the point where the corporal had ordered his section to stop and return fire.

Once during the retreat, Lachlan was suddenly confronted by a warrior who stepped from behind a tree with a musket and fired wildly. The shot missed.

Lachlan brought his rifle up to his waist and fired an equally wild shot, causing the warrior to step behind the tree for cover.

Lachlan kept moving forward until he reached the next designated position. He was nearing the end of his physical reserves. He knelt by Andrew, panting for breath through cracked lips. Would it ever end?

'The church,' he heard someone call and when Lachlan raised his head he could see the welcome sight of the fortified walls.

Sensing that they had run out of time, the Maori warriors suddenly broke off the fight and withdrew with their wounded. A couple of militia men came forward to carry Andrew's unconscious body to shelter.

'You put up one hell of a fight.' Lachlan immediately recognised Michael Duffy's cheery voice. 'I am sure your feat will impress the Von.'

'Michael,' Lachlan gasped, struggling to his feet. 'What the devil are you doing here?'

'I was sent by the Von to carry a message to our brother Rangers at Mauku. We could hear the gunfire and from my estimates I didn't expect to see any of you get here alive.'

'It was a bloody close-run thing,' Lachlan said, wiping his brow with the end of his sleeve.

'That fellow you brought in a friend of yours?' Michael asked gently.

'A good friend,' Lachlan replied bleakly. 'I hope he lives. He took a pretty savage blow to the head.'

'Well, I have to return to my company,' Michael said, thrusting out his hand. 'Take care.'

'You, too. Put in a good word for me,' he added. 'I want out of the militia.'

'If you join us the pay and conditions may be better but I can promise you long days of sitting out in the bush and getting your backside wet,' Michael grinned. 'See you soon.'

Michael left Lachlan to himself on the grassy slope just outside the church. Instinctively, he went to check his firearm and realised that his hands were shaking uncontrollably. In his head he could still hear the screams and shouts of dying men. He sat down and placed his head between his legs. He wanted to go to sleep and not wake up for a long time. And when he awoke, he would be back on the track with Duncan by his side at a camp site on the banks of a gently flowing river. But he knew this would not happen. He was in a foreign country, fighting a fierce race of people who refused to give up their land. For a moment Lachlan understood the sympathy expressed by an older, battle-seasoned Scot. *'It's a bit like when the Brits cleared us from our land in the Highland clearances after Culloden,'* he had said. *'Now we are doing it to the poor, wretched native people of this land in the name of the bloody British Empire.'*

That late afternoon two companies of the Waikato militia arrived from Drury, but too late to have any impact on the battle. The staff officers in Drury had not accepted the dire circumstances the defenders of the church had found themselves in.

Early next morning a reconnaissance party from

the church defenders found the bodies of their slain comrades stripped of their uniforms and equipment. The Maori warriors had laid eight bodies out in a row and a white haversack had been placed on a stick to mark their location. All the bodies displayed tomahawk wounds. Amongst the dead was Lieutenant John Perceval of the 1st Waikato Regiment.

TWELVE

Only the clink of tea cups against saucers and the ticking of a grandfather clock in the hotel's foyer disturbed the tranquillity. Outside in the spring warmth there were no sounds of cartwheels along the paved street. Nor the clatter of a trolley car being hauled by draught horses – or the shouts of street hawkers plying their trade.

John MacDonald sat in a comfortable leather chair with his cup of tea before him. It had become his ritual to peruse as many papers as possible for items that might assist him in his decisions for investment.

Having learnt about Lachlan's enlistment in the army and the identity of his commanding officer, John had been trying to decide the best way of dealing with the situation. Part of him wanted to jump on board the first ship and head over to New Zealand, but he realised that this might not be the most rational course of action to take. He'd been spending some time researching the country and its war and had added news of that country to his reading.

He picked up a copy of the *Daily Southern Cross* and read a report by the war correspondent William Morgan. The paper was dated Tuesday, 27 October, 1863.

The bodies of Lieut. Thomas Alabone Norman, Lieut. John Spencer Perceval, Corporal M. Power and Privates Obein, McIlleray, W. Williamson and W. Beswick — the officers and men who were killed in the affair at Mauku — were yesterday committed to the grave in the Episcopalian burial-ground. Having fallen in the same engagement, they were all interned in one common tomb. There were a large number of persons, consisting of Waikato Volunteers, Regulars and Marines in attendance, paying a last tribute of respect to these brave men. There must have been nearly five hundred present. The funeral was to have taken place at two o'clock, but it was nearly three before all the necessary arrangements were completed. Just before that hour, the rain — which had long been threatening — began to descend and it ceased not the whole of the time occupied by the interment. At three o'clock the firing party, fifty in number, belonging to various companies, were ordered to reverse arms and beat time and then the order was given to move on. The firing party, in command of Lieut. Minnington, headed the procession. The fifes and drums of the Royal Irish followed, playing the Dead March. The Rev. Mr Morgan walked in front of the corpses, each of which was carried by Volunteers. Officers of different Waikato companies acted as pall-bearers. In the rear

*came the Volunteer companies, the Regulars, and the
Marines, each accompanied by their officers. There was also,
notwithstanding the weather, a good many civilians present
to witness the affecting sight of so many comparatively young
men carried to their final resting place . . .*

John put down the paper, not bothering to finish
the article. It was impossible not to think about his
long-lost brother. He did not know it but Lachlan
had stood in the pouring rain at the funeral parade,
shivering as the water soaked through to the wounds
on his back.

John picked up another paper and flipped
through the pages advertising pills to prevent hysteria
in women, soap to make you smell fresh and many
varieties of Indian and Chinese teas. There was a further article on the New Zealand campaign, about
the militia volunteers and how they were in capable
hands with such British officers as Captain Charles
Lightfoot to lead them.

John threw down the paper in disgust. He
refused to sit by idly while Lachlan risked life and
limb in battle under his commanding officer who
was the murdering cur that had killed their brother
and father. If Lightfoot were to realise Lachlan's
identity, then his brother would be in mortal danger. John decided that he must travel to New
Zealand to see if he could do anything to bring
Lightfoot to justice before he killed his only
remaining brother.

How could he inform Nicholas of his decision to
sail for New Zealand? Nicholas would understand.

He was very wise in the ways of the world and John trusted his opinions.

There were times when the truth was best sought and this was one such time. John placed the newspaper on the table beside his cup of tea now grown cold. He would go to his room and compose a letter to Melbourne.

Amanda Lightfoot travelled to Drury to stay with her brother in a little cottage he had been able to acquire within the town limits. He had protested her desire to join him. However, Amanda had defied her brother, stating that she was growing bored in Auckland living amongst strangers. She was not about to tell her brother her real reason.

The only person Charles Lightfoot truly felt close to was his sister and eventually he relented. At least he would be able to better keep an eye on her, he justified to himself, even if Drury was on the front line of the war. There were other advantages too to having his beautiful young sister in close proximity. Amanda was an excellent hostess and had a way of charming all she came in contact with. It could not do his military career any harm to have her entertaining visiting senior staff officers and their wives.

Charles stood by the fireplace of their sitting room with a sherry glass in one hand and a cigar in the other as Amanda sat embroidering the small tapestry on her lap with pictures of flowers and butterflies.

'That young Scotsman of yours, Private

MacDonald, certainly redeemed himself in that skirmish at Titi Hill,' Lightfoot said, watching his sister's face carefully, puffing his cigar and taking a swig of the imported sherry.

'Who?' Amanda asked, distracted from the delicate needlework.

'Lachlan MacDonald, the boxer you championed in Sydney,' Lightfoot reiterated. 'You know, he is in my company.'

'Oh, how is he?' she asked, attempting to sound disinterested.

'Got himself into a spot of bother and had to be lashed for disgracing the Queen's uniform,' Lightfoot replied. 'But I was informed that at Titi Hill he personally killed two of the natives with his bare hands and carried out a comrade to safety, fighting all the way. Under other circumstances, he might have been recommended for the Victoria Cross except that has been negated by his previous disgraceful behaviour.'

Amanda had tried to put Lachlan from her mind but this did not work. She'd had many sleepless nights since Lachlan's visit to Auckland but the memory of his face and gentle ways persisted. However, she was a practical young woman and knew that he was too young and lacking the proper means to secure her love. Nonetheless, the thought that he might be killed was beyond her comprehension – as was learning of his punishment.

'Why was he lashed?' Amanda asked, hoping that her brother had not detected the tightness in her voice.

'He assaulted one of my sergeants,' Lightfoot

replied lightly. 'Mr Grimes sentenced him to fifty lashes, which I heard he took like a man. MacDonald was lucky not to be court-martialled and imprisoned.'

Amanda closed her eyes, attempting to put the vision of the cruel punishment from her mind. Lachlan was scarcely twenty years of age and this would mark him for the rest of his life.

'Is Private MacDonald posted to Drury?' she asked.

Lightfoot turned from the glowing flames of the hearth. 'Why would you want to know that?' he asked intently. 'He is not of any special interest to you, is he?'

'No,' Amanda retorted. 'It was nothing more than curiosity.'

'Anyway,' Lightfoot continued, 'he will not be in the militia for much longer. I have approved his request to be transferred to Von Tempsky's Ranger Company, effective as from the day after tomorrow. I granted him compassionate leave to remain so that he can see if his comrade, Private Hume, lives or dies. He was the man that MacDonald rescued in the fighting.'

Lightfoot felt smug in his decision. When he had agreed to his sister's request to join him in Drury he knew the best thing he could do was have MacDonald transferred out of his company to another unit posted well away from Drury.

Amanda sat very still, reflecting on what her brother had told her. Many thoughts raced through her mind but one above all persisted. She knew that she must see Lachlan before he left, although she did not know what she might say to him after their brief conversation in Auckland.

John opened the envelope and read the telegram that had been delivered on a silver platter to his room by one of the smartly dressed young boys on the hotel staff. It was from Nicholas in Melbourne, informing John that he had received his letter and was not to leave for New Zealand without him.

Walking down the stairs to the hotel foyer, John smiled at each person that he met. It was not the answer that he had expected to his letter, but one that pleased him very much.

Amanda found Lachlan on a wood-chopping detail. She had been directed to where he was by the corporal of the guard and had walked through the camp with its rows of white conical tents, past men drilling in the early morning sunshine on muddy fields and the camp kitchens steaming the day's stew in big pots over open fires. Her fresh beauty turned many a soldier's head.

Eventually she found the field. At the edge of a stand of tall trees a group of men stripped to the waist were chopping felled logs into usable sizes for the camp fires. Lachlan was not aware of her approach until one of his comrades ceased chopping to make a flattering but crude comment.

Amanda could see the wounds crisscrossing Lachlan's back. She knew that she had gasped at the sight, but repressed an urge to run to him and smother him with her sympathy. As the sister of a regular army officer, she knew to control her emotions.

Lachlan ceased wielding the axe and turned to face Amanda. Sweat ran down his chest although the morning was relatively cool.

'Hello, Lachlan,' Amanda said uncertainly, seeing both surprise and an enigmatic expression on Lachlan's face in her presence.

'Miss Lightfoot, what are you doing here?'

Amanda looked around at the half dozen men staring at her. Some knew that she was the sister of their commander and were respectful. Even so, Amanda felt awkward in their presence. 'Would it be possible to speak with you alone?' she asked quietly.

Lachlan placed his axe against the log. He knew that the soldier in charge of the detail would not object to him speaking to the company commander's sister for a brief moment.

Lachlan caught his eye, 'Permission to take a break?' he asked and the soldier in charge nodded.

'Get back to work,' he barked at the rest of the men gawking at the beautiful young woman.

Reluctantly, they did so as Lachlan quickly put on his shirt and accompanied Amanda towards the stand of trees. When they were sufficiently far enough away, Amanda was the first to speak.

'My brother told me of your fate in the last few weeks,' she said. 'It distressed me to hear that you had been flogged.'

'For something I was not guilty of,' Lachlan replied bitterly. 'But it is over now and the wounds will heal.'

Amanda stopped walking and turned to Lachlan. 'I feel that I am to blame for your misfortune,' she said in a trembling voice. 'I feel that you would not be here if it weren't for me.'

A savage smile came to Lachlan's face. 'You think I would not be prepared to receive a thousand lashes just to be in your company?' he said, looking down into her face. 'I cannot tell you that I love you as we do not know each other that well, but from the moment I first saw you I have been able to think of no one else.'

'Oh, Lachlan, your words are beautiful – but you must forget me,' she said, impulsively touching his cheek with her fingers. 'We are of different worlds, you and I. I know it is my duty to be courted by one with means – despite any personal feelings that I may hold.'

'For me, you mean?'

'If I answer your question I may give you false hope,' Amanda said. 'It may be that my feelings for you are the same as yours for me. You are like no man I have ever met before. You are strong, gentle and brave, but that alone does not sustain a life between a man and a woman.'

'Wealth and ambition are the answers,' Lachlan said with a bitter, short laugh. 'I am but a poor young man but I do at least have ambition. One day the world will know of my exploits as an explorer, then you may see me in another light.'

'You will earn land at the end of your enlistment,' Amanda said lamely. 'That is a start.'

'I am not a farmer,' Lachlan replied. 'I lived my

life roaming with a wonderful man on the dusty tracks of the colonies of Victoria and New South Wales. What beckons to me is the colony of Queensland. If only you could wait for me to achieve the fame and fortune I seek, I could show you that my ambition makes me worthy of earning your love.'

Amanda did not reply. She could see that he was ambitious but whether he made his dream come true was another matter. For now he was in the middle of a war and had to survive that before he could advance his hopes.

'So, why did you come here to see me?' Lachlan asked after a short silence between them.

'I . . .' Amanda dared not answer.

'This may cost me another session at the triangle,' he said. 'But it will be worth it.'

Before Amanda could react, Lachlan leaned forward, kissing her on the mouth. The kiss was returned and Amanda felt that she might faint, such was the beautiful shock of this intimate contact with the young soldier. She did not resist and when he broke the moment she wished he had not. The kiss lingered.

'I think that you should go,' he said quietly, knowing that his act had been observed by some of the men in the wood-chopping detail. 'Your brother would not approve of you being seen in the company of common soldiers.'

'Lachlan, I . . .'

Lachlan reached out to touch Amanda on the cheek with great tenderness. 'You do not have to say anything. Just promise that you will not forget me.'

Tears welled in Amanda's eyes. 'I promise. I will wait for you forever, my love. I will write every day to you – no matter where you may be,' she whispered and turned to walk away lest she burst into a fit of sobbing.

Lachlan watched her walk away towards the camp. 'I will come back to you, one day,' he said quietly, his soul soaring with the echoing words of her promise to him. 'And when I do, the whole world will know.'

Lachlan walked back to the detail and picked up his axe. Not one of the men said a word.

THIRTEEN

Private Lachlan MacDonald stood to attention, a cool breeze whipping scudding clouds overhead. Beside him he gripped the barrel of his new .537 Terry carbine and at his right hip was a holstered .44 five-shot Deane-Adams revolver. On the opposite hip in its sheath was a finely honed bowie knife, and on his head a pill-box cap with the badge of the Forest Rangers. His blue jacket was crossed with leather straps to hold the haversack mounted high on his shoulders. He wore knee-length boots, which actually fitted, as Michael Duffy had friends in the Quartermaster's office where uniform was issued.

The Forest Rangers were the eyes of the army, scouting for enemy positions, ambushing Maori war parties and protecting vulnerable supply lines from attack. Many of the regular British officer staff referred to the Rangers as colonial scum, considering them ill-disciplined, even if they were invaluable in this war which was being fought deep in the thickets of the New Zealand bush.

Captain Gustavus Ferdinand von Tempsky personally reviewed his company and Lachlan was impressed by his new commander. He was a tall, well-built former Prussian regular soldier who had fought in the guerrilla war against the Spanish army in Nicaragua, before coming to New Zealand to dig for gold. He was also an excellent artist and author who had travelled the world in his search for adventure. He had dark hair almost to his shoulders and a neatly kept moustache curling to the edge of his mouth. Lachlan could see how the handsome man might make women swoon but he was also popular with his men. They would have followed him into hell had he asked it of them.

Lachlan had seen an increase in pay since transferring to the Von's company. He was now being paid three shillings and sixpence per day and also was entitled to a double issue of rum. The camaraderie amongst the men also impressed him. It had not been easy to transfer but Lachlan had come to learn that there was a special bond between Michael Duffy and the Von.

'The natives call Von Tempsky *manu-rau*,' a Pakeha soldier had told Lachlan when he first arrived at the company. 'It means *many birds*, as the Maori say he is everywhere in the bush.' The soldier had lived for some time amongst the Maori people and was known as a *Pakeha Maori*. But he was just the kind of man the Von sought for his company of rangers; he knew the bush and he knew the Maori they now fought.

Lachlan instantly felt at home with his new comrades but his pleasure was tempered when he heard that his old friend Andrew Hume had been discharged from the militia because of his severe head injury. Lachlan might have saved his life, but Andrew was now prone to fits. The blow had done its damage and Lachlan had bid his friend a farewell before leaving the militia to join the Rangers. As far as Lachlan knew now, Andrew would return to the Australian colonies and travel on to Queensland to resume his life as a surveyor. He had been discharged with honourable mentions and would be employed by the new Queensland government for the service he had rendered in uniform for the Queen.

The parade was over and the Rangers dismissed to their quarters. 'Ranger MacDonald,' Michael Duffy called to Lachlan. 'Report to me.'

Lachlan shouldered his carbine and marched smartly to where Michael was standing alone on the parade ground.

'How are you settling in?' Michael asked warmly.

'I don't know how to thank you,' Lachlan replied. 'This is a lot better than being in Lightfoot's command.'

'You might not be thanking me in the next few weeks,' Michael grinned. 'We have orders to go bush again in the next few days. That will mean a lot of wet, sleepless nights stalking the Maori in his own territory. It is not like the militia where you return to a warm and dry stockade each night.'

'I don't mind,' Lachlan replied. 'I feel that what is ahead will prepare me for the life of an explorer when I eventually return to Australia.'

Michael shook his head. 'You have to survive this war first,' he chuckled. 'But I have to give you marks for your enthusiasm. Well, it is time to get some rest and hot food. So, join the men.'

Lachlan left Duffy, known to all as Sergeant Michael O'Flynn. When Lachlan felt self-pity for his own situation he only had to remind himself that Michael had lost much more than a woman in his life. He had lost his whole family and any hope of returning to Australia without fear of arrest on the false charge of murder.

'It was brought to my attention only today that you were seen to be acting in a somewhat common way with Private MacDonald some three weeks ago,' Charles Lightfoot ranted at his sister in the privacy of his cottage.

'I kissed him,' Amanda replied mildly. 'It was simply a sign of affection for the courage you told me he displayed.' She sat in her usual chair with her embroidery before the open fire.

'Is that all it was?' Lightfoot questioned, only partially satisfied with his sister's explanation. 'If I thought that he had forced himself on you I would have him immediately arrested and flogged to within an inch of his life.'

'No, dear brother,' Amanda frowned. 'It was I who delivered the token of my respect for his sterling service to the Queen,' Amanda persisted. 'If you have him arrested I promise that you will never see me again.'

'You sound as if you may be more than fond of the man,' Lightfoot said suspiciously.

'I am eighteen, old enough to know my own feelings,' Amanda said. 'It was nothing more than affection.'

'I will accept your word on the matter,' Lightfoot concluded but he now regretted allowing MacDonald to transfer to the Rangers. If he still had him in his command he was sure that Sergeant Samuel Forster would have some devious means of having the man put under arrest and suffer a spell in prison. Locked away, he would no longer be able to see Amanda. At least he could console himself that the life of a Forest Ranger was fraught with much danger and that the Maori warriors might just dispose of MacDonald once and for all. He could not afford his sister to fall in love with a commoner – when he had visions of marrying her off to Sir Percival Sparkes.

The ship dipped and rose in the heavy swells of the Tasman Sea. John had decided he would get some fresh air in an attempt to ward off seasickness and stood at the bow, gripping the rails. The steamer chugged and puffed to fight the seas in the night while the wind moaned in the rigging.

'I thought I would find you here,' Nicholas said, making his way carefully along the deck to grip the rails beside John.

'I needed the air and a chance to think,' John replied, staring into the darkness where horizon and sea met.

'Are you still worried about your brother's reaction if you find him?' Nicholas asked.

'That, and what I can do to fulfil my promise,' John said. 'If this Captain Lightfoot is one and the same as the man who murdered my father and brother, robbing my father at the same time, I do not know how I will exact revenge.'

'There are many forms of punishment,' Nicholas said. 'One does not have to kill one's enemy to punish him.'

John turned to glance at Nicholas, who was also staring out to sea. 'Possibly you could explain,' he said.

'Well, I doubt that you are acquainted with the use of duelling weapons, so you have to use some other means to inflict the vengeance your Gaelic blood cries out for. Find a weakness in your enemy – and exploit it.'

'Your explanation is still couched in vague terms,' John continued.

'For example,' Nicholas said, 'you are now a man of considerable means and that brings power. It has always been my experience that a man's greatest weakness is the woman in his life or his financial interests. Taking either one has the possibility of destroying him.'

John laughed. 'I doubt that I might take any woman from Lightfoot,' he said, 'considering who I am.'

'Then it must be his wealth,' Nicholas said. 'Destroy him financially and watch him rot in poverty.'

John liked the idea of seeing the man who had murdered his father and brother in dire financial circumstances. But how could that be achieved? he pondered. As if to answer his unspoken question, Nicholas spoke.

'Lightfoot does not know of my connection to you,' he said. 'I think when we arrive I should set up circumstances to befriend your enemy, gain his trust and let our combined power destroy him.'

'How will you do that?' John asked, his respect for the man in his life heightened by the way he was able to plot such schemes. He had witnessed how shrewd Nicholas had been in dealing with people in their business and had no doubt that he was capable of carrying out his plan – whatever it might be.

'You must trust me,' Nicholas said. 'Our contracts with the army in New Zealand mean I have contact with some very important people, both in the army commissariat and the government. No doubt I will be able to use them to get to Captain Lightfoot. Now, I think it is time that we joined the captain's table for a hand of cards. I am feeling lucky tonight.'

It was Lachlan who was first alerted to the extreme danger Michael Duffy might be in. He had been sitting with his new comrades from the Rangers outside their tents, smoking pipes, chatting and playing cards. They had been preparing for an operation into the dark forests of the Maori-held territory to seek out enemy positions and now they had some time off to relax.

A new recruit to the Rangers sat near Lachlan, puffing on a pipe and staring hard at Michael Duffy standing a distance away conversing with Von Tempsky.

'I know that man,' he said to the soldier beside him. 'He used to fight in Sydney.'

Lachlan froze when he overheard the comment. 'But he wasn't O'Flynn then,' the new soldier continued. 'His name was Michael Duffy and he was wanted by the Sydney traps for murder. Last I heard when I left Sydney was that he was still wanted for the murder and there was a reward for his arrest.'

Lachlan did not know how to react. Should he scoff at the new man's suggestion or simply ignore it, hoping that none of the others around them had taken any notice.

'I doubt that Sergeant O'Flynn is this man Duffy you are talking about,' the corporal with them said. 'He is a bloody good soldier and a good man. I'd say you got it wrong and if you know what is good for you, you will not go about making such accusations again.' The new man's statement had been met with some hostility from the rest of his comrades as well and Lachlan realised just how much respect the men had for Michael. He decided to wait until he could speak to Michael alone later that day and at last came across him beside the cookhouse where the army butchers had a carcass hanging on a hook from a tree.

'Michael,' Lachlan said when he had caught the Irishman's attention, 'a new man to the company has recognised you,' he said.

Michael sucked in his breath and frowned. 'It has always been something I knew would catch up with me,' he replied. 'New Zealand is too close to Sydney.'

'What are you going to do?' Lachlan asked.

'I have wondered that myself,' Michael replied, casting around him to ensure they could not be overheard. 'The Von knows who I am, and about the situation in Sydney. I think it is time that I moved on.'

'No doubt easier said than done,' Lachlan offered, surprised that their commander knew about Michael's real identity. 'Especially since we go bush tomorrow morning.'

'I will have a word to the Von,' Michael said. 'It is time to disappear.'

'If I can help,' Lachlan said, offering his hand, 'all you have to do is ask.'

'I thank you, Lachlan MacDonald,' Michael responded. 'We will see.'

John and Nicholas arrived in the port of Auckland and could immediately see the signs of war. All around them in the streets of the large town were red-coated soldiers, wagons full of war supplies and even Maori auxiliaries dressed in the uniform of the British army.

Nicholas had been astute enough to arrange accommodation for them before they left Sydney.

Such arrangements were vital in a town now crowded with farmers and families from the edges of the frontier, parts of which were controlled by the hostile Maori forces.

Although not fancy, the hotel's accommodation was comfortable and the food relatively good. John and Nicholas took separate rooms and settled in. When they were established, Nicholas went in search of men who until now had been simply names on contracts and invoices. His first contact was a captain from the commissariat supplying the army.

For John, his first contact was the British army headquarters to try to locate his brother. He was fortunate that a roll of all men enlisted for pay purposes was kept. It was not long before a clerk ran his finger down a roll of the Waikato militia to find Private Lachlan MacDonald, enlisted from Sydney.

'Last known posting was at Drury in Captain Lightfoot's company,' the clerk said. 'But our rolls take time to be amended in the event of transfers.'

John thanked the man and returned to the hotel.

'Lachlan is definitely a soldier in Lightfoot's command,' John said glumly.

'How convenient, you get to find your brother and meet your enemy all at the same time,' Nicholas responded with a faint smile.

'It is a queer coincidence,' John replied. 'I do not feel easy about the matter of Lachlan being in the command of the man who murdered our father and brother.'

'It might be wiser if I went to Drury to seek out your brother, in that case,' Nicholas said. 'It would not help my plans to have Charles Lightfoot meet with the man ultimately to be responsible for his downfall.'

John agreed.

'I will make arrangements to travel to Drury tomorrow,' Nicholas continued. 'In the meantime, you could use the time to visit some influential people I have met over here and seek out any possible ventures that we may turn a pretty penny on. War always has a market for items we take for granted.'

Lachlan pulled the greatcoat around his body in a vain attempt to keep from soaking to the skin. At least its bulk provided some warmth against the biting wind that whipped through the dank ferns. He kept his rifle covered to avoid moisture dampening the paper cartridges and his finger remained not far from the trigger as he sat peering into the gathering darkness of the coming night.

His section of Rangers had now been three weeks in the bush scouting for enemy camps and tracks. They had patrolled without any luck in the rugged, heavily timbered hills south of Auckland. Their luck had changed this day as one of the Rangers, a man who had once lived amongst the Maori, spotted signs of a track being used by war parties.

The Von was consulted and he decided that they would sit off the track with the intention of springing an ambush should it be used again. The company established a base camp with the pack horses hobbled and then moved three smaller sections forward to cover the area. Lachlan was one of the sentries posted. He could hear the faint sound behind him. Slowly, he turned his head and was relieved to see Michael Duffy, with one of the other Rangers, creeping forward to his position.

'Anything?' he whispered and Lachlan shook his head.

'Private Clyde is relieving you,' Michael said. 'Time for you to go down the hill for a hot cup of tea.'

Lachlan was thankful. His limbs were cramped from the hours of sitting in a hide of ferns, scanning the area for any movement. He was easing himself to his knees when all hell broke loose. The musket and shotgun fire that poured into the ambush site bespoke a sizeable force of Maori warriors who had somehow turned the tables on the outfit.

Lachlan immediately fell flat on his face, discarding the heavy, rain-soaked coat. Fragments of leaves and splinters of wood spattered his face. In his desperation he sought to see where Michael was and saw that he too was lying face down to avoid the incoming fire. A groan from behind Lachlan told him that Private Clyde had been hit.

'Get back to the base camp,' Michael shouted. 'I will cover you.'

Lachlan raised his head to protest and from the corner of his eye could see four Maori warriors advancing stealthily through the trees towards them. They were armed with muskets as well as their personal weapons of axe, tomahawk and war club.

Lachlan swung his rifle to lay his foresight on the

nearest man and fired. He was rewarded with the heavy bark of the Terry rifle and a thump in his shoulder but in the twilight his round went wide, smacking into a tree trunk beside the warrior. It was enough to make the Maori stop and take cover.

Beside Lachlan, Michael fired his rifle, dropped it and snatched his revolver from its holster. Rising to his feet, he roared in Celtic, firing his pistol at the Maori warriors as he did so. One of the warriors dropped his musket as a bullet caught him in the chest.

'Go now!' Michael yelled. 'Tell the Von what is happening. I will hold them.'

Reluctantly, Lachlan turned to crash through the bush in the direction of their base camp, knowing that the gunfire would most likely already have alerted the company commander to the skirmish.

As he ran, Lachlan pulled out his pistol and snapped off a shot in support of Michael, now standing alone over the private's prone body.

Lachlan was only part of the way to the camp when he saw the Rangers advancing up the hill in a skirmish line towards him. The Von was urging them on, waving a sword in one hand and holding a pistol in the other.

'Sir, Sergeant O'Flynn is holding on about a hundred and fifty yards up the hill,' he gasped. 'Private Clyde is down wounded.'

'Very good,' Von Tempsky replied calmly.

Lachlan could see a strange mixture of serenity and excitement in the former Prussian officer's eyes. It was as if such situations were made to fill his life.

With the night gathering fast, the skirmish line found itself being separated by the stands of trees. Lachlan almost stumbled into a Maori warrior and for a moment they stared at each other, mere feet apart. Lachlan fired three shots at point blank range, one of the bullets taking the warrior in the face. Lachlan fired again but his pistol clicked empty. In desperation he drew his long-bladed bowie knife, lunging at the man who was slumped, holding his face with both hands. Lachlan could feel the blade bite into yielding flesh and the man fell to the ground at Lachlan's feet.

'Fall back,' came the call, relayed along the line of skirmishers.

Lachlan quickly reloaded his pistol and picked up his rifle, not wanting to look at the man he had just killed. Obeying the order, he fell back down the hill and was joined by other Rangers.

Von Tempsky was already conversing with his NCOs, trying to account for any of his men that might be missing.

'Sergeant O'Flynn?' he asked.

'Nothing seen of him, sir,' one corporal answered. 'But we found Private Clyde. He has a gunshot wound to the face. He said Sergeant O'Flynn charged a group of Maori to draw them away from him. He says the sarge should get a medal for what he did, but we need to get the wounded man out of here now.'

Lachlan felt sick at hearing the soldier's recounting of the last sighting of Michael. It seemed so typical of the man to risk his life for another. But now he had disappeared.

The company commander briefed his NCOs to organise an all-round defence of their base camp and hold for the night. Lachlan had come to learn why the Rangers received the extra pay for their services. In the cold and biting rain, he huddled against a fallen log with another soldier and without his greatcoat shivered throughout the long night. Little wonder the Rangers had a reputation for being tough. The only thing that helped Lachlan bear the misery was the memory of the kiss he had stolen from Amanda. He would retreat in his mind to a place where they were together in the warm sunshine, and she was holding his head in her lap. It was not a place he knew but told himself it must be in the colony of Queensland, as travellers had told him that the climate of that colony was warm and sunny. Yes, he and Amanda were together in Queensland, he dreamed. She had expressed her love for him and they were living as man and wife under the tropical sun.

'Wake up,' the man beside Lachlan nudged quietly. 'I think the boss is on his way over.'

Lachlan snapped awake. He could see the glow of the lantern waving through the pitch dark towards them. Only the company commander had allowed himself a lantern, to minimise any signs of the camp, although they all guessed that the Maori warriors had probably spotted it.

'MacDonald?' Von Tempsky asked, the glow of the lantern lighting his face as he bent over the two men by the fallen log.

'Yes, sir,' Lachlan answered.

'Tomorrow morning, you will report to me at first light. I have a mission for you.'

'Yes, sir,' Lachlan replied dutifully, and then the Von was gone, moving in the dark to inspect his picquets.

What mission? Lachlan settled back behind the log to benefit as much as he could from its protection. He would learn the answer in the next few but long hours. In the meantime, he and his fellow Ranger snatched some sleep, taking turns to stand guard against an attack during the night.

Just before first light the rain tapered away to reveal a heavy mist rising from the wet ground, as the sun broke through the clouds, bringing some warmth to the men miserable with the cold.

A breakfast of cold water and equally cold hard biscuit was passed out as the men stretched their cramped limbs and rubbed their frozen hands together. Weapons were checked to ensure that they were still functioning and then the men formed up for a sweep of the hillside in the direction of the previous evening's skirmish.

Moving forward very cautiously, weapons at the ready, the Rangers made their way up the timbered slope, ensuring that they kept within sight of each other. Near where Michael had stood over their fallen comrade, Von Tempsky called Lachlan to him, directing the rest of the company to sweep along a gully for any signs of the Maori war party.

'Sergeant O'Flynn informed me that you knew of his secret and that he trusted you with his life,' Von Tempsky said quietly once they were alone. 'What

I am going to ask you is to support what I say in my report. I am going to say that Sergeant Michael O'Flynn fell here yesterday in a courageous one-man stand to buy time for us and protect a fallen comrade. You will verify that you saw him slain by the natives before you fell back on our line. As I am mentioning his bravery in my dispatches, I will do so under his real name of Michael Duffy – the man deserves that much. That part of the report will be true. Do I have your word that you will never disclose that the rest of my report is a fabrication?'

Stunned, Lachlan listened to the Prussian relate the conspiracy. 'Is Sergeant O'Flynn . . . Duffy, alive, sir?' he asked.

The Von nodded slightly. 'I hope so,' he replied. 'He had told me that he thought he might be betrayed by one of the new recruits to my company and we planned to give him the opportunity to slip away any time that might be opportune. As we have not found his body, I believe Michael Duffy is now on his way out of these hills to seek anonymity elsewhere. He is an extremely resourceful man. God go with him.'

'I will support your report, sir,' Lachlan replied without hesitation.

'Good,' the Von muttered, turning to greet a senior NCO moving towards them with his report of the sweep.

FOURTEEN

Nicholas Busby had been able to secure an interview with General Cameron, commander of the operations against the Maori rebellion. Nicholas found the general an easy man to talk to and they quickly established a rapport in their meeting at Cameron's temporary headquarters in Drury. He was surprised that the English general expressed doubts about the righteousness of the war, even stating that he felt he was simply fighting for greedy land-grabbers. As an honourable man, he did not conceal his opinions, but Nicholas knew that such beliefs were dangerous. They could lead to the general being replaced and sent home.

But Nicholas also knew that Cameron was not alone in his indignation at waging war against a courageous people fighting for their lands. Others in high places were also grumbling that the government could have sought other means of resolution.

The meeting led to an invitation for Nicholas to join the English general that afternoon at a tea party being held by Captain Lightfoot at his cottage on the outskirts of Drury. It would be attended by army and naval officers from the district, and a few influential civilians, Nicholas because of his services to the military commissariat being one of them.

'Three o'clock sharp,' Cameron said. 'Formal dress.'

Nicholas hurried back to his hotel, changed into a suit, found his way to the cottage and was welcomed at the door by a very pretty young lady.

'I am Miss Amanda Lightfoot,' she said. 'And how must I address you, sir?'

Nicholas was struck by her warm smile. 'Mr Nicholas Busby,' he said. 'Of Melbourne, and representing my firm, suppliers of rum and rations to the land and naval forces here.'

'Well, Mr Busby, on behalf of my brother, Captain Charles Lightfoot,' Amanda said, 'you are welcome here.'

This delightful lady was the sister of the man he had travelled from Auckland to meet Nicholas thought. She appeared to be such a nice young lady that he almost had doubts about his mission.

'General Cameron told me that your brother is responsible for the fine spread that I see before me,' Nicholas said as they walked together towards a gathering comprising mostly men in uniform and a few ladies wearing their best dresses. The men stood delicately balancing cups in their hands as they partook of the array of fine cakes. From the way some of the young men looked in Nicholas's direction he knew that he was not the centre of attention. Amanda had plenty of admirers.

'I know that you have already met General Cameron,' Amanda said, 'so I must introduce you to my brother.'

She led him towards a tall, handsome officer standing in the company of two young ladies. They were laughing and Nicholas felt a strange coldness creep into his soul. So this was the man John was sure had murdered his father and brother.

'Charles, I would like to introduce you to a guest, Mr Nicholas Busby.'

Lightfoot did not bother to extend his hand but simply looked Nicholas up and down dismissively as Amanda excused herself to greet General Cameron, who had arrived in the company of his orderly.

'And your occupation, Mr Busby?' Charles Lightfoot asked coldly.

'I am the man who puts rum in your troops' mugs and beef in their stew,' Nicholas answered. 'I was informed that you command a militia of Australian volunteers.'

'I do,' Lightfoot answered. 'The scum of the Australian colonies, according to some in government here. From your speech I gather that you are a fellow Englishman.'

'I was born in England,' Nicholas replied. 'But I prefer the climate of the Antipodes. Do you intend to return to England after this war, Captain Lightfoot?'

'It depends on where I am next posted,' Lightfoot replied. 'If I do not gain a commission to a good regiment then I might consider resigning to take up business interests in the Australian colonies. There appear to be opportunities available to men of good breeding and enterprise.'

'In terms of acquiring a sound return on investment I can assure you that you are right. I have recently availed myself of such an opportunity and doubt that I would have been as successful back in England. All one has to know is what people need, and then exploit the market. Take my card in the event you ever happen to be in Melbourne,' Nicholas said, producing one of his visiting cards and pressing it on the captain.

'I shall avail myself of your financial services if I ever return to the Australian colonies but if you will excuse me, Mr Busby,' Lightfoot said, accepting the card, 'I must return my attention to these two delightful young ladies.'

'I understand,' Nicholas said. 'I feel that I should use this time to make the acquaintance of your fellow officers and ask them about the quality of my company's products. Good day, sir.'

It was not long after the afternoon tea that General Cameron was to fight his most disastrous battle with the Maori rebels, at a place known as Rangiriri, just west of Lake Waikare on the Waikato River. The Maori defences were superbly sighted, with rifle pits running parallel to the river to cover any approach from that direction and heaped earthworks able to absorb the heaviest artillery bombardment. A series of ditches were positioned in front of the main earthworks to slow down an assault. Well-concealed trenches and parapets spread from the lake to the river in a continuous line and were manned by around only five hundred warriors. Under Cameron's command were approximately twelve hundred heavily armed British regulars. The general's strategy was to engage the Maori rebels in a decisive battle, bringing the rebellion to an end once and for all. To do this he planned to launch a two-pronged infantry assault from the front and rear of the Maori fortifications. This tactic would also ensure that none escaped to fight another day as had occurred at a battle near Meremere two weeks before.

The river had allowed Cameron to transport troops and heavy guns to the Maori fortifications. The small naval ships *Pioneer* and *Avon* towed two gunboats to support the assault but the troops on board arrived late and after a difficult landing assembled for the attack.

Earlier, Cameron had ordered a bombardment of the fortifications using his Armstrong artillery guns. This had little effect so he ordered in an attack by the 65th Regiment. The fighting was fierce and the Maori defenders relinquished some ground – only to counterattack and drive back the British.

Cameron conceded that the position was too strong to be taken and the British settled into a siege situation. But during the night many of the Maori defenders slipped away, foiling Cameron's aim of containment and destruction. He had commenced a sap to snake its way to the main redoubt, which was to be blown by engineers when the trench reached the outer defences of the pa.

The next day a white flag was seen fluttering from the Maori redoubt. The Maori were signalling that they wanted to negotiate. They knew they were in a strong position, but the British army took the flag as a sign of surrender and marched in. They captured one hundred and eighty-three Maori – but at a cost of forty-one of their own men.

As the long war dragged on, General Cameron continued to advance up the Waikato River to occupy the junction of the Waikato and Waipa rivers by the end of the year.

Private Lachlan MacDonald, along with his comrades from the Forest Rangers, was with the advance.

While bivouacked at the junction of the two rivers, Lachlan received his first letter from Amanda. The mail had been brought by pack-horse from Raglan, some sixteen miles away on the west coast.

With his rifle in his lap, Lachlan sat staring at the neat handwriting. With the edge of his knife, he slit open the envelope, carefully removing the letter inside.

My dearest Lachlan,
I pray that this reaches you safely and that no harm has come to you.
    Your kiss from the last time we were together

still lingers on my lips. Although we do not know each other as well as we should, I feel a strong bond to you. From the moment I first saw you on that paddock in Sydney I have always had you in my thoughts and, of late, in my heart as well.

I do not know what the future holds for us, as we are people of two very different worlds. My brother expects me to marry a man of means and I must confess that I owe him much for his kindness in supporting me since our parents died. I love my brother dearly and owe him my loyalty.

There are many times when I am out walking that I see the soldiers drilling and find myself searching their faces for your kind smile and beautiful eyes. But I know you are now with the Forest Rangers and live wild in the bush country, always in mortal danger from the natives.

My brother does not know that I have written to you and you must realise that any reply from you would jeopardise our secret. When it is cold and you are wet and miserable, please think of me, and the great affection I hold in my heart for you. I know when I am alone at night I think of you and the kiss you bestowed. No matter what happens I will wait for you to return to me and hope that we may share your dream of exploring those far-flung silent frontiers you desire to walk.

With my warmest affection
Amanda

Around Lachlan, men built beds of cut fern, spoke quietly and smoked pipes as they set up camp.

They were weary and wet from the rain that had drenched them on the march but for now Lachlan did not feel the harsh conditions around him. His heart was beating like a hammer and he wanted to cry with joy. He re-read Amanda's letter many times, finally slipping it back into the envelope and carefully placing it inside his jacket.

'Mac!' a soldier called softly to him. 'Time for you to go on guard duty.'

Lachlan raised himself stiffly from the wet ground and for once the irksome duty was bearable.

'I made discreet enquiries around Drury as to where your brother might be,' Nicholas told John in the comfort of their hotel by the harbour. 'It seems that he is no longer in Lightfoot's company but has transferred to a unit known as the Forest Rangers. Last heard, the Rangers were advancing with General Cameron up the Waikato River.'

John bowed his head and stared into his tumbler of whisky. 'At least he is alive,' he said, swallowing hard. 'I just wonder how I can make contact with him when he is in the field, so far from the possibility of being granted leave.'

'It is Christmas eve,' Nicholas said, attempting to lighten John's heavy heart. 'And my Christmas present to you is that I have met with your enemy and learned his weakness. That should cheer you up.'

John turned and stared into Nicholas's eyes. 'I know,' he sighed. 'But a better one would have been to have Lachlan and Phoebe here to share a drink with us. There's been little good news about Lachlan and none about Phoebe,' he said.

'Next Christmas, dear chap,' Nicholas said, placing his hand reassuringly on John's arm. 'By this time next year you will have your brother back and then together you can search for your sister. However, I must caution you that we should return to Australia soon. Our enterprises call for closer management. At the moment it is out of the question for you to attempt to travel to General Cameron's force. The best you could do is write a letter to your brother, as I know which unit he is in. At least that will establish a contact for the future when he returns from his service here.'

John had to agree. They had been away long enough from the running of the company. He would write a long letter and mail it to his brother before leaving New Zealand's shores.

Christmas passed as good as unacknowledged by the troops advancing like a spear towards the heartland of the Maori rebels. The Rangers found themselves at the point, scouting the forward areas and securing the flanks for General Cameron's regulars and militia men.

Each day for Lachlan was spent moving stealthily in the thick undergrowth, always alert to Maori war parties. It was a war of nerves. The advance had been slowed by the need to manhandle three six-pounder, Armstrong guns, twelve bullock drays and 196 pack-horses across gullies and streams. By the end of

January the officers and men of Cameron's 2185-strong force eventually reached the formidable pa at Pikopiko. They set up camp, only to discover an equally formidable pa at Paterangi when they manoeuvred in the vicinity of the Waipa River.

General Cameron surveyed the situation he found himself in. Paterangi, with Pikopiko on the north flank and the pas of Rangiatea and Te Ngako visible to the east, was in a position to command all the tracks and roads leading into the vital Waikato hinterland. Cameron realised how strategic was the Maori layout of fortifications and past, bitter experience made him more cautious.

He established his field headquarters on the Te Rore River around one-and-a-half miles from Paterangi and pushed out a force of 800 officers and men to construct entrenchments within 1500 yards of the Paterangi pa. From their earthworks the British carried out sniping and some shelling with their artillery. By now Cameron was also in possession of intelligence that suggested that Maori from the east coast were gathering to join the Waikato warriors he now faced. A force was sent to Tauranga in the Bay of Plenty and landed unopposed. Both British and Maori settled down to see what would happen next.

At the end of January John's letter, along with five from Amanda, reached Lachlan at the advancing front of General Cameron's force.

Mail has been – and always will be – one of the

most significant factors in a soldier's life. It can boost morale or, at times, cause a pain no bullet can equal in its intensity.

When the orderly room clerk distributed the all-important envelopes at mail parade, Lachlan could not believe his luck in receiving so many letters from Amanda. He sat alone to savour them. In the distance he could hear the occasional crump of the artillery guns firing and the muted voices of his comrades.

Army life had hardened Lachlan's body to a peak of fitness he had not known before – not even when he had trained for his fights in Sydney. He had grown a beard and his face and his hands were tanned by the New Zealand sun. Although he was not aware of it, he had become a different man from the one he left in Sydney. He had learned to discipline himself against the physical and mental hardships of living in the field, and the innocence of youth was long gone. He had killed many times and had watched his defeated foe die before his eyes. He no longer felt anything other than a hardness to the death around him, his dreams of becoming an explorer forgotten as he lived simply from day to day. Only the loving words from Amanda touched his soul. He had sealed her letters in a leather pouch which he always carried with him on the dangerous scouting missions. They were his good luck talisman – and a reminder of the reason to finish the war, so that he could go to her.

Now Lachlan stared once more at the letter on top of those from Amanda and was puzzled by the handwriting. He did not recognise it, but the envelope bore a postmark from Auckland. He had decided to read this strange letter first and then allow himself as much time as possible to savour Amanda's letters.

As Lachlan began to read, his heart felt as if it had stopped beating in his chest.

My dearest brother,

I pray that this letter reaches you, as I have not been able to. When I learned from our dear friends, the Duffys in Sydney, that you had volunteered for service in the New Zealand campaign, I shipped to this country to find you.

Alas, I was informed in Auckland that you are in the field with General Cameron's army and unable to be met in person. My financial ventures force me to return to Sydney with my business partner, Mr Nicholas Busby, but I have all hopes that we may meet in person upon your return to Sydney. The Duffys will know where I am if my business causes me to move around the colonies.

There is so much to say to you, but I feel that should be done in person. I am now well off and hold in trust your share of the money our father left to us. There was more, but I have recently learned that it was stolen by a man whom I now know as your former commanding officer, Captain Charles Lightfoot. Although he did not directly kill our father, he ordered a Samuel Forster to do so but it appears Lightfoot did strike our brother Thomas with a sabre, causing his lingering death . . .

Lachlan could hardly believe what he was reading. No wonder Lightfoot and Forster were close; they were bound by a long-held secret.

Lachlan read on as John sketched out his life and revealed how he had found the hidden coins. Finally, he wrote . . .

> *My greatest desire is to find our sister and unite us once again as a family. My heart is with you and I count the days until we meet in person. My only desire is that you remain safe and well.*
> *Your loving brother,*
> *John*

Lachlan put aside the letter and stared into the dark forest before him. So he was no longer alone and financial means were waiting for him in Australia. The only cloud on this sunny, warm day was learning of Lightfoot and Forster's role in the death of his father and oldest brother.

'To arms! Rangers on parade!'

The shouted warning snapped Lachlan from his reflections. He quickly stuffed the precious letters inside his jacket, snatched up his rifle and ran. He could see his fellow Rangers assembling in ranks. Von Tempsky was pacing up and down in front of the parade of around forty men while the senior NCOs ensured that all men who could be spared were on parade. Lachlan joined the ranks.

The colour sergeant called the parade to attention, saluted the Von and marched smartly back to take up his position behind the parade.

'Men,' the Von spoke loudly, 'we have a difficult job ahead of us. A section of our British brothers has been ambushed while bathing in the Mangapiko River. Reinforcements have been already dispatched to provide covering fire. We have the task of flushing out the natives from the bush. You will be briefed by your NCOs as soon as the parade is dismissed. Colour Sergeant.'

'Sah.'

'Fall out the parade to their duties.'

Lachlan fell out and joined his corporal for the briefing. The letters temporarily forgotten, he readied himself to go back into the dense scrub and once again engage the fierce warriors. He felt both fear and excitement – and a terrible, nagging sense of doom.

FIFTEEN

Lachlan quickly charged his revolver with powder and ball, ramming down the rounds into each chamber and packing in the musket balls. He rarely kept the pistol loaded in camp, lest the moisture soak the gunpowder charge. Satisfied, he finally slipped his bowie knife into its sheath and left his rifle with his kit. This mission required a hunt where reloading might not be fast enough to counter a threat that they all knew would be only a hand's distance away.

'Across the stream and up the slope, lads,' the corporal in charge of Lachlan's section said quietly. 'It's a grand day to go hunting.'

The section splashed across the stream, holding their revolvers high to avoid water entering the charged chambers. They struggled up the bank on the other side and fell flat on their stomachs to crawl through the fern undergrowth. The Maori warriors could be anywhere concealed in the dense forest around the old pa site.

Lachlan could hear gunfire to either side of him but it did not deafen the sound of his own heart beating. He slithered forward, pausing to listen for any suspicious sounds. Not hearing any, he continued to crawl forward on his stomach and then stopped. His vision was obscured by the ferns and he risked raising his head above them. As he did so a young Maori warrior lifted his head to face Lachlan only a breath away. The fear on both men's faces was cut short when the young Maori raised his shotgun to level at Lachlan. But he had managed to get his revolver in place and fire first. His bullet smashed into the stock of the Maori's shotgun, snatching it from his hands. Lachlan fired again, but was horrified to hear the click of the hammer striking a percussion cap. Despite all his careful efforts to keep his powder dry, water had neutralised the explosive powder.

Realising that he had been granted a second chance at life and now wielding a long-bladed knife, the Maori warrior did not hesitate to fling himself on Lachlan, who desperately attempted to roll away from the attack. Lachlan felt the knife blade rip through his jacket and slide along his ribs. Using his revolver as a small club, Lachlan struck the warrior, but his blow fell harmlessly against the Maori's shoulder.

Before Lachlan could bring his revolver into action again as a club, the Maori was straddling him, his knife raised. For a moment, both men locked eyes and Lachlan despaired. The young warrior had a look of triumph on his face, knowing that within a split second the blade would tear into Lachlan's chest, delivering death. But suddenly the look of triumph became an expression of surprise as the Maori toppled forward. When Lachlan struggled out from beneath, he could see that a bullet had entered the side of the warrior's head, killing him instantly.

Lachlan did not know who had saved his life but as he lay on his stomach, with trembling hands he cleared the chambers of his revolver and reloaded them with the powder he had been able to keep dry on the river crossing. When he attempted to crawl forward the pain stung in his side. He cried out with surprise and did not attempt to go any further. The injury was worse than he had expected. Gingerly, he slipped his hand inside his jacket to feel for the wound along his ribs. Blood was stiffening his shirt and soaking the letters he had so carefully folded. His hands touched a bloody laceration and the contact made him gasp. Would he bleed to death before anyone found him? Lachlan rolled slowly onto his back and stared at the shining sky through the lush canopy above.

Lachlan did not know how long he had lain injured but he figured that he must have lost consciousness. When he opened his eyes he could no longer hear gunfire but only the voices of his comrades around him.

Four men carried him carefully down the slope, across the river and back to their camp site, where they laid him under a tent made of blankets on a bed of cut ferns. When his jacket was removed the package of blood-soaked letters fell to the earth.

'Bad cut,' someone said. 'Need to get him over to the Waikato militia. They have a regimental surgeon who can take a look at him.'

A litter was produced and Lachlan felt himself being lifted into it. He lost consciousness again and when he opened his eyes was aware of the regimental surgeon looking down at him. 'Looks like a cut, not a musket wound,' he grunted in a satisfied voice to his assistant. 'He's lost a lot of blood but should recover. I'll need to stitch him. Private MacDonald, we meet again,' he said gently and continued probing the wound with his fingers.

The surgeon stitched the wound and wrapped Lachlan's chest with a bandage before moving on to the next patient awaiting his skills. Lachlan accepted the water poured into his mouth from a canteen by one of the Rangers who had brought him to the aid post.

'At least yer are better off than the soldier next to you,' he said, capping the canteen when Lachlan had drunk enough.

Lachlan turned his head to see the British soldier lying on a stretcher next to him. His face had been shot away from a blast that must have been delivered at point blank range. All that remained was a bloody pulp, without any recognisable features.

'With any luck,' the Ranger kneeling over Lachlan said, 'the poor bugger might die without much pain.'

Lachlan silently agreed with his comrade. The soldier next to him could just as easily have been him. His own mortality was something he no longer took for granted, although when he stared at the faceless man lying alongside him he knew that there were some things far worse than death.

'It seems that we lost around six and about the same number wounded but the heathens lost over thirty-five killed from what I hear,' the Ranger said before taking his leave. 'Get some rest, Mac, an' we will see you back in our lines.'

Feeling too weak and weary to respond, Lachlan fell into a troubled sleep. He was awoken by a murmur of voices in the dark.

'How are you faring, Private MacDonald?' he heard the Von ask in a concerned voice.

'Well, sir,' Lachlan replied optimistically, 'I will be back on my feet by the morning.'

'I hope so,' the Von replied. 'We are advancing again and I will need you to be ready for action.'

Lachlan was pleased that as far as his commanding officer was concerned he would not be evacuated to a rear area to recuperate. To be away from the Rangers for the campaign was unthinkable.

'Wake up, you lazy scum,' the voice snarled in his ear. 'No time to go slacking on the army.' Lachlan opened his eyes to find himself staring into the face of Sergeant Forster bending over him. 'I heard that the natives had tickled you with a knife,' he said. 'Scum like you was lucky this time.'

Rage rose up in Lachlan's chest. He suddenly had an urge to smash the sergeant with his fist, but remained silent.

'So, I have you back for the moment,' Forster said, standing to tower over Lachlan. 'Yer probably think yer a real soldier now that yer have seen some service with the Rangers. Not real soldiers though,' he continued, the contempt obvious in his voice. 'Just the scum who couldn't make it in the militia.'

'I am not under your command, sergeant,' Lachlan replied calmly. 'I intend to report back to my company today.'

'Pity,' Forster sniffed. 'I could have given you some work around here digging latrines.'

With some difficulty, Lachlan sat up. The effort brought a stab of pain to his side. He felt light-headed and thirsty.

'I have a question for you, sergeant,' Lachlan said bitterly. 'You were at the Ballarat goldfields when the rebellion occurred, were you not?'

Forster blinked. 'I was,' he replied. 'What's it to you?'

'You get to kill anyone there?' Lachlan asked, staring intently into the sergeant's eyes.

'I saw my share of fighting,' Forster replied warily.

'But did you get to kill anyone?'

'I stuck a rebel scum,' Forster answered. 'Some Scotsman like you. He . . .' Forster's expression suddenly altered dramatically. 'Now I know why I have never liked you,' he said softly. 'You look a bit like that bastard.'

'He was my father,' Lachlan replied quietly. 'And

I swear that there will be a reckoning between you and me one day.'

Forster stepped back and stared dumbly at the young Scot. He could see murder in his eyes and despite his rank knew that he was facing a very dangerous opponent.

'When Captain Lightfoot hears how you threatened me,' Forster replied, 'he will have your hide for garters, Private MacDonald.'

'I know about Captain Lightfoot's role in the murder of my father and brother,' Lachlan said.

Forster turned and stumbled away, leaving Lachlan to watch his parting back. When the surgeon approached the improvised tent, Lachlan called to him. 'Sir, may I see you?'

'What is it, soldier?' he asked, bending down to adjust the bandages binding Lachlan's wound.

'I request permission to rejoin my company, sir,' Lachlan said, suppressing the pain he felt.

'The wound looks clean, but I will have to put you on a light duties chit for a couple of days. That won't be so bad, will it?'

Lachlan liked the surgeon. He was a kind man with a real regard for the welfare of the soldiers in the company he was attached to. 'That will be fine, sir,' Lachlan replied.

'Good,' the doctor grunted and proceeded to scribble a note on a page from his notebook.

'Thank you, sir,' Lachlan said, taking the chit exempting him from heavy duties for a couple of days.

'Well, Private MacDonald,' the army surgeon

said, 'you Scots are a hardy bunch of souls. So far you have survived a flogging and a knife wound. I doubt that anything worse should befall you now.'

'No, sir,' Lachlan replied. 'I think my luck should hold for the rest of the campaign.'

Lachlan struggled to his feet and reached down for his bloody jacket. With some difficulty, he slipped it on over the bandages and sought inside for his letters. He could not find them. The doctor had moved on to visit his other patients by now and Lachlan stepped out to find his company.

He found his comrades where they had set up camp.

'Good to have you back, young Mac,' they said, slapping him on the back.

'I kept these safe for you,' the corporal said. 'They are in a bit of a mess, but I don't think that really matters.'

Lachlan nodded his thanks. 'Go and draw your firearms from the quartermaster,' the corporal said. 'We are on the move again.'

Lachlan suddenly felt a rush of warmth for the men he was with. Although he did not know them well, they had shown their concern for him by saving the letters and making sure that he got them. The looks of genuine pleasure at his return had cemented his membership of this very special brotherhood of men. Never before had he felt so proud to be a Ranger.

On his way over to the quartermaster's tent to retrieve his field kit, Lachlan took the chit he had been given by the surgeon and tore it up. He did not need to be left behind if they were on the move again. Despite the discomfort he suffered, he reminded himself how the wounds of the flogging had been worse and yet he had soldiered on. He now had another burning desire in his life besides staying alive and eventually seeing Amanda again. When he had dealt with the hated sergeant, he would find a way to settle with the captain.

Excusing himself from his comrades, Lachlan sought a quiet place to finally get the opportunity to read the letters Amanda had sent him prior to his wounding. He sat down under a tree and carefully parted each envelope from the next. When he opened each letter he was bitterly disappointed that his blood had blotted some of Amanda's words from the pages. For the moment he forgot that she was the sister of the man he had sworn to kill.

Sergeant Samuel Forster stood with Captain Charles Lightfoot away from the camp site of the militia volunteers.

'What do you want to see me about, Sergeant?' Lightfoot asked irritably. The odious sergeant's urgent plea for the meeting smacked of something he really did not want to know about.

'It's about Private MacDonald, sir,' Forster said, wiping his brow with the edge of his cap. 'I think there is something you should know.'

'Get on with it, man,' Lightfoot said, glancing back at his men going about their routines.

'MacDonald is the son of that rebel you had me

slay at Ballarat, and he knows about our role in his father's killing.'

Lightfoot visibly paled. 'How do you know this?' he asked in a strangled voice. The rebel Scot had a bad way of coming to his troubled dreams at night asking for his stolen money back.

'Coz the bastard told me himself, just after they brought him over from the Rangers to have our surgeon look at his wound,' Forster replied.

'Do you know if anyone else is aware of this?' Lightfoot asked. 'Do you think he would have told any of his comrades?' For a moment the difference in rank between the two men was forgotten.

'I doubt it,' Forster replied slowly.

'How can you be sure?' Lightfoot asked.

'Coz he has threatened to do away with me the first chance he gets.' The sergeant spat on the ground. 'I doubt that he would go telling the world anything if he intends to kill me.'

Lightfoot nodded. What the sergeant said made sense. At least fore-warned was fore-armed, he reflected.

'What are we goin' to do about MacDonald?' Forster asked.

'That is something better handled by you, Sergeant,' Lightfoot replied. 'I am sure that you will come up with something. After all, serving in a war makes it easy to be killed, with few questions asked.'

Forster stood silently pondering the captain's direction. After Lightfoot had taken the money from the dead Scot, he had given Forster a thousand pounds of his loot to ensure his silence. Never in his wildest dreams could he have imagined being in the same place at the same time with one of the sons of the murdered man.

'Leave it to me, sir,' Forster finally replied. 'It won't be easy and will cost you a thousand quid if I am goin' to stretch my neck out for the hangman.'

'Five hundred guineas – and not a penny more,' Lightfoot countered.

'That's a deal,' Forster replied, knowing full well that he could not argue for further money. He snapped off a salute to his commanding officer. 'MacDonald will be dead an' buried before the end of this campaign.'

The weeks passed and the Rangers grew impatient. Meanwhile General Cameron formulated his plan to bypass the hilltop pas and march on the rich farmlands at Te Awamutu twelve miles away. To seize these Maori lands would effectively cut off food supplies to the pas and starve out their defenders.

Lachlan did not see Forster or Lightfoot during this time, as the Von remained active in sending out scouting patrols to clear the dense forest of any possible war parties forming for an attack on the British positions. But he did not stop thinking about Amanda, his brother in Australia, and how he would first kill Forster and then Lightfoot. The trouble was the latter obsession could get him arrested, in which case the other preoccupations would become irrelevant.

Finally, General Cameron made his move. On a

night of drizzling rain, Lachlan and the rest of his comrades were given the order to move out. Cameron was going to bypass the fortified pas and march for the farmlands. And Lightfoot's company was moving to join up with the Rangers.

SIXTEEN

The order to advance came down just before midnight. Marching in single file, the troops of Cameron's assault force wound their way through fern wet from the steady drizzle of rain. Soaking fronds swished against the soldiers' legs as they crossed the flat areas to ford cold streams in the dark. Finally they emerged on a dray road approximately two-and-a-half miles from Te Awamutu.

But not all was well. A company of British regulars had become separated in the dark and the assault force had to wait for them to rejoin the advance. This cost Cameron two hours but finally Te Awamutu was reached and occupied without any resistance.

Cameron immediately ordered his force to continue the advance onto Rangiaowhia, an area where crops of wheat, maize and potatoes had been grown for the Auckland market. The rich cultivation land was prized by both European and Maori.

General Cameron made his assessment and realised that an attack on the well-defended Paterangi pa was out of the question. He chose to bypass it instead, using the moonless night to assist his force. A mixed-race man by the name of James Edward, who had lived in the district, guided Cameron's troops as quietly as possible past the Paterangi defence line.

Lachlan and his comrades had been given the task of defending the column from any attack from the rear. They had passed so close to the Paterangi sentries that they could hear the Maori warriors talking to each other.

The march continued throughout the night and by dawn Cameron's weary force found itself just outside the village of Rangiaowhia. Cameron ordered his cavalry ahead and in a short time Lachlan heard the sound of gunfire coming from the settlement.

'Looks like we're in for a hot time,' the corporal in command of Lachlan's section said reflectively, as the Rangers crouched on the early morning earth, still damp with the evening's coolness.

Lachlan gripped his rifle, experiencing the old fears that had become second nature to him. What were they up against? How many would die this day? As most soldiers do, he had come to learn that the waiting before an action was worse than being involved.

'On yer feet, Rangers,' their corporal said in a tired voice. 'The word has come down that we are to join the fight.'

Lachlan heaved himself to his feet. He had been hungry but his appetite was gone. Now he moved forward with his company to engage in the fighting ahead.

Most of the Maori men and women had fled the village of thatch-roofed buildings but a small, determined contingent had remained to fight it out. The Von ordered his men to assault the Catholic church. In ranks they poured fire into the building until a white flag was seen fluttering from a window. Reluctantly, the Von took the surrender and ordered his men on to the next objective.

In small groups of three or four men, Lachlan and his comrades moved through the village. Firing seemed to be coming from all directions. Lachlan found himself separated and when he turned a corner he came across Sergeant Forster, who was confronting a huge unarmed Maori warrior. It was clear the sergeant was about to execute his prisoner. He raised his rifle, shouting, 'Die, you heathen bastard.'

Here was the perfect opportunity for Lachlan to exact his revenge. He raised his own rifle but an unexpected, almost forgotten memory of another time and place suddenly froze him. It was a recollection of a ten-year-old boy seeing helpless miners being slaughtered by the red-coats and goldfields police. For a brief moment he was a long way away in his mind but the sight of the huge Maori warrior brought him back to the present.

'If you shoot, Sergeant Forster, I will shoot you down like the dog you are.'

Both Maori prisoner and Forster turned to stare. The young man had his Terry Callisher carbine to his shoulder and pointed directly at Forster.

Forster's mouth fell open in his surprise and an expression of rage came to his face.

'Go now,' Lachlan yelled to the big Maori, who blinked his surprise at his unexpected reprieve. 'Get away.'

'Thank you, Pakeha,' the Maori replied in English. 'You are a good man.'

Without hesitating, the warrior broke into a sprint between the houses and Lachlan unexpectedly found himself hoping that the man might live to rejoin his people. But the warrior stumbled into the path of a British regular corporal, who immediately took him prisoner.

Forster swung his rifle on Lachlan and the two men now faced each other in a deadly stand-off. Now, Forster thought, was the perfect time to kill MacDonald. He would say that he met his death at the hands of a Maori warrior. It was unlikely that anyone would question his version of the events.

Lachlan harboured a similar scheme, but he was prepared to fire the Maori shotgun, thereby concealing the rifle wound and making the sergeant's death from enemy action appear more credible.

Neither man had the chance to carry out his plan. A body of troops swarmed around the corner of the building, sweeping the two men up. The settling of accounts would have to be at another time.

Lachlan bent down, scooped up his cap and went

in search of his company, while Forster bent down and picked up the shotgun that had been left on the floor beside him.

The fighting had come down to flushing out ten courageous warriors holding out in a warehouse where they had succeeded in killing a British corporal who had tried to enter the building. Under a baking sun the troops poured rounds into the building, which soon showed signs of being alight. Although smoke poured from the door and windows, the Maori defenders refused to surrender.

A British colonel standing nearby was felled by a shot from the burning building as the gallant defenders continued to fight on. Eventually one of the defenders stumbled from the burning building, only to fall down dead a few paces from the doorway. The fight for the building was over but not the skirmishing which followed Cameron's retreat from the village.

Along with the rest of the column, Lachlan fell back sweating. The track to the little village of Te Awamutu had been stirred into a cloud of dust raised by the boots of the troops and the iron-shod hooves of the horses. All the time the men's jangled nerves, already cut raw by exhaustion, were constantly drawn taut by the sporadic Maori fire.

When they reached the village the order to fall out was given and Lachlan joined his comrades, collapsing gratefully onto soft patches of grass to rest their bone-weary bodies and reach for water canteens.

Lachlan lay on his back, his rifle across his chest,

staring with gritty eyes at the puffy clouds filling the blue of the southern sky above. He longed to fall into a deep sleep.

'Private MacDonald,' the corporal said, toeing Lachlan's boot with his own, 'the Von wants to see you.'

Lachlan groaned, slipped on his cap and struggled to his feet. He could not think why his commanding officer wished to see him.

Lachlan found the commander standing with the colour sergeant, a big, broad-chested Scot who was known to be firm but fair in his meting out of discipline to the sometimes unruly colonial volunteers. Both men were eyeing Lachlan with some expression of amusement as he approached. Lachlan came to a halt and snapped off a salute by touching the stock of his carbine.

'You are not reporting in regimental order,' the colour sergeant growled gently. 'You are out of uniform.'

Confused and dazed from his exhaustion, Lachlan could only stare uncomprehendingly at the big Scot who was twitching with feigned annoyance. Beside him, the Von smiled enigmatically.

'What the colour sergeant means is that you are not wearing your rank, Corporal MacDonald,' the Von said.

For a second or two his commanding officer's words did not sink in.

'It is my pleasure to inform you, Corporal MacDonald, that I had nominated you for promotion a while back, and orders have come down from

General Cameron's HQ that the appointment has been approved, as from midnight last night. You have earned your promotion based on what the senior NCOs tell me about your leadership with others in the company. For one so young, you have gained the respect of many.'

'So, laddie, get over to the quartermaster and draw your stripes,' the colour sergeant said warmly. 'It will be your shout tonight.'

Lachlan blinked, attempting to clear his head.

'Thank you, sir,' he half mumbled. 'I am grateful for your trust in me.'

'Just don't let us down,' the Von said. 'I heard about your conviction when you were with Captain Lightfoot's company but was assured by Sergeant O'Flynn . . . I mean Duffy . . . that you were inno-cent. I did not hold that against you when I put your name forward for promotion. Congratulations.'

As the significance of his promotion sank in, Lachlan thanked the Von once again. The colour ser-geant excused himself to attend to regimental duties, leaving Lachlan alone with his commanding officer for a moment.

'I did not believe that Mr Duffy was guilty of the charges levelled against him in Sydney,' the Von said quietly. 'He had proved himself a splendid soldier and a fine man. I have recently heard a rumour that a man fitting his description was seen aboard a Yankee whaling ship leaving Auckland,' the commander continued with a twinkle in his eye. 'Sadly, if he is sailing for America, he is sailing into another war and, knowing the man the way I do, I doubt that he will be able to stay out of it. I have read that the Irish make first-class soldiers on either side of the civil war over there.'

As tired as he was, Lachlan understood what the Von was telling him; Michael Duffy had been able to flee the British system of justice for a new land.

'You may fall in with your comrades, Corporal MacDonald,' the Von said, granting leave for Lachlan to get a quick nap.

Lachlan saluted smartly, turned about and marched directly to the store to pick up his chevrons.

Lachlan's promotion was well accepted by his comrades. He had earned a reputation as being cool under fire, with the quiet ability to inspire men despite his youth.

Many slapped him on the back to congratulate him and offered the young man a tot of rum. But Lachlan politely declined all offers of good Jamaican, remembering his promise to the old German, Max Braun.

His promotion carried with it extra pay – and extra responsibilities. He found that he had less time to sit down and write letters to Amanda, let alone resume his correspondence with his brother now living in Sydney. In one of his letters John had written that he and his business partner were using the city as a base to establish future enterprises in the colony of Queensland. Planting sugarcane would be one such enterprise and the establishment of their own rum distillery another. Not surprisingly, the letters between the two brothers were somewhat stilted. They were almost strangers. All they really had in common was their blood, and a mutual desire to avenge the murder of their father and brother at Ballarat.

Lachlan never stopped scheming as to how he might find a way to kill Samuel Forster, but now that March had come to the campaign it was a time of relative inactivity for the Rangers camped at Te Awamutu.

As it was, Lachlan found himself in charge of his own section. The men were more than glad to go bush on reconnaissance duties, scouting for Maori war parties. At least they were not being used on fatigue duties, gathering potatoes for the winter or building redoubts. But they did not locate any real signs of enemy activity on their long patrols and back in camp they were able to relax a little – more than welcome after the long, arduous hours spent in the rugged hills and dense bush.

Each time he returned from the patrols Lachlan hoped for a small pile of letters from Amanda. With them in hand, he would retire to a quiet section of the camp to sit under a tree and carefully open each letter in order of the dated postmarks. Her words continued to express her yearning for him. Lachlan only wished that he could go to Amanda, take her in his arms, gaze into her eyes and express his feelings with words, rather than ink on paper.

Despite the lull in the fighting, Cameron was reinforcing his army with troops from Auckland, and near the end of March, Lachlan found himself back in action, but this time with the responsibility of leading men in combat.

Cameron had received intelligence that Maori war parties had retreated north-east to the lower spurs of Maungatautari Mountain, flanked by the Waikato River. Mobilising a column of his troops, Cameron rendezvoused at Pukerimu with additional reinforcements and the river steamers *Avon* and *Koheroa* carrying siege artillery. Lachlan and the Rangers made camp overlooking the river and awaited further orders.

Outside his tent, over a folding camp table cluttered with maps and papers held down by a revolver as a paperweight, Captain Charles Lightfoot finished his briefing.

'Are there any questions?' he concluded, but none came.

'Gentlemen and sergeants, you are dismissed to your duties,' Lightfoot said, relieving his commanders to return to their men and brief them on their duties for the next day.

Sergeant Forster was about to rejoin his section when Lightfoot caught his eye and, with a movement of his head, indicated that he wished him to remain behind.

'I have heard that MacDonald is still with us,' Lightfoot said quietly. 'I had faith in your abilities, Sergeant Forster.'

'I almost had a chance back at Rangiaowhia,' Forster replied, toeing the soil with his boot. 'The bastard got the jump on me when I was occupied detaining one of those big heathens.'

'You know, of course, that the Von has seen fit to promote the cursed man,' Lightfoot added. 'And worse still, there is a rumour coming from the Rangers camp that he is corresponding with my sister. I am loath to believe it, however, as I would think that my sister has more integrity than to associate with such as he.'

'Women can be funny creatures,' Forster said, realising his error when he glimpsed the stormy expression on his commanding officer's face. 'But your sister is a true lady, sir,' Forster hurriedly added. 'She would never entertain such a thought, I am sure.'

'I will know soon enough,' Lightfoot muttered. 'I will be in Auckland very soon for a meeting with Mr Grey's government.'

'Good, sir,' Forster replied.

'But, for the moment,' Lightfoot continued, 'we have this unresolved matter of Corporal MacDonald. The man is like a burr under my saddle.'

'I have not forgotten, sir,' Forster said. 'I do have a plan.'

Lightfoot looked surprised. 'Well, spit it out,' he said.

Forster shifted his balance and gave a small cough, clearing his throat. 'We are deep in enemy territory and any man who should stray too far from camp could be slain very easily by some of them roving heathens. Need I say any more?'

'Not really, Sergeant Forster,' Lightfoot said. 'You

have my permission to free yourself of any duties that may impair your ability to resolve our mutual problem.'

'Thank you, sir. Be assured that with the plan I have put together – and some help – MacDonald will not see the sun rise tomorrow. I promise you that.'

Lightfoot dismissed his fellow conspirator and watched him march away. Whatever Forster had in mind, he did not want to know the details.

SEVENTEEN

Sergeant Samuel Forster had plotted his elimination of Lachlan MacDonald well. The bottle of good Jamaican rum had cost him ten shillings, but as a bribe it had paid off. Later, he would request reimbursement from the captain, along with his fee for removing the young Scot from their lives.

Shivering, he squatted in the dense bush, while drizzling rain ran down the back of his jacket. The temporary discomfort would be worth it, as soon as MacDonald came alone along the track towards the militia headquarters of his old unit. The time and place had been carefully selected. Forster knew a sergeant in the Rangers who was fond of rum and had given the bottle to him on the condition that he let MacDonald know there was mail waiting for him over at Lightfoot's company.

Accepting the gift with a shrug, the Rangers

sergeant had gone in search of the newly appointed corporal. There'd been some mix-up in the mail deliveries, Lachlan was told. He should sort it out with his old unit. Lachlan picked up his carbine and went in search of his missing mail.

Forster waited alongside the track that connected the Ranger company with its adjoining militia unit. For over a couple of hundred yards it was an isolated stretch through dense undergrowth and tall trees. As picquets had been posted further out to protect the regiment's perimeters, the track was considered relatively safe to negotiate. Even so, Lachlan moved warily, aware that the Maori warriors were only miles away and would be scouting their enemy's positions, attempting to ascertain strengths and weaknesses, as well as weapons and numbers of troops.

Forster waited in the dank semi-gloom of the forest. In the distance he could hear the faint sounds from the military camp – muted voices, the clanging of a blacksmith's anvil as a horseshoe was belted out, and a sad song being sung by some soldier, bemoaning the loss of a love.

In his hands, Forster cradled the deadly shotgun he had retrieved from the huge Maori. It was a beautifully crafted weapon that had obviously been purchased from a European source. Both barrels were loaded and the spreading shot was bound to hit a target at close range.

From his concealed position in the undergrowth, Forster expected to be able to fire both barrels at MacDonald from a distance of five paces. Needless to say, the massive wound would prove fatal – and the corporal's death could easily be attributed to a roving Maori warrior.

The squelch of wet grass underfoot alerted Forster. Someone was approaching. Carefully he shifted position to peer through the fronds. Lachlan was walking towards him, trailing his rifle. From his demeanour, it was clear his target had no suspicion that he had been lured into an ambush. Lachlan was still twenty paces away and Forster readied himself. He would let him pass, then step out behind him to deliver the discharge into the corporal's back. Forster's only decision now was whether he would warn the young man so that he would see the smile on the sergeant's face before he sent him to hell.

Forster held his breath, fading into the foliage as Lachlan walked past him. He was so close that Forster wondered if he should not fire now. Then Lachlan was past him and walking down the track.

Forster stepped out from his hiding place, raised the shotgun to his shoulder to ensure that his aim was accurate, and applied pressure on the triggers. He would simply kill MacDonald without seeing his face. It was so easy.

Preoccupied with the annoyance of his mail being sent to his old unit, Lachlan was completely unaware of the sergeant's ambush. Suddenly, every nerve in his body seemed to scream out a warning. Hearing a dull thud and the long, low moan of a man only paces behind him, Lachlan swung around in a semi-crouch, expecting death to be staring him in the face. His carbine was pointed at a huge Maori standing over the body of a soldier. A great war club was swinging at the warrior's side and he looked directly into Lachlan's eyes with the slightest of smiles on his broad, dark face. Lachlan knew that he was in a bad position. How many of the enemy would surround him if he shot down the warrior who had just felled a fellow soldier? But to Lachlan's surprise, the warrior dropped his club.

'You know me,' the Maori said in good English. 'You saved my life from the man I have just killed.'

In the gloom of the dying day Lachlan peered at the man, vaguely recalling his face from the fight in the settlement.

'My name is Matthew Te Paea and I have been to your country many years ago.' The Maori bent down and rolled the body of the soldier onto his back. Now Lachlan could see it was Forster. 'He had my gun and I wanted it back. It cost me a lot of money,' Matthew explained, retrieving the weapon. 'I think he was going to kill you.'

Lachlan lowered his carbine. It was a strange situation – two enemies talking to each other on the track when they should be fighting each other.

'I think that you are right,' Lachlan said, stepping forward to see more clearly the massive wound to the sergeant's head. 'You said that you have been to Australia,' Lachlan continued. 'I was on the Ballarat fields as a boy. Were you there when the British came to massacre us?'

Matthew shook his head. 'That was your fight, not mine,' he replied, going through the pockets of the dead sergeant and finding a pocket-knife and a wad of English money. 'I left with my cousin before the

British came and returned to my own land to fight the British who are stealing our sacred earth from us.'

'I remember seeing Maori on the goldfields,' Lachlan said. 'Maybe I first saw you then.'

'Perhaps,' the Maori warrior said, standing up to tower over Lachlan. 'But you saved my life and I've remembered your face from then. You are with Von Tempsky's Rangers and have our respect for your fighting tactics. You are not unlike us in that way.'

'I guess you are here to spy on our camp,' Lachlan said.

'As you spy on us,' Matthew retorted. 'That is the way of war.'

'Why didn't you kill me when you had the chance?' Lachlan asked.

'It would have been too easy – and besides, you did save my life. Now we are even, so when I next meet you on the battlefield I will kill you then.'

'When I last saw you, you were a prisoner. How is it that you are now here a free man?'

'It was not hard to escape,' Matthew replied with a soft laugh. 'No British will ever lock up Matthew Te Paea. This is my land – it does not belong to the Pakeha who have come to rob us.'

Lachlan did not reply. He had come to see the Maori point of view. Many of his comrades had grumbled that all they were really fighting for was the interests of the rich civilians and their greed for the fertile farming lands.

'What do we do now?' Lachlan asked, knowing that they could not remain on the track in conversation much longer lest another soldier ventured along.

'I will go. And you will tell your people that Matthew Te Paea killed the sergeant,' the Maori warrior said, cradling the shotgun in his arms. 'I have finished now and tomorrow we may meet again on the battlefield.'

Lachlan nodded. How ironic that he had plotted so long to kill the man now lying dead between them, and that the deed had been done not only in his presence but by one who was his enemy. Lachlan was at a loss for words.

'Maybe when the war is over, you and I go back to Australia to look for gold,' Matthew grinned. 'Then we buy England off the English.'

Lachlan thrust out his hand. 'Maybe we do that. I only hope that we both live to see that day.'

Matthew nodded and, letting go of Lachlan's hand, disappeared into the dark forest, leaving Lachlan with Sergeant Forster's body at his feet. Lachlan knew that he would have to hurry back to his own unit and report the matter. However, he would not divulge how he had engaged in friendly conversation with a Maori who had infiltrated their lines. The meeting had affected Lachlan more than he dared admit to himself. In the past he had thought of the Maori warriors only as savage fighters, bent on killing him. Now he had met a man who not only had once walked the same earth as he in Australia but also had saved his life. Somehow the cause he was fighting for had lost its meaning. All he wanted to do now was get out of the army, go back to Australia with Amanda and finally meet his brother. Together, they would go in search of their sister. But this was a dream – as Lachlan well knew. From the rumours circulating all in Cameron's force knew that they were facing a big battle and it was expected many would be killed. All he had to do for now was survive.

Captain Charles Lightfoot was in a rage, listening to his adjutant relate how Sergeant Samuel Forster's death at the hands of Maori had been reported by the Forest Ranger Corporal Lachlan MacDonald.

'Forster was murdered,' Lightfoot spat.

'I'm sorry, sir, I do not understand,' the confused young captain replied. 'It seems from what the Ranger corporal reported to his unit that Sergeant Forster died from a massive blow to the back of his head from what appears to be a heathen war club. I suspect that the Maori have been able to infiltrate our lines. Ensign Mair was able to get in close enough and listen in to the heathens' conversations.'

'Mair is a Maori lover,' Lightfoot grunted. 'He was born in this country and is not the most trustworthy man to send on such a mission. I have heard that he speaks their language fluently and has a great respect for their pagan ways. Such a man cannot be trusted to gain unbiased information.'

The adjutant did not agree. He knew William Mair and admired him. They had spoken of the incident where Mair had risked his life by creeping in under cover of darkness to the pa, where he covered himself in a blanket under a dray. Bullets had flown overheard throughout the night, killing some of the cattle around him. Mair had been so close that he had been able to hear the Maori sentries warning each other to hold fast and be cautious. The adjutant also knew of the hatred between the Ranger corporal and militia sergeant that had grown out of the flogging the corporal had received when he was a private in the militia. Despite this, he doubted that MacDonald would have risked his own life murdering Forster.

'I want you to report the matter to the Provost Marshal,' Lightfoot ordered. 'You can add to the report that I suspect Sergeant Forster was murdered by Corporal MacDonald out of revenge. Let MacDonald answer to the military police for his actions.'

The first stages of the skirmishing around Orakau had commenced before the arrival of General Cameron's forces. Days earlier, two surveyors had spotted the construction of Maori fortifications and reported their findings to Brigadier General Carey's headquarters.

The British officer immediately put together a force of around 1100 men. They would make an assault in what he perceived as a chance to defeat the Maori before they could finish their fortifications. A subordinate, Captain Ring, carrying out an assault on the Maori workers, did take them by surprise. But, under excellent leadership, the warriors fired disciplined volleys into the advancing British troops, causing them to reel back in defeat. Two more assaults were launched, but each time, Carey's men met with the same controlled volleys of fire, falling back with the taunting cries from the victorious defenders ringing in their ears. 'Come on, Jack, come on!'

Defeated, and leaving their dead and wounded on the slopes, the attacking troops soon realised that their Maori enemy was more than a match for their European tactics of warfare. Carey decided that he would need reinforcements if he were to finally bring the Maori rebels to heel.

Morale was high amongst the Maori warriors, but some of their leaders knew that the location of the pa had a fatal weakness. It had been situated too far from a supply of water. Carey also knew this and moved his troops as close as he safely could to the fortified embankments.

Now the British dug trenches, firing from them and in return being fired upon. A sap was begun, aimed at the heart of the pa and covered by a bombardment of artillery fire from three six-pounder Armstrongs. However, little damage was done, on account of the skills of the pa's builders. The Maori had layered fern between the mounds of earth to help cushion the effect of artillery shells when they exploded. At one stage, a small force of Maori warriors attempted to join their comrades in the pa, but they were denied access by the ring of British troops encircling the Maori fortifications. Understanding the grim position that their brothers had found themselves in, the Maori sat on a neighbouring rise of land and wept the death song in farewell to the defenders, who were being driven back hard by artillery fire.

The British continued their siege of the pa over a period of three days but Lachlan and his comrades had not been committed to the battle as yet. During the first night – when the Rangers had reached Orakau – they had spent an anxious time. During the night Lachlan would lie on his back, his rifle beside him and listen in awe to the thunderous pounding of the warriors' bare feet as they roared out their battle songs. The ferocious chants chilled each and every soldier's heart. They knew that they would eventually have to confront these men in hand-to-hand combat.

By the morning of the third day, the British had been unable to break either the spirit or the formidable defences of the Maori defenders. Once again, Cameron called on the skills of his young ensign William Mair to make contact with the warriors holding the pa.

Corporal MacDonald was sent forward with his section to observe Mair's success or failure at convincing the Maoris to surrender. Lachlan crouched with his rifle cradled in his arms at the end of a trench that had been dug to give the advancing troops cover. Mair passed him by and gave orders for the officer in charge of the sapping party to cease fire. Then he called out in the Maori language to the defenders.

'What's he saying?' Lachlan asked one of his soldiers who had lived amongst Maori and was fluent in the language.

'He's telling them that General Cameron has large reinforcements,' the Pakeha Maori replied. 'And that he wishes to save the Maori from being killed.'

A native voice replied and Lachlan's interpreter grinned. 'The Maori has asked who will be killed? Cheeky bugger. Mr Mair has told them that they will be killed by the cannons, so they had better hoist a white flag.'

Lachlan raised his head cautiously to see the row of dark tattooed faces peering over the wall of the pa. Such fixed expressions of defiance did not bode well, he thought. Mair remained exposed to the Maori and Lachlan could hear a low rumble of native voices discussing the offer. Suddenly, a voice called out from within the pa and Lachlan turned to his interpreter, who shook his head.

'Stupid buggers,' the soldier muttered. '*Rewi himself has said, friend, the Maori have only one word only to say, we will fight you forever and ever.*'

When Ensign Mair responded, Lachlan's interpreter simply answered his unspoken question. 'Mr Mair is wasting his time trying to reason with them. They have made up their minds and will fight it out to the end.'

Lachlan's attention was suddenly drawn to movement on their flank. The Maori warriors had used the truce to manoeuvre into a position of attack. He did not need to warn the rest of the men in the sap as others had also noticed the stealthy movement.

Mair ducked down, calling, 'They say they will fight to the death. Give it to them again, boys.'

A soldier near Lachlan cried out, 'Well done, we admire them for their pluck, we will give them what they want.'

The air was rent with the cracks of hundreds of rifles being fired and the crump of fused grenades exploding as they were heaved into the pa. As an Armstrong artillery gun added to the din, Lachlan remained crouched behind the earth wall, only a few yards from the enemy. It was time to fight.

Lachlan rallied his section and they advanced up the sap to meet the oncoming Maori warriors. Reloading, he and his section scattered some attackers from the sap but the fighting continued until the rest of the warriors had retreated to the pa.

Lachlan collapsed exhausted to the earth, now wet with blood from friend and foe alike. Wounded soldiers were being dragged past but he merely stared with unseeing eyes at the unfortunate men. He had fired all his ammunition and had a raging thirst, but it was time to remind himself of his responsibility. As a corporal he must look after the welfare of his men. With a great effort, Lachlan forced himself out of his strange lethargy and called on his men to rally around him. They had been engaging the enemy for the last four hours without a break. Resupplied with ammunition being doled out by a colour sergeant, Lachlan led his section down the sap and back to their lines.

'They've just broken through the 40th!' came the yell from a corporal running towards Lachlan and his section.

'Rangers stand to! To arms!' Lachlan immediately cried out and his men groaned in their exhaustion. The fight had flared up again and there would be no respite for them at their lines.

A daylight evacuation by the Maori defenders had not been expected by the besieging British troops. The war leader, Rewi, had planned the surprise break-out carefully. He had placed the women and children in the centre of a flying column pointed at the lines of the 40th Regiment. A hill had covered them and the sight of the silent, disciplined, fighting column of Maori warriors had completely startled the besiegers. Smashing its way down the slope through the British line, the advancing column broke through. The soldiers of the 40th had been able to fire only one volley.

Matthew Te Paea was amongst the leading warriors making the break-out. He could see a fence over-grown by fern before him and he scrambled over it. Then he saw the double rank of British soldiers waiting beyond the fence. Without a word, all fleeing the doomed pa broke into a sprint aimed directly at the line of muskets and bayonets. A rattle of fire erupted from the British troops and many of the charging Maoris fell, but Matthew had made it to the line.

A soldier attempted to bayonet him but Matthew parried the deadly tip with the barrel of his shotgun, firing at the same time. The soldier fell against the man next to him and another stepped forward to meet Matthew's charge. Matthew fired the second barrel of his weapon, felling that soldier also. Then he was through the line and running as fast as he could towards the relative safety of the tea-tree swamps and scrub.

Reaching the manuka bush, the Maori survivors broke up into smaller parties in an attempt to confuse any pursuers, all the time maintaining fire and movement to cover their retreat, and inflicting heavy losses on the British troops.

The swift-moving British cavalry, and the Rangers on foot, pursued the retreating Maori warriors. It was only a matter of time before Lachlan and Matthew Te Paea would once again meet.

EIGHTEEN

The British cavalry swept forward and the Forest Rangers followed, Lachlan leading his section of five men forward in pursuit of a small group of Maori.

'Careful not to hit the women and children,' Lachlan yelled back over his shoulder. From the corner of his eye, he could see a couple of cavalrymen gallop down a woman and child separated from the men. A Maori turned and fired his shotgun, unhorsing one of the cavalrymen, but he was unable to save the woman as the sabre swept down to cut deeply into her shoulders.

The party that Lachlan's section pursued disappeared into a stand of bush. Lachlan could hear the splash as they found the swampy ground underfoot. 'Careful, boys,' he yelled to his eager men as they followed their corporal into the thicket.

Lachlan found himself wading through rank, strong-smelling water that came up to his thighs. He could only hear the splashing ahead, his prey being concealed by the thick swamp scrub. The section had fanned out and Lachlan suddenly found himself alone, separated by the wiry trees that thrived in the fetid water. He knew he must keep within sight of his men, so as to be able to control their movement. All around him he could hear the shots and screams as the pursuers caught up with the fleeing Maori.

A volley of shots from his right side and the confused yelling of both Maori and European told Lachlan that the bulk of his section had stumbled onto the party that they were chasing. He swore in his frustration at not being with them and prayed that they had not shot down any of the women and children. As he went to step forward the Maori warrior suddenly appeared in front of him. Immediately, Lachlan raised his rifle to fire.

As if sensing his presence, the Maori swung and fired his shotgun, at the same time that Lachlan fired his carbine. In a split second, both men crashed backwards.

Lachlan lay on his back in the water, his mouth filling with putrid vegetation. He forced himself into a sitting position then struggled to his feet. The pain in his left arm hit him like a sledgehammer. Such was its intensity that Lachlan cried out in agony.

He hardly realised that the Maori warrior was also rising groggily from the waters of the swamp to stand, a puzzled expression on his face. Despite his pain, Lachlan recognised that he was still in mortal danger. His rifle was gone somewhere under the water, but he still had his pistol. With his right hand, Lachlan grasped the butt and swung it up to fire at the warrior facing him a mere ten paces away. But there was only the empty sound of a misfire. Slamming the pistol back into its holster, Lachlan grabbed the hilt of his bowie knife. Only then did he focus the face of his adversary.

'Matthew!' Lachlan gasped. He had hit Matthew Te Paea in the thigh; blood oozed from the gaping exit wound caused by the big lead bullet. For seconds the two stood eyeing each other. Matthew had not attempted to reach for his war club.

'I've got him!' a voice yelled from Lachlan's right. Lachlan swung around, to see one of his own men levelling a rifle at Matthew.

'Don't shoot!' Lachlan screamed. 'The man has surrendered, he is my prisoner.'

Reluctantly, the Ranger lowered his rifle. 'You are wounded, corporal,' he said, noticing the blood soaking the sleeve of Lachlan's jacket. 'You need to get help before you bleed to death.'

Lachlan knew that he was right. Blood flowed down his arm into the waters of the swamp. He had no control of it. The arm hung at his side like a useless appendage.

'Keep going,' Lachlan said to the Ranger. 'I will go back with my prisoner to seek aid.'

The Ranger nodded and disappeared deeper into the swamp.

'C'mon, Matthew,' Lachlan said gently. 'Come

with me as my prisoner and I will make sure our doctor looks at your wound.'

Without a word, Matthew waded painfully over to Lachlan. He could see the Australian was on the verge of fainting. Slipping a powerful arm under Lachlan's good shoulder, the Maori helped his enemy through the stagnant waters of the swamp, to emerge near the pa. By this time Lachlan had slipped into a state of semi-consciousness. He hardly remembered what happened next as the darkness and relief came to him.

'. . . should amputate. He took a considerable blast of shot in his arm,' Lachlan heard as he regained consciousness.

Amputate! Lachlan focused on a face hovering over him. It was the regimental surgeon from his old militia unit. 'Please, no,' Lachlan croaked, reaching up with his good arm to grasp the front of the surgeon's jacket. 'I am begging you, please don't amputate the arm.'

A medical aide grasped Lachlan's hand and broke his grip.

'You have had a bit of a rough trot, Corporal MacDonald,' the surgeon said gruffly, but with sympathy in his voice. 'Maybe we can keep it for a short time and see if any infection sets in. But I doubt that it will be very useful to you in the future. You have had a lot of muscle and nerve damage. There are still bits of lead shot in the tissue – but most I can dig out.'

Tears of gratitude flowed down Lachlan's face as he sank back on the wooden table. A pungent cloth went over his face and he sucked in the chloroform. Soon he was oblivious to the clatter of lead into an enamel tray as the surgeon removed the shot from his shattered arm.

When Lachlan came to, he could feel his body being jolted and bumped. Above him was a blurry sheet of canvas. The squeaking of wagon wheels told him he was probably in an ambulance. The after-effects of the anaesthetic had caused vomit to rise up in his throat. Lachlan tried to resist but despite his efforts he brought up the vile liquid.

'Yer awake, corporal,' a kindly voice said at his elbow. Lachlan tried to focus on the face a short distance from his. He could make out the uniform of a bandsman from one of the British regular regiments. 'Yer our only passenger on this trip,' the medical aide continued. 'All the rest have been transported to Drury.'

Drury, Lachlan thought. Where Amanda was living. His arm throbbed with pain and he bit his lip, lest he cry out at each jolting bump. At least he might get to see her.

'How long ago was the operation?' Lachlan rasped.

'Yer been out to it for a day,' the medical aide replied. 'The doc kept feedin' you large doses of laudanum to ease the pain in yer arm. Lucky yer didn't have it chopped orf. I have some with me if the pain gets too much for yer. Yer look as if yer could do with a sip.'

Lachlan eased his good arm to gingerly touch where his shattered arm still remained. He could only feel a great swab of bandages and a sling.

'There was a wounded Maori I brought in. His name is Matthew Te Paea.'

The medic put a water canteen to Lachlan's lips to ease the dryness.

'Don't know anything about any heathen warriors,' the medic replied. 'They had medical attention and then were sent under guard to Auckland. If yer brought him in, then he is probably destined to end up on one of them hulks in the harbour.'

The water ran into Lachlan's mouth. He was in terrible pain but the thought of being transported to a hospital in Drury made it bearable. He was finally going to see Amanda's beautiful face once again and be able to tell her of his love.

Weary from fighting the pain, Lachlan slipped once more into semiconsciousness. The last thing he remembered was the voice of the medic. 'It looks like the Maori are finished around here and yer fighting days are over, by the look of yer arm. Time fer you to pick up yer pay and go home . . .'

Lachlan lay in a hospital bed in Drury frustrated by the fact that he was only a very short distance from the woman he loved. At the first opportunity he would get leave from the hospital and visit her, he decided.

But he did not get the opportunity to carry out his plan. He awoke early one morning to see three men dressed in the uniform of the military police standing grimly over his bed.

'Are you Corporal Lachlan MacDonald of the Forest Rangers?' the sergeant among them asked.

Lachlan struggled into a sitting position. 'I am, sergeant,' he replied, confused by their appearance in the ward filled with other wounded soldiers from the Waikato campaign.

'The doctor has informed us that you are well enough to travel,' the sergeant said stiffly. 'You can consider yourself under arrest on the charge of murder.'

'Murder!' Lachlan blurted. 'Whose bloody murder?'

'That of Sergeant Samuel Forster, formerly of the Volunteer Militia, under the command of Captain Lightfoot,' the sergeant replied. 'On your feet and get dressed.'

Stunned, Lachlan shifted from the bed to his feet. How had events come to this?

After the fighting at Orakau, Captain Charles Lightfoot was given leave to return to Drury. He had noted Lachlan's name in the post-battle report, under the list of wounded and hospitalised. Now Lightfoot dismounted from his horse outside his cottage in Drury. Amanda was standing in the front door and her expression of concern was a welcome sight.

'Oh, Charles, I have heard the reports of your campaign,' she said, kissing him on the cheek. 'I have been praying to God to preserve you.'

'Thanks to your prayers – and my trusty sabre – I have returned,' Lightfoot replied, returning his sister's embrace. 'Now, I would welcome a hot bath and some good whisky. Where is the maid, Annie?'

Amanda's expression darkened slightly. 'She has run away,' she replied. 'I think she has gone to join her people on the east coast.'

'Damned natives,' Lightfoot snorted. 'Their loyalty is to their own kind and not the Queen.'

'Can you blame them?' Amanda retorted. 'We are stealing their lands and killing their women and children.'

Lightfoot was taken aback at his sister's defence of the Maori and felt an uneasy echo of a woman too independent for her own good in her words.

Amanda turned on her heel with a swish of her long dress and Lightfoot followed her inside their cottage, where he was pleasantly assailed by the scent of wildflowers. The cottage was a true sanctuary from the rigours of army life and Charles Lightfoot felt at ease. Well, almost at ease. Soon he would have to raise with his sister the subject of the young corporal. One way or the other, he would learn the truth.

After his bath Lightfoot lounged in front of an open fire in his smoking jacket. Balancing a tumbler in one hand and a large cigar in the other, he stared at the flickering flames. Amanda had joined him in the small, comfortable living room and sat quietly with her sewing.

'Is it true that you have been corresponding with that MacDonald chap?' Lightfoot asked at length, causing Amanda to prick her finger with the needle.

A tiny droplet of her blood splashed the embroidery in her lap.

'Why do you ask?' she said, placing her bleeding finger between her lips to stem the flow.

'Because I am your brother, and guardian, and that gives me the right to know your affairs,' Lightfoot replied. 'Is it true?'

Amanda removed her finger from her mouth. 'It is true,' she replied defiantly. 'Lachlan and I have exchanged letters, while he was campaigning.'

'Would those letters be of a romantic nature?' Lightfoot continued in a soft tone.

Amanda did not immediately reply. She had known that it was inevitable that he would eventually learn of her contact with the young Scot – and of her strong feelings for him. It had only been a matter of when.

'I love him,' she said quietly, bowing her head to avert her brother's angry stare.

'You cannot,' Lightfoot said in an almost gentle voice. 'Soon he will be facing execution for the murder of one of my sergeants.'

Amanda gasped. 'What are you saying?' she asked in her horror. 'What do you mean execution for murder?'

'Just that,' Lightfoot answered smugly. 'Oh, and I almost forgot to mention that your dearly beloved Ranger may have had his arm amputated by now. Makes it a bit hard to embrace you, don't you think?'

The news was almost more than Amanda could bear. She attempted to rise but felt faint and remained seated.

Lightfoot rose from his chair and brought his tumbler of whisky to his sister's lips, forcing her to take a mouthful.

'You are the only family I have,' he said, taking a puff from his cigar. 'As your brother, I have only your interests and welfare at heart. I do not gain any comfort from telling you these things about Mr MacDonald. You must believe me on that.'

Regaining her senses, Amanda wiped her mouth with a delicate handkerchief. 'I must see him,' she said quietly. 'You must know where he is.'

'That would be unadvisable. As soon as he is well enough to face an investigation, he will no doubt be facing the charge. It would not do your reputation – or mine – any good if your intimacy with him was known.'

'I beg you, Charles, that I be allowed to see him,' Amanda pleaded.

'I am sorry, Amanda,' Lightfoot said, shaking his head; 'that is not permissible. To ensure that you comply with my wishes, I will be insisting that you return to Sydney at the next most practicable time, and remain there until I return.'

'I will not do that,' Amanda flared, an icy determination in her eyes.

'You will,' Lightfoot said, his expression matching her own. 'I will make a promise to you. If you give me your word that you will never attempt to make contact with MacDonald again, as the officer pressing the investigation into his role in Sergeant Forster's death, I will be less determined to see a judicial outcome leading to a firing squad. In short, the life of your precious Corporal MacDonald is in your hands, dear sister.'

Amanda glared at her brother. She was well aware how much power an officer commissioned by the Queen held over the life of an enlisted man. Had not Lachlan already been flogged, even though he was an innocent man? Hatred replaced the anger in her expression. This was outright blackmail.

'Are you able to quash the investigation?' she asked coldly.

'I am afraid I cannot do that,' Lightfoot replied. 'But I can press my case less firmly.'

Puzzled, Amanda asked, 'Why would Lachlan want to kill your sergeant?'

'He was the man that MacDonald assaulted,' Lightfoot replied. 'MacDonald has had it in for him ever since the flogging and took the opportunity to settle the score at Orakau.'

'I do not believe that Lachlan would murder a man,' Amanda said stubbornly. 'He is a gentle soul with too much intelligence to risk his reputation over such a matter.'

'Well, he can explain all that to the military police,' Lightfoot said, hoping to conclude the matter. 'All I need is your word that you will take the first ship to Sydney out of Auckland and never again make contact with MacDonald. Give me your word and I will do my best to see that he does not go before a firing squad.'

'You have it,' Amanda answered in a beaten tone. 'But, you must promise me that you will do everything within your power to save Lachlan's life.'

'I give my word – as an officer and a gentleman,' Lightfoot replied, raising his glass of whisky in a salute. 'Needless to say, you have very little say in the matter anyway, as you are under twenty-one and I am your guardian until you attain that age.'

Charles looked down at his sister mercilessly. 'And another thing' he added. 'Sir Percival Sparkes has been enquiring after you.'

Amanda looked sharply at her brother with tears in her eyes, wondering what else he had in mind for her.

'I think it would be wise of you to see him on your return to Sydney to dispel any rumours of your affections for a convicted criminal.'

'Lachlan has been convicted of no crime yet,' Amanda retorted bitterly.

'That's correct, my dear,' Charles said smugly. 'And I'll try to keep it that way if you keep Sir Percival happy.'

Amanda bowed her head in defeat, knowing that the price, although heavy, was a small one to pay to keep Lachlan alive.

That night in her bed, Amanda sobbed until no more tears would come. She would have given her very life to see Lachlan and feel his arms around her just one more time. His letters had opened a window to him as a man and what she had seen through that window had made her truly love him. But to see him even once more could cost the young man his life. She would keep her word and leave New Zealand, knowing that she would never see him again and accepting that her future lay in the hands of her ambitious brother.

NINETEEN

Sitting in a tent alone, and guarded by an armed soldier outside the entrance flap, Lachlan pondered the strange twists of fate in his relatively short life. Had he not saved Charles Lightfoot that time many months ago, then he would not be where he was now, waiting to face a court-martial for murder. From what he could gather, the investigating officer had accepted the superior officer's word and felt that there were sufficient grounds for Lachlan to face the charge.

The flap was thrown aside and a sergeant from a regular British unit stepped inside. Lachlan rose to his feet from the edge of the camp stretcher.

'How is your arm?' the soldier asked kindly and Lachlan recognised his thick Scottish brogue.

'Good, Sergeant,' Lachlan lied, as the pain continued to throb. At least the visiting regimental surgeon had not detected any sign of infection, and to Lachlan's joy some feeling had returned to his shattered arm. Each day he would force himself to flex the arm and attempt to grip. Each day he found that he could do a little more.

'Well, laddie,' the sergeant said, 'I am to take you to see Lieutenant Goldsworthy. He is going to be defending you in the courtmartial.'

Lachlan had been confined to the tent for five days now and this was the first time anyone had offered assistance.

With an armed guard and in the company of the sergeant, Lachlan was marched to a stone building that was part of regimental headquarters. After a short wait outside standing to attention, he was ushered into a small office. He saluted the small, bespectacled man wearing the uniform of a commissariat officer.

'You are dismissed, Sergeant,' Goldsworthy said. 'The guard can take post outside my office.'

'Very well, sah,' the sergeant said, snapping off a smart salute.

When the sergeant and guard had exited the office, Goldsworthy gestured to Lachlan to take a chair on the other side of his desk.

'I am Lieutenant Goldsworthy,' he began, 'and I will be defending you at the courtmartial. Do you have any objections to me defending you, Corporal MacDonald?'

Lachlan sat down carefully, lest he bump his arm in the sling. 'No sir,' he replied. 'But do you have any legal experience?'

'A fair question,' the officer replied with the trace

of a smile. 'As a matter of fact I have been admitted to the bar in England, although I have not had much time in the Queen's courts defending felons. I mostly carried out probate and conveyancing work for my firm in Sydney. However, we have a mutual friend there, Mr Daniel Duffy.'

At the mention of Daniel's name, Lachlan sat up. 'Have you seen Daniel lately?' he asked.

'Not since I volunteered for service in New Zealand some six months ago. He just happened to mention that you had been writing to him and his family at the Erin, and when I saw your name come up in the provost marshal's report, I put my name forward to defend you.'

'I appreciate that, sir.'

'Did you kill Sergeant Forster?' Goldsworthy asked without any more preamble.

'No sir, I swear on the graves of my family that I did not kill Sergeant Forster.'

The young officer lifted a sheet of paper from an open folder in front of him. Adjusting his spectacles, he perused it for a short time before speaking.

'Captain Charles Lightfoot has stated under oath that he has overheard you verbally threaten the said sergeant's life on an occasion while you were still in his command.'

Lachlan's face reddened with indignation. 'That is a lie, sir,' he replied with controlled anger. 'I have never threatened Sergeant Forster in front of anyone.'

'So, you had at some stage threatened Sergeant Forster,' the officer commented quietly, catching Lachlan off guard. 'You must tell me only the truth in this matter – if I am to save you from a firing squad.'

'Yes, sir,' Lachlan answered contritely. 'I once told Forster that I would kill him. It was just after I was wounded the first time, but none were around to hear my threat.'

'Yet you say that you did not lie in ambush on the track and kill him with a blow to the back of the head with some heavy object.'

'Sir, I did not kill him, although I did witness his death at the hands of another.' The officer looked sharply over his glasses. 'If what you say is true, then who did kill the sergeant?'

'A Maori warrior,' Lachlan replied. 'With a war club, in the manner that you have described.'

'How is it that you did not say this in your initial report?' Goldsworthy asked, sitting back in his chair with a frown on his face.

For a moment, Lachlan listened to the bawling voices of NCOs drilling men on the parade ground. He was reluctant to incriminate the big Maori with whom he had formed a strange friendship.

'You must tell me all,' the officer gently prompted. 'I am your only hope of reprieve and must know all the facts.'

'I knew the Maori warrior who killed Sergeant Forster,' Lachlan almost whispered. 'He has become a kind of friend – although he is also the reason for my wounded arm.'

'How extraordinary!' Goldsworthy exclaimed, removing his glasses to peer at the young Ranger sitting opposite him. 'How is it that you have befriended one of those we consider the enemy?'

'I saved him from being murdered by Sergeant Forster some time ago at a village called Rangiaowhia. Apparently he escaped, and we met again some weeks ago when he was on a scouting mission for his leader, Rewi, on the eve of the battle we had for Orakau. He killed Sergeant Forster to get back his shotgun that Forster had taken from him when he was about to kill him at the Rangiaowhia village. I was spared because he recognised me as the man who had intervened on his behalf, but I could not report that I had allowed an enemy to go. I did not think that it would be of any consequence when I reported finding Sergeant Forster's body on the track.'

The commissariat officer replaced his spectacles and picked up the statement made by Lightfoot. 'Captain Lightfoot has queried why you were making your way towards his lines at the time,' he said without looking up. 'According to what you told your commanding officer, you were going to retrieve some misplaced mail but the Captain says that this is not true, as there is no evidence of mail addressed to you ever arriving in his unit. His orderly room clerk has corroborated this fact in a separate statement. What is your answer to that?'

Lachlan was stumped by the question. He desperately tried to recollect who from the Rangers had passed on the message to him.

'Sergeant Lingard!' Lachlan exclaimed. 'It was Sergeant Lingard of the Forest Rangers who passed on the message to me. He can support my story of why I was on the track to my old unit.'

Goldsworthy scribbled down the name of the man mentioned. Hopefully, he would corroborate Lachlan's excuse for leaving his unit lines that evening.

'I don't suppose that we can be lucky enough to have access to your chief witness, the Maori warrior who you say killed Sergeant Forster?' Goldsworthy asked with a wry smile.

'I took him prisoner – after I shot him,' Lachlan replied quietly. 'His name is Matthew Te Paea.'

With a start, Goldsworthy looked sharply at his client. 'You even know his name?'

'Yes, sir, but I would rather he did not come forward lest the army punish him for an act of war.'

'If they attempted to do that,' Goldsworthy said, 'then I promise you that I would defend him. It has been widely accepted by the British army that this enemy are not simple savages but men of great courage and honour. What he did in killing Sergeant Forster in a time of war between us and his people is legitimate. Otherwise, the Maori could, in turn, have us put on trial for the occasional killing of their women and children. No, I doubt that he would be in any trouble if he bore witness in your defence. Possibly one day the judicial systems of the world will conspire to bring about a law which holds soldiers responsible for their acts against innocent civilians. I personally pray that this will one day eventuate. But, back to matters before us. You said that you once threatened Sergeant Forster's life. Was that because he had you flogged?'

'No,' Lachlan answered, shifting his weight in the chair to ease the constant, nagging pain in his arm. 'Many years ago, at the Ballarat goldfields, he murdered my father during the uprising. I have evidence of that and may eventually have settled the score with him and Captain Lightfoot, who was also involved in the slayings. But I did not get the opportunity to personally settle with Forster.'

'You have an interesting story to tell about the deceased and your accuser, Captain Lightfoot,' Goldsworthy said, sitting back in his chair. 'Let us hope that I am able to acquire statements from Sergeant Lingard and the Maori warrior. I think that Te Paea's statement is the most important one and should convince the good officers of the court-martial board that you are innocent. Nonetheless, I do not think that it is wise to mention your vendetta against the two men. It would appear as if you were trying to lead the court away from the matter before them. I doubt that would reflect well on your case when what you say cannot really be corroborated.'

'Thank you, sir,' Lachlan replied, sensing that his interview was at an end.

'You are dismissed, Corporal MacDonald. I will chase up our evidence to corroborate your innocence.'

Lachlan rose from his chair, saluted and was escorted back to his tent by the sergeant and armed guard. He sat down on his bunk and stared at the light coming through the open flap. It was a bright, crisp day. All he could do now was wait and pray that all went well in his defending officer's investigations. He had no duties due to his wound and wished that he had something to read. At least he was able to write letters to his brother. He had already attempted to send a message to Amanda, but had been unsuccessful until he found he could bribe a guard who said he would drop off a letter to Amanda's cottage in Drury and ask about the lady from neighbours.

When the guard had returned, he told Lachlan that no one had been home and a neighbour had informed him that Miss Lightfoot had travelled to Auckland to sail for Sydney.

This news almost shattered Lachlan. Surely she must have known that he was back in Drury? So why did she not attempt to make contact with him? There was no answer – only a nagging suspicion that her brother had something to do with it.

Two days passed before Lachlan saw his defending officer again. This time he came to Lachlan's tent just after the regimental surgeon had departed, having changed the wound dressings and examined the wounds to the arm. At least his prognosis had been positive.

Lachlan rose to his feet when Lieutenant Goldsworthy entered the tent.

'Corporal MacDonald, how are you faring?' he asked politely, but from the expression on his face Lachlan already knew that he was bearing bad news.

'Something has happened, sir?' he asked.

'I am afraid so,' Goldsworthy replied. 'Sergeant

Lingard has died of an illness in the field and it seems that your friend, Matthew Te Paea has escaped – again. I was told by the military prison people that he has a rather fierce reputation of being able to avoid confinement. It would appear that he only surrendered to you so that he could receive medical treatment for the wound that you inflicted on him. As soon as he thought he was well enough to leave, he did just that. Now he could be God knows where. I must confess that our case is looking rather bleak at the moment.'

Lachlan did not reply but stood staring ahead, his mind a whirl of sickening thoughts. The officers of the court-martial board would no doubt accept the word of the senior officer and he would be found guilty of murder on circumstantial evidence.

'Thank you, sir,' Lachlan dutifully replied. 'I know that you would have done your best.'

'Your commander, the Von, has spoken very highly of you and is prepared to give character evidence in support of your case,' Goldsworthy added, but the flatness of his delivery belied any hope of him winning the case. Indeed, Goldsworthy was already formulating how he would plead for a life sentence over execution. 'Your hearing is tomorrow,' he concluded bleakly. 'You will stand before the board at ten o'clock to answer the charge.'

With that, the young officer departed, leaving Lachlan to reflect on how long he might have to live after the case was concluded against him. He had only a few regrets. Amongst them the thought that he would die in disgrace even though he was an innocent man. This thought was as painful as knowing that he would never get to see his brother or kiss Amanda ever again.

Three senior army officers sat behind a table facing Lachlan and Lieutenant Goldsworthy. Nearby sat a captain who would act as the prosecutor. Lachlan could see that the man was not from a front-line regiment but had been drawn from a logistics unit based in Auckland. Behind Lachlan and his legal defence stood the Scottish sergeant. Other than the panel of military judges, guard, prosecutor and Lachlan with his legal defender, the large room was empty. The improvised courtroom had once been a storage shed and a pigeon fluttered in the rafters overhead, seeking a way out.

Lachlan's arm was still in a sling and the sight of it elicited sympathetic looks from the three military men. He was at least recognised by them as a real soldier, one who had faced death many times on the battlefield.

Goldsworthy was quick to pick up on the thinly concealed looks of empathy for a fellow fighting man, as the three judges were also men who had faced danger many times in their careers. Before them was not a soldier belonging to the commissariat or a behind-the-lines man.

The charges were read and the plea entered of 'Not guilty'. Now it was time to get down to the war of words. When the prosecuting captain stood to address the panel, he recited the facts at hand.

Lachlan could hear the echo of Captain Charles Lightfoot's lies. He knew that he would have to rely on the cleverness of his defender, Lieutenant Goldsworthy, to untangle the web of deceit.

The first witness was the militia unit clerk who worked in Lightfoot's orderly room. He gave evidence that at no stage were there any letters accidentally sent to his unit for Corporal MacDonald.

'If there had been letters misdirected to Corporal MacDonald's former unit, would they have possibly been sent from Captain Lightfoot's sister to Corporal MacDonald?' Goldsworthy asked the orderly room clerk.

'Objection!' the prosecuting captain said from his table.

'Accepted,' came the response from the president of the court-martial board. 'I doubt that the witness would have an answer to such an irrelevant question,' he continued.

But raising the captain's sister's name, linking it to the man being court-martialled, brought expressions of surprise – even curiosity – to the faces of the presiding judges, just as Goldsworthy had wanted.

'Sirs, I beg your pardon,' Goldsworthy responded, smirking as he turned his back to glance at Lachlan who also registered a look of surprise. 'I have no other questions of the witness,' he concluded.

Throughout the day, other witnesses came forward to give evidence: the officer of his own unit to whom he had reported the death of Forster, the two soldiers who had been dispatched to fetch back the body, and the regimental surgeon who made a cursory examination of Forster's body when it was recovered for burial. He gave his evidence that the sergeant appeared to have died as a result of a massive blow to the head. When asked by Goldsworthy whether any instrument was recovered that could be consistent with the injury inflicted, the surgeon said that he was not aware of any such instrument at the scene. He added that the wound was consistent with having been inflicted by a Maori war club.

Goldsworthy attempted to capitalise on this fact but the prosecution put forward that Corporal MacDonald had plenty of opportunity to have in his possession such a club – and also had plenty of time to dispose of the evidence before reporting the matter of the sergeant's death. Even Goldsworthy was forced to concede to the prosecution's argument on these matters.

Around three o'clock the president of the court-martial board called it a day, adjourning the case until the following morning, when the last witnesses would give evidence. It would be a quick case with a finding within forty-eight hours, Goldsworthy reckoned when he spoke to Lachlan when he was back under guard in his tent.

'How do you think it is going, sir?' Lachlan asked.

'Neither way,' Goldsworthy replied. 'The prosecution's star witness is Captain Lightfoot. Much will depend on what he says tomorrow morning.'

'He will lie,' Lachlan sighed in despair. 'And it will be the word of an officer against a common corporal.'

'The law does not see rank in a case like this,' Goldsworthy hastened to reassure him. 'His evidence will carry no more weight than your own.'

'I wish I could believe that. From my experience, the gentry stick together, despite all that you have said about the law being blind to prejudice. They will take his version over mine.'

Although the young officer did not say so, privately he agreed. If only he had a witness who could corroborate MacDonald's story.

Goldsworthy left Lachlan with his guard and retired to the officers' mess. But he had little appetite, knowing what was likely to ensue the next day.

TWENTY

The following day Lachlan was marched back to the courtroom. He took his chair beside Lieutenant Goldsworthy and stood to attention when the members of the military board entered the room to assume their positions.

A door opening behind him caused Lachlan to feel more than a chill from the cold breeze entering the room. He instinctively knew that Captain Charles Lightfoot was present, a suspicion confirmed when the immaculately dressed officer came into view. He hardly glanced at Lachlan but smiled brightly at his fellow officers on the tribunal.

Sworn in, Lightfoot outlined his accusation and recounted the alleged conversation that he had over-heard between Lachlan and the now deceased sergeant. Lachlan listened intently as both the prose-cutor and his own defence examined the captain's statement, but Lightfoot did not deviate from his allegation. When Lachlan glanced at the faces of the three officers sitting in judgment of him, he could see from their expressions that they believed what Lightfoot was saying.

Frustrated, Goldsworthy returned to the table. From his demeanour, Lachlan knew that their case was looking more hopeless by the minute. Finally, Lightfoot was excused and left the room.

'Is there anything else to add to the defence, Mr Goldsworthy?' the president of the board asked.

'No, sir,' Goldsworthy replied glumly.

'Then, if that is the case we shall break for the moment and allow for summations to be delivered after the midday break. Sergeant, escort the prisoner back to his quarters.'

The Scottish sergeant marched forward with two soldiers to escort Lachlan from the improvised courtroom. Goldsworthy did not stand but remained seated at the table, staring at the sheets of paper before him.

'Too bad, laddie,' the sergeant muttered under his moustache. 'If it's any consolation, I dinna believe that you are guilty of what they say.'

Lachlan merely nodded his head. His mind was in turmoil. How was it that an innocent man could be executed on the mere word of an officer of the Queen's army?

After lunch, the sergeant returned to escort Lachlan back to the court. Lachlan knew in his heart that the board had already made up its mind and the only decision now would be where and when his execution would be carried out.

When Lachlan sat down beside Goldsworthy, he was surprised by his defender's expression of barely concealed delight. Goldsworthy half turned to Lachlan and beamed a reassuring smile.

'Gentlemen, are you ready to deliver your summations?' the president of the board droned, satisfied that all was over, other than the formalities of delivering the guilty verdict.

'I am, sir,' the prosecutor replied, rising to his feet, clutching sheets of paper.

Goldsworthy scraped back his chair and stood to answer the question.

'No, sir,' he replied, causing all present to suddenly stare at him. 'I have one more witness to be sworn in.'

'This should have been brought to the court's attention before the break,' the prosecutor said in an annoyed voice. 'I move that the request be denied.'

'I would accede to that point, sirs, except that the person who actually killed Sergeant Forster wishes to address this court.'

The expressions of annoyance on the faces of the members of the tribunal turned to looks of disbelief. Finally, the president spoke. 'If what you say is true, Mr Goldsworthy, then I feel that in the interests of military justice, your witness should be allowed to address this court-martial.'

'Thank you, sir,' Goldsworthy said, turning to address the sergeant standing guard in the court. 'Please, bring in the witness.'

All craned to see who would enter the room –

including Lachlan. Matthew Te Paea was dressed in old European-style clothing and limped badly from the bullet wound inflicted by Lachlan. When Matthew caught Lachlan's eye, he broke into a smile then looked away.

'This is Matthew Te Paea,' Goldsworthy said. 'He is the man who killed Sergeant Samuel Forster, and will relate how he did so.'

Matthew stood and assured the court that he could swear the truthfulness of his statement on the Christian Bible. The officers sitting behind their table had to admit Matthew cut an impressive figure. Each and every one of them had a healthy respect as they listened carefully to Matthew relating the events of the killing. When he had concluded his evidence, the prosecuting captain attempted to tear his account to pieces. But Matthew held firm and responded to every question thrown at him in a frank and open manner. Eventually the prosecutor resumed his seat with an audible sigh of frustration. Then Lieutenant Goldsworthy led the big Maori through the vital aspects of the evidence.

Lachlan's fate was back in the hands of the board. With the usual courtesies, the officers adjourned the court to consider all the fresh evidence. Would they accept what the proud Maori warrior had told them? Lachlan did not entertain much hope of this happening.

Lachlan stood swaying in the crowded, noisy bar. He had broken his oath to old Max Braun and knew only that he was getting very drunk.

'Here's to a close-run thing,' the Scottish sergeant said above the din of the crowd. 'Here's to an innocent Scot being freed from the shackles of the Sassenach legal system.'

Lachlan attempted to raise his glass but swayed too far and slammed into a soldier standing beside him.

'To Matthew Te Paea,' Lachlan responded, struggling to regain his balance and dignity. 'God bless the big heathen and those soldiers who accept that honour is still a reason to march a man into battle.'

A grumble of agreement rose around him. It was a rare thing for an accused man to walk away from a courtmartial, rare still for court-martialling officers to accept the word of an enemy over that of one holding the Queen's commission. Maybe there was hope for the British army yet.

But a question still nagged Lachlan. It had been the big Scottish sergeant who had tracked Matthew down in Auckland and secretly brought him before Goldsworthy at the very last moment. The young warrior was a man well known to many and not so hard to locate. When he had heard of Lachlan's plight, he had not hesitated to volunteer to step forward in his defence. If nothing else, Matthew Te Paea had a sometimes misguided trust in English justice, if not the British Empire.

As Forster's killing had been committed as a legitimate act of war, the tribunal had no choice but to excuse the slaying, although they were quick to conclude that Matthew should be immediately arrested as a prisoner of war. Goldsworthy had leapt to his feet and made a deal with the tribunal that, if the Maori warrior gave his word not to ever again take up arms against the British Crown, he be granted a military parole. Matthew agreed to the conditions and walked from the courtroom a free man, albeit a bitterly disappointed one. He would have given his left arm to be allowed to continue fighting the British. However, Matthew also understood the meaning of an oath – in any language.

'Why did you do it?' Lachlan asked the sergeant now.

The Scot swigged his whisky and looked Lachlan in the eye. 'Because it were right,' he said. 'And you are a fellow Scot. The Sassenachs may employ me to fight for them, but my heart is still with the heather and glens. It were right to give you a chance.'

Lachlan did not question him any further. All he knew was that his life had been spared because of a shared heritage. In his gratitude for this kindness, Lachlan felt he might break into tears. He quickly made an excuse to leave the bar and broke into the noisy night of the Auckland street. Now Lachlan knew why he had taken the oath to abstain from liquor. The last thing he remembered before waking up in the military hospital was the night swirling around him like a heavy, stifling coat.

'You have a bad fever. I feared as much with the wounds you received.'

Lachlan recognised the voice as belonging to the kindly surgeon from his old militia unit.

'How long?' Lachlan croaked.

'Three weeks,' the doctor replied. 'You have been in and out of the fever since you were brought here.'

'My arm?' Lachlan asked in a weak voice.

'You get to keep it,' the army surgeon gently replied. 'The fever is abating and your wounds appear to have healed, although I doubt you will have the same strength in it as before. For the moment I will leave you in the care of the orderlies, but I think when you are discharged from the hospital, your days of soldiering are over.'

Lachlan smiled and closed his eyes. Around him he could hear the soft murmur of voices, broken only by the shouts of a wounded man a couple of beds from him. The man was obviously in a state of shock.

''E was at Gate Pa,' came the explanation from the bed beside Lachlan. 'The big heathens shot him down in the trenches. Where did you get yours?'

Lachlan opened his eyes, turned his head to see a bandaged head with only the eyes watching him.

'Orakau,' Lachlan replied. 'Got shot in the arm. How about you?'

'Gate Pa,' the British soldier replied. 'Me name's Corbett. I'm with the 43rd.'

'I was with the Forest Rangers,' Lachlan said. 'My name's MacDonald.'

'You a colonial then?' the British soldier asked. 'I thought you might have been a Scot.'

'I am,' Lachlan said. 'But spent most of my life in the colonies. What happened at Gate Pa?'

The soldier turned his head on the pillow. The brightness in his eyes had faded.

'We got the chop from the Maori. We was over Tauranga Harbour way where the heathens built a pa right under our noses. They was taunting us to come and fight them but old Cameron brought up every gun we had and bombarded the hell out of them. It looked like nothing could survive. Every inch of the pa had been shelled.

'Finally, we went in. We thought all we had to do was pile up the bits and pieces left over in the trenches. At first we had only a bit of resistance when we went over the top but suddenly they were firing into us like rats trapped in a barrel. We lost seven officers killed and God knows how many of me mates killed and wounded.

'The Maori had been as snug as bugs in their underground shelters and the artillery didn't even mess up their hair. The fighting were so fierce that we had to get out and leave our wounded to the mercy of the natives. Young Henry over there, screaming his lungs out, swears that a native woman who could speak English came to him when he was lying wounded in the trench and gave him water. Some of the other boys tell the same story.

'The Maori aren't like other heathen natives I've soldiered against. The worst thing was that after they repelled us they all got away. Old Cameron is saying we had a victory, coz we took the trenches, but every one of us knows that the Maori won on account of so many casualties.

'It was a nightmare in them trenches. I just want to go home.'

Corbett sighed and closed his eyes. The next morning, the orderlies came to remove his body.

Due to his half-useless arm, Lachlan found himself discharged from the army. Not that he minded, as his heart was no longer in soldiering. In common with many prominent men in the New Zealand government, Lachlan could clearly see the real reason for the war against the courageous Maori warriors – the stealing of valuable native land for a handful of rich speculators – and he was relieved to be no longer a part of it.

Besides being discharged with an honourable record, and his severance pay, the government had provided him with a ticket home to Sydney. Lachlan had a day before his ship sailed the Tasman. Sober, and dressed in civilian clothing, he set out to find Matthew Te Paea. The kindly Scottish sergeant had informed Lachlan that he might find the former Maori warrior living in a shanty town on the outskirts of Auckland.

It was a place of dispossessed Maori – men, women and children awaiting the end of the Waikato campaign, before attempting to bring normality to their shattered lives. So far, it appeared that the campaign was far from over. Cameron and his force had not been able to bring the rebels to a confrontation where he could deploy his forces to crush the resistance once and for all.

Lachlan found Matthew living with another former warrior in a tin shack.

'I see that you are able to use your arm a bit,' Matthew said, greeting Lachlan.

'And I can see that you are able to walk well enough,' Lachlan replied with a slow smile.

The two men stood some paces apart appraising each other. 'I see that you are no longer fighting for Cameron,' Matthew continued.

'And you are no longer fighting for the Kingites,' Lachlan said.

'It was not really my fight,' Matthew said softly. 'I am of the Ngati Kahungunu people from the Hawkes Bay region. I only went to help the Waikato tribes to show them how real warriors fight.'

Lachlan nodded. So they both had volunteered to fight for a cause that was not theirs.

'What are you going to do now?' Matthew asked as a cluster of Maori watched with curiosity the two men in their midst conducting a conversation in English.

'I am returning to Sydney. There, I will meet my brother and after that travel to Queensland to become an explorer,' Lachlan answered, not mentioning that in fact his first task would be to seek out Amanda, having been told she had returned there.

'Good,' Matthew grunted. 'I think that maybe I will go to Queensland one day. I have heard that it is warm there – even in the winter. It was not warm at Ballarat when I was there.'

'If you ever travel to Queensland,' Lachlan said, 'you must look me up and we can reminisce about our fighting days.'

'I will do that,' Matthew said. 'We will meet again.'

Lachlan extended his hand but Matthew reached out to draw the young man close, touching his nose with his own.

'Our way of saying goodbye,' Matthew said.

Lachlan stepped back, nodded, then turned to walk away, wondering at this strange friendship that he had formed with a man who had tried to kill him on the battlefield – yet saved his life in a courtroom.

When Sydney came into sight, Lachlan was standing at the bow of the ship, watching the rise and fall of the great sandstone cliffs that acted as the gate posts to the bustling city on the beautiful harbour. It was early morning and, despite the onset of winter, the sun shone over a gentle, rolling sea.

Soon the ship was being secured to a wharf at Circular Quay. Lachlan was acutely aware of his wounded arm, now out of a sling but hanging limply by his side. He wondered how Amanda might react to seeing him now that he'd been injured and squeezed his eyes tight. It was not something that he wanted to think about. He would exercise it as much as possible, but too much movement brought on almost unbearable throbbing pain. At least he could raise it and grip with his fingers. He leant down to sling his swag over his shoulder and with his free hand took out a scrap of paper to once more read the address written on it. Lachlan had decided that he should attempt to meet up with his brother before seeking Amanda's whereabouts. He needed a place to stay and also wanted to discuss the inheritance John had written to him about.

As it was, the hotel was not far from Circular Quay, and Lachlan made his way up the street. The hotel was one of the better places in Sydney and when he entered the foyer the man behind the reception desk looked startled at the appearance of this broad-shouldered young man carrying a swag and wearing rough, working man's garb.

'I'm afraid we have no vacancies,' the man behind the reception desk stated disdainfully when Lachlan approached. 'You should try another establishment.'

'I believe that a Mr John MacDonald is a resident in this hotel,' Lachlan said, ignoring the expression of contempt.

'Who may be in residence here is confidential,' the man sniffed.

'Well, I am his brother, Lachlan MacDonald, and have just returned from the Maori wars,' Lachlan growled. 'You can get a message to my brother that I am here.'

'I shall see what I can do,' the man replied, stepping back from the desk.

Lachlan turned his back and walked over to a comfortable leather chair. He sat down, dropping his swag beside him. Around him, well-dressed men and women passed by.

The man behind the desk gestured for a young, smartly dressed boy to come to him. He whispered something and the boy disappeared up the curving staircase. Within minutes Lachlan looked up to see a well-dressed man stop at the bottom of the stairs and glance around the spacious foyer. John and Lachlan's eyes met and a broad smile broke out on John's face as he walked quickly forward to greet his brother.

'Lachlan?' he asked, with hope in his voice.

'John.'

They stood staring at each other – a distance of years and experiences separating them and neither sure how to bridge the gap.

After a few moments John stepped forward and grasped Lachlan's arms. 'It has been a long time and we have much to talk about,' he said with tears glistening in the corners of his eyes. 'Harold,' John said, turning to the man behind the reception desk, 'I want your best room for my brother – and no excuses.'

'Very well, Mr MacDonald,' the receptionist said. 'For you, it will be done.'

Lachlan broke into a grin. He'd felt so alone for so long but now he had his brother back again. He had a family.

Throughout that evening and into the early hours of the morning, John and Lachlan caught up on the lost years, sitting on the verandah of the hotel with a bottle of brandy between them. Lachlan did not speak of his experiences in the New Zealand campaign. That part of his life held too many ghosts. And nor, for the time being, did he speak of Amanda.

'Now, if we could only find Phoebe,' John sighed, 'then we would all be together again.'

Lachlan experienced a twinge of guilt at the mention of his sister's name. But John was right, they would have to do all they could to find Phoebe.

'This is such a big country,' Lachlan commented.

'But it has a small population,' John countered. 'Between us, we will find her and she will be able to claim her share of what was left to us. But what are your immediate plans?'

'I hope to catch up with the Duffys at the Erin, and then find a lady I once met in Sydney before I volunteered,' Lachlan replied, swirling the brandy in his tumbler.

'Do I detect the sound of Cupid's wings?' John asked with a twinkle in his eyes. 'May I ask, who is the young lady?'

Lachlan stiffened. He knew how he felt about Amanda, but he did not understand her leaving New Zealand without attempting to contact him and could not guess at how she would react to seeing him again. 'She is no one that you would know, and I don't know what will happen when we next meet,' Lachlan finally replied. 'It is just something that I have to do.'

Lachlan did not want to go into any details. He knew of his brother's hatred for Lightfoot and it would be better that he did not reveal Amanda's identity until he was able to sort things out between them.

When Lachlan finally retired to his room he fell into a sleep racked by dreams of sweating men engaged in hand-to-hand combat. In his dreams he could not use his arm and a Maori war club was about to descend on his head. Lachlan woke in a sweat. Why was it that the terrible things of the battlefields should haunt him even now that he was safe? For a moment, he lay on his back staring at the darkened ceiling of the hotel room, frightened that his dreams were some sign of madness. It did not make sense that the past could intrude so easily into the present.

Lachlan slipped from the clean, crisp bed linen to sit at the edge of the bed. He reached for the remaining brandy. When he found it, he swilled down the last drops.

If anyone would know where Lachlan might find Amanda, it would be Daniel Duffy. The next morning, Lachlan shared breakfast with his brother, who suggested that he invest in a set of smart clothes befitting a young man who had inherited a small fortune. Lachlan took his advice and visited a gentleman's clothing shop. He returned to the hotel, brightly bid the snooty hotel receptionist good day and went to his room to change. When he came down the stairs the expression on the receptionist's face told him he made a suitable impression. No longer a bedraggled former soldier, he was now a well-dressed man about town.

Lachlan caught a cab to the Erin Hotel, where he was joyously welcomed by Bridget, Frank and old Max Braun, who was forced to turn away with a sniff lest anyone mistake the glistening in his eyes for the onset of a tear or two. Bridget fussed over Lachlan's wounded arm with suggestions of applying goanna oil to help in its recovery, while Frank located his best Irish whiskey to toast the adopted member of the Duffy clan.

In the kitchen where so many important matters had been spoken of in the past Lachlan knew what the first question would be. 'Did you get to see Michael when you were over there?' Frank asked, leaning forward.

'I did,' Lachlan replied, taking a swig from his glass. 'We served together in the Forest Rangers. I wanted him to write to you but he said that it was better that you think he was gone for good. He was worried that any contact with him might have brought the law down on you all here.'

'The stupid lad,' Frank sniffed. 'We were not concerned with what the law might try to do to us. All we care about is Michael. He's been like my own son since his father was killed in Queensland. Were you present when Michael was killed?'

Lachlan feared this question, as he had sworn a sacred oath to Michael that he would never reveal – not even to his family – his whereabouts.

'I was,' Lachlan replied quietly. 'If it had not been for Michael holding them off, the Maori warriors might have inflicted many more casualties on us. He died like a hero. Unfortunately, we were unable to retrieve his body.'

'I will never believe Michael is dead,' Bridget said firmly, 'unless I actually lay his body out myself.'

Lachlan cast her a quick look, avoiding the woman's eyes. He wished that he could have told her Michael was still alive and probably somewhere in the Americas. But his oath held back any reassurance to Michael's beloved aunt.

That evening Daniel returned home after his long

day at the law firm. At the sight of Lachlan, he broke into a broad smile and hugged him affectionately.

'It is good to see you!' Daniel exclaimed. 'We all feared that you might suffer the same tragic fate as Michael.'

After Frank and Max excused themselves to tend to their duties in the bar, Daniel removed his coat, hung it on a stand by the kitchen door and sat down at the kitchen table with Lachlan. He could see that the young Scot had been drinking, despite his promise to Max, but was still quite sober.

'Why did you not write that you had come across Michael?' Daniel asked quietly, pouring himself a whiskey.

'Michael made me swear not to mention it,' Lachlan answered. 'He had his reasons and I did not question them. You of all people must respect the sanctity of an oath.'

'As his friend, you did the right thing by keeping his secret. I understand that.'

Lachlan felt relief. He had hated keeping Michael's secret. Now he could relax and engage in normal conversation. 'Michael died a hero,' Lachlan said, closing any further questions on the subject. 'Now, as regards another matter, I was wondering if you had heard anything of the whereabouts of Miss Amanda Lightfoot?' Lachlan asked.

'You don't know?' Daniel replied, a dark shadow clouding his face. 'Miss Lightfoot was wed last week to Sir Percival Sparkes. Her brother gave her away.'

Lachlan felt like he'd been hit with a sledge hammer. As his nausea rose, Daniel could see the terrible impact the news had on his friend. The young Scot must have strong feelings for the lady. 'I'm sorry, Lachlan,' he said awkwardly. 'I did not realise that you may have held a fondness for Miss Lightfoot.'

'I simply thought that she was a nice lady,' Lachlan lied lamely. 'It was nothing of any importance.'

Daniel did not know what to do. He excused himself from the room, leaving Lachlan alone. For a time, Lachlan stared at the wall of the snug little kitchen, finally placing his arms on the table. Laying his head on his arms, he broke into sobs. So much he had given to win her love and all for nothing. She had promised him that she would wait forever – she'd lied. His dream had been shattered as much as his left arm. Lachlan wept until there were no tears left. When he lifted his head from the table, it was to swear that one day he would destroy Amanda and her brother. He did not care how long it would take but he would see them both rot in hell before he died.

Part Three

THE EXPLORER

1874

The Colony of Queensland, The Northern Frontier

TWENTY-ONE

He was virtually blind and the stinging in his eyes caused Lachlan to grit his teeth, lest he cry out and allow his enemies to know that he was injured and almost helpless. He sat on the rough stone pebbles of the tiny beach by the tropical creek, clutching his big Colt revolver in his right hand. Lachlan knew the terrain he was in, as he had been able to see it before the poison took its effect some hours earlier. He was deep in the rugged rainforest country of northern Queensland, his young Aboriginal companion had been killed by a twelve-foot spear through his chest, and it was unlikely any help would be forthcoming.

Above him on the steep slope running down to the creek bed the forest was silent. The only sound Lachlan could hear was that of water gurgling over the rounded stones and the rustle of the three hobbled horses nearby, grazing on a bank covered in native grasses. The silence brought back ominous memories of the fern forests of New Zealand where, ten years earlier, he had fought against the Maori in the Waikato. Silence in any forest was not a good thing.

Lachlan had spent the last nine years of his life roaming the northern lands of the Australian colony of Queensland. Not in the grand tradition of the great explorers lionised by the press, but in private employment, seeking out potential farming land for the company of MacDonald & Busby. His secondary task was also to seek those places that might hold traces of gold and it was this that had brought Lachlan to country not before trodden by Europeans.

Further north, the Palmer River gold rush was well and truly under way and Lachlan had launched himself into a frantic expedition to explore regions just south of the Palmer for any other potential fields. He had set out with the fifteen-year-old Jupiter, the boy having attached himself to Lachlan when he was on a previous exploration in the northern rainforests. That had been four years earlier when he had found the boy, the only survivor of a massacre near the strange geological formation of black granite boulders piled into a hill south of the Endeavour River. Since then, the boy had accompanied him on all his expeditions and had proved to be a valuable companion in the densely forested ranges where the tribesmen fought for every foot of ground. Many times Lachlan had been forced to fight for his life against the brown-skinned warriors but this time it appeared that his luck had run out.

He and Jupiter had been traversing a ridge, away

from the camp site they had established on a broad section of a gently flowing tropical creek, and had stumbled onto a well-trodden track in an unknown tribal area. The track had been beaten out by many bare feet, and clearly over a long period of time.

'Blackfellas!' Jupiter hissed.

Lachlan felt the hairs stand up on the back of his neck. An old instinct told him that they were being watched. Drawing his revolver from his belt, Lachlan swung around. Five huge warriors wielding spears and clubs stood with spears raised only twenty paces away. Before Lachlan could react, he heard the rattle of the hardwood missiles in the air. Miraculously they all missed – except one. Jupiter's cry of anguish took Lachlan's attention off the warriors for a split second as he turned to see Jupiter on his knees, clutching the long shaft protruding from his chest. Such had been the power of the arm that hurled the spear that it had exited through the youngster's back. He swung his eyes on Lachlan, a pitiful pleading for help, before toppling forward, the shaft of the spear snapping under his weight.

Lachlan swung again to face the threat. The warriors had advanced, armed with the war clubs. Raising his pistol, Lachlan aimed for the closest of the advancing men and fired. The heavy lead bullet took the warrior in the chest, causing him to stop in his tracks with a puzzled expression on his face. The other warriors faltered in their attack and when they saw their companion pitch forward, they turned and fled.

Lachlan's shot had caused enough panic to ensure

that he was momentarily safe. He knelt by Jupiter and turned him over, but the boy was dead.

'Oh, you poor little bastard,' Lachlan moaned, tears welling in his eyes. There was little else he could do except fetch a shovel and bury his faithful Aboriginal companion.

One of the spears still lay on the ground at Lachlan's feet. He picked it up to examine the lethal barbed notches at the point. From his long experience in the northern forests he was often able to identify a tribal grouping by the way they carved their spears. He ran his hand along the barbs and then flung the spear away. It was not one that he knew and he started to walk back to the camp site by the creek.

Sweating from the steaming heat of the tropical forest, Lachlan wiped away the perspiration running into his eyes with the back of his hand – only to feel the smarting effects of the poison from the barbs of the spear. He blinked rapidly but to no avail. Within minutes he was losing his vision. By the time he reached the camp site he was virtually blind, despite flushing his eyes with water.

Lachlan cursed. He had been careless on two occasions this day – the first had cost Jupiter his life and now the second mistake had cost him his eyesight.

The cooling air warned Lachlan that evening was approaching and his finely honed instincts told him that the tribesmen were most probably watching him from the cover of the rainforest. It was only a matter of time before they attempted an attack – especially if they twigged to his blindness. He knew that he must feign normalcy.

Lachlan rose to his feet, tucked the revolver back into his belt, and edged cautiously towards where he guessed he had left the saddle bag with his supplies. Somehow, he would attempt to find the remainder of the damper he had baked that morning. But he would not light a fire.

When Lachlan found the bush bread, he bit off a piece and leaned back on the saddle bag. He would at least light his pipe. Within minutes the slightest clink of creek pebbles nearby caused him to reach for his revolver and fire in the direction of the sound. The echo rolled around the walls of the steep banks. But nothing followed and Lachlan wondered if he had let his imagination take control. At least the blast told the warriors he still had the weapon.

As sleep began to overcome him, Lachlan drifted into another world. Tears of disappointment rolled down his tanned cheeks. If only he had been allowed to live just a little longer he might have been able to make his mark in the history of exploration in the colony. He had been a fortunate man to have a brother like John, however – a kind and caring brother who had never forgotten his oath to find him and his sister. But the search for Phoebe had proved unsuccessful. Using his money and influence, John had secured many leads, but all turned out to be false. Phoebe would be around twenty-five years of age by now, Lachlan reckoned. She could be married with her own family.

Lachlan had often wondered at his brother's lack

of interest in the fairer sex and once he had asked John directly why he had not found a good woman to settle down with. John had stared out the window of his office in Sydney. 'My energies are caught up in expanding the companies,' he had replied. 'Maybe one day I will take a wife.'

Lachlan accepted the answer. But as time went on, and Lachlan noticed how his brother related to Nicholas Busby, a horrifying suspicion crept into his thoughts. Was his brother one of those who preferred the company of other men? But his brother was a gentle, caring soul and so Lachlan would dismiss any thoughts about John's private life. Over time, he accepted that his brother would never marry, and was consoled by John's discretion about his relationship with Nicholas.

John had risen to great wealth in partnership with Nicholas but always insisted that Lachlan share in his good fortune. Reluctant to accept more hand-outs, Lachlan had convinced his brother that he could be employed by the company to work as a private explorer, seeking out new lands for their enterprises, which now included mining and agriculture. He had proved to be successful, locating prime land in the north, which was then purchased by the company for resale. The ever-expanding frontier was a place of limitless possibilities and the company's profits grew at a rapid rate.

Lachlan had only one real regret – that he had known love and lost it. His long years of wandering the frontier of Queensland's north had left little time to go in search of love again. He had known the passion of a woman's body in occasional encounters in the frontier's whore houses, but time and again had been disappointed. Love was something very different, he had come to understand, and he yearned for it even though securing a woman's true affections would mean giving up his current way of life. How could he expect any woman to wait for him while he went on the dangerous, long expeditions into places where he might not return?

Now as he sat blinded in the dark, he suddenly thought about Amanda. It had been ten years since he last saw her and although he had once vowed to bear hatred for her betrayal, he always carried her letters with him. His anger had mellowed somewhat over the years. Perhaps if they met again he would even wish her well. But for now, all he had to do was survive.

The young woman – her face pinched by hunger and her hair hanging like a greasy mat to her shoulders – knelt by the camp stretcher holding the cold hand of the man lying on his back, his eyes partially closed. Had she not been suffering the privations of her current life, any man seeing her would have been struck by her pretty face.

She was now a widow at the age of twenty-five. Behind her stood a little boy and girl, six and five years of age respectively, their clothing in rags. Her husband's body was thin and wan; he had fought a terrible struggle with the fever that took his life.

Phoebe had been crying, but her tears were now

dried up. She had loved this man, whom she had met in Adelaide seven years earlier, and who had taken her from the life of working as a housemaid for a wealthy family in the growing capital of the colony of South Australia.

George Meers had been a clerk working in a bank and, although he was not a rich man, he had a wonderful view of life, that one day he would become a bank manager and possibly a director on the board of bank governors. Phoebe loved his happy smile and gentle ways. She had been in her teenage years when they met at a picnic and fell in love. Soon they were wed and the pretty young woman eventually bore him two children.

The little girl, Nelly, stood behind her mother sucking her thumb while her brother, William, held his sister's hand. He was frowning. Why was his father lying so still and silent? Phoebe could hear life going on as usual in the camp site on the goldfields of the Palmer River. The raucous voices of the miners and their families carried to the tent across the clatter of shovels. This place of dust and searing heat was so far from what could be called civilisation that Phoebe and her children could have been in a different country altogether. It was dangerous country, beset by bouts of famine, deadly fever and, for those who ventured into isolated gullies in search of gold-bearing ore, the possibility of sudden death from a tribesman's long spear or wooden club.

Phoebe could hear the call of the itinerant pedlar, a sound which always evoked her childhood with her family on the goldfields at Ballarat. Some twenty years had passed since that terrible day when she had last seen her father and brothers.

A friendly man and his wife had taken her by the hand and led her away from the confusion. They had no children of their own and were returning to their home in Adelaide, having sold their mining lease. They had made their money and now it was time to leave. Phoebe did not remember much apart from the long journey in the wagon and the kindness the couple showed her. They raised her according to the tenets of the Methodist church, and Phoebe grew to love both of them dearly. They provided for her as if she were truly their daughter.

When Phoebe was fourteen she had been placed as a housemaid with a rich family who attended the same church. The years of drudgery were forgotten when she met George. They married in that same church, and their first couple of years of wedded life had been good. Phoebe was happy in their little cottage but George became discontented with the little that he made as a bank clerk. When the word raced around the colonies that a major gold find had been made on the Palmer River in Queensland, George, like many others, had thrown in his job. Taking a gamble with their meagre savings, he sailed for the colony with his young family, hoping to find the gold nuggets waiting for the taking in the creeks and gullies of the Palmer. Like so many others, however, he was ignorant of the conditions to be faced on the savage frontier.

There had been no gold for the latecomer. Only death from a tropical fever that had racked his body for three days before he died. His young wife and family were left destitute.

Phoebe rose stiffly from beside the camp stretcher. A couple of miners had kindly offered to take George's body away and bury it.

'Ready, Missus?' a gruff but kindly voice asked from the entrance flap to the tent.

Phoebe turned to see the two bearded miners standing outside.

Answering with a nod, Phoebe pulled her two young children to her dusty dress. The men entered awkwardly, removing their battered hats out of respect for the deceased. One of the men bent and wrapped an old, threadbare blanket around George's body. He took a large sewing needle and quickly stitched the edges together.

The two men lifted the body between them and carried it outside. Phoebe stood with her children at her side. She did not want to see the men dig the shallow grave from the hot earth. She wanted to remember the man she had loved, the times they had shared amongst the shadows of the tall gum trees by the river where they had first met. This wan, lifeless body seemed so alien. She could never have imagined that they would come to this place only for her husband to die.

That evening, after Phoebe had put her two children to sleep in the tent, she sat by the camp fire. She felt numb. Outside, by a sea of camp fires, people were laughing and singing. Phoebe stared at the flicker of flames and reflected on her situation. The last of her supplies had been used and the very little money remaining hidden away. There was barely enough to buy food for the children. George's long hours of hard work had come to nothing.

So absorbed in her despairing thoughts was Phoebe that she did not hear the man approach from behind her. 'If yer need any help, Missus,' he said softly, 'you only just have to ask.'

Phoebe turned her head. It was one of the men who had taken her husband's body earlier that day. She did not even know his name.

'My name's Ken Hamilton,' he said. 'I'm packing it in and heading back up the track to Cooktown the day after tomorrow. Thought it wise to get out of here before the wet returns. If yer like, you and the young'uns can accompany me.'

'Thank you, Mr Hamilton,' Phoebe replied. 'Your offer is very generous and I will accept it.'

Phoebe guessed him to be in his late thirties and he had a kindly face behind his beard. 'Well, I had better get back to me mates. Give yer time to sell off yer gear before we go,' he continued awkwardly.

'I do not think that I will be able to pay you,' Phoebe said before he departed.

'I wasn't expecting any pay, Missus,' he said. 'Maybe you could cook up a good meal from time to time. That is all I expect.'

Phoebe smiled sadly. Hamilton was a total stranger, but she could not refuse his offer. Alone, with only the children, there was a good chance that they might be killed, whether it be by vicious white men preying on the helpless along the track or roaming tribesmen.

Phoebe and her two young children trudged behind the pack-horse.

Fortunately the children took to the man as they travelled through the rugged scrub on their way east towards the coast. Hamilton was cheerful and around the camp fire at the end of each day's journey, he would regale them with tales of his years travelling the world as a sailor. Phoebe would sit by the fire mending their clothing or simply sipping tea, listening to the former sailor entertain her children. Her grief had not been spent, but still she was grateful that she had been fortunate enough to meet Ken Hamilton. He had proved to be a true gentleman.

Phoebe had been able to sell up all her mining gear and tent before leaving, but the small amount that it had fetched was not enough to secure their passage to South Australia. By the camp fire each night, she wondered what would become of her and the children once they reached Cooktown.

'Time to sleep,' Phoebe said gently to her children.

'Just one more story,' William protested, reluctant to leave the colourful world of Mr Hamilton's adventures. 'Please, Mother.'

'No,' Phoebe replied firmly. 'We have many miles to journey tomorrow, and you need all your strength.'

With a shrug of defeat, William wandered over to the blankets that were laid out as a bed.

'Didn't mean to keep them up,' Hamilton apologised.

'You did not interfere,' Phoebe replied. 'Your stories have helped with their grief at losing their father. You have been able to distract them.'

'And what about your own grief?' Hamilton asked gently. 'It's always hard for a man to see a woman suffer.'

Phoebe glanced at him across the flickering soft glow of the flames of the fire. 'I cannot go back and change what has happened in my life,' she said sadly. 'All I can do now is consider what I must do to protect my children. That is what George would have expected.'

'Fair enough,' Hamilton said, reaching with a dry twig into the flames to obtain a light for his pipe. 'What will you do when you reach Cooktown?'

'I will seek work – until I have enough money to purchase a ticket to travel back to Adelaide with my children,' Phoebe replied. 'I believe that God will find a way to look after us. He has before.'

'I have some friends in Cooktown,' Hamilton said, puffing on his pipe. 'That is, if they are still alive in that hellhole of a place. Maybe I could help out.'

'Thank you, Mr Hamilton,' Phoebe said. 'I believe God sent you to us back on the Palmer and for that I am grateful.'

Hamilton did not reply. His thoughts were troubled. The young woman appeared to be ignorant of what Cooktown really held for her and he feared for her fate in the violent, sinful town.

TWENTY-TWO

It was only tiny, but at least Lachlan could see it – a beautiful flash of light from the multi-hued wing of a kingfisher swooping on the creek. Despite his fear, Lachlan had slept through the night and was still alive. The tribesmen had not attacked him and he was regaining his sight.

Stiffly, he rose to his feet, squinting to see if the blurred world would take on a more defined shape. At least he had enough vision to make out the rain-forest trees looming above him and the water flowing in the creek. These at least gave him some sense of direction.

Fumbling around where he had left his stores, Lachlan found his tea-making gear and set up a billy. He groped around for some dry kindling and made a fire to brew some tea. Even as he sat sipping the hot tea, he was able to see more clearly. He washed out his eyes with the remainder of his tea when it had cooled. The tea leaves spattered his face but the water was soothing on his eyes.

By mid-morning he had recovered enough vision to locate the horses and prepare them to shift camp. He agonised over the decision to leave Jupiter's body unburied but considered it would be unwise to go back up the track that had led them into the ambush. It was time to return to Townsville to deliver his report on this current expedition's findings.

John MacDonald sipped his coffee, turning the pages of the newspaper on the table in front of him. It was quiet in the big, rambling house in the harbourside suburb. Only the ticking of a clock on the wall disturbed this time he allocated to reading before making his way to the city office that he and Nicholas had established in Sydney. They had decided to relocate from Melbourne so the company would be closer to their rapidly growing interests in sugarcane and beef production in Queensland. It also made it easier to manage their growing trade with the rest of the world. They had progressed from simply supplying the British army in New Zealand with rum and beef to purchasing prime land in the new colony up north and then establishing wool stores along Sydney's waterfront to export the bales. Nicholas's business acumen was second to none and their wealth and growing political power in the colonies achieved recognition when they were accepted for the prestigious Australia Club. It was here that much of their business was conducted.

A headline caught John's eye. He placed his cup on the table and flipped open the paper to better peruse the item. The article reported that Major Charles Lightfoot, hero of the Waikato campaign, had returned to Australia with his sister and her husband from England. John took a deep breath. Before him was a name he had almost forgotten. The old feelings of anger welled up. Years earlier he had learned from Lachlan of Samuel Forster's demise at the hands of a Maori warrior and had been strangely pleased to learn that the cruel man's death had occurred in his brother's presence. Half the score for the murder of their father and oldest brother was settled, but Lightfoot's very existence still nagged John. Although a gentle man by nature, the very thought of this murderer who could also add common thief to his name rankled John's strict sense of justice.

'I can see from your dark expression that you have read the article about your old enemy,' Nicholas said, entering the room with his own cup of coffee balanced in his hand.

John folded the paper and placed it on the table. 'It is something that still causes me pain,' he admitted as Nicholas walked over to a wide window to gaze at the peaceful yet busy harbour.

'Do you still entertain thoughts of revenge?' Nicholas asked quietly, without turning.

'Until the day either Lightfoot or I meet our Maker,' John answered, 'it is a sworn blood oath.'

'Something you heathen Scots seem to be good

at,' Nicholas said with a grim smile. He turned to face his business partner and companion of many years. Their love for each other had not abated with time.

'Well, I also made a promise to you many years ago,' Nicholas said, 'that I would assist you in the destruction of Lightfoot. That promise is still valid.'

'I love you for your unconditional support, dear Nicholas,' John sighed. 'But I'm still perplexed as to how you could do that.'

A slow smile creased Nicholas Busby's face. 'Many years ago, when we were in New Zealand searching for Lachlan, I met Lightfoot. I gave him my card and lo and behold, he has managed to track me down after all the years that have passed. I have received correspondence from him that he wishes to avail himself of my expertise in investment matters in the colonies – one gentleman to another.'

John looked shocked, until slowly he realised that his conniving partner would not be meeting with Lightfoot unless he had a well-thought-out plan. He would trust Nicholas's judgement.

Phoebe had heard of Cooktown's terrible reputation from the miners on the Palmer fields. When she and George had arrived on the Queensland coast they had disembarked at Townsville and taken the long overland route to the Palmer. This track had been dangerous enough. Through arid lands of stunted, desiccated scrub they had constantly fought off thirst and many times she had wondered if they would even reach the famed goldfields. But they had survived.

George had often spoken of going to Cooktown once he had found their fortune, but such a journey with her husband was never to be. Phoebe was unprepared for the noise, squalor and seeming disorganisation of the town. She was assailed by the sounds of drunken brawling and the raised voices of women chiding inebriated men. An alien scent wafted on the steamy breezes coming from the muddy Endeavour River. It was not unpleasant but reminded her of rich spices.

'Chinese quarter,' Ken Hamilton muttered, seeing the expression of curiosity on Phoebe's face as she walked beside him with the children in tow.

The miner led his horse through the sea of tents at the outer limits of the sprawling town. The camp had sprung up to cater to the thousands who had come up north seeking their fortunes. Businesses of every kind from butchers to gun traders had flourished in the town. But the establishments that were predominant were the brothels and bars. It was said that there were even more brothels than establishments selling hard liquor – but looking at the bark and tin buildings, Phoebe could not tell if this was so.

However, it was immediately apparent to her that this was a dangerous place for a woman on her own. She looked at the man striding towards the main thoroughfare, Charlotte Street. Ken Hamilton was a strange one, she thought. Not once had he attempted to force his attentions on her while they had traversed the track to Cooktown. At all times he had proved to be kind and considerate, to both her and the children, although he had no real reason to do so. Now that they were in Cooktown, she wished that she had shown him a little more attention, but she was still grieving for George. Clearly Mr Hamilton understood this.

'Mr Hamilton,' Phoebe said, clearing her throat, 'I don't know how I will ever repay you for the great kindness you have shown myself and my two children in our hour of need.'

'No need to thank me,' Hamilton said gruffly. 'I was just doing what would be expected of any good Christian under the circumstances. Now I have to find you quarters and maybe somewhere for you to earn your keep.'

'Even though you have done so much for us already, I would appreciate your assistance,' Phoebe replied. 'I must admit that Cooktown frightens me.'

'You have good reason for your fears,' Hamilton said, as gently as he could. 'This is a place where you could get your throat slit for the shoes you are wearing.'

He did not elaborate any further. It was enough that Mrs Meers was here and almost destitute. She had enough to contend with.

Hamilton stopped walking when they reached the entrance to a side street that led into the Chinese quarter. 'Mrs Meers, I am going to propose something that may help your situation, but I fear that it will not meet with your approval.'

Startled, Phoebe swung her attention to the

bearded man's face. She could see pain in his eyes. A terrible thought crept over her. Had she over-estimated this man?

'Make your suggestion, Mr Hamilton,' she said in a low, angry voice.

'It's just that you need somewhere safe for you and the two little'uns to stay and I have a friend here who can provide cheap but good quarters for the moment. I know what I am about to advise you to do is abhorrent to most Christians, but it is only a suggestion,' Hamilton said awkwardly.

'Go ahead and speak your thoughts,' Phoebe said, instinctively clutching her two children to her side.

'Well,' Hamilton said, removing his hat and scratching at his bushy hair, 'my friend is a Chinaman. He has a place down this road and I know he and his family would take you in. He is keen to have a white person teach them how to speak our language, as he plans to stay on in Queensland. Mr Lee is a trader and as fine a man as I have ever met, although many of my fellow country-men might not agree. He . . .'

Phoebe gripped his arm and smiled. 'I would be honoured to meet Mr Lee and his family,' she said, throwing the tough miner off guard. 'If a fine man like yourself recommends Mr Lee and his family, then that is good enough for me.'

'Hell and high water,' Hamilton chuckled. 'I thought that you might despise me for suggesting that you stay with a Chinaman's family. Most people would.'

And so, Phoebe met Kwong Lee, his gentle little wife and their two almond-eyed sons, who were approximately the same age as her own children.

Lachlan dropped his swag on the bed, sat down and stretched out his legs. He was in his old room at the Criterion Hotel in Townsville and it felt like home. Roaming the frontier, he had not required a permanent place of residence and so he had used his brother's generous expense account to set himself up at the hotel, where he was assured of a good meal and a place to meet old friends.

The hotel was a two-storeyed building with spacious verandahs to provide shade from the hot tropical sun. Expecting a visitor, Lachlan quickly shaved after his hot bath. He changed into clean clothes and went out onto the verandah to gaze down on the rutted street below. Bullock wagons and horse drays lumbered past as well as horsemen and the occasional horse-drawn gig.

'Hello, old boy,' a voice greeted cheerfully from the end of the verandah. 'It has been a while since we last met.'

Lachlan strode towards his old friend and former military comrade, Andrew Hume. 'It is good to see you again, Andrew,' he said, shaking his hand. 'It must be around a year.'

'Around that,' Andrew said. 'I heard that you lost Jupiter a while back.'

The mention of the young Aboriginal's death brought a dark cloud to Lachlan's face. 'Up in the jungle country, south of the Palmer,' Lachlan replied. 'He was a good and faithful companion.'

'Sorry to hear about your loss,' Andrew added. 'You up for a drink?'

'That sounds like a good idea,' Lachlan said. 'Maybe raise a toast to Jupiter's soul – wherever it may be roaming right now.'

They went downstairs to the hotel's bar, where Lachlan ordered a bottle of rum. Time had brought a softness to his friend who had once been a lean, hard soldier in New Zealand. Now Andrew Hume was a highly-placed government officer. He and Lachlan had met again when Lachlan had first stepped ashore at Moreton Bay after leaving Sydney. Their meeting had been opportune, as Andrew was at the time employed by the government to process government land grants and leases for new settlers in the colony.

For his part, Andrew had not forgotten how Lachlan had stood by him back in Waikato and this bond now carried into their lives as civilians. With Andrew's help Lachlan had been able to identify regions of interest yet unexplored by Europeans. After mapping them, he had always been able to peel off the choicest land and purchase it from the government at a very reasonable rate for the MacDonald & Busby enterprises. In return, the company had always paid a generous, albeit secret, commission to Hume. This had been a welcome supplement to his meagre government pay, especially now that he had a wife and children to care for.

Lachlan produced the hand-sketched maps of his last expedition from his leather satchel, as well as his personal written observations on the flora and fauna. His love for learning had given him the basis to make detailed, accurate reports on all that he observed. Besides being an explorer, he was also an amateur botanist and geologist of some note.

'I did not see much evidence of gold,' Lachlan said, sipping his rum as Andrew finished reading the report. 'But I suspect that another expedition back into the same country might change that.'

Andrew closed the folder with its jumble of papers and sketches and picked up his drink. He could see that the harsh conditions of the wild parts of northern Queensland had taken a toll on his old friend. The young man's face was burned a deep brown and carried tiny scars. Lachlan had lost weight, too, but his powerful physique was still apparent. Andrew could also see that Lachlan was still troubled by the war wound that had weakened his left arm.

'So, you are going back,' Andrew said, sipping his rum. 'Have you ever considered quitting before some wild blackfella spears you, or you get a fever and die out there alone?'

'Not much else worth dying for,' Lachlan said with a grin, raising his glass. 'Maybe one day the government will build a monument to me.'

'I doubt it,' Andrew said. 'The motive for your explorations is to find land for your brother's companies. The government does not see that as worthy of recognition.'

'So what motivated all the others who have written their name into history?' Lachlan said with a touch of anger. 'They might have espoused noble ideals of venturing into unknown lands for the sake of furthering mankind's knowledge but in the end it was simply so that the colonial governments could send settlers in their footsteps to claim that very same land.'

'I agree with you,' Andrew soothed. 'The difference lies in who commissioned the expeditions. In the case of the others who got the glory, it was a government, or some geographical society. In your case, you are financed by a private company, so your discoveries don't count in the eyes of the public.'

Lachlan knew that Andrew was right. His dream of fame and recognition might never be realised, but at least he was actually going to places no other European had been before.

'Oh, by the way,' Andrew said with a slight smile on his face, 'while you were up north trudging around in the bush, there has been a man looking for you. I overheard him yesterday asking at Jacob's store. It seems that he heard that you were in these parts, and claims that you two met in New Zealand. He would very badly like to make your acquaintance again.'

Lachlan knew his friend well enough to know that he was savouring something at his expense. 'Who?' Lachlan asked suspiciously.

'Not someone I would like to meet up with again, if I were you,' Andrew shrugged.

'Who are you talking about?' Lachlan repeated, suspicion turning to exasperation.

'Some bloody big Maori cannibal, who says his

name is Matthew Te Paea. He is staying at the stables down the road,' Andrew said. 'He says you gave him his gammy leg.'

Lachlan was stunned by the news. 'Yeah,' Lachlan retorted with a grin. 'And he gave me this gammy arm.'

Now it was Andrew's turn to look surprised. 'God almighty!' he exclaimed, looking to the doorway of the bar. 'He's here!'

Lachlan turned to look over his shoulder. The doorway was almost blocked by the bulk of the man filling it. Slowly, Lachlan rose to his feet as Matthew strode towards him.

'Hello, brother,' Matthew said with a broad grin. 'I finally found you.'

Lachlan hardly knew how to reply as Matthew grabbed him in a powerful hug and rubbed his nose against Lachlan's. Andrew drew away. He had a fleeting memory of Maori greetings and they were not for the likes of him.

TWENTY-THREE

The meeting between Nicholas Busby and Charles Lightfoot took place in the offices of MacDonald & Busby in Sydney.

Lightfoot appeared to have aged somewhat from how Nicholas last remembered him at their meeting in New Zealand. He still had his thick hair but it was now shot with grey and his once handsome, aristocratic features showed the lines of a dissipated life. He carried a silver-topped cane and wore an expensive suit tailored in England.

'Mr Busby,' Lightfoot said when he was ushered into the office by a clerk, 'it is good to make your acquaintance once again.'

Nicholas rose from behind his desk.

'Major, a pleasure to see you again. I'm so glad you decided to take me up on my earlier offer to contact me on your return to Australia. I trust that you've had a pleasant time in the homeland? Please, take a seat.'

Lightfoot sat down in a chair, crossing his legs. 'England is always far superior to the colonies in both culture and society,' Lightfoot replied arrogantly. 'While I was there it appears I encountered a mutual friend, Lord Summers, at a regimental dinner in London,' he said, glancing around the spacious, well appointed office. 'He informed me how you had pointed him in the right direction for the investment of some of his capital.'

'Ah, yes,' Nicholas said, touching the end of his nose with his finger. 'Running sheep for wool production. Lord Summers purchased quite a few acres of prime land near Goulburn. He was a friend of the family many years ago.'

'A charming chap,' Lightfoot said ingratiatingly. 'We did a spot of grouse shooting on his estate in Scotland.'

'I was never one for the blood sports,' Nicholas commented. 'My youth was spent in books, rather than my father's gun cabinet. But so much for recollections of our youth in the old country. I gather that you are here to see me for financial advice.'

'You have a way of getting down to business that I admire,' Lightfoot said with a strained smile. 'Yes, that is correct. I have returned to the colonies with my sister and her husband to explore business opportunities. Needless to say that after having met you in New Zealand originally and coupled with Lord Summers' very high recommendation, I had hoped that as a fellow countryman you might be of some assistance.'

'One must always be of assistance to a fellow countryman,' Nicholas replied.

'Good show, old chap,' Lightfoot said, visibly relaxing.

'Well, the best way to start is to consider just how much capital you have to invest,' Nicholas said.

For a brief moment, Lightfoot appeared to be uncomfortable. 'Not exactly my capital,' he said, clearing his throat. 'I am acting on behalf of my brother-in-law, Sir Percival Sparkes.'

'So you are working on a commission basis in this matter?' Nicholas asked.

'An arrangement similar to that,' Lightfoot replied. 'Whatever enterprise that Percival establishes will be managed by me.'

'You have a very trusting brother-in-law. A man who allows another to invest his money must have great faith – even if related by marriage.'

Nicholas's edge of sarcasm made the former army officer nervous. 'Percival has no reason not to trust my judgment,' Lightfoot sniffed. 'We have known each other long enough for him to have faith in any investment that I should deem worthy of putting his money into.'

'I do not doubt your honesty, Major Lightfoot,' Nicholas said reassuringly, rising from behind his desk to indicate that their meeting was coming to an end. 'Family is family. I will give you the best advice that I can. Shall we meet again next week to discuss what I can come up with?'

'Thank you, Mr Busby. Hopefully, next time we meet I may also have the pleasure of meeting with your partner, Mr MacDonald.'

'Mr MacDonald is currently unavailable,' Nicholas said, walking with Lightfoot to the door. 'However, when I see him next I shall pass on your regards.'

When Lightfoot was gone from the office, Nicholas walked to the window looking down on the street. He could see the major enter a fine carriage drawn by two matched greys.

'So, the rat has smelled the cheese,' John said behind Nicholas.

'You heard our conversation then?' Nicholas asked, turning away from the window.

John nodded, taking the chair vacated by Lightfoot. 'Do we advise a worn-out gold mine or a worthless tract of swamp land?' he asked with a smile on his face.

'Nothing so crude,' Nicholas replied. 'Whatever we do, it has to guarantee that he is totally destroyed. My plan will be absolute in its outcome. Trust me.'

A thousand miles north, Lachlan awaited a reply to his latest report. He had forwarded it by mail to his brother in Sydney and in the meantime rested in Townsville, regaining his health and spending time with Matthew Te Paea. They would go fishing together and Lachlan learned how the Maori had decided to travel to the Australian colonies to join the gold rush along the Palmer. Not having had any luck, he had sought work back on the coast at Townsville to pay his way home. He had found some work on the wharves, but the pay was just enough to cover food and accommodation.

'You think that you would be interested in coming with me on my next trip into the forests?' Lachlan had asked. 'It's dangerous work.'

'Any worse than what we did in the Waikato?' Matthew retorted.

'About the same,' Lachlan replied. 'Except out there we are on our own.'

'Then, brother, I will go with you.'

It was a letter that turned John's life upside down. Postmarked from the colony of South Australia, it arrived at his office and he read the contents with growing excitement. Six months earlier he had tracked his sister's possible whereabouts to Adelaide. He had the means to employ a man in the colony to attempt to seek out his sister and it had paid off. John read that his sister was now married to a Mr George Meers and had two children. Meers had been employed by a bank but inquiries led John's private investigator to learn that the young man had sold up all that he owned and headed for the Palmer River goldfields. He had foolishly taken his family with him despite the advice of friends and family, the report concluded.

John placed the letter on the desk and stared at the clock on the wall opposite. He now knew his sister's new name and the names and ages of his nephew and niece. According to his calculations, his sister must now be somewhere in the tropical north of the Queensland colony. So too was his brother, Lachlan.

John stood and stretched his legs. He strolled over to the window that gave him a view of the street below. Gazing out the window, he allowed the turbulent emotions to swirl around in his mind. Lachlan could go to Cooktown and the Palmer to search out his sister, he thought. He would cable north with the news and arrange to join his brother in the search for their beloved sister. Yes, it was certainly time that he once again reunited with his brother, whom he had now not seen for five years. Deep down, John had a good feeling about the news. He was within easy reach of upholding the oath he had made so long ago.

'Thank you, Lord!' John shouted in exhilaration.

The office door opened and his personal assistant poked her head in.

'Did you call for me, Mr MacDonald?' she asked in a puzzled tone.

John smiled at her. 'Not unless you command the hosts on high,' he replied, 'thank you, Gertrude.'

Nicholas Busby's campaign to assist Charles Lightfoot with his brother-in-law's investments had got off to a good start. A real estate deal in Sydney had returned a 200 per cent profit, giving Lightfoot good reason to trust the entrepreneur's business acumen. Nicholas was also able to put forward

Lightfoot's name for membership to the Australia Club. This night, they met in the plush surroundings.

'Well, old chap, here is to you and your very sound financial advice,' Lightfoot said, raising his glass in a toast.

'My pleasure,' Nicholas responded. 'Anything to assist a fellow countryman of such impeccable reputation.'

Lightfoot looked pleased with the compliment. 'I have a great favour to ask,' he said. 'To do with a possible future investment.'

'It would be a pleasure to be of assistance, Major,' Nicholas said with a fleeting, enigmatic smile. 'You only have to ask.'

'The thing is,' Lightfoot started, 'Sir Percival is somewhat of an amateur geologist and has a desire to travel to Cooktown and view a geological formation in that area called Black Mountain. He has asked me if you might know of someone trustworthy to act as his guide up there. I feel with all your contacts that you might be able to steer me in the right direction. I have to confess that I know little about his peculiar interest but he has informed me the mountain is of sufficient significant geological importance to warrant exploration.'

A name came immediately to Nicholas's mind, but he dared not speak it. 'If you give me time I shall make some inquiries,' he replied. 'I am sure that I can satisfy Sir Percival's request.'

Lightfoot settled back to enjoy the conversation at the club. It had as its members some of the most influential and wealthy men in the colonies.

He knew that he was in good company and looked forward to swelling the capital his brother-in-law had entrusted to him. Charles felt the smugness of one who had always known what was best for his sister – and the marriage he had arranged had proved one of his best investments, following the decline of his own small fortune. Too many losses at the card table and the expenses of living the life of a gentleman around London had sapped his finances. Through his brother-in-law he had a chance to redeem his fortune and the opportune meeting with Nicholas Busby in New Zealand had been God sent.

That evening, Nicholas related the conversation that he had with Charles Lightfoot and told John about Sir Percival's request.

'You seem to have Lightfoot's trust,' John said. 'My brother would be more than capable of acting as a guide, but Lightfoot would be bound to recognise him.'

'As far as I know Lightfoot himself is not travelling north; it would be Sir Percival alone. According to Lightfoot, he would be very generous when it came to payment.'

John gave the matter serious thought. Would it be safe to have Lachlan escort the English adventurer to Black Mountain? What advantage would there be in allowing him to do so? It would not be the money; Lachlan was already well off. His inheritance had been invested wisely and grown considerably. Indeed, Lachlan had enough income to settle down to his own business or simply retire on the interest his money was bringing in.

There was also the possibility of Lachlan going to the Palmer goldfields in search of their sister to be considered. 'Maybe it would not hurt to contact Lachlan and put forward the proposal,' John finally relented, having formulated what he would do about seeking out Phoebe. 'It could do no harm and might even put him in a position to monitor Lightfoot.'

'You mean collect intelligence,' Nicholas said, pouring a sherry from a crystal decanter on the sideboard. 'I hope that I never make the mistake of crossing you, John.'

'Not so long as you remain faithful to me,' John replied with the faintest of smiles. 'We Scots are well known to carry a grudge – even to the grave. I would haunt you forever if you ever sought another to take my place.'

'That will not happen,' Nicholas sighed. 'Even with all my vices, loyalty and love happen to be two of my greatest strengths.'

'I know,' John said, rising from the chair and walking across to Nicholas. He placed his arm around the Englishman's shoulders and hugged him. 'We will be together until the day one of us should die. Oh, and I have decided to book a berth north to visit my brother for a short while.'

'You are not intending to travel with him to the Palmer, are you?' Nicholas asked, shocked at his partner's decision.

'Why not?' John smiled. 'I think it is about time that I visit those wild places in the north he seems to love so much.'

'It's dangerous!' Nicholas exclaimed. 'I have heard

tales that the savages up that way are cannibals – not to mention the abundance of ruffians who would cut your throat for little else than the clothes you wear. Do you think that your decision is wise?'

'I may not be the heroic figure cut by my brother but I have another reason to go to the Palmer – I am in receipt of information that my sister may be on the goldfields.'

'Then that makes all the difference,' Nicholas said. 'I can see why you would risk much to find her.'

'I knew that you would understand.'

Within weeks, Lachlan received a long letter from his brother outlining all that had occurred in Sydney since the arrival of Charles Lightfoot, his brother-in-law and Sir Percival's wife, Lady Amanda Sparkes.

Lachlan felt his heart skip a beat when he read that Amanda was back in Australia. Had he not sworn years earlier to destroy Amanda and her brother? The old wound reopened and once again he felt the terrible emotional pain that her betrayal of her promise to wait for him had wrought. Bitterness rose like bile and Lachlan consoled himself that at least he would not be seeing Amanda again.

John had also mentioned in his letter the matter of him joining Lachlan to search for Phoebe, and that Sir Percival was in need of a guide to Black Mountain. Lachlan knew of the eerie place – a low hill composed of a jumble of huge, black rocks about twenty miles south of Cooktown. Jupiter had been born in the shadow of the hill and had often told

Lachlan stories of its evil magic. Once he and Jupiter had sat astride their horses, observing the hill from a distance. When Lachlan had suggested that they ride to it, Jupiter had shrunk away. 'My people call it the place of the spear,' he said. 'That really means the place of death. Do not go there.'

Lachlan gazed across the verandah of the hotel at the shimmering heat on the railing. Why not, he told himself. Maybe just to do so would honour Jupiter's spirit and besides, Matthew had been nagging him to leave town for the bush. Their friendship was an important part of Lachlan's life and the big Maori was eager to go exploring. He was as restless as Lachlan; sitting around town had bored him.

'So brother, when do we go bush?' Matthew asked when he next met Lachlan.

'We have an assignment to travel to Cooktown, where we will meet with a rich Englishman by the name of Sir Percival Sparkes,' Lachlan said. 'We will then escort him to Black Mountain, just south of Cooktown.'

'He looking for gold?' Matthew asked.

'No, he just wants to go and see the hill,' Lachlan replied.

Bemused, Matthew shook his head. 'He must be mad to just go and look at a hill without scratching for gold.'

'Yeah,' Lachlan echoed. 'Mad and rich.'

No matter what the Englishman was, Lachlan knew that he was taking the assignment only for the chance to see what sort of man Amanda had married. But it would be good to share with Matthew this country that he had come to love, despite its many dangers. He would always be a man of the frontier, regardless of his personal wealth. Although maybe one day he would discover that piece of the colony where he would be prepared to settle.

TWENTY-FOUR

$\mathbf{M}$r Lee had employed Phoebe to teach his wife and children English as well as educate the children in the basics of a European-style education. It had not been easy at first, but the two Lee boys seemed to master what they were taught and were learning English at a good rate. The family had proved to be generous and warm-hearted towards Phoebe and her children and the little space that had been allocated for them at the back of Lee's store was clean and comfortable.

However Phoebe soon came to learn why Ken Hamilton had been somewhat reluctant to place her in the company of the Chinese family. Her first lesson came when Phoebe volunteered to take Kwong Lee's children for a stroll down Charlotte Street after a couple of weeks staying with the Chinese family.

When Phoebe exited the Chinese quarter, it was

returning to the country that she once knew. Rough and rowdy miners mixed with bullock drivers on the streets while by the Endeavour River those who had experienced the horrors of the Palmer goldfields jostled each other to obtain a berth on one of the ships preparing to return south. Such was the desperation of some, they would even resort to leaping into the crocodile-infested water to swim to the ships.

The four children watched wide-eyed. Phoebe's children clung to her hands as they walked along the jostling street.

'A Chinee lover,' a male voice suddenly sneered from behind Phoebe. She gripped her children's hands more tightly and glanced anxiously at the two Chinese boys walking beside her.

'Hey, Missus,' the voice said loudly, 'why don't you stop and buy a real human a drink?'

He was close enough now for Phoebe to smell the alcohol on his breath. Then she felt his hand on her shoulder, spinning her around. The man stank and his rheumy eyes spelled many days and nights in the town's bars. From his tattered clothes, Phoebe could see that he was a man down on his luck.

'These bloody Chinamen are doing honest miners out of their bread and butter,' the man said angrily, pointing at the two small boys with Phoebe.

'I hardly think so,' Phoebe replied coldly. 'Please take your hand off me,' she added, attempting not to be intimidated, although she was feeling real fear for the safety of herself and the children.

'What are you goin' to do about it?' the man hissed into her face.

When Phoebe looked over the assailant's shoulder she suddenly felt a surge of hope. Striding along the street towards her was Ken Hamilton with a fierce look on his face.

'Let the lady go,' he roared when he was about ten paces away.

The man released Phoebe, swinging around with a long-bladed knife in his hand. 'Want yer guts sliced out?' he snarled at Hamilton.

Ken Hamilton reached under his shirt and produced a small pistol from behind his waistband. 'Want your head blown off?'

The man lowered his knife to slink away into the crowds around them. It had all happened so fast that very few on the street had been aware of the confrontation. Ken Hamilton quickly slipped the revolver back into his waistband.

'Are you all okay?' he asked. His sudden appearance brought expressions of delight to young Nellie and Hugh's faces.

'Mr Hamilton,' Phoebe said, 'you must be our guardian angel.'

Hamilton looked sheepish. 'I was just lucky enough to find you,' he said. 'I went to see Lee and he said that you had planned to take the kids for a look at the town. So I came looking for you. I wanted to inquire how the last couple of weeks have gone.'

'I must thank you once again,' Phoebe said gratefully. 'The Lees are such a fine family. They have been wonderful, although I must admit it does feel strange to be amongst their people.'

'Yeah, well,' Hamilton drawled, 'I got to admit that I felt a bit strange living in their world when I first met Lee. But he is a Christian man – as you most probably know by now. He got his education and what English he had from Methodist missionaries in China. Now he wants to establish a trading company in this part of the world. He believes that China and Australia have a lot to share in the years ahead. Sadly, I do not think he will ever see his dream come true. Too many people despise the Chinese because they are different from us.'

'You do not appear to be one of those people, Mr Hamilton,' Phoebe said.

'Like I said,' Ken Hamilton replied, 'I had the chance to live in China many years ago and found the people not much different from us. They love their families, want to work and live in peace. That's about what all of us want.'

'You sound like you should have been a missionary, Mr Hamilton,' Phoebe said with a faint smile.

'Don't get me wrong,' Ken Hamilton said quickly, 'I don't go for that religion stuff. I kind of put my faith in a strong back and good rifle living up these ways. But I do like the Chinese for their ways – God knows why.'

'Would you like to walk with us?' Phoebe gently asked.

'I would be honoured,' Hamilton replied, suddenly aware that little Nellie had taken his hand.

'Will you marry me when I grow up?' she asked seriously, looking up at him with her big eyes.

Hamilton suppressed his laughter and glanced at

Phoebe. 'Maybe,' he said, 'I will have to ask your mother first.'

'Good,' the little girl said happily and continued to cling to his hand.

'You seem to have a gentle way with children,' Phoebe remarked. 'How is it that you do not have a wife and family of your own?'

'My life at sea did not allow me much time for such considerations,' Ken replied. 'I chose to come ashore to seek gold and was lucky,' he continued. 'I guess that I gave up the sea to seek a steadier life. Now that I have made my money, it is a case of going south to start a boat-building yard – maybe around Moreton Bay. I like the weather in the colony.'

'I think that you would be a wonderful husband for some fortunate woman,' Phoebe sighed. 'You are a rare gentleman.'

'Would you be interested, Mrs Meers?' Ken quietly asked.

'Oh, I did not mean to insinuate that I was asking,' Phoebe quickly said, her face reddening. 'I suppose I was saying that you are a man who . . .'

Suddenly Phoebe was lost for words, realising that she was revealing more of her feelings than she dared. Still mourning the loss of her husband, she felt such thoughts were improper. But when she looked up into Hamilton's face she noticed his strong features and the wisdom in his eyes. He appeared at least fifteen years older than herself – a man in the prime of his life – and one who had seen so much of the world. She appreciated how in his quiet way he had helped her and the children after George's death.

Yes, she thought, Ken Hamilton was a desirable man in many ways.

'What I meant to say, Mr Hamilton,' Phoebe said, 'is that I would like you to be around to see the children. They have taken a liking to you.'

'And you?' Ken asked, a twinkle in his eye.

'I suppose that I have missed your company,' Phoebe admitted.

'In which case I should visit my old friend Lee a bit more often.'

Weeks later, the telegram to Townsville gave Lachlan the name of the coastal steamer that his brother would be travelling on. He waited at the wharf as the passengers were rowed ashore with their luggage.

'Top hats are not very practical up here,' Lachlan said, stepping back to appraise his brother. 'We will have to get you kitted out for the journey ahead.'

John was also appraising his brother, dressed in knee-length riding boots, trousers and a loose-fitting cotton shirt. He was surprised to see how the climate seemed to have agreed with Lachlan. He looked fit and well. His weakened left arm seemed to have recovered from the terrible injury and Lachlan's clean-shaven face was tanned to a golden colour. His long hair, tied back, was dark and lustrous. Wearing his dark suit, John suddenly felt out of place. The other Queenslanders greeting passengers from down south were similarly dressed to Lachlan. It seemed that civilised customs stopped north of Moreton Bay.

Moreover, some of the local men were wearing guns in their belts.

'It is wonderful seeing you, Lachie,' John said, using his pet name for his little brother. 'You look so well.'

'I have spent a few restless nights waiting for your arrival,' Lachlan replied, guiding his brother to a pile of suit-cases off-loaded onto the shore from a separate rowboat. 'All we have to do is clear you with our customs people and then we can go back to the hotel. I have booked your accommodation.'

After paying the excise duty for some goods in John's possession, the two men walked to a light wagon Lachlan had hired from the stables. Matthew sat in the driver's seat and his fearsome appearance startled John. Lachlan grinned when he saw the expression on his brother's face. 'This is Matthew Te Paea,' he said, 'the man who gave me my wounded arm in New Zealand, but you will observe that he has a slight limp, which I gave him.'

John did not know what to say, but reached up to the grinning Maori and shook his huge hand.

'Welcome, brother,' Matthew said.

'Pleased to meet you, Mr Te Paea,' John responded, casting his brother an inquiring look.

'Well, time to get back to the verandah for afternoon drinks,' Lachlan said, hauling himself into the back of the wagon while John took a seat beside Matthew.

Sitting beside his brother on the hotel's verandah, John found a strange peace. He had no desire to live in the tropics himself but could understand why Lachlan found the hot climate of Australia's north so appealing. Here, life seemed to lose its frenetic pace. Compared to the busy world of commerce down south in Sydney, everything here seemed to move so slowly – even the lazy drawl of conversation around him.

'I noticed that a lot of the men around here are carrying guns,' John remarked, watching the sun sinking in a mauve mist on the western horizon.

'The ones going back into the bush do,' Lachlan said. 'A necessity – if you don't want to be skewered on a wild blackfella's spear. This isn't like New South Wales or Victoria. It gets more dangerous the further north you go,' Lachlan continued. 'Around the Palmer, the Merkin have claimed many a miner's life. I would suggest that you get a good rifle before we leave for Cooktown. Maybe one of those new Yankee repeating rifles, or at the least a Snider. I will also give you the name of a man who will guide you to the Palmer. He is an experienced bushman I would trust with my life. I only wish that I had not taken the assignment to escort this Sir Percival Sparkes. I should be with you.'

'I will take your advice,' he said, sipping his gin and tonic. 'And I thank you for your concern for my welfare. But I will be all right. We MacDonalds are made of stern stuff.'

The two brothers spoke well into the evening, mostly catching up on the news of the company's growing fortunes, but also speaking softly of their hopes for finding their sister. At length the subject of Lightfoot came up.

'Nicholas feels that he will find a way of ruining him,' John said. 'If anyone can, it will be Nicky. I have not met the man, as Nicholas feels to do so might jeopardise his plans for him.'

'Nicholas is wise,' Lachlan said. 'I think if I saw Lightfoot now, I would up and shoot him. The slimy bastard almost had me shot.'

'I know that you were rather fond of his sister,' John said quietly. 'Does it not bother you that you are escorting her husband?'

'I do not think about Amanda anymore,' Lachlan said, not wanting to reveal that since he had learned the news of her arrival in Australia he had not been able to get her out of his mind. 'I would rather not talk about the matter,' he added quickly.

'I have to admit,' John said sympathetically, 'that I have not had to confront such a situation with the fairer sex.'

'Would you possibly feel the way I do if Nicholas were to leave you?' Lachlan asked.

John fell silent for a short time, gathering his thoughts. The subject of his relationship with Nicholas had never come up before, although he suspected that Lachlan must have some inkling of its true nature.

'Do you condemn me for who I am?' John asked.

Lachlan turned to gaze at the last remnants of the sun sinking below the horizon. 'I do not agree – or even understand, for that matter,' he replied. 'But you are my brother and have more than enough demonstrated how much you care for me – and for Phoebe. I do not know of any other man who would have done what you have to find us. No matter what you have chosen to be in life, you are my brother and I love you for that.'

John was touched by his brother's acceptance but glad even so that it was dark on the verandah. He did not want Lachlan to see the tears that were streaming down his face.

TWENTY-FIVE

Lachlan, Matthew and John travelled north on horseback, trailing a string of pack-horses carrying their supplies. Not only did the journey give Lachlan the opportunity to teach his brother the ways of the bush, it was also a time that drew the two brothers even closer. Fording streams, hacking through dense rainforest and being ever alert to hostile tribesmen, they shared hardship as well as the serenity that came at the end of the day around a camp fire.

Matthew was in his element, although his fear of the snakes that inhabited the north was a constant source of amusement for Lachlan. Having hailed from a country where such reptiles were unknown, Matthew couldn't help but be fearful. He had heard all the tales told by the old hands of how the fearsome creatures could strike without being seen and bring a slow, agonising death to the unwary.

Lachlan placed a snake's carcass in Matthew's bedroll one evening, but the jest did not elicit any laughter from the Maori when he found it. But it brought gales of merriment from Lachlan and John, who rolled around on the ground, laughing at the spectacle of the big Maori leaping in the air and screaming like a girl.

'So where is the warrior I once knew?' Lachlan asked, wiping away the tears streaming down his face. 'You can easily see that it is dead.'

Matthew stomped away, growling Maori curses and sat down, his arms folded across his great chest. 'One day I will get you, brother,' he muttered. 'One day.'

Their trek north took them past the small outposts of Port Denison and Smithfield, where they stopped to resupply their stores. Eventually, their journey brought them just south of Cooktown and within sight of Black Mountain.

'So that is what Sir Percival wants to see,' John mused from astride his horse, gazing at the giant black landform rising above the scrub to form a low hill. 'Just looks like some giant has piled up a store of stones to build something and forgotten what it was.'

'Not the time to go exploring the hill now,' Lachlan said, wiping the sweat from his brow with the back of his hand. 'We have to keep moving if we are to meet the boat bringing Sir Percival to Cooktown.' With that, Lachlan spurred his horse forward through the scrub.

'This place has got a bad feeling,' Matthew

muttered. 'We have places like this at home where you don't go.'

'Bloody heathen rubbish,' Lachlan threw back across his shoulder. 'It's just a strange-looking pile of rocks – nothing more. Maybe Sir Percival will tell us how the hill was formed.'

'The devil made it,' Matthew replied softly. 'That is a place of dead people who come out at night to snatch you away.'

Lachlan shook his head. He had spent long enough in the bush to know that the dangers to him were tangible – not spiritual. But that night, having fallen into a deep sleep beside the camp fire, Lachlan had a strange dream. In his nightmare, the dead did indeed come out of the crevices between the rocks. They had the almost forgotten faces of the Maori warriors he had killed and were led by a decomposing Sergeant Samuel Forster. He awoke with a shout, waking the others in fright, expecting a shower of Aboriginal spears to fall on their camp site. Snatching a rifle, Matthew looked across the dying embers of the camp fire.

'What is it?' John yelled.

Lachlan was now fully awake, sitting up and rubbing his eyes. 'Nothing,' he replied. 'I just had a bit of a bad dream. Nothing to worry about.'

The following morning over a mug of hot tea, Lachlan glared at Matthew sitting on a log, poking the fire with a stick.

'You know that trick we played on you with the snake,' Lachlan growled. 'Well, you got me back last night you big heathen bastard. I wouldn't have had my nightmare if you hadn't put it in my head with your talk about the dead coming out of Black Hill.'

'I was serious,' Matthew answered, continuing to poke the embers and without looking up at Lachlan. 'There are the spirits of dead people in that place.'

'I thought that you were a Christian,' Lachlan said.

'I got my education from missionaries,' Matthew smiled. 'I didn't say I was a Christian.'

'Thought so,' Lachlan sighed. 'I let myself go bush with a heathen Maori who is probably a cannibal on top of everything else.'

'I didn't say I wasn't a cannibal,' Matthew grinned.

John had listened to the banter between the two men and noted their camaraderie. He could see that for some strange reason the two men – once former enemies – were as close as any two brothers. He could only surmise that it had grown from the bond that develops between men who have known the horrors of armed conflict, regardless of which side they fought on. He envied Matthew for his relationship with his brother, but was also grateful that Lachlan had such a man by his side. He had Nicholas by his, and seeing the closeness his brother shared with Matthew he was beginning to appreciate more his own relationship with Nicholas. Where Lachlan and Matthew were men of action, however, Nicholas's strength lay in his mind and the ability to manipulate the world around him. That was what he was doing now, John mused, rolling up his blanket, working towards destroying Major Charles Lightfoot.

How, John was only vaguely aware but he knew all would be revealed in time. Whatever scheme Nicholas was working on was guaranteed to succeed. Nicholas was not a man to lose.

'My company was going to purchase this stretch of estate,' Nicholas Busby said, standing in the street with Charles Lightfoot gazing at the long row of empty warehouses on the harbour foreshore. 'But we are committed to another investment and a bit over-extended at the moment. So, I remembered you and, as a great favour, put your name first on the list to possibly buy the land before it comes on the market. It will be worth a fortune to anyone with the money to snap it up now and resell within a month.'

Charles Lightfoot cast his eye over the vast stretch of vacant buildings. 'How much is the vendor asking?' he queried. 'That is a lot to ask,' Lightfoot replied when Nicholas gave him a price. 'To do so would be using all Sir Percival's capital.'

'Ah, but I predict that when you resold you would triple your return,' Nicholas replied. 'You would have to act fast, for when the sale is announced it will not remain on the market for long. The buildings are ready to use for any factory or storehouse business on a large scale. There are plenty in Sydney with financial means and prepared to take a gamble – although I do not see the purchase, of this tract of land as being much of a risk when I know the current market here.'

Lightfoot frowned. He knew that he had access

to the amount required for the purchase but it was everything that Sir Percival had shifted to the colonies. In his mind, he quickly calculated his commission on the transaction, and the frown evaporated from his face. It was enough to live off for a couple of years in the lifestyle suited to a gentleman. 'You say it could be put back on the market almost immediately after purchase for triple the price I might pay?'

'That's right,' Nicholas said, cupping his hand to light a cigar. 'You would not even have known about this deal if I had been in a position to buy it myself.'

'I would have preferred to have spoken to my brother-in-law first,' Lightfoot said.

'I believe he is probably up in Cooktown by now, getting ready to have a look at his hill,' Nicholas said, blowing smoke into the still air. 'Maybe you could consult his wife – your sister,' he suggested.

'That is a bit hard, old chap,' Lightfoot mused. 'At the last moment, my sister insisted on travelling with him to Queensland. She said that she would be bored waiting for him in Sydney.'

Nicholas paled. From what he had heard, Lightfoot's sister was well acquainted with Lachlan MacDonald and would surely come across him in Cooktown. To do so might cause suspicion and ruin Nicholas's long-contrived plan to ruin Lightfoot. Already Nicholas was considering telegraphing Lachlan to warn him of the unexpected development. Or was it already too late?

'I will go ahead with the purchase,' Lightfoot said.

'Sorry, what did you say?' Nicholas said, his mind focused a thousand miles north, rather than where he stood with Lightfoot.

'I said I will go ahead with the purchase,' Lightfoot reiterated. 'No doubt you are able to assist me with that.'

'Wise decision,' Nicholas replied. 'As a matter of fact, I have just the solicitor in mind who will handle the paperwork. A young chap by the name of Daniel Duffy.'

Ligthtfoot nodded. He was both excited and frightened by his decision. But Nicholas Busby had already proved his worth as a man who knew how to make money and if he recommended the purchase then that was good enough. But a small fear continued to nag him. What if something went wrong? It was a long drop from riches to rags. If Sir Percival had not been so besotted with Amanda, then he himself would not even be considering such a huge outlay of another man's money. But it was an easy way to make an income. One did not have to work for the return like a common person. After all, money made money.

'Sir Percival Sparkes is over there,' the crewman from the coastal steamer told John.

He, Lachlan and Matthew had gone down to the jetty on the Endeavour River to await the boat's arrival. When it docked, John had approached the gangplank while Lachlan and Matthew had remained with the wagon they had hired to transport the

Englishman's luggage to the accommodation they had arranged for him. Through the crowd, John could see a tall, well-dressed, handsome man with an aristocratic bearing, standing by a large pile of trunks. Beside him stood a striking young woman wearing a free-flowing dress of pure white and a sun-bonnet and carrying a parasol. For a moment, John was puzzled. Who was she? Suddenly he had the answer. It had to be Sir Percival's wife, Amanda. He gasped. His first thought was to warn his brother and find someone else to guide Sir Percival to his mountain. But this thought was curtailed when Lachlan suddenly appeared beside him.

'Thought I should come down to help our visitor with his luggage,' Lachlan said lightly.

'Lachlan, I have . . .' John started, but was cut short.

'God Almighty,' Lachlan gasped. The beautiful woman had swung around and her eyes fixed on Lachlan. From the expression on her face, it was clear that she had recognised him immediately. Her eyes were wide, as if she had been frightened by a ghost, and for a brief moment it appeared that she might swoon.

'Damn!' Lachlan swore under his breath. 'What in hell is she doing here?'

'I doubt that it matters now,' John answered glumly. 'The cat is out of the bag – as they say. Well, we may as well go over and introduce ourselves to Sir Percival and Lady Amanda Sparkes.'

As they pushed their way through the crowd milling around the jetty, Amanda's expression did not change. Lachlan tried to remain stony-faced.

'Sir Percival,' John said, thrusting out his hand. 'I am John MacDonald and may I introduce my brother and your guide, Mr Lachlan MacDonald.'

'It is a pleasure to meet you, gentlemen,' Sir Percival said warmly. 'I would like to introduce my charming wife, Lady Amanda.'

Amanda smiled wanly and averted her eyes. She had said nothing about already knowing him and for this Lachlan was grateful.

'Well, Lachlan has arranged a wagon to take you and your luggage to the best hotel that had a vacancy. I hope it is suitable, although we were not expecting Lady Amanda to be accompanying you on this expedition.'

'I have always had an interest in seeing new places,' Amanda spoke up. 'I have had the good fortune to see much of the world and was not going to miss out on visiting this part of the colony. I once even spent time in New Zealand with my brother, during the Waikato campaign.'

'Ah, yes,' John said, clearing his throat. 'So did my brother Lachlan.'

'Did you soldier there?' Sir Percival asked with interest.

'I did,' Lachlan replied quietly. 'I was with Von Tempsky's Rangers company.'

'Ah, then you would not have known my brother-in-law, Major Charles Lightfoot. He was a captain at the time of his service in New Zealand.'

Lachlan caught Amanda's eye for a fraction of a second. 'I'm afraid not.'

'I served in the Crimea with my father's regiment,' Sir Percival said. 'But I did so as a mere ensign. Did you hold a commission?'

'Corporal,' Lachlan replied, reaching for one of the heavy chests. 'I finished my service around '65 and returned to Sydney.'

'Then you would have received the campaign medal for New Zealand,' Sir Percival continued in a chatty mood.

'I was not much interested in medals,' Lachlan said. 'My brother made application for it on my behalf. He said that it was good for the family inheritance.'

'Something for your wife and children, no doubt,' Sir Percival said.

'I have neither wife nor children,' Lachlan replied, hefting the chest onto his shoulder and noticing just the slightest change in Amanda's expression.

Loading the wagon, Lachlan tried to remain calm, but he now had to admit to himself that he had never stopped loving Amanda despite his vow to ruin her. He only hoped that his legs would not give way as he hoisted the chest onto the tray.

Lachlan quickly introduced Matthew to Sir Percival and Amanda. He had never mentioned Amanda to the former Maori warrior but at least it was out in the open that he had served in New Zealand. It was one less lie to hide.

John took over settling their guests and their luggage into their hotel, but all the while Lachlan and Amanda did not speak to each other. However, the tension in the air was palpable. Lachlan longed to be with Amanda alone so he could ask the question that had haunted him for over a decade. Why? Why had she so suddenly and inexplicably broken all contact with him, after professing her love in such tender terms through her letters?

The opportunity to speak to Amanda alone did not arise while they were in Cooktown. Lachlan was occupied arranging for extra supplies now there was an additional person accompanying them on the trip south to Black Mountain. He was also kept busy ensuring that John's trek to the Palmer goldfields was well organised and locating the Dutchman who would guide his brother. By the time he had completed his work, it was well into the evening. He returned to the stables, where John was standing guard over their precious supplies.

'Have a drink,' John offered.

Lachlan accepted the bottle passed to him.

'Your party is settled in,' John said. 'They will join you tomorrow at first light.'

Lachlan nodded, taking a long swig from the rum bottle and wiping his mouth with the back of his hand.

'Lady Sparkes was quite a surprise,' Lachlan said. 'At least she did not let on to her husband that she knew me.'

'We can't be sure that she will not inform her brother that you are here,' John said. 'The telegraph can be a blessing or a curse.'

'I don't think she will tell him,' Lachlan said, gazing out at the dimly lit street. 'I think that she will try to pretend to herself that I don't really exist.'

John made no comment. He found it hard to accept that a woman could be that insensitive, considering the little that he knew of his brother's past love for her.

'We will part for the time being in the morning,' John said quietly. 'I just wanted to tell you how much I have enjoyed sharing this country with you, my dear brother.'

Lachlan gazed at his brother's face in the dim light of the kerosene lantern. John's tender gratitude brought a lump to his throat.

'Be careful,' Lachlan replied. 'It can be very dangerous in the lands that you will be passing through. Always keep your gun handy.'

'I will,' John smiled. 'I have given the rifle a name. It's called Lachie.'

Lachlan broke into a broad grin. 'Good name,' he said. 'Well, time to find Matthew and get him home for some sleep before we ride out at dawn.'

'Do you know where he is?' John asked.

'I have a good idea,' Lachlan replied. 'I made the mistake of paying him his wages today and when I last saw him he was heading in the direction of a house of ill repute.'

'Take care, and I will share breakfast with you before we leave,' John said, settling down to a bed he had fashioned from loose straw.

Lachlan found Matthew exactly where he had expected him to be. He was just in time, as the Maori was standing toe to toe with a powerfully built American prospector, arguing over a girl. Reluctantly, Matthew left the establishment, throwing a stream of Maori curses over his shoulder.

'Time for us to head back to the stables,' Lachlan said. 'We have an appointment with the Black Mountain.'

'I still don't like that place,' Matthew mumbled. 'It has a bad feeling.'

TWENTY-SIX

The following morning, with his brother gone, Lachlan remained with Matthew at the stables. Although they had been supposed to depart Cooktown at first light it was almost mid-morning before Sir Percival arrived with Amanda.

'Sorry to be late, old chap,' Sir Percival said cheerily. 'But I had to send a telegram south to my brother-in-law, to inform him that we had arrived safely in Cooktown.'

'That's okay,' Lachlan growled. 'You are paying.'

If the English aristocrat had detected Lachlan's surly comment, he ignored it. Lachlan regretted being so churlish. He hoped the English aristocrat had not mentioned him in the telegram. But it was too late to worry if he had. On the trip up from Townsville, John had detailed the plan to ruin

Charles Lightfoot and Lachlan felt no guilt that should it succeed the scheme would also drag Sir Percival into financial devastation. Although it would also probably mean Amanda finding herself in dire straits, Lachlan was not too troubled. It would be a fitting fate for the woman who had hurt him so deeply. This morning Amanda was dressed in riding boots and a long dress tied at the waist with a sash.

'I hope that you have a side saddle,' she said to Lachlan.

'I was able to find one yesterday,' Lachlan replied. 'Your horse is already saddled.'

They were the only words that passed between them before they departed from Cooktown.

Nicholas had arranged to meet with Lightfoot at the Australia Club. Over dinner, Lightfoot told him that the contracts for purchase had been examined and all seemed to be in order. The settlement date had been agreed for the next week.

'Good,' Nicholas said, raising his claret. 'Here is to your windfall.'

'You are sure that this deal will pay off?' Lightfoot asked.

Nicholas sensed the other man's nervousness. 'All business is a gamble, my dear chap. I am sure that you will reap what you deserve.'

At this reassurance, Lightfoot relaxed. He was looking forward to surprising his brother-in-law with the good news of the purchase that he had made in his name and its subsequent resale for a huge profit.

Lachlan called a halt to set up camp for the evening. It had been an arduous day traversing the dense rain-forest tracks, but Sir Percival had proved to be a competent horseman and appeared to be at home in the terrain. His background as a young officer in Her Majesty's army had clearly prepared him for such conditions.

'I had the opportunity to hunt tigers in India,' he said when Lachlan begrudgingly complimented him on his skills. 'It is a pity that you do not have such game in the colonies.'

'We have a big bird up here called a cassowary,' Lachlan said. 'You don't want to get on the bad side of one without a good gun to defend yourself. It's a bit like an emu but its axe-like horn can smash your chest.'

'With any luck we may come across one that I can bag,' Sir Percival said, emptying a hip flask of whisky into an enamel mug and passing it to Lachlan. 'Here, old chap, have a swig. You have done pretty well yourself today.'

Lachlan accepted the mug and poured half its contents into another mug, passing it to Matthew.

'Cheers,' Sir Percival said, raising his flask. 'To sighting the mountain on the morrow.'

Lachlan glanced across the flickering flames. Amanda appeared exhausted at the end of the day. Riding side-saddle along the narrow tracks had sapped her strength. Wisps of hair had come free and fallen across her dirt-smeared face.

'You appear ready to put your head down,' Lachlan said.

She glanced up at him with a wan smile. 'I am very tired,' she admitted. 'I think that I shall retire to leave you gentlemen to your own devices.'

'I will ensure that your tent is clear of snakes or spiders,' Lachlan volunteered.

'I would be grateful for that,' Amanda said.

'With your permission, Sir Percival,' Lachlan said, rising from beside the fire with a lit lantern.

'You have it, old boy,' Sir Percival replied, content to sit and sip his whisky.

Amanda followed Lachlan to the tent that had been pitched to accommodate her and her husband.

'You have not revealed that you knew me in the past,' Lachlan whispered when he calculated that they could not be overheard.

'I do not think that is necessary,' Amanda replied quietly. 'The past is the past and cannot be relived.'

As Lachlan opened the flap of the tent for Amanda to enter, she stumbled, falling backwards against Lachlan. He quickly put his arm around her waist to steady her.

'Why, Amanda?' he asked in a hoarse whisper. 'Why did you suddenly leave New Zealand without a word to me and marry another? You know, when I returned to Sydney I swore that I would hate you for the rest of my life.'

'And do you?' she asked, gazing directly into his eyes.

Lachlan released his grip on her and stood back. 'No,' he sighed. 'That feeling disappeared a long time ago, when I was deep in the rainforests. I had the opportunity to remember how your letters kept me going in the war. All I could think of was seeing your beautiful face for that first time in Sydney.'

Amanda looked away. 'That was a long time ago, Lachlan, and much has changed. You can see that I am a married woman.'

'I understand your marital position, but do you love your husband as you once professed your love for me?' he asked.

'It should not matter to you how I feel about my husband,' she replied, biting her bottom lip. 'What we had is past, you must accept that.'

'I never thought that I would see you again,' Lachlan said.

'And I believed the same. I thought that I might faint when I saw you standing with your brother at the river.'

'So, you still feel something for me?' Lachlan asked.

'It does not matter about my feelings. I am married and will remain so as long as my husband is alive.'

'Please,' Lachlan said in a pleading voice, 'I do not want you to think that I am asking anything of you other than an answer as to why you left me without a word.'

Amanda looked at Lachlan with tears welling in her eyes. 'I did so only because my brother threatened to use all in his power to have you shot – and

I know that he was in a position to do so. I could not bear the thought that my presence might cause your death. When I returned to Sydney, Charles pressured me to marry Percival. My brother had squandered much of our inheritance on the card tables and saw my marriage as a means of redeeming himself. I was obliged to accept Percival's proposal to help my brother, who had always supported me after the death of our parents. The marriage has proved to be convenient, as my husband has often been away on his trips. This is the first time I have actually accompanied him. I wanted to return to the colonies, which I have grown fond of. Meeting you again is something I never expected to happen. I always wondered about your fate and prayed that you would find the happiness you deserved.'

Lachlan was stunned by Amanda's revelation. There were so many things he wanted to say to her, but he couldn't find the words. She had sacrificed her love for him rather than see him dead. 'I do not see anything here that might harm you,' Lachlan finally said quietly. 'So, I will bid you a good evening.'

'Ah, all safe in the tent?' Sir Percival asked when Lachlan returned to the camp fire.

'Nothing to worry about, Sir Percival,' Lachlan replied, taking a seat on a log, his mind still reeling.

'Your man here was telling me the extraordinary story of how you two met in New Zealand. I believe you both tried to kill each other. And now Mr Te Paea informs me that he considers you a brother. What a tale to tell the chaps back at my club in London.'

Lachlan glanced at Matthew, who ducked his head sheepishly. They were friends, but Matthew had never expressed the true depth of his feelings in that way before.

'It was a bad time for . . .'

Lachlan did not finish his sentence but reached for his revolver as Matthew snatched up his shotgun.

'What in the devil . . .' muttered Sir Percival, startled at the sudden urgent action on the part of his companions by the fire.

'Hello there!' a voice said from the dark. 'We smelt yer coffee and was wonderin' if you had any to spare for a couple of poor travellers on this dark night.'

Lachlan had his pistol levelled at two figures who had appeared at the edge of the light thrown off by the fire. The strangers were dressed in dirty clothes that reflected they'd been a long time in the scrub. Neither appeared to be armed, but Matthew kept his shotgun in his lap pointed in their direction nonetheless.

'Come,' Lachlan said, slightly dropping the barrel of his revolver.

The two men shuffled forward, wary of the guns pointed at them. They squatted on the opposite side of the fire. 'You got any coffee or tucker to spare?' the older one asked. His companion appeared to be around his late teens and sported a wispy beard.

'Help yourself,' Lachlan said. 'There is a damper loaf you can share.'

'Thanks, matey,' the older of the two said, reaching for the flat loaf. 'Been a while since we had any tucker.'

'Where you from?' Lachlan asked.

'Been on the Palmer but didn't have any luck,' the older man said, stuffing his mouth with a chunk of the warm bread. 'Now headin' south to Townsville lookin' for work.'

Lachlan stared hard at the two men. They did not look like they had been starving. Indeed they both looked well fed.

'Where are you lot travellin'?' the man asked, wiping his mouth with the back of his hand.

'Just travelling,' Lachlan replied, noticing that the younger man seemed very interested in everything around the camp site. He did not speak but his eyes flitted from one thing to another. Lachlan did not trust the two – there was something wrong and he would be glad to be rid of them.

'You can take a tin of coffee, a bag of flour and some sugar and a tin of treacle with you,' he offered politely but firmly.

The older man rose from where he squatted and Matthew passed him the items Lachlan had nominated.

'Thanks, matey,' the man said, accepting the small hessian bag. 'Me and me mate will be off. Hope you have a good trip.'

'Don't trust them,' Matthew muttered as the two men disappeared into the dark. 'I thought I heard horses a while back before they turned up.'

'I agree,' Lachlan said. 'Sir Percival, are you armed?'

'I have this,' Sir Percival said, producing a small-calibre revolver from his trouser pocket.

'Keep it close by you tonight,' Lachlan cautioned. 'There are some pretty desperate types who roam these areas. A traveller can go missing and the police would have trouble finding any evidence of foul play in these lands.'

'Quite agree, old chap,' Sir Percival replied. 'Do we post a guard tonight?'

'Matthew and I will keep a lookout,' Lachlan said, easing the hammer off his pistol. 'I am sure all will be well. If those two had been making a reconnoitre of our camp, then they would have seen that we are well armed. Maybe they will move on.'

Although Matthew and Lachlan took turns to stand watch through the night, the only sounds that came to them were the mournful cries of the curlews and the howls of dingoes deep in the scrub. At sun-up Lachlan organised striking the camp and after a breakfast of tinned meat with damper they saddled up the hobbled horses to continue south to the Black Mountain.

Although Amanda did not avoid Lachlan, they had little opportunity to speak privately on the trip. Lachlan felt the pain of seeing her riding just behind the man she admitted marrying for her brother's sake. Lachlan had to stop himself from telling her all that he knew about her murderous brother. It would only sound like sour grapes to do so. He could no longer hate her, but still he would be glad when the assignment was over and Amanda would forever leave his life.

At a rest break around mid-morning, Matthew signalled to speak with Lachlan in private.

'I think that I should drop back and sit off our track,' Matthew said quietly. 'Then I will catch up with you when you camp tonight.'

'You have the same feeling as me,' Lachlan replied. 'It could be blackfellas, but I don't think so. Jupiter told me most of his clan were wiped out around this area.'

When the break was over, Lachlan approached Sir Percival. 'Matthew has to go back down the track for a while,' he said. 'We might have lost one of our loads from the pack-horses. He will catch up to us when we camp tonight.'

'Nothing wrong is there, old chap?' Sir Percival asked with a frown. 'Not those two we met last night by any chance?'

'No,' Lachlan lied, wanting to spare Amanda any concern. 'We will mount up and head on to the Black Mountain. All going well, we should reach it about mid-afternoon.'

Sir Percival stood in his stirrups to gaze at the low jumble of black boulders that made up the hill. 'By Jove, it certainly is an interesting outcrop!' he exclaimed in his excitement. 'I can hardly wait to have a close look at it.'

Lachlan glanced at Amanda, who looked weary, and decided that he should pitch camp to establish a base for Sir Percival. With a hand from Lachlan, Amanda slid from the saddle.

'Thank you,' she said. 'I think I should have a drink of water.'

Lachlan passed her a canteen and she drank in great gulps.

'Sit in the shade of a bush while your husband and I pitch camp,' Lachlan said, observing that Amanda appeared to be suffering a touch of heat stroke. She did not protest as Lachlan helped her across to a small tree, Sir Percival seemingly oblivious to such matters as keeping an eye on the condition of his wife.

'My husband does not agree that ladies should be on such an expedition,' she said. 'He believes that our place is in the parlour or bed only.'

'Well, if you are to be here he could at least keep an eye out for you,' Lachlan growled.

'I know that you are doing that,' Amanda said. 'That is enough.'

Her words bit deep into Lachlan's heart and he turned quickly away.

Just before sunset, Matthew rode into the camp and slid from his horse. Lachlan strode out to meet him at the edge of the clearing amongst the low scrub at the base of the hill.

'Five of them following us,' Matthew said, bending to examine one of his horse's hoofs. 'The two that came to the camp last night and three others. All are armed. They are being cautious, hanging back so we don't see them.'

'Did they see you?' Lachlan asked.

'Did you see me when I killed that bastard, Forster?' Matthew grinned.

'So you think that they are up to a great mischief?'

'More than likely, brother.' Matthew straightened his back and gazed at the great rock pile. 'I told you this place has bad spirits.'

Lachlan ignored his friend's observation and walked back to the camp with troubled thoughts. Was he being over-cautious or did he have a genuine reason to fear these men? He questioned himself. He was less afraid for himself than for Amanda. The worst any man could do to him was kill him. But five men could do far worse to Amanda before killing her. The odds were not looking good.

TWENTY-SEVEN

Lachlan did not embark on the exploration of the hill that day. Instead he spent much time carefully setting out the camp site. The arrangement soon attracted Sir Percival's attention. 'If I did not know better,' he said, walking the perimeter of the cleared area and beyond, 'I would say that you are establishing lines of fire around our bivouac.'

Lachlan ceased striding through the scrub to stop and retrieve his pipe. 'Just normal precautions in this country,' he said, tamping down a plug of tobacco with his thumb. 'There is always the danger of some hostile tribesmen launching an attack on the unwary.'

Sir Percival accepted Lachlan's explanation. After all, the man had once been a soldier in the famed Forest Rangers.

That evening dinner was prepared and eaten in relative silence. Amanda was less weary from travelling that hot day and appeared to be acclimatising to the rigours of the journey.

When she and Sir Percival retired to their tent for the night, Lachlan and Matthew rostered themselves on guard duty.

Lachlan sat away from the camp fire, in the shadows of the night. He regretted that he had not brought dogs on this trip as he had on some of his other explorations. They were the best early warning system he could have and several times had saved his life from prowling tribesmen.

The constellation of the Southern Cross was low on the horizon as Lachlan sat out his watch, his rifle across his knees and his Colt revolver close at hand. All seemed well in the scrub immediately surrounding their camp, but when he looked to the southern horizon he could see the sinister outline of the hill. He suddenly felt uneasy, as if the geological formation was watching them, waiting for them. Lachlan cursed himself for thinking such ridiculous thoughts. It was just a strange formation and nothing else. Lachlan remembered the stories Jupiter had told him of the hill's creation. One was of a man who had been a cannibal and devoured a popular young chief of the local clan. He had been banished to the surrounding hills but would occasionally sally forth to snatch the unwary. On one of his forays he turned into a goanna to escape his tribe's wrath but was struck by a bolt of lightning, causing him to explode and shower the earth with burnt rocks. Yet another story told how the creation of the hill came about as a result of two brothers getting into a fight over a girl they both desired. They had rolled huge rocks down the sides of hills until they eventually formed the great pile that was now the mountain.

Jupiter's last version of the story was somewhat ironic, Lachlan thought. That two men fighting over a woman would create a mountain. No matter how strongly he might feel about Amanda, he was not in a position to fight for her love. She was married. Fate had dealt a cruel hand but he must accept how things had transpired, even if in his heart he knew he would never forget her. If only matters had turned out differently.

'Granite,' Sir Percival said, stroking a huge black boulder.

The previous evening had passed without incident and after breakfast he, Amanda and Lachlan had set out on foot to explore the boulders. Matthew had been more than happy to remain with their camp, as he still eyed the strange rock formation with foreboding.

The great rocks were beginning to warm under the rising sun and a shimmer of heat haze lay over the scrubby hill as the trio scrambled up the first layer of stones. Amanda did so with some difficulty, encumbered by her long dress.

'That terrible sound,' Amanda gasped when they stopped for a rest above a crevice. 'It sounds like someone is moaning.'

Lachlan felt the hair on the back of his neck stand up. He too could hear the faint sounds emanating from deep in the crevices. 'Could be the wind blowing through the cracks,' he said. 'Or it could be bats.'

'Wind, most probably,' Sir Percival said, tapping the surface of the boulder he was perched on with a small geological hammer. A hollow, ringing sound echoed around them. 'No earth to absorb the transmission of a knock,' he continued.

He was like some schoolboy opening his Christmas presents, Lachlan thought. Amanda cast him an exasperated look at her husband's seeming indifference to all around them except the hill. Looking down at the crack between the rocks, all Lachlan could see was an infinite darkness. He was about to stand when the popping of gunshots drifted to them on the tropical breeze.

Peering over the sea of low trees, Lachlan could see a tiny wisp of gunsmoke rising above their camp.

'What the blazes is happening?' he heard Sir Percival ask from above him.

'We're under attack,' Lachlan said, reaching for his revolver. 'Get Lady Amanda under cover.'

With a frightened face, Amanda looked from Lachlan to her husband. 'Get down in the crevice,' Sir Percival said, reaching for his wife's hand.

Lachlan scrambled down the rocks, his pistol drawn. When he reached the bottom he pushed through the scrubby trees in the direction of the camp. He could still hear sporadic gunfire. It was obvious that Matthew was fighting an unequal battle and Lachlan had a good idea against whom. He prayed that he would reach his friend in time. But before he could reach the camp he became acutely aware that the gunfire had ceased. It was not a good sign.

Lachlan heard a slight noise behind him and spun with his weapon levelled at its source.

'I'm coming with you, old chap,' Sir Percival said quietly, his own small revolver gripped in his hand.

Charles Lightfoot could not sit down. In his agitated state he paced Daniel Duffy's office, muttering under his breath.

'It would be easier on yourself,' Daniel said calmly from behind his desk, 'if you took a seat and composed yourself, Major Lightfoot.'

Charles ceased pacing and swung on Daniel. 'Did you know of this?' he demanded, his eyes almost bulging from his head.

Daniel kept a poker face. If only you knew, he thought, eyeing the former English officer with contempt. He had been briefed by John MacDonald before he departed for the north. Aware of who Lightfoot was and why John wanted his downfall, Daniel had agreed to assist Nicholas in his clever scheme. 'I am afraid what we have discovered comes as a shock to me too,' Daniel said, doing all he could to hide his smugness. 'But, in business, one has to accept that there is always a gamble involved when investing large sums of money. We only found out today that the property you purchased is being resumed by the government.'

'They are paying a pittance of compensation compared to what I have outlaid on the purchase,'

Lightfoot said, spitting out his words. 'I am ruined unless something can be done. The money was nearly the sum total of my brother-in-law's capital.'

'Well, at least it was not your money,' Daniel shrugged. 'You must be grateful for that.'

Lightfoot stepped to the edge of Daniel's desk and glared down at him. 'Sir, I once held the Queen's commission and thus I was deemed to be an officer and a gentleman. Gentlemen do not throw away a trust granted to them by someone like Sir Percival Sparkes. How can I tell him of the loss?'

'I am sorry for the situation that you find yourself in,' Daniel said, trying to sound sincere. 'But all you can do is take it on the chin, and write off the financial loss to experience. I think you may have been a better soldier than a businessman.'

Lightfoot finally slumped into a chair. 'Is there nothing I can do to recover even some of the money?' he pleaded.

'We could appeal in the courts,' Daniel offered. 'But that could take years and a great amount in legal fees.'

'So, you are saying I would be wasting my time,' Lightfoot sighed.

'To be honest,' Daniel replied, 'it would be a waste of time, unless you had resources to fight the government.'

'Why was there no warning of the resumption?' Lightfoot asked.

'Just one of those matters lost in the red tape of a colonial government,' Daniel shrugged. 'About all I could suggest at this stage is for you to return to your hotel and have a stiff drink. No doubt you will have to contact Sir Percival and inform him of the loss.'

Lightfoot rose wearily from his chair. His demeanour reminded Daniel of the defeated boxer leaving the ring after a terrible beating and he almost felt sorry for him. But Daniel's tragic family history also had its roots in that bloody day at the Eureka stockade when his uncle, the legendary Patrick Duffy, had stood against the British regiments and goldfields police. This matter was as personal to him as it was to his friends the MacDonald brothers.

As Lightfoot entered the foyer of his hotel a desk clerk waved a telegram at him.

'It came today,' the clerk said, handing it to him. 'All the way, relayed from Cooktown,' the clerk continued, clearly impressed by the marvels of modern technology.

Lightfoot accepted the telegram without much enthusiasm. If it was from Cooktown, then it had to be from his brother-in-law. He pocketed the envelope and went to his room.

Taking off his coat and top hat, he sat down at a desk. The telegram was indeed from Sir Percival, saying that he and Amanda had arrived safely and were preparing to go on the expedition to the Black Mountain. But what Sir Percival had added chilled Lightfoot. His brother-in-law had been fortunate in acquiring the services of a well-experienced guide by the name of Lachlan MacDonald. In fact, their guide was a former Forest Ranger, who had served in the same campaign as Lightfoot.

'Lachlan MacDonald!' Charles Lightfoot whispered, dropping the telegram to the floor as if it were a poisonous snake. He had tried to dismiss the young Scot from his mind after the unfortunate incident with Forster's murder trial, which had left him looking like a liar in the eyes of the court. That was besides the impudent scoundrel's influence over his sister. It had taken a lot of threatening to get Amanda to agree to marry Sir Percival Sparkes on their return from New Zealand and he suspected she still harboured feelings for the young soldier she had loved all those years ago.

What was Lachlan doing acting as a guide for Sir Percival Sparkes? Hadn't it been Nicholas Busby who recommended the man? The same Nicholas Busby who had recommended such a 'sound' financial investment which had now ruined his brother-in-law?

And then the pieces started to fall together in the bitter officer's mind; Busby & MacDonald – surely it was no coincidence that Nicholas's business partner shared the same name as the man he held such enmity for? Lightfoot suddenly felt the chill of a conspiracy. He had been set up!

Leaping to his feet, Lightfoot gripped the table, toppling it over in his rage. By God! They would all pay for their devious treachery. He would have his revenge. From a small travelling chest, he took a pistol. He was ruined and had nothing more to lose.

• • •

Cautiously, Lachlan and Sir Percival moved through the bush towards the camp. Now they could hear voices and calculated that they were about a hundred paces from the clearing.

'The bastard slew Jimmy,' Lachlan heard one voice raised in anger. 'Cut the heathen's throat.'

Spurred by the urgency of getting to his friend, Lachlan burst from the scrub to see three men standing around Matthew, who lay on his back on the ground. Without hesitating, Lachlan raised the pistol and fired into the group. Four shots scattered the startled men, but they had no chance to return fire, so intent were they on seeking the cover of the scrub. Lachlan was reassured when he heard Sir Percival's revolver providing covering fire.

Matthew raised his head and groped for the shotgun lying a few feet from where he had been felled by a bullet. 'Get away!' he shouted at Lachlan. 'They will shoot you!'

Lachlan sprinted across the camp site and dropped to his knees. Blood was oozing from the big Maori's chest where a bullet had entered his right side. Lachlan had seen enough of the signs in war to know that his friend was in trouble unless he could get him medical help.

'They jumped me,' Matthew rasped in his pain. 'But I got one of them – over there.' He nodded in the direction of the tents, where Lachlan could see a young man splayed on the ground, staring with sightless eyes at the sky.

A volley of shots from the scrub nearby and the shouts of men encouraging each other to shoot made Lachlan acutely aware of how vulnerable he was. 'Take cover, you damned fool man,' he heard Sir Percival shout to him from the edge of the clearing.

'I will come back for you,' Lachlan said, laying Matthew's head gently on the earth. 'Just keep your head down.'

Lachlan sprinted to where he had left his rifle and cartridge belt by his saddle. He scooped up both as bullets plucked the grass around his feet. At least he now had a weapon to hold off the men.

Joining Sir Percival and loading the Snider, Lachlan swung on the scrub where the shots had come from. For a fleeting second he saw a figure blur in the bush and he fired. Luck was with him when he heard the man scream, 'I'm shot!' As the gunfire abated, Lachlan guessed that the man's companions were going to his aid. Five men the day before but now that number had most likely been reduced to three, he calculated.

This time, his opponents were careful not to reveal their presence and Lachlan waited behind a log for a target to reveal itself. The wait was agonising. In front of him was Matthew and behind him he had left Amanda. Were the attackers even now doubling around the camp to go directly to the hill of stones seeking out Amanda? Lachlan moved his head to peer into the shimmering grey scrub. A volley of shots plucked at the trees around him, answering his unspoken question. Then he heard the sound of horses' hooves thundering away. It seemed that the men had departed.

Warily, Lachlan rose from behind the log.

Turning to Sir Percival, he froze. The Englishman lay on his back. A small dark spot on his forehead marked where one of the shots from the departing volley had entered. Lachlan immediately dropped to his knees and stared at Sir Percival's motionless body. The bullet had killed him instantly. Closing the dead man's eyes gently, Lachlan shook his head. Walking towards Matthew, he could see his chest rise and fall. The big Maori was still alive.

Charles Lightfoot stood over the body of Nicholas Busby, the smoke curling as a wisp in the still air of the hallway. Blood was forming a pool around Nicholas's head and soaking into the carpet.

Staring at the man he had just shot dead, Lightfoot felt very little. Busby had attempted to play him for a fool, but had at least admitted that his partner was indeed the brother of Lachlan MacDonald. When Lightfoot had produced the pistol, Nicholas had tried to reason with him – but to no avail. Although Lightfoot had promised him his life in return for the information that he required, he had still shot him at point blank range between the eyes, once he was satisfied that he had learned all Nicholas Busby could tell him.

Did they really expect him to do the right thing and shoot himself? Lightfoot smiled grimly, staring at the body at his feet. If so, they had also underestimated the former soldier. Well, there were others who would pay for treacherously leading him to financial ruin. It would not be hard to hunt down the MacDonald brothers before losing himself in the hordes drifting between the goldfields and Cooktown. He still had enough money to purchase a ticket north, and enough after that to flee to the Americas. But he would first exact his revenge.

It was time to tie up loose ends.

TWENTY-EIGHT

There was nothing Lachlan could do for Matthew at the moment, except make him comfortable, so he turned his attention to Amanda. With his rifle and revolver, he ran back to Black Mountain.

'Amanda!' he shouted from the base of the hill, but received no response.

Lachlan clambered up the rocks until he reached the last place he had seen her. He called down into the wide crevice, but still no response. Cold fear gripped him. He must return to the camp to fetch a kerosene lantern, having no other choice than to go down into the heart of the hill itself.

Returning with the lantern, Lachlan lit the wick and, leaving his rifle on a rock, carefully lowered himself down into the crevice. He could feel earth beneath his feet when he slithered to the bottom and glanced around at the shadows flickering on the smooth granite walls. There appeared to be a series of tunnels, varying in size.

It looked as if Amanda had been there. He cried out her name again but still did not get any response. Suddenly there was a whir of sound around him. Huge bats flitted past his head, disturbed by his presence. Lachlan ducked to allow them to pass.

Holding up the lantern, he could make out a steady decline in the slope that seemed to lead to a narrow set of tunnels. Lachlan bent down to see where Amanda's tracks led.

As he carefully followed the trail ever deeper into the centre of the hill, he was forced at times to stoop to negotiate the passages, aware all the while that he must keep the lantern alight. Without its illumination he would surely be a dead man. Again and again Lachlan called out, but the only answers he received were the muffled echoes of his own voice.

An overpowering, musty stench was all around him. Lachlan guessed that it was the excretions of bats. In the distance he could hear the moaning growing louder. Every instinct warned him to leave the place. 'God help me,' he muttered in his fear, desperately wanting to find his way out. But leaving Amanda in the entrails of the hill was not an option he could take.

'Lachlan.'

The cry was faint and he had to force himself to believe that he had heard it. 'Amanda,' he responded and heard Amanda call out to him again. When he lifted the lantern, there were four tunnels before him. Lachlan called out again. 'Amanda, keep calling my name.'

She did so and Lachlan's hopes were raised. Her cries became louder the further he went, until he entered a relatively large cavern. Amanda was huddled on the floor, covered in dirt and bloody scratches. She blinked at the light and Lachlan went to her, taking her in his arms to hold her in a crushing hug. 'Thank God,' he almost sobbed in his relief. 'I have found you.'

Amanda was so racked with sobbing she could not at first reply. Finally she regained her composure.

'I fell down. I've been groping along the tunnel. I . . .' Amanda broke into another fit of sobbing. 'I want to get out of here. Please, Lachlan, get me out of here.'

Lachlan helped Amanda to her feet and together they back-tracked along the trail of footprints Lachlan had left in the musty earth.

Eventually they could see the sun shining down through a narrow crack in the rock. With some difficulty they were able to climb up the crevice, at last bursting into the warm sunshine of the day.

They sat on the rocks, surveying the scrub around the base of the hill. Never before had it looked so good, thought Lachlan, reflecting on how close they had come to being trapped inside the hill. If nothing else, sharing the same tomb as Amanda would have meant they were joined in death. Banishing the macabre thought from his mind, Lachlan spoke forthrightly.

'Your husband is dead,' he said, gently placing his arm around Amanda's shoulders. 'He was shot and

I am not sure if the bastards who killed him are gone. They may attempt to kill us in revenge for the death of one of their own. Matthew has been seriously wounded and I have to get him back to Cooktown as fast as possible.'

Amanda swung on him with tears in her eyes. 'I must go to my husband's body,' she said.

'I think that the best option is to return to Cooktown as quickly as possible and inform the police of what has happened here,' Lachlan said. 'We don't have much other choice. Hopefully, Matthew will survive until then.'

When they returned to the camp, Lachlan quickly buried the body of the silent young man who had come into their camp previously. Amanda went to her husband's body alone. Lachlan watched as she knelt beside him. She seemed to be saying prayers over the body of the man she had married. Finally, he intruded on her privacy to heft Sir Percival's body onto one of the pack-horses. He then was able to assist Matthew to mount a horse. On a second examination of the wound, Lachlan was pleased to see that the bullet had passed through the flesh, leaving a clean wound.

'You will live,' Lachlan muttered.

Matthew grinned weakly. 'I had better,' he said with some effort. 'We have many places to explore together.'

On their return to Cooktown, Lachlan immediately sought out a doctor. He made a cursory examination of the wounded Maori before turning his attention to Lachlan.

'Your big heathen friend will live,' he said, 'so long as he rests and the wound does not take on any infection.' Lachlan thanked the doctor, bid his friend a farewell, then joined Amanda outside to ride to the police station with Sir Percival's body.

After taking statements, the police promised to organise a party to go in search of the gang. Lachlan then led Amanda to a relatively clean and reputable hotel, where he secured her accommodation. He stood awkwardly in her room, his hat in his hands. 'I wish it had been me and not your husband,' Lachlan said. 'From the little that I learned of Sir Percival on our expedition I got to like him.'

'I know it is a cruel thing to say,' Amanda said softly, 'but if I had to choose between you and my husband, I would have chosen you to live. Oh, I was very fond of Percival,' she said. 'He was a good man. But I always knew that one day he would leave my life on account of his foolish searches. In that way, you and he have much in common. You are both restless men.'

'What will you do now?' Lachlan asked.

'I must arrange to have my husband's body shipped back to Scotland,' Amanda said. 'I made him a promise that should he die on foreign soil his body would be buried on the family estate. I suppose I will accompany his body and take over the management of my husband's properties.'

'I guess that there is little else you can do,'

Lachlan said, standing by the door as Amanda sat in a chair with her hands in her lap. 'If I can be of any help, you only have to ask,' he added.

'What will you do?' Amanda asked quietly.

'I have to return to Townsville as soon as my brother returns from the Palmer,' Lachlan replied. 'Maybe he has found our sister by now. If so, that shall bring some light to the darkness presently upon us.'

'Will you return to your life of exploring?' Amanda asked.

'I think that I will, as soon as I get the chance to speak with my brother,' Lachlan answered.

'I always remember those beautiful letters you wrote to me in New Zealand, where you would pour out your dreams of becoming a famous explorer,' Amanda said gently. 'I wish you well. I will never forget you, Lachlan MacDonald. It seems so cruel that just when I had thought you were forever out of my life, fate should cast us together in this place. I will have to try and erase you from my heart one more time.' Amanda turned away, tears welling in her eyes. 'I think that I would like to be alone now,' she whispered.

Was her grief just for her husband or was it for losing each other again? Only Amanda had that answer. For now, Lachlan would go to a hotel with the hope that alcohol would help assuage his own pain of lost love. How could God be so cruel as to allow him to once again meet with the only woman he had truly loved and snatch her away from his life again? But now he had become the betrayer. It was probably only a matter of time before Amanda would learn that he was implicated in destroying her brother. He could not find any reason why she would not hate him after that.

Lachlan sobered up two days later in the stables where he had organised the expedition for Sir Percival. He washed, shaved and found clean clothes, but when he checked at Amanda's hotel he was told that she had been able to secure a berth on a ship going south.

'She said if you came looking for her,' the hotel owner said, 'you were to have this.'

The man held out an envelope to Lachlan.

Lachlan took the envelope and opened it to find a letter inside. He walked out onto the verandah.

My dearest Lachlan,
I could not bear to again say farewell to you. As much as I was fond of my husband, seeing you again so unexpectedly only brought back feelings that I thought I would never know again. My words to you written so long ago have as much meaning to me now as they did when they burst from my heart all those years ago in New Zealand. I still carry the little book of poetry that you gave me and often think of you whenever I read Donne's words of love.

I wish that we could go back to when we first met and that life had not taken so many tragic turns for us both. I pray that you may find

happiness and know that there is someone in this
world who loves you.
  Amanda

Lachlan read the letter only once. The pain
was almost too much to bear. He carefully folded
the letter and placed it in his shirt pocket over his
heart.

Three days later, John returned to Cooktown. He
looked leaner and harder than he had in many years,
the arduous trek to the Palmer and back having
eaten away the excesses of the soft city life. He was
now sporting the beginnings of a thick, bushy beard,
and his face and arms were tanned.

'It is good to see you,' Lachlan said to his brother
when they met at the stables.

'And you too,' John replied, embracing his
brother in a great bear hug.

'Well?' Lachlan asked.

'I am afraid I was too late,' John said, shaking his
head sadly. 'I was told by miners who knew our sister
that she was indeed on the fields with her husband.
But, alas, her husband died from a fever and she and
our nephew and niece departed in the company of
another miner by the name of Ken Hamilton. As far
as I could ascertain, this Hamilton was providing an
escort for Phoebe back to Cooktown, where she had
told one of the miners she intended booking passage
back to South Australia.'

'How ironic,' Lachlan snorted. 'You travel all the

way to the Palmer when she might well have been here all the time.'

'You seem to be at odds with life,' John frowned. 'Am I perceptive in this matter?'

'I guess you could say that while you were away things did not go well at this end. I lost Sir Percival.' Lachlan went on to describe all that had occurred in the past few weeks: reaching Black Mountain, the clash with the bushrangers, the death of Sir Percival and the serious wounding of Matthew, who was even now still recovering. He did not mention Amanda's name other than that she had been with her husband on the expedition. John was quick to pick up on this.

'What has happened to Lady Amanda with the death of her husband?' he asked.

'She has packed up and taken passage back to Sydney to join her brother,' Lachlan replied.

'Was she not the woman you told me that you had once loved?' John asked gently.

'The same woman,' Lachlan replied, glancing away to stare at the bright patch of light marking the stable entrance.

'I'm sorry,' John said, placing his hand on his brother's shoulder. 'I can see that her appearance once again in your life has caused some pain.'

Lachlan's slight nod confirmed John's suspicions about his melancholy. Not so much for his own failure to find Phoebe, but the loss of Amanda from his life once again. 'C'mon, I have paid a fortune for you and I to stay in the town's best accommodation until I take passage back to Sydney. Tonight, we will dine at French Charley's and drink champagne. We will raise a toast to dear, departed friends and get rolling drunk. The treat is on me, little brother.'

Lachlan tried to smile. He loved this strange man who was his brother. It was a bond that could never be severed – even by death.

Even as the two brothers walked from the stables with their swags over their shoulders, Charles Lightfoot stood in Charlotte Street. He had been able to secure passage on one of the quicker steamers going north. He would ask around about the MacDonald brothers and do all he could to find them. Then he would finish what he had started. No one made a fool of Major Charles Lightfoot and got away with it. He hefted his carpet bag and went in search of temporary lodgings. He did not intend to stay in this frontier town for very long.

TWENTY-NINE

John still felt confident about finding Phoebe in Cooktown. But, if it appeared she and her children had already left, he would arrange to return to Sydney, and from there go on to the colony of South Australia.

'I need to pick up some supplies before I ride south for Townsville to meet with Andrew Hume regarding that land purchase you and Nicholas are going to close on there,' Lachlan informed his brother over breakfast. 'There is a store just down the street from here.'

'I will come with you,' John said. 'I might even ask a few questions.'

Above the store door, painted on a board, was a description of the shop's wares and the name Eureka Company. The two brothers stepped into the relatively spacious room. There was just about everything a settler or prospector could need on the frontier: pots and pans, shovels and picks, bags of flour and candles. They were greeted by a pretty young woman with red hair tied up in a bun and a smatter of freckles across her cheeks. But it was the tall, lean man with the scar tracing a line down his face who immediately caught John's attention. From his drawling accent, it was clear that he was an American. Something about him struck John as familiar. When the stranger turned around, John suddenly remembered where he had met him.

'Mr Tracy.'

Luke Tracy stared at John for a moment, puzzled. 'Have we met, sir?'

'Then it is you,' John said. 'It was at the Ballarat goldfields in '54. You attempted to save my brother, Tom, after the British massacre.'

Luke Tracy's face suddenly lit with recognition. 'You were that little fella with his sister,' Luke said with a broad smile. 'God damn! And here you are now.'

Lachlan looked on in confusion as the men shook hands.

'This is the man who risked his life for us after the British went hunting for survivors,' John explained. 'He helped get Tom back to us, until he was forced to flee himself to avoid capture. It was Mr Tracy who kept the secret of where the money Da had left us was buried, even though he could have retrieved it himself.'

Lachlan stepped forward to shake the American's hand. 'Well, it is good to meet you, Mr Tracy,' he said.

'My brother and I owe you a lot more than we can adequately say.'

'It was no big thing,' Luke shrugged off. 'What any Christian would do under the circumstances.'

'Not all men are good Christians,' John parried. 'Your act of courage and kindness changed our family fortunes in ways I would be here all day explaining. Thank you, Mr Tracy.'

'I would feel more comfortable if you called me Luke and must confess that I have forgotten your name,' Luke said.

'It's John MacDonald and this is my brother, Lachlan, who was tragically separated from us on that terrible day.'

'But I see that you are now together,' Luke replied. 'I should introduce you to Mrs Emma James, who is the manager of this store,' Luke said. 'Mrs James's husband is an old friend – as is Emma herself. Henry was once a sergeant with the Native Mounted Police.'

'As Mr Tracy is boarding with us, I think that it is only right that you dine with us tonight,' Emma said with a warm smile. 'I have a feeling you three have a lot to talk over.'

Having accepted the invitation to dinner, that night John and Lachlan met Henry James, the former police sergeant. He was older by many years than his wife but was still strong and fit, although he walked with a noticeable limp – a legacy of fighting with the British army against the Russians in the Crimean Peninsula in the same year that the British army attacked the Eureka stockade. When he learned of

Lachlan's military career in New Zealand, the two men warmed to each other, as only former soldiers can.

After dinner, the men retired to a verandah. Over cigars and brandy, John raised the subject of possibly seeking Henry's assistance in tracking down Phoebe. If anyone could find a missing person, it had to be a former policeman, John explained and although he offered money for the assistance, Henry declined the money. He would do it as a favour for a friend of Luke Tracy.

The evening drew into early morning before the four men reluctantly curtailed their swapping of stories. John and Lachlan had learned meanwhile that Luke Tracy had returned to the Australian colonies to go to the Palmer fields in search of gold. On their way out, Emma James quietly informed them that she thought Luke was really heading out along the Palmer–Cooktown track in search of Kate O'Keefe – his one and only true love.

The two brothers walked down the hill and back into the still carousing town. When they reached their hotel, they were met by a sleepy desk clerk.

'A telegram arrived for you, Mr MacDonald. It came just after you left.'

John took the envelope. 'Probably from Nicholas,' he said, slitting open the envelope with his finger. 'Wanting to know when I will be returning to Sydney.'

Suddenly, John staggered sideways as if hit by a bullet. Lachlan stepped quickly to his brother's side.

'What is it?' Lachlan asked in his alarm.

'Nicholas has been murdered,' John replied in a hoarse whisper. 'It seems that Lightfoot slew him.'

Lachlan took the telegram from his brother's trembling hand and read the contents. It was from John's personal assistant, who had sent the message days earlier. Busby's body had been found by a maid, almost immediately after he had been shot. The maid recognised Major Charles Lightfoot, who was leaving the house just as she arrived, but the police suspected that Lightfoot had fled the country on a ship that same night to a destination unknown.

'C'mon,' Lachlan said gently to John, guiding him up the stairs to the rooms. John moved like a sleep-walker, allowing his brother to usher him to a chair in his room. Lachlan retrieved a bottle of gin that John had packed in his travelling chest, poured a glass and handed it to him.

'Drink this,' he said. 'You need it.'

'It's my fault,' John said, taking a long swig of the fiery liquid. 'I got him into this years ago, and now it has come back on me. He was the only man that I could have spent the rest of my life with.'

'Lightfoot is a cold-blooded murderer. We know that from what he had done to our father and Tom,' Lachlan said, standing over his brother with his hand on his shoulder. 'I have personally experienced his evil. You were not to blame for Nicholas's death.'

'But I allowed him to get involved in my oath to destroy Lightfoot,' John said, staring down at the rough floorboards. 'Otherwise he would still be alive. I killed him – not Lightfoot.'

Lachlan did not reply at first. What his brother

said was partially true, but he could not tell him that he thought the same thing. Anyone close to them was in peril, he thought. 'Maybe you should have another drink and get a good night's sleep,' Lachlan gently suggested.

'I have to return to Sydney as soon as possible,' John sighed. 'I have the funeral to attend to, besides the business. Under the terms of our arrangement, whoever survived the other inherited our companies. I should inform you now, in the event of my demise, you and Phoebe would inherit the companies, with you managing the estates.'

'Yes, well I do not see that happening in the near future,' Lachlan said, assisting his brother to his feet. 'You will be around for a long time yet. More chance me being killed somewhere out there in the forests from a native spear or nulla.'

'Promise me,' John said, gripping his brother's arm fiercely, 'that if anything happens to me you will continue the search for Phoebe and take control of the companies.'

'Of course I promise,' Lachlan replied, helping his brother to the edge of his bed, where he sat him down with another glass of gin. 'I swear a blood oath to you that I will do both, but it is a moot point when you will be looking after both matters for a long time to come yet.'

John swallowed down half the glass and pulled a face. He only wanted this moment to disappear from his life, but he knew that the news of Nicholas's terrible death would not allow him to sleep.

When Lachlan had laid his brother fully clothed

on his bed, snuffed out the lantern and closed the door behind him, he heard the first sobs coming from the darkened room. Although he would never truly understand how one man could love another, he did understand his brother's grief.

Lachlan retired to his room next door and lay down on his bed. He found himself staring at the ceiling in the dark, but sleep did not come easily. Something in his brother's manner had disturbed Lachlan, who had heard similar talk from men before a battle. It was as if they were foreseeing their own deaths and had resigned themselves to their fate.

Lachlan did not know why he came awake with a start. Maybe the many months of campaigning in enemy territory had honed his senses for survival. He blinked away the last remnants of his torpor and realised that he could hear the soft murmur of voices coming from his brother's room and recognised his brother's voice. Suddenly the voices became raised and there were curses, followed by a strangled cry for help from John.

'John!' Lachlan screamed as he flung himself out of bed and through his door to tumble into the hall-way. Lachlan had gone to sleep fully clothed but he was devoid of a weapon.

Lachlan flung himself at his brother's door, feeling it give way at his onslaught. He fell forward into the dark room and saw a shadowy figure standing over his brother and the dull sheen of a knife blade in the stranger's hand reflected from the hallway light. The figure did not wait for Lachlan to regain his footing but crashed through a glass window adjoining the outside verandah. For a second Lachlan was torn between following the intruder and seeing to his brother.

'John!' Lachlan gasped. 'Are you hurt?'

'Stabbed,' John gasped. 'In the chest. It was Lightfoot, Lachlan. He's here.'

Fumbling in the dark, Lachlan found a box of matches alongside a candle and quickly lit the taper. The light it threw revealed John gripping his chest, blood spreading between his fingers. Pain racked his face.

To examine the wound Lachlan pried his brother's hand from the spreading stain. He had seen many similar wounds and was relieved to note that the blade seemed to have been deflected by the ribs. If Lightfoot had been planning to stab John in the heart, he had missed by a good four inches and merely grazed his chest.

'You will live,' Lachlan said grimly, covering the bleeding with a torn fragment of the sheet. 'But I have to get you to a doctor immediately.'

The ruckus had wakened the publican, who filled the room's doorway with a lantern held high. 'What the bloody hell is going on?' he snapped, irate at being torn from his much-needed sleep by the sound of yelling and breaking glass.

'Fetch a doctor,' Lachlan shouted over his shoulder. 'My brother has been stabbed.'

'It was Lightfoot,' John said again and grimaced in his pain, grasping his brother's arm. 'He woke me to gloat about how he had killed Nicky. He wanted me to know that before he killed me.'

'He failed,' Lachlan said gently. 'I swear that Lightfoot will be brought to account for doing this to you.'

Lachlan remained with his brother until the doctor arrived and tended to his brother's wound. John was given a sedative and Lachlan remained by his bed, armed with a pistol and silently vowing to bring to justice the man who had caused his family so much heartache.

The police were summoned and Lachlan gave his statement to a grizzled sergeant.

'I believe it was a man by the name of Major Charles Lightfoot,' Lachlan said, standing outside the room where his brother still slept. 'As far as I know, he is also wanted in Sydney to be questioned regarding the murder of my brother's business partner.'

The sergeant licked his pencil and recorded the name in his notebook. 'Do you have any real evidence as regards this Major Charles Lightfoot being the man who stabbed your brother?' he asked.

'My brother said that the man admitted his identity to him before he attempted to kill him,' Lachlan replied.

'Ah, it was dark and your brother could have been confused. Besides, there are a lot of ruffians in this town,' the police sergeant said, 'who would cut your throat for a couple of shillings.'

'I don't doubt it,' Lachlan replied sourly. He could see that the police investigation was only half-hearted. 'But I am sure you will do your best to apprehend the man who has done this terrible thing to my brother.'

The sergeant left and Lachlan entered John's room. His brother was awake but looked very pale from loss of blood. John attempted to struggle into a sitting position but Lachlan eased him back gently, reaching for a pitcher of water and helping John drink.

'I know business should be the last thing on my mind,' John said weakly, 'but I was due to go to Townsville to meet with Mr Hume to settle a very important land deal.'

'I will do that for you,' Lachlan replied. 'What you have to do is get a lot of rest before you leave this room. I will organise for someone to tend to your needs while you are recuperating.'

John nodded his head and closed his eyes. He felt secure in his brother's care and confident that Lachlan was capable of looking after the company's financial interests.

Before long, Lachlan was visited by both Luke Tracy and Henry James, who had heard of the attempted murder.

Lachlan sat with them on the verandah of the hotel and explained how he knew that Lightfoot was the would-be assassin.

'I will ask around,' Henry said when Lachlan had finished describing Lightfoot. 'I have a few friends in the pub business and other places who might have seen him about.'

'What do you intend to do now?' Luke asked.

'I have to go to Townsville on a business matter

for my brother,' Lachlan replied. 'Then I will return to John and see how your inquiries regarding the whereabouts of my sister are going.'

'Well, Henry and I will keep looking for your sister and her kids and we'll keep an eye on John for you,' Luke said. 'When I have to leave, Henry will keep up the search.'

'You don't know how much that means to my peace of mind,' Lachlan said. 'Can you also keep an eye on Matthew while I am gone?'

Both men agreed and Lachlan watched them walk away. Lightfoot was out there and while he lived neither his brother nor he would ever be safe. Lachlan knew his former commander would not stop until he had killed them both.

THIRTY

On the verandah of his hotel, Ken Hamilton plugged his pipe, lit the contents of the bowl and puffed on the stem until the tobacco glowed and threw off a haze of grey smoke. The sun was high over the hills surrounding Cooktown and Ken Hamilton knew that in a matter of hours he would be viewing the tropical hills from the deck of a steamer sailing south for Moreton Bay, with Phoebe and her two children beside him.

But he still had time to peruse the local paper while he puffed his pipe before he paid for his hotel bill and went to the Chinese quarter to meet with Phoebe.

The news was much the same as it had always been in the paper. Many advertisements proclaiming the essential wares for prospectors and a few luxuries available to those who had struck it rich. He flipped the page and idly read an article by the editor concerning the lawless nature of the mining town, and how a prominent businessman visiting the north to search for his long-lost sister Phoebe MacDonald . . .

Ken sucked in more than a mouthful of the strong tobacco and spluttered. Could *his* Phoebe be one and the same woman?

The livery keeper eyed the well-dressed gentleman who stood before him. 'So you want some information?' the livery man asked suspiciously, wiping his grimy hands on his leather apron. 'Why do you want to know about Lachlan MacDonald?'

The livery man knew Lachlan and liked him. Lachlan was always prompt in his payments and had a winning way about him.

'We soldiered together in New Zealand,' Charles Lightfoot said with a friendly smile. 'I was hoping to make his acquaintance again.'

The livery man sniffed, stared at the earth strewn with hay before answering slowly. 'Well, seeing as you is a friend of Mr MacDonald I don't see any harm in telling you that he rode out a couple of hours ago to travel to Townsville on business. It was a bloody awful thing that happened to his brother, though.'

'What was that?' Lightfoot asked, cupping a cheroot in his hand and lighting it.

'His brother almost got himself killed a couple of days ago by some ruffian.'

'That's too bad,' Lightfoot replied, watching the

smoke from his thin cigar-like cigarette waft to the rafters of the stable. 'But it would be taking something of a risk to put one's head down in the hotels of Cooktown. Now, I'd also be interested in purchasing a horse, my good man.'

After some discussion about the former soldier's needs, the livery man fetched his best mount and eagerly accepted the bank notes Lightfoot paid him. He included the rest of the equipment Lightfoot needed for an extra roll of notes and watched the stranger saddle his horse.

With practised ease, Lightfoot swung himself into the saddle. 'You wouldn't know which track Mr MacDonald took out of town, would you?' he asked from astride his mount.

'He took the south track,' the livery man replied, picking up a rake.

As Lightfoot swung his mount around and trotted away without a further word, the livery man commenced raking the earthen floor. Suddenly he paused in his task. Surely it was nothing, he told himself. But he did not remember mentioning that Lachlan MacDonald's brother had been attacked in a hotel.

Lachlan's journey took him out of a valley and over a small, heavily forested range. The foliage dripped with water. Tears of the forest, Lachlan thought as he brushed against the wet leaves. The trees were crying for all that would come to their lands and for all those who had not left them alive. Hobbling the horses to graze on the native grasses, he prepared his camp for the night, unaware that he was being watched.

Lachlan was glad when morning arrived after a wet night of huddling under a sodden blanket. The rain continued into the morning and Lachlan realised he must press on with his journey south with some haste if he were to cross the small creeks that could quickly become raging torrents. He rose from under the blanket and stood stiffly.

Lachlan was hardly aware of the sound, but the impact of the bullet spun him around. Fighting to stay on his feet, he instinctively bent to reach for the rifle lying within reach against a log.

'Don't even try!' a voice called to him from a clump of scrub trees at the edge of the clearing.

Lachlan straightened. The pain in his shoulder throbbed and blood trickled down the front of his shirt.

'I thought that I would kill you with my first shot,' the voice said, closer this time. Lachlan half-turned. 'It must have been the rain that put off my shot,' Lightfoot said, standing a mere few paces away with his revolver levelled at Lachlan. 'After all these years, Corporal MacDonald, I thought that you would be better prepared against ambush.'

Lachlan stared with frustrated fury at his tormentor. Lightfoot was right. He should have been more alert, suspecting that his brother's killer was at large.

'I would expect no less than to be shot in the

back by you,' Lachlan spat. 'You wouldn't have the guts to face a man'

'I hunted you,' Lightfoot said. 'The same way you hunted the heathen Maori in New Zealand. With stealth and cunning – the soldier's way.'

'Was it the soldier's way to murder a poor miner and his son at Ballarat?' Lachlan asked, glaring at the barrel of the pistol.

'That was a legitimate military action to suppress a rebellion,' Lightfoot answered.

'And attempting to kill my brother?' Lachlan said wearily. He stood in the rain holding his hand over the bleeding wound. The pain was getting worse. 'Get on with it,' he continued. 'We have nothing more to say.'

'You are right, Corporal,' Lightfoot said, raising the pistol.

Lachlan did not close his eyes but stared with all the malevolence he could muster at the Englishman. These were the last seconds of his life. He heard the shots, but this time did not feel any pain.

Lightfoot's expression of surprise seemed strangely mild to Lachlan. The former English officer stood staring at Lachlan, before toppling forward into the muddy earth. A pool of blood formed on the damp ground. A bullet had entered his spine and exited from his chest.

Lachlan was stunned. He blinked against the rain and saw two men astride horses emerge from the scrub. Both held rifles to their shoulders, and Lachlan could make out Luke Tracy's features under his hat, pulled down low against the rain. On the horse beside him rode Matthew Te Paea. They brought their mounts forward and gazed down at the body sprawled at Lachlan's feet.

'I presume that is Major Lightfoot,' Luke said, sliding his rifle back into the holster attached forward of his saddle. Still in shock at the dramatic turn of events, Lachlan could only nod.

'Hello, brother,' Matthew said, a wide grin across his broad, brown face. 'I reckon it was my shot that got the bastard but Mr Tracy reckons it was his.'

Luke slid from his horse. 'We were only minutes away when we heard the shot,' Luke said. 'So we hurried up to see him pointing his pistol at you. I was taking a chance with the range, but figured we only had one. If I missed, then I hoped that Mr Te Paea might get him. Otherwise, it looked as if you were going to be a dead man.'

'That is Lightfoot,' Lachlan finally spoke. 'From what I had heard from my brother, you seem to be in the right place at the right time to rescue us MacDonalds. Guess it was my time to be saved.'

'I never thought of it that way,' Luke grinned. 'But I wasn't only riding out after you to save you. I was hoping to catch up before you got to Townsville, to say that your sister, Phoebe, has found your brother. Thought you would want to know before going all the way to Townsville. I stopped by the livery and was talking to the owner, who just happened to mention that his previous visitor had been asking after you. When I asked him to tell me what the man was like, he painted a picture of this Lightfoot character just as you'd described him to me. I was about to leave when Matthew also turned up. He insisted on riding with me, so I got him a horse and lent him one of my rifles for the journey. It seems that fate has led us here just in time.'

'You seem to need a bit of patching up,' Matthew remarked. 'How bad is it?'

'I think it passed through,' Lachlan grimaced. 'Not the first time I have been shot.'

'Yeah, well I will have a look at it,' Luke said.

The wound was bleeding but not profusely. Luke made a bandage from an old shirt Lachlan had in his kit and when he had attended to the wound, Lachlan sat down on a log to regain his strength.

'I think that it is best we all head back to Cooktown,' Luke suggested wisely. 'Get a doctor to have a look at you and order your friend here back to the hospital tent.' He glanced across at Lightfoot's body. 'What do we do about the Major?'

'We can take him to the hill over there,' Lachlan said, waving to Black Mountain. 'People have a way of completely disappearing in that hill.'

Luke Tracy glanced up. It was the first time he had actually seen this place. He had heard Henry say it was one of the cursed places in this ancient land. He had a feeling Lachlan was right. Anyone who went into the hill would most likely never be seen again.

The black hill held too many bad feelings for Matthew and he refused to assist in disposing of the body. Instead, he remained with the horses while Lachlan and Luke got rid of Lightfoot's body down a crevice. They set his horse free and then tossed the little equipment he had been carrying down the crevice as well. By now the rain had eased off. Lachlan saddled up his horse to ride north once again.

Freshly bandaged with his arm in a sling, Lachlan went with Luke to the Chinese quarter of Cooktown to meet his sister.

The reunion had been joyous as they fell into each other's arms and tears flowed freely. Lachlan met the Chinese family who had been caring for his sister and her two children. Nelly and William stared with shy eyes at this fierce-looking man who had been shot and was introduced as their uncle. But he had a kindly way and it was Nelly who took his hand in a gesture of acceptance. 'Are we going to visit Uncle John?' she asked.

Lachlan swept up the little girl. 'We certainly are,' he said with a broad smile.

Before Luke Tracy departed for the Cooktown–Palmer track, a heated argument broke out between him and Matthew. They could still not agree on whose bullet had killed Lightfoot. Hearing the argument raging between the two men, Lachlan produced the medal he had been awarded for his service in the New Zealand wars. 'This is for you, my heathen brother,' Lachlan said, pinning the medal to Matthew's shirt. 'In recognition of assisting in saving my life.'

Matthew beamed with pride at the award, all argument forgotten. He was at a loss for words.

After concluding the land deal initiated by his brother, in Townsville, Lachlan walked away from the bank and into the broad, dusty street.

'Hey, Mac,' a voice called and Lachlan turned on his heel to see one of the long-bearded frontier men smiling at him. He was a settler Lachlan had met in one of his many travels. 'I heard that you got a million pounds and have decided to go south.'

Lachlan broke into a broad smile. 'You heard wrong, Schmidt,' he called back. 'I'm putting together an expedition to go west. You have me confused with my brother, John.'

'Good on yer, Mac,' the man astride the horse replied before turning his mount and wheeling away into a canter.

Lachlan sighed and continued walking towards his hotel. Oh how he would have given it all for just one chance to tell Amanda how much he loved her. All the money in the world could not buy the love that comes from the heart alone. What good was fame and fortune if it could not be shared?

EPILOGUE

Two Years Later
A Place in the Scottish Highlands

The sky was heavy with the promise of snow and the soft click of the tough little pony's hooves echoed against the row of low stone walls bordering the lane. On the driver's seat of the gig sat two men well clothed against the biting cold that swept in from the nearby loch.

'So ye know Lady Percival?' the Highlander driving the gig asked his passenger.

'We have met,' Lachlan replied, pulling his collar up against the cold wind and eyeing the dark skies.

'Poor lady. A pretty widow so young. There is a rumour that Sir Percival lost a lot of money in the

Australian colonies. At least he still had his estates here for Lady Amanda to retain.'

'I heard that,' Lachlan replied, feeling somewhat uncomfortable knowing that Sir Percival's financial ruin had been the doing of his brother John and his business partner, Nicholas Busby. The proceeds from the sale of the land had actually gone into the coffers of MacDonald & Busby and was now theirs to keep.

'She just stays up at the manor,' the driver continued. 'A nice lady for a Sassenach, though. Never seems to be interested in any of the local gentry although she could have the pick of any one of the local gents.'

Lachlan only half-listened to the chatty Scotsman. His thoughts were in turmoil. After returning to Sydney his brother John had ensured that the vast spread of enterprises were well managed. Both he and John were pleasantly surprised to learn that Phoebe was expecting another child to her husband, Ken Hamilton, who was prospering with his boat-building enterprise at Moreton Bay.

From Brisbane, Lachlan set out for the north again – the silent frontier. In the depths of the rain-forested mountains Lachlan found peace – and often enough danger. His reputation as an explorer was now well established and he was acquiring a legendary status among the tough Queenslanders.

But in the silence Lachlan realised his life was empty. He would sit by a camp fire and remember the face of Amanda Lightfoot. The guilt of knowing he had been party to her financial downfall kept him from going to her. Besides, he feared finding her, only to lose her once more. At least he could still dream that they would one day grow old together in this tropical paradise.

One day, Lachlan returned to Sydney and with his brother's help was on a boat to England. He had made his choice to travel to Scotland in search of Amanda, but with little hope that she could forgive him for being involved in the plan to ruin her brother. Now his journey had brought him to the cold, bleak Scottish Highlands. To Greystones Manor – the Scottish home of Sir Percival Sparkes.

'We're here,' the driver said, reining the cart to a halt.

Lachlan leapt down, stretched his legs and reached into his pocket to pay his fare.

The driver accepted the generous sum. 'Would you like me to stay and take you back to the village?' he asked, pocketing the coins.

'No,' Lachlan replied, gazing at the imposing double-storeyed building. 'I was born not far from here,' he said. 'I still have memories of this place.'

'So ye be one of the MacDonalds from up around the hill,' the driver said, impressed that this son of Scotland who had travelled to far-off places had roots in the district. 'Then you must be the son of Hugh and Mary MacDonald. I heard he met his Maker in the colonies.'

'I am,' Lachlan replied.

He turned and strode up the gravel driveway to the house. Never before had he experienced the fear he now felt for the unknown. Not even before a battle in New Zealand or facing hostile tribesmen on the Queensland frontier. What if Amanda rejected him after he had journeyed halfway around the world to meet with her again?

'There is a stranger approaching the house, Lady Amanda,' the elderly maid said, standing by the window which looked down on the driveway. Amanda, sitting by the coal fire reading a book of poetry, glanced up. 'Do you not recognise him, Meggie?' she asked, putting aside the book.

'No, ma'am,' Meggie replied. 'But I will send him away if you wish.'

'Only a foolish or lost man would be this far from the village on a day like this,' Amanda said, rising from her chair. The first flurries of snow began to fall from the heavy skies and Amanda focused on the man's face.

'Dear God!' she exclaimed.

Meggie glanced at her mistress with alarm. 'Should I fetch the constable?' she asked, seeing the enigmatic expression on Lady Amanda's face.

'No, Meggie,' Amanda replied and her sudden, impulsive hug startled the maid. 'No, let the man in. He is no stranger. He is a man who does not know the tyranny of time or tide.'

Before leaving Australia with her husband's body, Amanda had learned of her brother's murderous rampage. Lachlan's knowledge of the scheme to bring about her brother's ruin was also discovered. Two years had passed and nothing had been heard from Charles. Even in the Scottish Highlands rumours circulated that he had escaped to the Americas.

Lachlan's apparent duplicity had shocked Amanda when she had learnt of it, but more than that, it had hurt her. But time had healed her emotions and when her anger had dissipated she realised that above all she missed the young Scot. In her heart she had always known he would come.

Lachlan stood hesitantly at the great wooden doors of the manor. Had he come too far? He wondered whether he should turn around and go back to the Scottish village where he had temporary lodgings. But he did not have time to answer his own question.

The door opened. There was Amanda's beautiful face before him.

'Lachlan, my dearest, do not say anything,' Amanda said and reached out to embrace him with a passionate kiss that startled even the tough bushman. It was enough to tell him that his journey of searching had finally come to an end.

AUTHOR'S NOTES

Never before or since has an Australian involvement with New Zealand been more significant
than when 2500 Australian recruits crossed the
Tasman to fight in the Waikato campaign. The men
recruited by Colonel Pitt were accompanied by
around 1000 women and children, although the
majority of the recruits were single men. I have met
New Zealanders who can trace their roots back to
those Australian soldiers who took up land after their
service to become Kiwi citizens. Years later,
Australian and New Zealand soldiers and sailors
would fight side by side in the South African war at
the turn of the century. Fourteen years after that a
combined force became known as the ANZACs.

It is interesting to note that the Waikato campaign is not acknowledged as an Australian feat of
arms; most military historians view the volunteers as

acting more in the mercenary soldier role, unlike the New South Welshmen who later fought in the Suakin campaign of the 1880s.

It was not my intention to write about the politics of the land wars of New Zealand, which had flared sporadically from 1848 to the last shots being fired in 1916. This has been done by many fine New Zealand historians.

During the course of my research I came across a wonderful collection of DVDs which comprehensively cover the New Zealand wars. I would recommend the set to anyone with an interest in military strategy. The New Zealand historian, James Belich, has written and produced through Landmark Productions this thoroughly entertaining and informative series entitled *The New Zealand Wars*. A search of the Internet will lead those interested to the distributors.

Of all the colonial wars the British army faced in the 19th century, the war against the Maori people was not one that they could claim as a victory. The same army that could take on the might of the African armies and defeat them found itself in a guerrilla war against a people of incredible courage and intelligence. At the time Maori entrenchments were easily more sophisticated than those used in the American Civil War. It is ironic that it was the Maori who paved the way for a new form of deadly defence to be seen again in 1914. Sadly, the lesson to the British army had been forgotten and would cost them the loss of many good men in the trenches.

Amongst some of the many sources used, I must single out a few: Leonard Barton's *Australians in the Waikato War: 1863–1864*, Library of Australian History, Sydney: 1979; Neil Finlay's *Sacred Soil: Images and Stories of the New Zealand Wars*, Random House NZ, Auckland: 1998; and James Belich's *The New Zealand Wars*, Penguin Books, Auckland: 1988. In these books I was able to read actual eye-witness accounts of the battles described. I have attempted to place my fictional characters in these real events as accurately as possible.

For readers interested in the events of the 1854 Eureka stockade I recommend Bob O'Brien's *Massacre at Eureka: The Untold Story*, Australian Scholarly Publishing, Kew: 1992.

An interesting fact of history pertinent to this novel is that it was indeed a little known and unsung Australian who helped pioneer the system of refrigeration. The use that my characters have put the invention to in the novel is purely fictional, however, although other references to its use are fact. Our beer was chilled by the new invention!

Lachlan MacDonald's role as an explorer on the Queensland frontier was heavily inspired by the almost forgotten true-life character of Christie Palmerston. The best source about this remarkable man's life is Paul Savage's *Christie Palmerston: Explorer*, James Cook University, Townsville: 1992. The fictional incident with Lachlan being blinded is based on an event that happened to Palmerston, as recorded in his diaries.

As for further stories of our colourful Queensland

frontier I continue to recommend the books by Hector Holthouse and Glenville Pike.

Black Mountain is a real place and its sinister reputation is well deserved. Many have visited it over the years never to be seen again. It lies just south of Cooktown in the Black Mountain National Park.

A postscript to the story here is that General Cameron eventually resigned in protest at what he saw as an unjust war against the Maori people. The Von was killed in an attack on a Maori pa in 1868. Major Charles Heaphy, a New Zealander, won that country's first Victoria Cross in recognition of saving a soldier's life on the banks of the Manapiko River in 1864.

Peter Watt
Cry of the Curlew

I will tell you a story about two whitefella families who believed in the ancestor spirits. One family was called Macintosh and the other family was called Duffy . . .

Squatter Donald Macintosh little realises what chain of events he is setting in motion when he orders the violent dispersal of the Nerambura tribe on his property, Glen View. Unwitting witnesses to the barbaric exercise are bullock teamsters Patrick Duffy and his son Tom.

Meanwhile, in thriving Sydney Town, Michael Duffy and Fiona Macintosh are completely unaware of the cataclysmic events overtaking their fathers in the colony of Queensland. They have caught each other's eye during an outing to Manly Village. A storm during the ferry trip home is but a small portent of what is to follow . . . From this day forward, the Duffys and the Macintoshes are inextricably linked. Their paths cross in love, death and revenge as both families fight to tame the wild frontier of Australia's north country.

Spanning the middle years of the nineteenth century, *Cry of the Curlew* is a groundbreaking novel of Australian history. Confronting, erotic, graphic but above all a compelling adventure, Peter Watt is an exceptional talent.

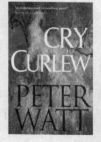

Peter Watt
Shadow of the Osprey

On a Yankee clipper bound for Sydney harbour the mysterious Michael O'Flynn is watched closely by a man working undercover for Her Majesty's government. O'Flynn has a dangerous mission to undertake . . . and old scores to settle.

Twelve years have passed since the murderous event which inextricably linked the destinies of two families, the Macintoshes and the Duffys. The curse which lingers after the violent 1862 dispersal of the Nerambura tribe has created passions which divide them in hate and join them in forbidden love.

Shadow of the Osprey, the sequel to the bestselling *Cry of the Curlew*, is a riveting tale that reaches from the boardrooms and backstreets of Sydney to beyond the rugged Queensland frontier and the dangerous waters of the Coral Sea. Powerful and brilliantly told, *Shadow of the Osprey* confirms the exceptional talent of master storyteller Peter Watt.

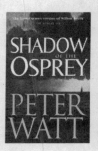

Peter Watt
Flight of the Eagle

No-one is left untouched by the dreadful curse which haunts two families, inextricably linking them together in love, death and revenge.

Captain Patrick Duffy is a man divided between the family of his father, Irish Catholic soldier of fortune Michael Duffy and his adoring, scheming maternal grandmother, Enid Macintosh. Visiting the village of his Irish forbears on a quest to uncover the secrets surrounding his birth, he is beguiled by the beautiful, mysterious Catherine Fitzgerald.

On the rugged Queensland frontier Native Mounted Police trooper Peter Duffy is torn between his duty, the blood of his mother's people – the Nerambura tribe – and a predestined deadly duel with Gordon James, the love of his sister Sarah.

From the battlefields of the Sudan, to colonial Sydney and the Queensland outback, *Flight of the Eagle* is a stunning addition to the series featuring the bestselling *Cry of the Curlew* and *Shadow of the Osprey*, with master storyteller Peter Watt at the height of his powers.

Peter Watt
To Chase the Storm

When Major Patrick Duffy's beautiful wife Catherine leaves him for another, returning to her native Ireland, Patrick's broken heart propels him out of the Sydney Macintosh home and into yet another bloody war. However the battlefields of Africa hold more than nightmarish terrors and unspeakable conditions for Patrick – they bring him in contact with one he thought long dead and lost to him.

Back in Australia, the mysterious Michael O'Flynn mentors Patrick's youngest son, Alex, and at his grandmother's request takes him on a journey to their Queensland property, Glen View. But will the terrible curse that has inextricably linked the Duffys and Macintoshes for generations ensure that no true happiness can ever come to them? So much seems to depend on Wallarie, the last warrior of the Nerambura tribe, whose mere name evokes a legend approaching myth.

Through the dawn of a new century in a now federated nation, *To Chase the Storm* charts an explosive tale of love and loss, from South Africa to Palestine, from Townsville to the green hills of Ireland, and to the more sinister politics that lurk behind them. By public demand, master storyteller Peter Watt returns to his much-loved series following on from the bestselling *Cry of the Curlew*, *Shadow of the Osprey* and *Flight of the Eagle*.

Peter Watt
Papua

Two men, sworn enemies, come face to face on the battle-fields of France. When Jack Kelly, a captain in the Australian army, shows compassion towards his prisoner Paul Mann, a brave and high-ranking German officer, an unexpected bond is formed. But neither could imagine how their pasts and futures would become inextricably linked by one place: Papua.

The Great War is finally over and both soldiers return to their once familiar lives, only to find that in their absence events have changed their respective worlds forever. In Australia, Jack is suddenly alone with a son he does not know and a future filled with uncertainty, while the photograph of a beautiful German woman he has never met fills his thoughts. Meanwhile, the Germany that Paul had fought for is vanishing under the influence of an ambitious young man called Adolf Hitler, and he fears for the future of his family.

A new beginning beckons them both in a beautiful but dangerous land where rivers of gold are as legendary as the fearless, cannibalistic tribes, and where fortunes can be made and lost as quickly as life: Papua.

A powerful novel from the author of *Cry of the Curlew*, *Shadow of the Osprey*, *Flight of the Eagle* and *To Chase the Storm*.

Peter Watt
Eden

Jack Kelly and Paul Mann have survived one world war – will they survive another? When the Japanese threaten to invade the Pacific the two men know that they must do everything in their power to protect their country and their loved ones from an ambitious and merciless enemy.

Lukas Kelly and Karl Mann are like brothers – just like their fathers – and both are determined to do their part for the Australian cause. While Karl works undercover in espionage, Lukas trains to be a pilot. The two men have also inherited their father's passionate natures, and romantic entanglements raise the stakes even further.

Four men, with ties closer than blood fight to hold on to love, and a world that is gradually disappearing. When the war finally explodes terrible tragedies, courageous deeds and enduring friendships will change their lives forever.

A new war, a new generation and an old enemy meet in this thrilling and poignant novel of love, loss and hope written by the bestselling author of *Papua*.

PHOTO: DEAN MARTIN